SINGAPORE FLING
WITH THE
MILLIONAIRE

MICHELLE DOUGLAS

To all the readers who've ever dropped me a line to tell me how much they've loved my books, who've left reviews, and who've shared their enthusiasm for the romance genre with me. You are all awesome.

SINGAPORE FLING WITH THE MILLIONAIRE

MICHELLE DOUGLAS

SECRETS OF FOREVER

MARIE FERRARELLA

MILLS & BOON

First Published in Great Britain 2020
by Mills & Boon, an imprint of HarperCollinsPublishers,
1 London Bridge Street, London, SE1 9GF

Singapore Fling with the Millionaire © 2020 Michelle Douglas
Secrets of Forever © 2020 Marie Rydzynski-Ferrarella

ISBN: 978-0-263-27901-6

1020

MIX
Paper from
responsible sources
FSC™ C007454

This book is produced from independently certified FSC™ paper to ensure responsible forest management.

For more information visit: www.harpercollins.co.uk/green

Printed and bound in Spain
by CPI, Barcelona

CHAPTER ONE

CHRISTY MINSLOW TRAILED behind the other business-class passengers—among the first off the plane because *business class*—and told herself she was *not* taking advantage of James Cooper-Ford or his high-end fashion label Molto Arketa.

She glanced back and bit her lip. *Business class.* Why had the man sent her business class? Did he think it'd sway her into signing his contract?

The thought had her eyebrows lifting. *Not in this life-time, buddy!* There was no way that Beach Monday and Molto Arketa were *ever* going to do business. And she'd told him as much. Nicely, of course. So Mr Cooper-Ford could pamper and flatter her until the cows came home and it wouldn't sway her. She wasn't some naïve school-girl with stars in her eyes. Not any more.

A little shiver of delight refused to be repressed, though. *Business class.* She'd felt pretty damn pampered when the flight attendant had handed her a cocktail menu, and definitely flattered by the speed with which her Singapore Sling had arrived. She'd chosen a Singapore Sling because Singapore was her destination and it seemed the polite thing to do.

Polite? She bit back a grin. If the Cooper-Fords wanted to throw their money away, who was she to argue?

She halted by the luggage carousel and folded her arms, tried to push away the frown that wanted to settle over her. She *wasn't* taking advantage of James Cooper-Ford. People like her didn't get the opportunity to take advantage of people with double-barrelled surnames. But her suitcase was one of the first to drop to the carousel, and it had her shoulders inching a fraction closer to her ears as she tried to fight off the guilt needling through her.

As she manoeuvred through the airport, her eyes started to widen. There were trees. *Inside the building.* She wasn't talking little standards in pots here, but towering trees. And a wall of cascading water. Not to mention tubs of orchids everywhere. She pressed a hand to her chest. It all looked so calm and beautiful. It left her feeling revitalised and oddly restored. Drawing a breath into lungs that felt as if they hadn't had a chance to breathe properly in months, a tiny flicker of hope flirted at the edges of her consciousness. Maybe Singapore would help her find her creative mojo again.

Staring every which way, she tried to take it all in. According to her guidebook this wasn't even the most beautiful part of the airport. The Jewel on the airport's eastern side held an amazing tropical forest garden spanning five storeys and an extraordinary waterfall—the tallest indoor waterfall in the world. She was definitely seeing that before she found a taxi and headed into the city proper. She wasn't coming all this way and not experiencing that.

Oh, really? said that voice in her head—she could see it fold its arms and tap its foot. *And what does that tell you?*

Her hand clenched around the handle of her suitcase. She had nothing—*nothing*—to feel guilty about. It wasn't possible to take advantage of a company like Molto Arketa. The iconic luxury fashion label was worth billions of dollars. It had men and women in sharp suits, and a board of directors, and the world's most feted designers…not to mention a raft of up-and-coming bright young things.

And they wanted her.

Or, more to the point, they wanted her company—Beach Monday. Though the likelihood of her selling Beach Monday to a company with MA's appalling record of workplace exploitation was laughable.

She'd still accepted this two-week junket in Singapore to 'discuss' things, anyway.

But that didn't mean she was taking advantage of the company. She hadn't hidden how she felt. Besides, she was just one tiny person—no billions or millions.

Her fledgling Beach Monday business might be considered one of the hottest new things around at the moment, but the key word in that sentence was *fledgling*. Every cent she had she'd poured into her business, and she'd have to watch every penny while she was here. She wasn't risking everything she'd worked so hard for over the last nine years to make a mistake now. She'd be frugal with her money and on her guard. She had no intention of letting the attention of such a prestigious company go to her head or slip under her guard.

Uh-huh, and you claim you're not taking advantage of anyone? You're in Singapore under false pretences. Is that what you'd call ethical?

At that exact moment she glanced up to see her name held high on a gold-embossed placard by a man dressed in a dark suit. Beside him stood another man in another suit and although she wasn't *that* kind of designer she could tell that the difference between those two suits was the difference between owning a nice house in the suburbs and owning the world.

Her heart sank. Not only had James Cooper-Ford sent

a driver for her, he'd come himself to welcome her. *In person*.

People like him—people who owned the world—could afford to send drivers, they could afford to offer two-week trips to Singapore, and they could afford to buy whatever they damn well pleased. But no matter how much she reminded herself of that fact, guilt continued to drill away at her insides.

She should turn around and jump on the next flight back to Sydney.

And then what? She needed to make a decision about Beach Monday, and soon. That was the reason she'd come to Singapore. She'd thought of it as a breather—a chance to straighten her head out. But she should've done it on her own time, not on James Cooper-Ford's.

Before she could turn tail and run, however, James, as if aware of her scrutiny, glanced across at her. Not wanting to appear an utter ninny, she forced herself forward. 'Mr Cooper-Ford.'

If her appearance surprised him, he didn't betray it by so much as a flicker of an eyelash. 'Ms Minslow, it's a pleasure to meet you in person.' His hand was cool and his clasp firm, but not too firm, and the economy of his movements made her feel gauche and uncoordinated and travel soiled. To hide how she felt, she held her hand out to the other man.

He blinked but shook it. 'I'm Robert. Your driver, ma'am.'

'Pleased to meet you.' She turned back to her host. Assessing blue eyes raked her face. The man was utterly, *utterly* impeccable—like a model in a glossy Molto Arketa fashion spread. She doubted a single dark hair on his head would dare flip out of place. Which, perversely, had her aching to reach up and mess it up.

He was the most perfectly beautiful man she'd ever seen in the flesh. Not in a modern Hemsworth brothers kind of way, but in a young Gregory Peck kind of way. Yesterday she'd have sworn she preferred the Hemsworth look, but she'd have been wrong. Even now she tried telling herself she preferred the breadth of Thor's shoulders, but it was a lie. There was absolutely nothing wrong with the breadth of Gregory Peck's shoulders. Or James Cooper-Ford's.

A frown appeared in his eyes, though it did nothing so vulgar as crease his brow. Dear God. She was staring. *Stop staring!*

'I trust your flight was a good one, Ms Minslow?'

Did he have to be so polite? Was it really necessary for him to have gone to so much trouble? 'Please, call me Christy. And the flight wasn't just good, it was glorious.' *Worse luck.* 'I mean, *truly* glorious. I have to go online now and give the airline and staff the best review ever.'

He looked a tiny bit shell-shocked. 'You leave…reviews?'

'Of course I do. And if you're happy with the service you receive, so should you,' she added stoutly.

Dear God, what was she doing? *Rein your mouth in, Christy.*

He bent towards her slightly, the frown in his eyes deepening, and her mouth went dry. 'I'm pleased your flight was so pleasant. However… Christy—' the hesitation before he said her name made her pulse stutter and start '—forgive me, but is something wrong?'

His soft American vowels did something strange to her insides. *Damn it!* Why did he have to come and meet her at the airport as if she were a VIP? 'I just… I didn't expect you to send a driver for me, let alone meet me at the airport in person.'

His fingers flexed and stretched as if in defiance of

the iron will that controlled them. 'I'm sorry if that's unwelcome.'

'Of course it's not unwelcome. But…'

He leaned towards her a fraction again and from the corner of her eye she saw Robert rein in a smile, and she knew he understood her dilemma.

She gestured. 'There you are in your perfectly impeccable suit looking perfectly…impeccable. And here I am in my yoga pants and Minnie Mouse T-shirt looking… well, not looking perfectly impeccable. If I'd known you were going to meet me I'd have slipped to the restroom and donned my perfectly impeccable suit too.'

He smiled—for real—and it made her realise that everything that had come before had been a polite sham. 'That doesn't matter in the slightest. You're not supposed to look perfectly impeccable after an international flight.'

'Says the man behind a designer fashion label,' she said as Robert took her suitcase. 'So I don't believe that for a moment.'

She said it to keep him smiling, but her words had the opposite effect. 'You can wear your suit tomorrow when I take you to see the Orchard Road store.'

She kept her chin high.

Please don't let him start talking business already.

'Wear my suit tomorrow? I'm sorry, but it's too late now.' No way was he seeing her off-the-rack suit. He'd loathe it. And it might in fact make him feel as if he had an advantage over her. *That* wasn't going to happen. 'The only way I can possibly regain any kind of ground now is to devolve to type.'

'Which is?'

'Retro-boho eccentricity—the staple for all us arty types.'

As Robert led them to the car the warmth and humidity

of a Singaporean afternoon enfolded them, and she kissed her tropical forest and waterfall experience goodbye. It was October, so spring in Australia, which meant the weather had warmed—but not like this. This was like… She closed her eyes and dragged in a breath, her feet slowing to a halt. It was like a big beach hug on a summer day.

When she opened her eyes again she found both James and Robert staring at her. Heat rushed into her face. With a shrug, she kicked back into motion and fell back on the standard excuse of creative types since time immemorial. 'Inspiration…research…nothing is too small to spark an idea. It's important to savour every new experience.'

Which was something she'd barely had time to do in the last two years, and it occurred to her now with renewed force that it wasn't the way she wanted to live her life. Being her own boss was supposed to have been a liberating experience, not a prison sentence.

Stop being a drama queen.

She glanced at the man beside her. Being a bigwig boss seemed to suit him. It *should* suit her too. Maybe studying him would give her some pointers and—

She dragged her gaze away with a gulp. At the moment all she seemed capable of was studying the length of his legs, the power of his thighs and the breadth of his shoulders—all very impressive. And yet noticing those things was far from professional. She focused on trying to not be so aware of him. Everything about him was a little too much.

He had to be busy—must have ten times more demands on his time than she did—and yet he'd taken the time to come and meet her and welcome her to Singapore. And no matter how much she told herself that it wasn't personal— it wasn't because he knew her or liked her—it didn't help. Because what it did reveal was how much he wanted her to sign on his dotted line. In the service of that he was prepared to make her feel important, special.

The knowledge was oddly seductive—it'd be glorious to let herself sink into it and really enjoy it. But she couldn't. She'd made the mistake of letting her guard down once before and it'd led to disaster. She wasn't risking that again. Besides, if she let herself enjoy all of this too much she'd feel beholden to him.

You haven't promised him anything. Not yet.

They sped along a highway lined with neat hedges of flowering shrubs, and with huge trees arching majestically above them. She fished her phone from her pocket to snap a picture of a tree. It'd remind her to find out its name later. And then she murmured, 'Hollywood,' into the dictation app on her phone. Gregory Peck and the golden age of Hollywood…? Could it become her next theme? Ideas had been few and far between over the last twelve months and she had no intention of letting a single possibility slip through her fingers. She was grabbing every teensiest tiniest scrap of an idea—even half an idea—when she could.

James raised a perfect eyebrow. His perfection was starting to set her teeth on edge. 'If I don't record my ideas as they strike, I'm worried I'll forget them,' she explained.

That eyebrow lifted even higher. 'Hollywood?'

She tucked her phone away. 'Don't ask. If I try and explain where my inspiration comes from it sounds startlingly banal—to both my listener and me—and I lose the magic.'

'I see.'

Did he? She doubted he cared. All he wanted was her signature on his contract selling Beach Monday to Molto Arketa. End of story. *And don't you forget it.* Except her signature wasn't a given and—

'Oh, my God!' She pointed, a thrill shooting through

her, her train of thought abandoned. The Marina Bay Sands Hotel rose against the sky in all of its splendour and it left her momentarily speechless.

In her excitement at seeing the iconic building she'd leaned forward, drawing dangerously close to her host. She couldn't read the blue of his eyes at all, but she could read only too clearly the sudden cramping of her lungs, the butterflies that assaulted her belly and throat, and the warm fizz that enlivened her blood.

Oh, no, no. *That* wasn't going to happen.

She eased back. 'I've seen pictures, of course. And I've read all about it, but I didn't realise it'd be so *big*. It really dominates the skyline.'

'You've not been to Singapore before?'

She shook her head. 'How many times have you been?'

'Five or six.'

He didn't know for sure?

'If you'd like to stay at the Marina Bay Sands, that can be arranged.'

He'd put her up in five-star luxury? Absolutely not! Regardless of how she tried to justify it, that *would* be taking advantage of him. 'I assure you that I'll be more than happy with whatever arrangements you've made.'

James couldn't get a handle on Christy Minslow at all. She oscillated between a seemingly innate, self-deprecating exuberance to a withdrawn, hunched-shouldered silence that he associated with socially inept introverts—socially inept like a fourteen-year-old adolescent boy who was standing in front of the girl he had a crush on trying to muster the courage to ask her on a date.

He glanced again at his puzzling guest. Instinct told him social ineptness wasn't something she battled with.

And she was about as far as one could get from a fourteen-year-old boy.

For no reason at all, his tie tightened about his throat. He wished he hadn't worn the tie. He wished he hadn't worn the suit. He wished he'd warned her that he'd be meeting her at the airport. Except it hadn't occurred to him that she'd think otherwise. Damn it! He'd wanted to make her feel special, not ill at ease.

He needed to find out why his unexpected appearance at the airport had made her so uncomfortable, and then he had to fix it. Whatever *it* was. He needed her to sign his contract. He *needed* Beach Monday. The extraordinary reputation Christy's company had gained for its progressive stance on environmental accountability and social equity coupled with the links that she'd forged in developing countries was enviable. What was more, there was more demand for her products than she could currently meet.

If he could bring Beach Monday under the MA umbrella, it would prove to his recalcitrant board that incorporating progressive practices didn't have to correlate to falling shareholder profits. Furthermore, it'd halt the groundswell of public outrage at MA's outmoded policies and procedures. That groundswell was gaining momentum, but his board had become too entrenched in the old way of doing things to recognise the danger it presented. Not for the first time he cursed his mother's refusal to look beyond the bottom line and for allowing a board full of dinosaurs, and his father's memory, to hold sway.

Enough of that. He needed to focus on Christy, not his mother.

He watched as she bit her lip and turned a three-hundred-and-sixty-degree circle in the middle of the living room of the apartment he'd organised for her. MA owned both this apartment and the penthouse apartment above it, which was where he was currently installed. The complex was a charming six-storey colonial building painted a bright white, its window shutters sporting a variety of bright colours— pastel blue, red, yellow, pink. The shutters of this apartment were an inviting green. For the life of him he couldn't remember the colour of the shutters in the apartment above.

It occurred to him then that the silence had stretched too long. Social ineptitude might not be Christy's weakness but it was something he constantly had to guard himself against. 'If the apartment isn't to your liking—'

'No!' She swung to him. 'It's fabulous. I *love* it!'

Her words sounded sincere, but something lurked in the depths of those amber eyes and her riot of red curls seemed to momentarily droop as she stared at the gourmet fruit basket that adorned the small dining table—a fruit basket he'd personally selected. She didn't like fruit?

No, that was ridiculous. Who wouldn't enjoy all of that exotic freshness? He had the oddest yearning then. He wanted to see her smile again.

What on earth…? His gut clenched. While there was no denying that his guest was an attractive woman, that was *not* the way he did business. He needed to stay focused. There was too much at stake to risk muddying the waters with anything else. Signing Christy would be an unmistakable indication of the new direction he meant to take MA. It'd show the world that he was serious about making significant grass-root changes to the company's current policies. And it would prove to the board that their out dated notions no longer held sway in this brave new world.

He moved across to the window to gesture at the view. 'That's Clarke Quay down there—it comes alive at night with a remarkable array of bars and eateries.' She came to stand beside him and her scent rose up all around him—

warm and inviting like a vanilla cupcake. 'And that's the Singapore River.'

He schooled himself to not breathe in too deeply. He wanted to find that sweet vanilla scent too cloying. Rather than edging away, though, he leaned in closer to draw as much of it into his lungs as he could. Once he realised what he was doing, he snapped away. 'A twenty-minute walk along the river will take you around to the marina.'

'Right. Wow, look at all the boats.'

He stared at the colourful assortment of boats lining the banks. 'River cruises are popular with tourists.'

'Oh, that sounds nice.'

He supposed it did if you were into touristy things. Which he wasn't. 'I can organise one for you if you'd like.' Where Christy and Beach Monday were concerned, nothing was too much trouble.

'Oh, no, there's no need for that.'

She said it quickly. Too quickly. Maybe she wasn't into touristy things either. But then he recalled her face when she'd first spied the Marina Bay Sands Hotel and shook his head. She was *exactly* the kind of person who'd revel in a boat cruise.

He was also getting the distinct impression she'd like him to leave her alone now. As an introvert himself, he understood the need for peace and quiet. Setting his business card on the coffee table, he turned back towards her. 'I'll leave you to rest after your flight. Call me if there's anything you need or if you have any questions.'

She eyed his card as if she expected it to bite her. 'Thank you. That's very kind.'

'As I mentioned earlier, if you've no objections I thought we'd visit the Orchard Road store tomorrow.' He intended the new MA store to knock her socks off.

'That sounds great.'

She was lying. But he was confident he could change her opinion. She might be in two minds whether or not to sign the contract he'd offered her, but tomorrow she *would* be impressed.

'Why don't I collect you at ten o'clock?'

The smile she pasted on was big and fake. 'Sounds perfect.'

As James pounded through the park that ran behind the apartment block an hour later, he wasn't any closer to working Christy out. Exercise hadn't helped. And it was too hot—even in the late afternoon—to keep running at the pace he'd set himself. He'd finish with a walk by the river to cool down and—

He halted when Christy emerged from the apartment building, her red curls spilling down her back and creating a halo around her face. Her backpack was clutched to one shoulder, and she glanced around almost…furtively?

It made him frown. Something was wrong.

She was going the same way he was, but he didn't try to catch her up. She'd made it clear earlier that she didn't want company. But when she ducked downstairs to the underground railway he found himself following. Something in the slope of her shoulders had foreboding stirring in his gut. It occurred to him now that the expression in her eyes earlier had been guilt.

Why the hell would Christy Minslow be feeling guilty? Unless…

His nostrils suddenly flared. Was she meeting with one of his competitors while she was here? He knew Maddox was interested. And Bella Falconi from Jasmine's would make a move too if she could. But he thought he'd got a jump on all of them.

Acid pooled in his gut. Was it so damn impossible to find one honest person in this business?

He bought a train ticket that covered all zones, because he had no idea where she was headed. But if she was going to double-cross him, he wanted to know about it.

He boarded the same train she did, one carriage behind. Surveillance wasn't his super power, but she seemed too caught up in her own thoughts to notice she was being followed.

God, he thought in sudden disgust. Was he really following her? This was akin to stalking.

What did he mean...*akin*? It *was* stalking. His mother would applaud his tactics if she ever heard about them and that *wasn't* a comfort. What he should do was get off at the next stop and go back to the apartment, leave Christy to her own devices. Even if those devices were nefarious.

He dragged a hand down his face. Except there was so much at stake. If he couldn't turn the current tide of negative public opinion directed at MA around then he'd find himself in charge of a sinking ship. He'd promised his father he'd do everything in his power to protect and promote MA's interests, ensure its continued success.

He squared his jaw, resolution solidifying in his gut. This was his best chance of dragging MA out of its morass of negative publicity and winning back public favour. He wasn't going to lose that without putting up a fight.

He remained on the train. He wasn't following Christy to hurt her. He didn't even blame her for being tempted by a bigger, better, shinier offer. But he was determined that his offer would be the biggest, shiniest and most tempting of all.

He didn't trust his competitors' tactics or their morals as far as he could throw them. They played by the same rules his mother always had. She'd had her reasons, he reminded himself. An ugly set of circumstances had shaped his mother. He understood why she acted the way she did. But it wasn't the culture he wanted to cultivate at MA, and he wasn't letting this deal with Christy fall through without having done everything possible to convince her otherwise.

She disembarked at the airport.

What the hell...?

Was she taking off back to Australia? Just like that? Without a word to him?

A quick check of his phone told him he hadn't received any messages from her. Wait, she didn't have her suitcase... Though, he supposed she could've sent it ahead—or left instructions back at the apartment.

A rock settled in his gut. If she was leaving, what had spooked her?

Christy, however, didn't make her way to the check-in area. She turned instead in the opposite direction.

He followed her through the airport. She eschewed the internal train to walk the fifteen minutes it took to reach The Jewel complex. She entered the tropical rainforest garden, and he stood to one side, screened by palms and orchids, as she sat in front of the waterfall and stared about with wide eyes, as if drinking it all in. He could feel himself growing grimmer and more forbidding as he waited to discover whom she was meeting.

And he kept right on waiting. For the next twenty minutes Christy didn't glance at her watch once, she didn't cast searching glances at the entrances or at the people who walked past her, and James finally had to conclude that she wasn't meeting anyone.

She'd wanted to see the rainforest garden? Something in his chest cramped. Why hadn't she said anything earlier? They could've made a detour here before leaving the airport. Had she thought he'd mind?

He turned to leave. He'd infringed enough on her privacy, but hesitated when he glimpsed the slump of her shoulders. Something was troubling her. She was alone in a strange city in a foreign country, something was troubling her and—

Before he could think the better of it, he found himself winding his way through the garden to take a seat on the bench beside her.

She glanced at him—idly, preoccupied—and then did a double take. 'Mr Cooper-Ford!'

'James.'

'I— What are you doing here?' And then those hot brown eyes raked him from the top of his head to the tips of his trainers and back up again. He felt scorched, a low thrum of heat buzzing through his blood. He couldn't push a single word past the constriction in his throat. Her sudden smile, bright and sincere, knocked the breath clean from his body.

'You're wearing normal clothes!'

The curve of her lips told him the discovery delighted her.

'I—' he cleared his throat '—was out for a run.'

Her eyebrows shot up. 'Here?'

'No.' He had to tell her what he'd done. It'd be too underhanded otherwise. Sordid. But if she walked away... He ran a hand over his face. If she walked away it'd serve him right. 'I followed you.'

She eased away a fraction. 'You *followed* me?'

'I didn't mean to. At least, not initially. You were coming out of the building as I was coming back from my run. I was heading down to the river.'

She shuffled away another inch. 'What happened to heading down to the river?'

His stomach clenched. 'You were acting oddly.'

She remained silent.

'I could tell something was bothering you. You were acting…well, almost guilty, I guess. It made me suspicious.'

Her gaze dropped.

'I thought you were slipping off to meet with one of my competitors.' The admission burst from him. 'I wouldn't blame you for being tempted,' he hastened to add as startled amber eyes collided with his. 'But I wanted the lowdown if that was happening so I could put a new plan into place and—'

'You wouldn't blame me?' Her mouth fell open. 'Are you serious? I would! It'd be an appalling way to behave. You're putting me up in Singapore for two whole weeks, James. That has to buy a certain amount of loyalty, surely?'

He'd hoped so, but hard experience had taught him that wasn't the way the world worked. 'When you got off here—at the airport—I was worried something had spooked you and that you were going home.'

'That's a little closer to the mark.'

Her words brought him no comfort.

'But I can promise you I wouldn't leave without telling you first—preferably face to face.'

But those words did. 'Thank you.'

'When did you work out I wasn't meeting anyone?'

'Probably five minutes after you sat down.'

Her brow crinkled. 'Then why did you come over? Why didn't you just leave? Why confess to what you did?'

'I shouldn't have followed you in the first place. It was a reprehensible thing to do, and I'm sorry.' It was an effort to maintain eye contact but he forced himself to do it. 'It seemed only right to apologise.'

She stared at him for a long moment. Eventually she nodded. 'Okay, apology accepted. But it can't happen again.'

'It won't,' he promised.

Her gaze sharpened as if she sensed there was something else on his mind. 'And?'

He hesitated. 'Forgive me if this is out of line, but I can't help thinking that something is troubling you. You're alone in a foreign country and I'm your host. If there's anything I can do to help…'

She lifted her hands before letting them drop back to her lap. 'And see? That, right there, is my problem. I didn't know that you'd be so…*nice*.'

He didn't understand.

'The reason you think I've been acting guilty is because I *feel* guilty. I've been sitting here having a silent argument with myself. And holding an imaginary discussion with you in my head.'

For some reason her confession didn't scare him. His every instinct told him Christy Minslow had integrity. Somehow he'd find a way to allay her concerns—whatever they were.

He made himself smile. 'Wouldn't it be better to have a real-live discussion with the real-live me right now instead?' he offered, his every instinct shifting into fix-it mode.

CHAPTER TWO

MAYBE. MAYBE NOT.

But it had to be done whether Christy liked it or not. She didn't care if James was here representing some hugely prestigious company. Taking advantage of someone, regardless of how much money they had, was still taking advantage of them. Money and status didn't change that fact and they didn't justify it.

She glanced at him again. He looked so much more *human* in a pair of shorts and a sweaty T-shirt. And while his running shoes probably cost every bit as much as the polished leather Oxfords he'd worn earlier, they seemed a better fit for his skin.

She gestured. 'I like this look better.'

When he folded his arms and imperceptibly moved away, she mentally kicked herself. 'You look a bit scary in your designer suit.'

He relaxed again. 'It's a truly perfect suit, isn't it?'

'Flawless.'

'My mother informs me that as a representative of the MA brand I need to look the part.'

'Wow, speaking of scary things—your mother is terrifying!'

That made him laugh, but it wasn't the kind of laughter

that warmed his eyes, and something shifted inside her. Something that felt a lot like sympathy.

He sent her a lopsided smile. 'You should meet her in person.'

Uh…no, thanks. Denise Cooper-Ford had retired earlier in the year, passing the reins of CEO to James. It was why his apparent *niceness* had thrown her. She'd expected James to be more like his mother—driven, ruthless, cold and calculating…a shark. Denise's ruthlessness had been legendary. There had been something almost admirable in her single-mindedness. It occurred to her that Denise was probably a tough act to follow.

Or she could have James all wrong. It wouldn't be the first time she'd made such a mistake. James could simply be better at presenting a friendlier and more genial image than his mother. He could still be a wolf in sheep's clothing. While it had been a relief to not be immediately bludgeoned with all the reasons she should sell Beach Monday to Molto Arketa when she'd disembarked from the plane, it'd be foolish to trust him.

And none of that changed the fact that if his offer to meet with him in Singapore had come at another time, she'd have refused it. Her desire for a temporary break—the childish desire to run away from it all—had made her jump at the chance. In her eagerness, had she given him the wrong impression and led him on? Led his *company* on, she amended.

Pressing her hands together, she turned to face him more fully. 'James, I'm really sorry, but I feel like I'm here—in Singapore,' she clarified, 'under false pretences.'

Nothing in his gaze changed, but his eyes roved over her face and a prickle of awareness shifted through her. It was disconcerting to be the focus of his full attention. Just for a moment her breath became tangled in her throat, knotting her chest. It occurred to her then that his tactics might be even more lethal than Denise's. She really, *really* needed to stay on her guard.

Dragging her gaze away, she swallowed. A pretty face wasn't going to sway her. She wasn't letting another man take advantage of either her talent or her good nature to further his own agenda. If James thought he could seduce her into either compliance or submission, he was in for a nasty shock.

Get over yourself, Christy. Stop being so sensitive.

James hadn't made any kind of move—or hinted at making one. The tightness in her chest loosened. She didn't have to trust the man, but she shouldn't be immediately casting him in the role of villain either.

'I'm going to need to unpick that statement a little,' he said now, almost apologetically. His disinclination to offend or distance her made things inside her soften despite her best intentions.

'Always give a person a chance. Try and expect the best rather than the worst.'

They were words her mother always used to say to her when she'd been growing up. She pulled in a breath and nodded. After Lewis it'd been hard not to tar every man with the same brush. It wasn't fair to project all of that onto James.

Expect the best.

She pulled in a breath. She'd try. 'Unpick away.'

'You *are* Christy Minslow, right, and not her identical twin sister sent here on her behalf?'

That made her smile. 'I am she. I don't have a single solitary sibling, I'm afraid.'

'And you are still currently the owner of a business called Beach Monday?'

She stared at the majestic waterfall that fell from the roof of this extraordinary indoor forest and nodded.

'And you do mean to visit the new Orchard Road store MA is opening so you can see first-hand how we plan to showcase your designs if you decide to sign with us?'

She swallowed and nodded again. Molto Arketa was like that waterfall—huge and magnificent—while she felt as insignificant as a single droplet of water.

He remained silent after that and she dragged her gaze back to his. A frown had appeared in his eyes. He had beach-blue eyes—eyes made for smiling and fun. And it seemed wrong that he had to chain them behind perfect suits that diluted their essence.

'I'm sorry, but I don't see how you can feel you're here in Singapore under false pretences.'

'I'm going to put this bluntly—and I don't wish to offend you.'

'Taken as a given. And appreciated.'

She had to fight the quick smile his words sent rising through her. 'The thing is, ethically, MA's and Beach Monday's brands don't align. I could never sell Beach Monday to a company that—'

She broke off, not wanting to be downright offensive.

His lips twisted. 'Who rapes the land and screws its overseas labour force while its shareholders grow fat on the profits.'

'Um…yes.'

'Correction, Christy, our *current* strategic visions don't align, but I'm planning on changing that. It's my top priority. The culture you've created on a micro-scale is the kind of culture I want to incorporate large scale at MA.'

Yeah, right, and he had a bridge he wanted to sell her. And big pink elephants floating through the stratosphere were about to become the next trendy mode of transport.

She paused, and then pulled out her phone. 'Pink elephants,' she dictated. And then sent James an apologetic grimace as she stowed it away again. 'Sorry. Inspiration isn't always convenient and—'

He waved her apology away.

She didn't want to have this conversation, but the sooner it was over, the better. 'Look, I know you think I'm going to sign on the dotted line.' The words blurted out with an appalling lack of finesse, but she hated prevarication. 'I feel guilty because I feel I've led you on. I get two weeks in Singapore and you get…well, I expect you're going to get nothing.'

Molto Arketa can afford it.

Not the point!

'Have you made a definitive decision to reject MA's offer?'

She thought of all the hours she'd spent over the last two years with her accountant, and the public relations firm she'd hired, not to mention all the hours dealing with manufacturers and wholesalers. She recalled again her shock and disillusion at discovering that her office manager, Rosa, had been stealing from her. It'd been the last straw.

A weight bore down on her. The fact of the matter was she had so little time any more to spend on what she truly loved—designing. The money MA was offering was tempting. *Very tempting.*

'If I assure you that everything I've just told you is true—that I'm determined to make significant grass-root changes at MA?'

If that were true…

She pulled in a breath. 'No,' she said. 'If that's true then…no.'

He didn't reply immediately, as if her words had given

him pause. 'Has another company made you a more attractive offer?' At the shake of her head he continued. 'So at the moment you're trying to decide if you're going to sell Beach Monday to me or if you're going to continue running the business yourself?'

'I've pretty much decided to sell my company.' It'd been confronting over the last two years to discover how much she loathed the business side of things. It was equally confronting to discover she didn't trust anybody enough to take over the management of Beach Monday to free her up to focus on the design side of things either. Something had to give. But what?

'It's now just a choice of who I decide to sell to.' She glanced at him. 'I've had offers from other companies.' Companies whose practices were more in keeping with Beach Monday's. 'It's just that your offer to come to Singapore was…persuasive,' she finished with a weak shrug.

Her words made him smile—a crooked half-grin that jolted her pulse. 'It was supposed to be persuasive. Christy, I understand you're keeping your options open, but it's evident to me that MA is still in with a chance. In your mind that chance might only be slim, but I'm confident we have a lot to offer you.'

Unfortunately, so was she. But she couldn't just think about herself here. She had women in remote communities throughout the world relying on the business she sent their way. Their needs had to be taken into account too.

'You say you get two weeks in Singapore. In return, though, Molto Arketa gets the opportunity to pitch to you. That's all that's expected here. As far as I'm concerned, you've met or are planning to meet the terms of our agreement. I knew this wasn't a done deal just because you agreed to come. I was simply hoping a trip to Singapore would sweeten the deal. I'm happy to pay for your time so

I can go over in detail all the reasons I believe you should sign with MA.'

He made it sound so reasonable. Maybe it was.

'Christy, your beach umbrellas are works of art. We love your designs—your sarongs, beach bags and espadrilles. Your products align perfectly with our resort wear. As you already know, we're prepared to pay very handsomely for the privilege of buying your company. We'd also be delighted if you'd come to New York and join our stable of designers. You'd have the opportunity to make a name for yourself there that'll be recognised in the most exalted circles.'

He named a salary that had her gulping back an automatic expletive. It couldn't be denied that working for MA would look ridiculously impressive on her CV.

In the next moment her heart dipped again. What about Molto Arketa's appalling record when it came to issues of social equity and labour-force exploitation, though? Those things mattered to her, and she needed to know he was paying more than lip service to the issues at hand. Earlier in the year MA had been lambasted in the media. She might long to sell Beach Monday, but was she really prepared to go against her own moral code and sell out to a company like MA?

Absolutely not. She'd rather sell for a lower sum. Or she could make changes to Beach Monday's internal structure so she could focus on what she loved. That thought, though, made her feel exhausted so she pushed it away.

'There's a lot to consider,' James continued. 'Obviously you need to decide what's right for you, but there's time for you to explore your options.'

She forced herself to meet his gaze and nod.

'And you've no need to feel guilty about taking your time in coming to that decision.'

He was doing his best to reassure her and she appreciated it. 'You make it all sound so reasonable.'

'Why wouldn't you think it's reasonable?'

'I wanted to get away. Things have been crazy back home. So I jumped at the chance of two weeks in Singapore.'

'That's just serendipity. It doesn't make you beholden to me. I jumped at the chance of two weeks away too. My board of directors have been driving me insane.'

Yeah, but the primary difference was that he'd come to Singapore to work. She'd used the trip as an escape.

Still, he was right. Just because she'd agreed to come to Singapore didn't make her beholden to him. Somewhere along the way she'd lost perspective. Glancing at the man beside her, she couldn't imagine him ever losing perspective. 'Why have they been driving you insane?'

'Apparently I'm too young and hot headed. Too full of new-fangled ideas. They've been trying to keep me on a tight leash and—'

He broke off as if surprised he'd said the words out loud.

Sympathy welled at the bitterness she sensed beneath the calm exterior he projected. If what he'd said earlier about changing the culture at MA was true then he had a heck of a fight on his hands. It was all she could do to keep from squeezing his arm to offer him encouragement. At least she didn't have a board to answer to.

James was proving quite a revelation. She hadn't expected him to be so kind and understanding. Still, she guessed berating her or becoming impatient wouldn't help his end goal.

She stared at the waterfall and reminded herself that none of this was personal. It was just business.

Heat flooded her cheeks then and she had to suppress a groan. She could hardly have been described as businesslike today, could she? She searched her mind for a plausible excuse to explain what must appear to him to be completely erratic behaviour. 'I'm sorry; I've been terribly unprofessional. The thing is, I haven't had a holiday in, well…' she fought a grimace '…years.'

He stared and then smiled that pulse-jolting smile that had the breath catching in the back of her throat. 'Well, there you go. That's a point in MA's favour. The money we'd pay for Beach Monday would provide you with the means to have a *very* long holiday if you wanted.'

She laughed. Because he said it lightly, like a joke, so laughter was expected, but they both knew the truth of his words.

'And,' he continued, 'if you *did* join our team of designers there'd be fringe benefits like annual leave, not to mention overseas travel.'

Which sounded divine. The practical, selfish part of her urged her to snap the offer up and sign on the dotted line. It was the path of least resistance—the easiest thing to do.

'But if it's years since you've had a holiday, then you must be worn out.'

Her more noble self reminded her of the links Beach Monday had forged with village cooperatives around the world, reminded her of the charities Beach Monday supported and the difference she was helping to make in the world. All of that meant more than money and rest.

'And nobody makes their best decisions when they're running on empty and in danger of burning out.'

She glanced at him. Why wasn't he taking advantage of that? His mother certainly would if she were here and still at MA's helm. Except… She could be wrong, of course, but she was starting to think there was more to James than just a cold-hearted businessman.

She bit back a smile. Maybe he was only a shark when

he dressed the part. In which case it'd be in her best interests to find ways to keep him out of his suits.

Heat suddenly scorched her cheeks. Dear Lord, *not* like that. She meant finding ways to keep him in casual clothes. Not...*not naked*! Perspiration prickled her nape and she lifted her hair off the back of her neck. She needed to keep her mind on track.

He raised a quizzical eyebrow at whatever he saw in her face and she rushed into speech in the hope it'd hide the source of her confusion. 'Why do you care if my decision is a bad one or not?'

He folded his arms. 'You're expecting me to ruthlessly railroad you into signing with MA.'

She didn't bother denying it. 'Seems a sensible assumption to make.'

'Which means you think the bottom line—profits for MA's shareholders—is what matters most to me.'

'Isn't it?' Wasn't that where his loyalty should lie?

'And you think that said bad decision for you—as a result of me putting pressure on you—would be to sign the deal.'

He was a hundred per cent correct.

'While I think the opposite is true. I think signing with MA is the smart decision.'

She didn't ask him why—she already knew all the arguments.

'So when I voice concern that you're too exhausted to make a good decision, I'm worried you'll make a bad decision and *not* sign with MA.'

His words made her blink.

His mouth tightened as if he read her momentary confusion, and had registered her suspicion. 'One question if I may, Christy. Why—?'

'I've a question for you first,' she inserted, refusing to

allow him to run this show. 'What *is* more important to you than your shareholders' profits?'

'Professionally?'

She nodded. She didn't want to know what mattered to him personally.

'I want MA to adopt ethically sustainable practices. The same kind of practices Beach Monday has incorporated so seamlessly. Like I said earlier, *that's* my top priority.'

'Since when? MA hasn't exactly been known for its progressive attitude on such issues.'

'Since I became CEO.'

That was news to her, and too convenient for her to credit. And she didn't care how suspicious and uncharitable that made her.

'I believe MA's shareholders can take a minor hit on their profits in the interests of social justice. What's more, I think it's the only way forward. If MA doesn't start incorporating changes like this now, it'll have an impact on the company's bottom line in the future. It's the financially savvy decision to make, as well as the moral one.'

Now *that* sounded far more believable. But she didn't trust it. For too many years now profits had been MA's primary focus, not people and certainly not moral codes and ethical standards.

'May I ask my question now?'

She nodded.

'Why, when you have all the splendour of Singapore at your fingertips, did you come here to have your private argument with yourself?'

The grimace she gave was almost comical, but nothing about Christy or what she'd said since he'd sat down beside her had made James want to laugh.

'The truth of the matter is...' The delicate line of her throat bobbed as she swallowed. 'Until I decided what I was going to do—whether I was going to leave or not—it didn't feel right to let myself enjoy anything beyond the airport.'

He wanted to swear.

'Like I said. I felt like I was taking advantage of you.'

He wanted to swear and not stop. *Damn it all to hell!*

He *wanted* her to enjoy herself. He *wanted* her to revel in the royal treatment. Not tie herself up in knots. He needed her to relax enough so he could show her exactly how he meant to transform MA into a company she'd be proud to be associated with. He'd missed neither her scepticism nor her suspicion when he'd outlined his plans for MA, and if he couldn't find a way to get her to unwind, every instinct he had told him their negotiations would end in failure.

And that was an outcome he refused to consider.

What would his mother have done in this situation?

His lips twisted. She'd do exactly what Christy had expected of him—take advantage of her exhaustion and put immediate and intense pressure on her to sign. It was true that he could follow his mother's example.

Except…

How screwed up would it be to start working towards a fairer, more equitable world, but achieving it at the expense of someone else's happiness? He didn't want to achieve his end goal by making Christy miserable or having her regretting signing with MA.

MA was offering her a deal of a lifetime. Most designers would leap at the chance he was offering her. Christy, though, needed to come to that conclusion herself, in her own time. He ran his hand over his face and counselled patience.

He glanced across to find her gazing intently at a nearby spike of pink orchid flowers, and then back at the waterfall.

She pulled her phone from her pocket, her fingers flying over the keyboard as she made notes.

When she realised he was watching, she sent him an apologetic shrug before snapping a couple of pictures.

'Do you get ideas all the time?' He didn't have a creative bone in his body, but the creative mind fascinated him.

'I used to.'

A silent *but* hung on the air.

She shook herself and sent him a smile that didn't reach her eyes. 'It goes in fits and starts. But it definitely started firing the moment I stepped off the plane.'

'Is it fun?' He had no idea what prompted him to ask.

'It's wonderful.' Her eyes glowed and it was as if all the colours of the rainbow suddenly sparked from her. 'This garden and that waterfall are amazing. It might not be a Merlion or a grove of Supertrees, but it doesn't feel like a consolation prize, that's for sure.'

She wanted to see the Merlion and the Supertrees while she was here?

Of course she did.

'Definitely inspirational,' she added.

He glanced around, then frowned. She was right. It *was* lovely here.

She clapped her hands to her knees. 'Right, well, evidently I'm now going to stay. So we'll visit your Orchard Road store tomorrow, and—'

'No.'

She blinked.

'You need a day of sightseeing first.'

'I can sightsee afterwards.'

'I insist.'

Her chin came up. Not in challenge, more…as if she was assessing him. 'I wish I could get a better handle on you, Jamie Cooper-Ford.'

He blinked at that *Jamie*. Nobody called him Jamie, and yet she'd made it sound like the most natural thing in the world.

'You're so…unflappable. It makes you hard to read.'

He'd been raised by two distant parents. He suspected it made him distant too. And cold. 'What are you trying to see? What do you want to know?'

'What your intent is, your motivation? On the surface this seems very kind, but maybe you're playing a deeper game to win me over.'

'The truth is I don't want you accusing me of railroading you into a decision you come to regret. If you join the team at MA I want your wholehearted commitment—the brand deserves your wholehearted commitment. If you became disaffected with MA and were publicly critical of the company, the publicity would be damaging.'

She nodded slowly. 'That's true.'

'I want the opportunity to prove to you that I'm serious when I say I want to rewrite MA's mission statement. For that to happen, I need you to be willing to listen to me.'

She bit her lip at his words. 'I don't blame you for your scepticism,' he inserted as smoothly as he could. 'Given MA's track record, your mistrust is warranted.'

She peered into his eyes with an intense focus he did his best to return. Eventually her lips curved upwards. 'So… In pursuit of getting me suitably softened up to listen to you, I get to enjoy the sights tomorrow?'

He made a spur-of-the-moment decision, going with a gut instinct. 'No, you're going to take a whole week off.'

'A *week*?'

Her shock couldn't hide her delight at the prospect of a week's worth of sightseeing and downtime and he congratulated himself on this unorthodox piece of strategy. In a week's time she'd be only too happy to listen to him.

'Absolutely.'

She blinked.

'I'll still have Robert collect us at ten in the morning. And he'll take us wherever you want to go.'

'Us? You're planning on coming too?'

The muscles in his shoulders bunched. Why did she find that so surprising? 'I have an investment to protect.'

'Are you going to ditch the suit?'

'Absolutely. Suits are hardly relaxing holiday attire.' He mentally went through the contents of his suitcase. He might need to order a few things in.

Speculation grew rife in her eyes. He glanced at the way perfect white teeth bit into the plump pink flesh of her bottom lip and had to swallow. 'What?' The word emerged from his throat choked and raspy.

'You want me to have a nice time this week.'

'Absolutely.'

'Does that mean we can do Singapore my way?'

If that was what was going to make her happy… 'That's exactly what that means.' He frowned. 'What does doing Singapore your way mean?'

'Who knows? I'll probably make it up as I go along.'

He fought the urge to roll his eyes. These creative types were all the same. What he wanted to know was what was wrong with an agenda and a checklist?

'But the one thing I do know is that it doesn't involve a chauffeur.'

Right. He'd ditch the suit *and* the driver.

James paced the foyer of the apartment building the next morning as he waited for Christy to arrive, checking the list he'd made on the note-taking app on his phone—a list of all the sights that he thought Christy would like to see. He knew she'd said that she wanted to do Singapore *her way*, but he wanted to be prepared with a back-up plan if her inspiration flagged.

'You know, if you have work to do, Jamie, I'll understand. You don't need to feel obliged to babysit me.'

He gave a start to find Christy standing at his elbow. She wore a pair of navy capris and a white T-shirt, which should make her look crisp and cool. Except the shirt sported a huge pink glitter heart on the front and a line of red hearts hemmed the capris. His mind blanked.

She eased back to let out a low whistle. 'I'm loving this new version of you—we'll call it "Jamie in holiday mode", shall we? What?' she added when he remained silent. 'Did I say something wrong?'

'I...no. I'm just not used to anyone calling me Jamie.'

She grimaced. 'Sorry, it's an Aussie thing. As a nation we can't seem to resist shortening someone's name or riffing on it in some way. As if a name isn't perfectly acceptable as is. I'm sorry, I'll call you James if that's what you prefer.'

'Jamie is fine.' He liked her Jamie. Not that he intended admitting as much.

'If it's any consolation the impulse is a friendly one— meant to make you feel like one of the gang.'

One of the gang? The notion was so foreign that he was momentarily speechless.

'But while I approve wholeheartedly of your cargo shorts and boat shoes...'

The smile she sent him warmed him to the soles of his feet, and made him glad he'd spent some time considering what to wear today to put her at her ease. She was a designer—a visual person. What she saw impacted her on a visceral level.

She nodded at his phone. 'I'm also aware that you're a busy man who has a lot of demands on his time.'

He turned his phone towards her. 'I'm not checking my work emails.'

She glanced at the screen and pursed her lips. 'You're a list maker.'

For no reason at all, his mouth went dry. 'There's nothing wrong with that.'

'No.'

But she drew the word out a beat too long. When she didn't add anything else he released a slow breath. He had a feeling "list making" wasn't high on her inventory of attractive traits. Not that he wanted her to find him *personally* attractive. But as selling MA to her was his current goal, he sure as heck wanted her to find him professionally attractive.

He pushed his phone into his pocket. 'So, Christy-who-likes-to-change-people's-names, what would you like to do today?'

Ten minutes later he found himself seated on top of a double-decker open-air bus on one of the ubiquitous hop-on, hop-off tours that operated within the city.

'So…this is how you orient yourself?'

She adjusted the brim of her cotton sunhat. It was mint green and embroidered with big white daisies. It was a ludicrous hat. But whenever he looked at it, he wanted to smile. It didn't go with her outfit, but her breezy lack of concern informed him that didn't perturb her at all. Though he supposed one could make a case that it went perfectly well with her white tennis shoes.

'Orient myself? No! This is just for fun. I can use a map to orient myself. I spent quite some time last night studying my map of Singapore and doing exactly that.'

She stared at him as if expecting him to say something. 'I've no intention of casting aspersions at your map-reading abilities if that's what you're waiting for,' he said.

That made her laugh. 'Being up here in the open air—above the street—in this amazing city feels like being on holiday.'

It did?

'Close your eyes.' She closed her eyes so he didn't bother closing his. 'Feel the breeze in your face…and the warmth of the sun on your arms…and smell of the scents that are in the air.' Her brow furrowed. 'It smells so different here than it does in Sydney—blossoms and spices and things I just don't recognise.'

He stared at her rapt expression and an ache started up in his chest.

'It all feels so wonderfully exotic and foreign. So far removed from ordinary life.' Her eyes sprang open. 'I bet you didn't even close your eyes.'

He kept his mouth shut.

'It's also interesting to know what a tour company thinks a tourist should see in their city. So, Mr List Maker, we're going to do a complete circuit on this bus, and only then am I going to decide where to get off and what to explore further.'

She looked so utterly at ease with her plan that he couldn't help smiling. She was right. The breeze ruffling his hair did feel good. He hadn't lied to her when he'd said he'd wanted to get away too. The office had become a battleground. One he wished he could walk away from.

Except he couldn't. He'd promised his father he'd take care of business. And that was exactly what he would do. He had no intention of making the same mistakes his father had, or regretting his life the way his father had. He clenched his jaw.

'I expect you do something very different for your holidays.'

He didn't take holidays.

'You probably loll on some gorgeous beach some-where—California, Florida…the Maldives.'

Her voice dripped with longing and he found himself shaking his head. 'You have a very idealised view of my life. I don't have time for holidays. And I sure as heck don't have time for the beach.'

She froze. Very slowly she turned from the view of Singapore's Eye that was currently being pointed out to them by their tour guide, to stare at him. 'You're CEO of one of the most luxurious fashion brands in the world, a brand whose reputation is built on beach and resort wear, and yet you don't *have time for the beach*?'

'Sorry to disappoint you, but the reality and the fantasy rarely meet, I'm afraid.'

He became aware then that her entire body had started to shake. His collar tightened in foreboding.

Outrage flared from her every pore. 'Why on earth would I hand my gorgeous beach umbrellas and accessories—my Beach Monday business—to someone like you; someone who doesn't have *time for the beach*?'

He swore silently. He'd made a major misstep. It was testament to how exhausted he was and what a toll the last few months had taken on him. He should never have al-lowed himself to relax in her company.

'My umbrellas are the work of my heart.'

She slapped a hand to her chest. He followed the ac-tion and swallowed, reefing his gaze back up to eye level.

'But to someone like you they're just dollars and cents.'

Rescue the situation! 'But they mean more than dol-lars and cents to MA's customers. *That's* what I'm paid to focus on.'

He wished he could rewind this entire conversation. How the hell had he got into such a mess? And how in the blazes was he now going to get back out of it?

CHAPTER THREE

JAMIE PULLED HIS FACE into what Christy suspected was a deliberately thoughtful aspect. 'Now that I think about it, though… You're absolutely right.' He nodded for good measure. 'I should make time for the beach. I should be getting in touch with my…beachy side.'

He was so clearly not to be believed she almost laughed. Except…

Every instinct she had told her to grab Beach Monday with both hands and run for the hills. Or the beach where he'd never have the time to find her!

He dragged a hand down his face with a groan. 'God, must do better,' he muttered, as if realising how patently transparent his words had been.

He lifted his head. 'You know that whatever my attitude to the beach or holidays, it has no bearing whatsoever on my ability to sell your extraordinary umbrellas or the fact that I can introduce them to a huge number of new customers.'

'Logically, yes,' she managed, because she'd been quiet for too long and, whatever else happened here, he *was* giving her Singapore.

'But?'

His eyes had gone sharp and shrewd. His 'I don't have time for the beach' confession had been a slip. And, she suspected, out of character. She couldn't help wondering what had made him slip.

She shook the thought away. 'The thing is, if you don't have time for the beach or holidays, what on earth can you know of your customers' desires and needs for such things? How can you empathise with them and, therefore, shape in any meaningful way your company's mission statement—its very promise? If you don't have time for the beach then maybe you don't have time for things like the environment and climate change and the exploitation of factory workers.'

Pulling her hat from her head, she scratched both hands back through her hair, which was always a mistake as it was too curly, too wild, to simply slip one's fingers through. It always tangled. She shook her fingers free with a wince.

Stop it, she berated herself. She was making a proverbial mountain out of nothing more than a molehill. 'Obviously you're only a fashion brand, not a cure for cancer or any of the world's other ills,' she said, pulling in a breath. 'And it's crazy to expect…*more*.'

He blinked.

'And your customers are largely the mega-rich—you have the luxury end of the market rather than that of the common man—so we're probably not talking about people in desperate need of some R & R anyway.'

He was just one man. There'd be a whole machine behind him that took care of marketing and PR and all the other bits and pieces. Whether he loved the beach or loathed it was neither here nor there. He was just the guy who closed the deals.

'Christy—'

'No, I know you're right. I'm being silly.' It would be wise not to trust Jamie—they were in business negotiations, for heaven's sake, regardless of whatever he said about this week being a holiday—but that didn't make him a villain either. He wasn't the bogeyman.

His job was to sign her. Her job was to come to a decision. End of story. She should be more objective. But it was impossible for her to be objective about Beach Monday. It meant too much to her. She'd known she'd find the cold practicality of these negotiations confronting. She needed to toughen up.

She bet he didn't have any trouble being tough. Except... There'd been bleakness in the depths of his eyes when he'd mentioned not having time for the beach, and she'd bet he hadn't even been aware of it. A sidelong glance confirmed to her that he had no idea—had absolutely no clue as to what he was missing in not having time for the beach. It twisted something in her stomach, twisted it up tight and hard. She recognised that bleakness because it existed in her too. It was why she'd started Beach Monday—to help ease that bleakness for people like her. It'd just never occurred to her that someone as rich as Jamie could experience it too.

The distinctive shape of the Marina Bay Sands Hotel with its three columns and boat-shaped top riding the sky came into view and it made her smile. 'Every city should have a boat in the sky, don't you think?'

He turned to stare. 'And a CEO who embraces his company's promise,' he agreed slowly.

'You don't have to embrace the beach, Jamie. But I can't help thinking everyone needs a special place that helps them unwind and makes them feel happy.'

He nodded, but she could tell he was only being polite. She fought a frown, fought the way her stomach had started to sink. She wanted him to understand what he was missing. 'The thing is, Jamie, Molto Arketa is like the pinnacle of my beach dream.'

Those blue eyes turned back to her and she sensed she had his full attention.

'It's like…' She searched for the right words. 'If I won the lottery, MA would be the first place I'd shop before heading somewhere exotic like the French Riviera or Tahiti or…'

'The Maldives,' he finished for her.

She didn't understand the sadness that momentarily lurked behind his words. She wondered if he even knew it was there.

'I've been to the French Riviera, the Costa del Sol, the Greek islands—but I've not been to Tahiti or the Maldives.' He smiled. 'So if there's anything you want to know…'

She shrugged. 'If you don't have time for the beach then you can't tell me what I want to know.'

'That's a black mark I'm never going to be able to erase, isn't it?'

The man was so impossibly beautiful she had to force herself to gaze away, needing something to focus on beyond that tempting mouth and a rugged jaw that had her palms itching to slide across it. 'It's nothing of the sort. Just a case of apples and oranges.'

The bus jolted to a halt and their shoulders collided briefly. She tried to turn her swift intake of breath at the contact into a gasp of appreciation. She pointed. 'Look, it's the Merlion.'

As she stared at the statue the feigned appreciation all too quickly became real. She clasped her hands beneath her chin. 'Oh, my God! Isn't it just perfect? I've read about it, of course, but—'

Her words petered out at the way his brow pleated, and just for a moment one side of his mouth hooked up and it made her blood race. If he could appreciate the whimsy of a Merlion then the man couldn't be an utterly lost cause, right?

All too soon, though, his face assumed its carefully polite lines again, reminding her that his decision to come along to 'protect his investment' hadn't meant that he'd thought he'd have fun too. She'd bet he'd meant to pretend to enjoy himself—to put her at her ease, maybe while moving chess pieces across that imaginary chessboard that squatted between them, to further his cause. She'd be foolish to forget that.

He glanced back and his eyes narrowed. 'Did I say something wrong? I agree with you—the Merlion is splendid.'

Yeah, right. She waved his words away and stared instead at the city of Singapore as the bus trundled along, doing her best to ooh and ah at the glimpses of Chinatown that they caught from their seats. She wanted to put Jamie and his perplexing attitude out of her mind and focus on the here and now for a little while. The bus drove all the way out to the Botanical Gardens and she laughed when they had to stop and wait for a large lizard to cross the road. The entire time, though, she was aware of Jamie, and the fact that he studied her rather than the landscape.

Eventually the bus headed down Orchard Road—one of the richest shopping strips in the world. Her heart sped up and her stomach churned. 'Which one is...?'

He pointed and, as if in sync, their tour guide promptly described the building as one of the largest and most iconic malls in all of Singapore, boasting the kind of designer stores that made her head spin. The thought that her beach umbrellas and other bits and pieces could be featured in such a store seemed utterly amazing—the stuff of dreams.

The fairy-tale quality faded when she glanced at Jamie again, and the reality of the decision she was being asked to make struck her anew.

Not too long afterwards the bus pulled to a halt outside Raffles, which was where they'd boarded. The white colonial building shone bright in the sunlight, looking like an oasis of cool sophistication.

She turned to Jamie. 'You didn't enjoy that at all, did you?' The man simply didn't know how to do R & R.

He started. 'I didn't *not* enjoy it.'

Not the same thing. Even if he meant every word he'd said about changing the grass-roots culture at MA, *and* could achieve all he wanted, she couldn't risk handing over her company to a man who in all likelihood was going to burn out within five years. Not that she could say as much, of course. 'You've been very quiet,' she said instead.

'I'm not a natural chatterbox.'

Ouch.

'And I'm still trying to decipher your comment about me not being able to tell you about the French Riviera or the Greek islands.' His eyes narrowed. 'You've been frank with me, so I'll be frank with you—that comment sounded passive aggressive. Was it meant to?'

'No!' She went to push her hands through her hair again, but managed to stop herself at the last moment. 'I just meant you'd have been there for work, not fun, right?' Before he could answer she ploughed on. 'You can't tell me what those places smell like or whether the sun feels different in Greece than it does in Sydney or on which beach the people smiled the most and looked the happiest, or which of all the beaches in those places you'd go back to if you had a spare week.'

He stared at her as if he had absolutely no idea what she was talking about. 'See?' The word shot out of her like an accusation. She tried to temper her tone because, of course, he couldn't see and *that* was the problem. 'Those things—the scent of a beach, the sounds and the quality of the light…the feel of the sun—are what feed the creative soul. Or, at least, *my* creative soul. I need that kind of downtime to spark inspiration. While you…' She shrugged. 'Why were you in the Greek islands?'

'We were shooting an ad campaign.'

'And the French Riviera.'

'Closing a deal with an investor.'

'Did you swim while you were there?'

His Adam's apple bobbed and she had a feeling that he wished himself a million miles away. 'Only in the hotel pool, I'm afraid.'

No doubt after a session in the gym. She didn't roll her eyes. It'd be beyond rude. But it was an effort to remember her manners.

'Look, I was there for business.'

His glare might've scorched a lesser person. And… okay, it left her feeling a tad singed around the edges but she had no intention of letting him see that. 'You're in Singapore for business, but you're playing hooky today.'

Except he wasn't, was he? He was *protecting his investment*.

With what looked like a superhuman effort, he shrugged and spread his hands wide. He even managed a smile. 'See? There's hope for me yet.'

For no reason at all, her mouth dried and her pulse started to race. It made no sense, but she felt on some primal level as if she knew this man—as if something inside them was made of the same stuff. She didn't know why it felt so important to her that he learned the art of R & R. But she ignored the impulse to take on the role of his tutor. The man was an adult. If he wanted to take a holiday and loll on a beach, then he could. She had no right to hassle him to do any such thing or to reprimand him for the choices he made in his life.

'So,' he said when she made him no answer. 'Where have you decided to alight?'

'The Merlion.' It was the only place, other than Orchard Road, that had cajoled any kind of response from him. 'And then we're going to walk around to the Marina Bay Sands Hotel…and from there into the Gardens by the Bay because the one thing I want to see above all others is the Supertree Grove. Have you seen it?'

'Only from the hotel's rooftop terrace.'

'The photos look amazing.' She couldn't believe he'd been content with seeing it only from a distance. How had he been able to resist?

Work, Christy. He's only ever been here for work. The man lives for his work. Not sightseeing.

'It occurs to me how different our lives have been, Christy.'

'In what way?'

'I've grown up with a lot of privilege. Money has never been an object in my world. I live a charmed life. I'm not sure people like me need holidays—not when our lives are so enviable and we have so many advantages.'

She eased back to stare at him. 'You're joking, right?'

'I think you'll find I rarely joke.'

Absurdly then she wanted to cry for him. Working twenty-four-seven wasn't living a charmed life. Couldn't he see that? 'I did an online search on you, you know?'

His mouth opened and then closed. He frowned. 'And?'

'And the conclusions I came to—as far as one can make such conclusions—is that you work hard. Driven seems to be the general consensus. You have a privileged life, sure—' a life she could only dream of '—but you work hard for it. So while I know you have an apartment in Manhattan with views of the East River, I'm wondering if you ever get the time to enjoy them.'

'If you want to see the Merlion, this is our stop.'

She followed him up off the bus and lifted her sunglasses so she could meet his eyes directly. 'You don't lead a playboy lifestyle, you don't skive off midweek to…to…'

His lips finally twitched. 'To?'

'I don't know what rich people do to skive off,' she confessed.

'Have long lunches over some ridiculously expensive champagne in a swish restaurant overlooking the boat lake in Central Park.'

Um… Right.

'Or head up to Martha's Vineyard midweek to get away from Manhattan madness.'

Had she read him all wrong? Did he have a beach house in the Hamptons that he frequented, um…frequently?

'Or stay out late in some trendy nightclub that serves drinks in test tubes.'

'That was the nineties thing,' she said.

'It's coming around again.'

Well, who knew?

He gestured to the path that led down to the waterfront and she kicked herself into action. 'So, you do all those things?'

He grinned as if enjoying throwing her off balance. 'Of course not. You're right. I don't live the playboy lifestyle, but I know what it looks like.'

She laughed; absurdly relieved she hadn't read him wrong. 'I thought you said you rarely joked.'

'All of this sun and your sightseeing fever must be rubbing off.'

She managed to choke back a snort. Just. And then

she simply stopped and stared as the marina came into view. For a moment she had to pinch herself. She was in Singapore. What was more, she was in Singapore being courted by a famous fashion brand. There might be some downsides to the situation. But this—right now—was a serious high point.

'What do you think?'

Dark water sparkled with a million points of light, while opposite the Marina Bay Sands Hotel loomed, impossibly majestic. She moved as if in a dream until she stood at a railing. She stared at the water flashing below and gazed at the pretty tour boats scattered across the bay. Beautiful flowering shrubs lined the paths all the way around the marina—the pinks and whites and oranges of the blossoms festive and fragrant. Everywhere she looked people were smiling.

'It's beautiful,' she breathed. 'Really beautiful.' She glanced at him. 'What do you think?'

He nodded. 'It's lovely.'

The beauty couldn't be denied. They both continued to gaze at it all as if held spellbound.

'I *should* be making time for the beach.'

His words floated on the air and she did a double take. *Whoa, what?*

He frowned, rubbing his brow, before swinging to her with a decisive nod. 'You and I, Christy, are going to the beach—Sentosa. It's supposed to be amazing. I'll organise it for later in the week. And I'm going to prove to you that I'm *exactly* the man who can appreciate a company like Beach Monday.'

Dear God. She had a feeling that she should just surrender now and admit defeat. When the man looked at her like that she had a feeling he could talk a mere mortal like her into anything.

* * *

It wasn't until his phone rang that James realised he and Christy had been staring at one another in a kind of suspended daze. He pressed the phone to his ear, barking a curt, 'Hello,' while mentally noting he'd better get a hat. He'd evidently caught too much sun this morning.

'Mr Cooper-Ford, it's Lien Marsh.'

'Is there a problem, Lien?' Lien was the manager of MA's new Orchard Road store opening in a month.

'I'm afraid so. I'm afraid there's been a…spot of vandalism overnight.'

'What?'

The way Christy snapped away from taking photos of the bay to stare at him told him how sharply he spoke.

'How did this happen? How did the perpetrators get past security?'

'I don't know, sir.'

Misery threaded her voice and he made a concerted effort to check his impatience as outrage swelled in his chest. 'Have you called the police?'

'They're on their way.'

'I'll be there as soon as I can.'

'What's wrong?' Christy asked immediately.

'Just let me call Robert first.' He organised for his driver to collect him and then pulled in a deep breath. 'There's been a spot of bother at the new store.'

'*Spot* of bother? You asked if the police had been called.'

'I don't have any further details beyond knowing there's been some sort of vandalism. It's nothing you need to worry about. I want you to enjoy your day and—'

'I'm not abandoning you at the first sign of trouble. Today was supposed to be for you too.'

'But—' His protests were cut short as she took his arm and turned them back the way they'd come so they could meet Robert at the prearranged meeting point. He gestured back behind them, trying to ignore how the touch of her fingers sent a ribbon of warm heat flowing through his veins. 'The Merlion, the Supertrees—'

'Can all wait until another day.'

This woman had unbalanced him from the first moment he'd clapped eyes on her. Some respite now would be welcome. He gritted his teeth as the heat in his blood gathered momentum. Several hours' respite from Christy would be *very* welcome. 'There's nothing you can do, Christy. And—'

'I can offer moral support.'

Damn! How was he supposed to extricate himself from that? He didn't want her seeing the store in anything less than tip-top condition. But to reject her offer of moral support would offend her. Mortally, he suspected. And that would have a direct bearing on her decisions regarding Beach Monday. Hell, it'd probably ring a death knell on their negotiations. Grinding back a scowl, he forced himself to meet her eyes. 'That's unnecessarily kind of you.'

He could see that his words puzzled her, but he didn't know why.

'I appreciate it,' he added.

'Come on, Jamie.' She sounded as if she was trying to rally him. 'You've just told me we're going to Sentosa— which is dream-come-true material. This is the least that I can do.'

He was so used to people wanting something from him that for a moment he didn't know how to respond. He eventually found his voice. 'Thank you.'

His words seemed to satisfy her. And as they drove through the traffic towards heaven only knew what mess, he found some of his tension slipping away. He wanted her to see him as a man she could relate to. Perhaps this was a step in the right direction.

Fifteen minutes later he stared around the new store in horror at the mess that greeted them, a knot of anger balling in his chest. Such wilful destruction! It took an effort to turn towards Christy. Her pallor made him wince, and had him choking back his anger. She deserved gentleness—needed it, he suspected.

'Christy, I will get to the bottom of this.'

'They've…they've utterly destroyed my—' she swallowed convulsively '—my beach umbrellas.' She turned to Lien and tried to smile, and it slayed him completely. 'And no doubt the beautiful displays you were setting up.'

The horror on Lien's face speared into the centre of him, the glance she sent him agonised. He nodded briefly to assure her he had this, would take care of it, and that she could leave them to it. Her genuine distress that the artist in question was with him had found a home inside his own chest. Christy shouldn't have had to witness this.

'Christy, I—'

'They've wrecked *everything*.'

And the result was hideous, a travesty. In amongst the luxury beach towels, funky swimwear and silk caftans, Christy's Beach Monday umbrellas had been shredded and then strewn around like so much litter. Like sacrifices. Even the hardest-headed artist would find this devastating, and, while she was valiantly trying to hide it, he could tell that Christy was rocked to the soles of her feet.

'It looks as if they've *deliberately* targeted Beach Monday.'

'It looks worse than it is.'

She spun to him, eyebrows raised.

'What I mean is your designs look deliberately targeted because we were setting up a special display to showcase them. We'd ordered in a multitude of your stock—' all of it now in bits and pieces about the shop floor '—so we could make a statement and wow you.'

Damn it all to hell! Whoever had done this would pay. He and Lien had taken such pains yesterday to set this out to perfection. Especially the umbrellas, which were Christy's pièce de résistance. He'd wanted Christy to be dazzled by the store's displays. He'd wanted to seduce her with the glamour and beauty of it all. He'd wanted to make a big impression.

His hands fisted. They'd made an impression all right. *Please, God, don't let her cry.*

He'd understand it if she did—he sure as hell wouldn't blame her for it, but...

She turned to him, her brow pleating. 'Jamie,' she started slowly, 'do you get the feeling someone doesn't want the two of us doing business?'

He stared. 'You're coming over all Nancy Drew on me rather than dissolving into—'

'I prefer Phryne Fisher,' she shot back. When he said nothing she added, 'You might not know her. She's an Australian creation. A daring private investigator in 1920s Melbourne who wears—'

'I know who she is.'

'Good. Then we're straight on who I'm channelling here.'

He wanted to hug her. Though, perhaps, that wouldn't be such a good idea. With all of that honeyed skin of her arms and neck on display she looked far too tempting.

His skin tightened and perspiration prickled his nape. He was far too professional to do anything crazy like kiss a woman he was doing business with—he couldn't imagine anything more fraught. Especially when so much hung in the balance. In his experience, hugging could lead to kissing. *So no hugging.*

Besides, while she might be coming over all stoic and efficient he'd seen the shock in her eyes and the devastation that had flitted across her face. Some designers likened their creations to children—he didn't know if that was an accurate analogy or not—but an inordinate amount of time, patience, care, frustration and commitment had gone into the designing of Christy's beautiful beach umbrellas and other accessories. To see them so heartlessly and wilfully destroyed had to have hit her in a place that…

His hands clenched and unclenched. In a place that wasn't hard, wasn't protected by armour. A soft place where one held their dreams and other soft things that the realities of the world tried to compromise or destroy.

He also noted that, despite the valiant angle of her chin, her hands shook.

'Lien,' he called out—softly, as he didn't want to startle either woman. The mess and destruction were enough to make anyone jumpy. He, however, was six feet of hard muscle and anger—he could hold his own. Christy would be…what? Five five if she were lucky. And while she had a really nice— *Don't!* While she had excellent curves in all the right places, she wouldn't weigh much. And slim Lien at five two would weigh even less. He made a mental note to send Lien home for the rest of the day and to hire a security guard for the store until the opening. As a rule, this centre had excellent security, but it evidently wasn't foolproof. It helped to know that when he spoke with the centre manager his demand for extra security and extra vigilance would be heard.

'Yes, sir?' Lien appeared in the doorway that led to the storerooms and the staff kitchen.

He tried to find a smile, though doubted it reached his eyes. 'Please, Lien, you can call me James.'

Lien promptly burst into tears. Christy hurried over and pulled the sobbing woman into a hug, which only seemed to make his store manager cry harder. 'It must've been the most awful shock to walk in and see this mess this morning,' Christy said, as if it hadn't been the most awful shock for her. 'Why don't we go out the back where we don't have to see it?'

She led Lien, whose sobs had started to ease, out the back and James trailed along behind. Lien dried her eyes on a big red hanky with white polka dots that Christy pulled from her handbag. For some absurd reason that hanky was so *her*, and it made him want to smile. Had she made it herself? Could MA move into the designer handkerchief market too?

'You wanted to ask me something, sir?'

He didn't tell her to call him James again, despite the fact he was doing his best to alter the former formality his mother had instilled in all MA staff. He didn't want to give rise to a fresh bout of crying. 'I was just going to ask if you could put some tea on to brew.' He wanted both women to drink sugared tea—it was supposed to be good for shock, right? 'But I'll do it.'

She pointed to a pot. 'Already done, sir.'

'Then I'd like you two ladies to sit down while I pour you both a cup.'

'Oh, sir, I—'

'I find it's better to just do as he says,' Christy said, pulling out a chair at the tiny table for Lien and taking the one opposite. No sooner had her backside hit the seat, though, when Christy bounced back up. 'Ooh, look! They haven't managed to kill all of my umbrellas.'

He winced at her word choice—*kill*—but in one sense

she was right. The debris on the shop floor wasn't salvageable. She skipped over to a stack of rolled-up beach umbrellas carefully packaged in plastic. She lifted one and turned it in her hands, and then her lips curved into a smile that had his heart surging against his ribs. She glanced across at him and Lien. 'May I?'

They both nodded. He noted that Lien looked as dazed as he felt. He poured three cups of tea and liberally sugared them before taking them to the table and seating himself in the spare chair.

He watched her unwrap the outer packaging carefully as he sipped his tea, enjoying its sweetness—it occurred to him that he rarely indulged his sweet tooth. He wondered why, before discarding the thought as ludicrous. Maybe he was in shock too.

He forced his focus back to Christy. Her beach umbrellas deserved a much grander title. They were works of art. Like other beach umbrellas, Christy's had a central pole that anchored them in the sand, and they had a canopy that shaded the people beneath it. But there all likenesses to normal beach umbrellas ended. The canopies weren't necessarily round—they could be any shape. One of her bestselling designs was a castle with parapets rising above the canopy. Parapets!

Christy didn't just execute a design of a single flower, for instance, she did a whole garden. Flowers and leaves would emerge above the canopy and flap in the breeze above its lucky owner's head. Perhaps trailing ivy would form an exotic fringe. You might discover a woodland creature peering out. Her umbrellas were full of whimsy—the same kind of whimsy he recalled feeling for merry-go-rounds as a child.

He held his breath and waited to see what she would bring forth now. He could see her measuring the width of the room, but in terms of staff kitchens it was generous, and she carefully and with tantalising slowness opened the umbrella. What emerged was a gold canopy and rising above that was a red Chinese dragon. Chinese symbols hung from the canopy's fringe and he knew that an explanation and translation of each one was in the accompanying booklet.

He stared at it, and the longer he stared, the lighter he started to feel. A glance at Lien told him it was having the same effect on her.

Carefully, Christy leaned it against the wall in such a way it stayed upright, and then moved back to the table to sip her tea. She didn't wrinkle her nose at its sweetness either. Instead her lips lifted in appreciation as she inhaled the steam. Something in his chest started up a low hum. He forced his gaze from her and back to the beach umbrella.

'I'm proud of this design. It took some ingenuity to get the dragon to sit so triumphantly. There were a lot of less than stellar attempts at first. I came up with this idea during the Chinese New Year festivities in Sydney two years ago.'

'Your Chinese series,' he murmured. 'You did a red lantern that—' He tried to find words to describe it. 'It just blew me away.' The words felt lame even though they were true.

The smile she sent him, though, was anything but lame. It blew him away too.

He swallowed, forced his gaze back to the umbrella. He needed to be careful—seriously careful. Not only was Christy beautiful, but he suddenly realised what she'd done. She'd gone out of her way to make him and Lien feel better, to momentarily forget the disaster that was lying out there on the shop floor. It should be *him* who was trying to make *her* feel better.

Attractive *and* kind. He shifted on his chair. It'd been a long time since he'd felt the kind of interest for a woman that he was starting to harbour for Christy, but it'd be folly to let it grow or to give into it. He had to keep things strictly professional. He *wasn't* his father. And he owed MA his very best efforts—*he'd promised*.

CHAPTER FOUR

CHRISTY LET OUT a slow breath from choked lungs as Lien and Jamie's tension visibly eased. Glancing at her Chinese dragon again, she felt some of the weight pressing down on her lift too. Her designs had always helped people to… feel better—helped them to see the lighter side of life. She didn't understand how she was able to forge such magic, but she was grateful for it.

She cocked her head to one side. 'You know, while I'm in Singapore maybe I could develop a few ideas for a Singapore series.'

Just imagine if she had a chance to visit all of the world's beautiful places. She could dedicate a series to each of them. How much fun would that be?

Not that it could ever become a reality until she passed the reins of Beach Monday to someone else—until someone else had the responsibility for balancing the books and coordinating advertising campaigns and…and hiring and firing staff.

The fact she was away from all of that, if only for two weeks, was deliciously liberating. For this moment in time she could pretend she was just a designer and nothing more.

'Lien, you wouldn't happen to have any paper here, would you?'

'Yes,' Jamie and Lien said at the same time.

Lien handed her a pile of printer paper, and Christy pulled a pencil from her handbag. Jamie stared at her as if she were a magician. It made her warm all over. She rolled her shoulders. She had to stop that, noticing every little thing about her disturbing host. She couldn't let herself be beguiled by his attention. It didn't mean anything. This might feel like a holiday—and she might flirt with the pretence of being nothing more than a designer—but she couldn't forget she was in Singapore on business. She'd forget that at her own peril. And the peril of everyone relying on her.

'You have an idea for your Singapore series already?'

His words snapped her back. 'Absolutely.' And that in itself was a mini-miracle. Not to mention a relief. She'd been mortally afraid her creativity had packed its bags and deserted her for greener pastures. 'It struck me as I was walking through the airport—*such* a beautiful airport.'

'Hollywood?'

She shook her head, not meeting his eye. 'That's a different idea.'

She pressed a finger to her lips for quiet, and did what she could to ignore the quickening of her pulse. His beautiful voice—deep and assured—distracted her, brought to mind full-bodied red wines, autumn leaves, and Tuscany. A combination that made no sense. But she jotted the words down all the same.

Focusing her mind, she turned her attention to the paper in front of her. Visualising the airport again, she sketched a quick picture of a grove of orchid blossoms—not staked but ballooning and cascading over a rock. Some of the dangling blossoms and leaves could become bunting or a fringe. People loved things that fluttered and took on a life of their own in the breeze.

For a little while she lost herself to her sketch—art had always been her go-to when she'd felt down and unhappy or stressed.

She held it out at arm's length when she was done and viewed it critically. This would make a rather fine print for beach towels and sarongs too. 'I don't have my colour pencils with me, but I'm thinking the blossoms should be shaded in pale pinks and lilacs...with darker hearts. Maybe I'd have a spear of orchids rising up from the canopy here—' she pointed '—just for fun.'

Though, it'd look a bit phallic. She glanced at Jamie and heat suddenly scorched her cheeks.

Oh, for heaven's sake, Christy, don't even go there.

'That is beautiful,' Lien breathed, reaching out as if to touch the paper and then pulling her hand back at the last moment, as if afraid she'd ruin it.

Christy handed the other woman her sketch to study in closer detail. 'What colours would you choose?'

'Pink and purple, like you said. But you could make this in a range of colours and that way customers could buy one in their favourite colour.'

'That's not the way Christy's Beach Monday designs work,' Jamie said.

She glanced up. He'd done his homework. It shouldn't surprise her.

'She does one unique design, and that's it.'

Of course he'd noticed. He wanted to buy her. He'd have had a market appraisal and feasibility study done on Beach Monday. Or had some minion do so.

The thought had her mind glazing over. Lord, why hadn't anyone ever warned her how unbearably monotonous and...*boring* it could be to run your own business? She did what she could to stop her nose from curling.

Be professional. Be businesslike.

She managed a quick smile for Lien. 'It'd seem like cheating.' Staring at her sketch, her mind suddenly started to race. 'But...' She seized her phone and quickly made a note. Could she create slipcovers for this design? The umbrellas could come with an entire range of differently coloured slipcovers that its owner could choose from to suit their mood.

Heaven, it'd take some ingenuity to work it out but...

She made a few more notes and things inside her that'd felt bound and chained for too long started to stretch their wings and take flight. When she was finished she eased back in her chair. Coming to Singapore...was that all it took to have her creativity firing again? *Seriously?*

In her heart she knew it wasn't coming to Singapore but being away from what had become a soul-destroying daily grind. If she'd needed further proof that selling Beach Monday was the right decision for her, then she had it. She just had to make sure nobody in her production chain was materially damaged by such a decision.

'But?' Jamie's voice broke into her reverie.

She shook herself, straightening. 'Just another idea.' An idea she wasn't sharing until she decided to whom she was selling Beach Monday. Instinct told her that Jamie wouldn't steal her ideas or designs, but...

Recalling the mess on the shop floor, she winced. Today industrial espionage seemed an ugly possibility.

Lien handed her back the sketch. 'It was a privilege to watch you do that.'

Jamie surveyed them both as they finished their fragrant sweet tea. 'Lien, I'd like you to take the rest of the day off.'

'Oh, Mr Cooper-Ford, that isn't necessary. I'll wait until after the forensic team is done and—'

'James,' he corrected gently. 'And I'll take care of the forensic team.'

Lien had already given her statement to the police before Christy and Jamie had arrived, and they were sending a forensic specialist to fingerprint the store.

Lien still looked pale, and Christy loved that Jamie was giving her the rest of the day off to recover from the shock. 'You could come to the Gardens by the Bay with me,' she offered.

Lien smiled shyly. 'That is very kind of you, but… It would be nice to visit my grandmother. She hasn't been well and seeing her always makes me feel better.'

'Then you should absolutely do that,' Christy agreed.

After Lien had gone, Jamie turned to her. 'And you should go and visit your grove of Supertrees.' He scanned her face, his eyes narrowing. 'But you're not going to?'

She didn't want to mar her memories of Merlions and Supertrees with today's vandalism. She'd visit the Supertrees another day. Tomorrow maybe. 'It hardly seems fair to leave you alone to deal with all this.'

'It's what I get paid the big bucks for. Besides—' he waved towards the front of the store '—you don't need to keep seeing that ugliness.'

He was right, but she had a feeling what she really needed was a time-out from him. He'd started to disturb her in ways she hadn't envisaged—and in ways no man had in a long time. 'I might just go for a stroll…maybe even walk home—enjoy the sun and sights.'

'If you want a driver…?'

'Not at all, I can get a cab or take the underground if I get tired. My map tells me it's only a half-an-hour walk back to the apartment.' She posted on a big smile. 'I might even do some shopping.'

Men always thought women loved to shop, right? But Jamie didn't look convinced. 'I'm sorry this has marred what was supposed to be a fun day of sightseeing and R & R.'

Those ocean-blue eyes of his saw too much. She shrugged. 'It isn't your fault.'

'Let me make it up to you.'

Despite herself, she couldn't help feeling intrigued. 'How?'

'Let me take you to dinner. Somewhere special. Like the rooftop terrace of the Marina Bay Sands. The view up there is extraordinary. You'll love it, I promise. And then we can watch the laser show in the bay.'

She bit her lip. It sounded wonderful. 'What would I have to wear? Is it super formal up there on top of the world?'

'What you have on now would be perfect.'

She clasped her hands beneath her chin and forced herself not to bounce from one foot to the other. 'Then that sounds wonderful.' She was going to dine at the Marina Bay Sands? *Yes!*

His low chuckle heated her from the inside out. 'You do know that if you needed a formal dress you have all of Orchard Road at your disposal.'

And all of it outside her price range too, no doubt. She was being as frugal as she could with her money at the moment. Shopping for a new frock wasn't on her agenda. Nevertheless, she slapped a hand to her forehead and rolled her eyes. 'Doh! Of course I do.'

'I'll collect you at seven.'

'I'll be ready.' She almost leaned across to kiss him on the cheek. It felt like the natural thing to do. Hauling herself back, she gave a tiny wave and raced away before she did something so stupid.

Christy sipped her iced water until the waiter moved away. Only then did she set it back down and glance up to meet

Jamie's gaze full in the face. 'Right… So… Who resents you enough to vandalise my umbrellas?'

She winced as the words left her—they sounded even more bald and uncompromising out loud than they had in her mind.

Jamie raised an eyebrow. If her words rocked him, he didn't show it. 'Me?'

'I don't mean you personally, of course. I mean Molto Arketa.'

'What makes you think MA is the target? The police think it might be a random act.'

The vandalism hadn't looked random to her—it'd looked targeted. 'Do *you* think it was random?'

He pursed his lips and then shook his head. 'No. Try the wine.'

He lifted his glass to his lips and awareness skittered across her skin as the candlelight played across the planes of his face, highlighting the angular jaw and high cheekbones. Michelangelo would've gone into raptures if Jamie had ever modelled for him. She was in raptures just sitting across from him.

'It's very good.'

With a start, she realised she'd been staring. Seizing her glass, she lifted it to her lips, doing her best not to spill it down her chin. He'd chosen a cool dry white and notes of oak and passionfruit exploded across her tongue. She closed her eyes on a groan, momentarily transported. 'It's delicious.' She took a second sip before setting it down and topping her water glass up from the carafe on the table and downing half a glass in one go. At his amused smile, she pointed to the wine. 'Best wine ever. I want to savour it, not gulp it down to quench my thirst.'

'We can always get a second bottle.'

'In which case you'd have to carry me home, and that

would be seriously inappropriate considering we're in business negotiations.'

He shook his head. 'For the next six days you're on holiday.'

She smiled before turning back to the view. As he'd promised, it was spectacular. It felt as if she could see all of Singapore from up here, and the beauty of the place stole her breath. When she'd first emerged onto the Marina Bay Sands' rooftop terrace she hadn't been able to speak. The view had filled her heart to almost bursting. 'Have I mentioned how amazing this view is?'

'Once or twice.' Those blue eyes danced but in the gathering dusk they looked more midnight than noon.

He'd said she was on holidays, but the moment she'd walked into his store this morning all holiday breeziness had fled. 'I'm not wanting to be difficult, but are you trying to deflect me from asking any more questions about the vandalism?'

He sighed and set down his glass. He did it with such an easy elegance envy gathered beneath her breastbone. He had beautiful hands and—

Sudden and explicit images rose in her mind, images of those hands on a woman's body—her body. Her breasts tightened to painful sensitivity and she could barely catch her breath.

Stop it!

'It's true I'd like to take your mind off what you saw at the store today. I wish I'd insisted on you taking your walk around the marina.'

She refused to look at his hands.

'But you showed a lot of pluck, Christy.' She met eyes full of warmth and admiration. 'I'd not have blamed you for histrionics and tantrums.'

No way was she telling him that after she'd left the store

she'd gone back to her apartment and cried for ten minutes straight. 'I sometimes think I'm a failure as an artist,' she confided. 'I completely missed out on the drama-queen gene.' She sipped more of the gorgeous wine, memorising its flavour, wondering if she could somehow capture its taste in a design. 'And I was impressed with you too. You were calm and very kind.'

'I felt neither. But you and Lien didn't deserve me stomping around venting or shouting.' He pulled in a long breath. 'Okay, I understand you need to talk about what happened this morning. So tonight we talk about it and then draw a line under it, agreed?'

Could she do that? She needed to know if a potential vendetta against MA could impact on Beach Monday. She might loathe the day-to-day running of her company, but she loved Beach Monday. She'd do whatever was necessary to protect it.

She glanced at the lights of the city shining before her, at all of the twinkling and sparkling on the bay. Fixating on the vandalism, though, wouldn't do any good. She met his midnight gaze again. 'Will you keep me informed if the police discover anything?'

'I promise.'

'Then…agreed.'

His lips pursed. 'I don't want to upset you—' she waved his concern away '—but why are you so sure *MA* is the target? Are you sure you don't have any jealous ex-lovers or resentful colleagues who'd want to sabotage you?'

She snorted. 'The boyfriend got what he wanted so there shouldn't be any resentment from that quarter,' she said before she could think the better of it.

He stared at her for a long moment. 'But there is on your side.'

It was more statement than question, and she winced at how bitter she must sound. The truth was she did resent what Lewis had done. Deeply. She wasn't letting anyone use her like that again.

She waved his words away. 'It's ancient history, and it's far from flattering. I've no desire to revisit it, but I can assure you there's no reason an old boyfriend of mine would do anything to hurt me. As for fellow artists or other colleagues in the business.' She paused to think, racking her brain. 'There are no toes I've trodden on or any vendettas I'm aware of. And as for anyone who cares for me who might try and take matters into their own hands to persuade me to follow a particular course of action...' She shook her head. 'They just wouldn't.'

The confidence that laced her words and the conviction in her gaze sent an unexpected wave of loneliness sweeping through James, making him feel suddenly empty. What must it feel like to have such confidence in your community of family and friends, to truly believe they had your best interests at heart?

Get over yourself. His parents had given him *so* much. He knew his mother loved him. So what if she loved MA more? As for his friends... If he suddenly announced he was retiring to the Californian hinterland to become self-sufficient would they still be his friends? Not that he had any intention of doing such a ridiculous thing, of course, but that wasn't the point.

He glanced back at Christy. Her trust and confidence weren't universal, though. What had she meant when she'd said her ex-boyfriend had got what he wanted? His hands clenched, betraying an inexplicable desire to strangle something. Today had shown him that Christy was the kind of woman who put others' needs before her own, who did her best to make things better. She wasn't selfish, she wasn't self-involved, and she wasn't some princess expecting the royal treatment.

He hated the thought of someone taking advantage of her.

And she saw him as someone with that same potential. The realisation left a bitter taste in his mouth. He had to prove to her that he was trustworthy. He had to prove to her that MA would treat her designs and her vision with every respect and make her a star. He had to prove to her that he meant it when he said he planned to incorporate progressive strategies into MA's future policies.

Warm brown eyes met his gaze again. 'That's why I think the perpetrators are targeting you rather than me. I know I've been featured in a couple of industry magazines and won a couple of awards, but I'm still small fry. MA is in the big league.'

He was saved from having to respond when their food arrived. When they'd first taken their seats, Christy had barely been able to drag her gaze from the view to peruse the menu. She'd finally turned to him, all at sea. 'I've no idea what to choose. Every single thing sounds amazing.'

'Do you like seafood?'

'Love it.'

'As I'm familiar with the menu, would you like me to choose?'

'Yes, please. But no appetiser for me, thank you. I'll have a main and if I'm still hungry I might be wicked and have a dessert.'

He didn't know why, but the exchange had made him smile. He'd chosen the grand seafood platter for two. She stared at it now and visibly swallowed, her eyes wide. 'I think you just knocked dessert off the menu.' She leaned towards him as if to make sure no one could overhear her. 'This looks *amazing*,' she whispered.

He stared at the food spread before them and frowned. It really did.

'Do you eat like this all the time?'

He nodded because…yeah, he did. 'I mean, not *all* the time, but a lot of the time.'

'Nice.' She selected a couple of oysters and put them on her plate. She pronounced them utterly delicious and then peeled a shrimp. 'So do you have any business rivals who'd like to sabotage you, or any grumpy colleagues at MA?'

'Yes.'

Her hands stilled. 'In *your own company*?'

Her face fell and for the briefest moment a tiny part of him agreed with her—it should bother him that, professionally at least, some people wished him ill. When had he become hardened to it? 'It's a dog-eat-dog world in business, Christy. I'm a major shareholder plus I'm the CEO, but it doesn't mean I'm popular with MA's other shareholders or the board of directors. Everyone is jockeying for position and power. I'm the youngest CEO in the company's history by quite some way and it's created resentment in more than one quarter. It doesn't help that I've not been backward in criticising the status quo either.'

'Wow, so you really know how to become Mr Popular, then.'

He wasn't interested in winning a popularity contest. What he wanted to do was keep the promise he'd made to his father, and that meant making changes to MA's internal policies and the company's stance on economic sustainability. If those changes weren't made —and soon—MA would be in danger of becoming extinct, of sliding into oblivion. *That* wasn't happening on his watch. Still, it occurred to him now that he might've had more success if he'd taken a gentler approach. He ground back a sigh. It was too late now.

Christy ate her shrimp, frowning. But then, as if she couldn't help it, her face lit up. 'This is some of the nicest seafood I've ever eaten. Try some.'

He demolished several oysters, trying to ignore the fact that in several cultures they were considered an aphrodisiac. And doing what he could to ignore the way her silk shirt—a vibrant orange that should've clashed with her hair but didn't—dipped into a tantalising vee, highlighting the curve of her breasts. He swallowed a generous mouthful of wine hoping it would dampen the heat building inside him.

'What about jealous ex-lovers?' she asked.

He shook his head. He only ever dated women who were as cold and unattached as him.

'Good. You shouldn't date anyone who'd do crazy stuff like that.'

Her words made him smile. 'The problem with that, though, is you don't know they're crazy until after you date them.'

'True. I think following your instincts, though, is generally a pretty good guide.'

What did her instincts tell her about him?

'So…of these rivals who'd like to hurt you or your business, does anyone specific spring to mind?'

He huffed back a sigh, but rested his elbows on the table and met her gaze squarely. 'Who else besides MA has approached you? Who else wants to sign you?'

She named two well-known companies.

'It's conceivable that someone on either of their teams would try and kibosh any deal happening between you and me.'

Her gaze narrowed. 'But?'

'I can't imagine Ms Falconi stooping to something like that. As for the Portollinis… The youngest son is reckless, but his father would eat him alive if he pulled a stunt like that.'

'So, there's some honour among thieves?'

He smiled at her word choice, and reached across to place a piece of perfectly cooked salmon onto her plate, before placing a second piece on his own. 'Is that how you see us—as thieves?'

She helped herself to the salad before passing it across to him. Her nails were short and unpainted, and he wanted to drag each finger into his mouth and suckle it, to stare deep into her eyes, letting his questing tongue tell her what else he'd like to do.

The collar of his shirt tightened about his throat. He had to stop fantasising about this woman. There was too much at stake to consider a dalliance with Christy. She was nothing like the women he normally dated. She'd play by different rules.

Are you sure of that?

Well, of course he wasn't. But it was beside the point. He wasn't having an affair with a woman he was doing business with. End of story. It was a recipe for disaster. He had too much riding on this deal to mess it up.

'Would you stoop to something nefarious to gain an advantage over a business rival?'

Her words were like a bucket of ice, which was exactly what he needed. He searched her face, tried to find the reason she'd ask such a question. 'No.'

Her eyes plumbed his just as intently, as if drilling into his very soul. Eventually she shrugged. 'It's probably crazy, but I think I believe you.'

He slumped when she turned her attention back to her

plate, some unknown tension inside him relaxing and letting him breathe again.

'What about your mother?'

Everything snapped tight again. 'What about her?'

'Would she stoop to such tactics?'

In a heartbeat. Loyalty prevented him from saying as much. 'As she's now retired that's hardly a consideration.' The way Christy's brows rose at his words, though, told him that as far as she was concerned it was definitely still a consideration.

They ate in silence. James tried to concentrate on his food, tried to appreciate it the way Christy did, but he couldn't seem to manage it. He was too aware of her.

'Can I ask you something?'

He glanced up to find her staring at him, a frown in her eyes. For no reason at all, his mouth dried. 'Sure.'

'Why are you so interested in issues of sustainability and the environment *now*?'

There was a note of criticism, of scepticism, in her voice that stung. He set his knife and fork down with a snap. 'It's not *sudden*. I've been lobbying the board on the issue for years.'

'Then why didn't you make your opinions public? Why haven't you been openly critical of MA's policies and agitating from the inside?'

His hands clenched. He hated this—hated that she had every reason for her lack of faith…her disapproval. 'It was agreed, *from the inside*, that MA needed to provide a united front.'

'Because, they weren't issues your mother deemed important.'

His mother had been an old-school type of CEO. 'During my mother's reign she was primarily concerned with securing shareholder profits and steering the company into more stable waters.' Christy opened her mouth, but he forged on. 'I know that sounds cold and clinical, but she came in as CEO at a tricky time and she had to fight hard not only to earn the board's respect, but to bring the company out of very rocky waters.'

Her eyes narrowed. 'I'm not criticising your mother on a personal level.'

Yes, she was. And he couldn't really blame her.

'I'm aware of how highly she's held in business circles.'

'Exactly. But I'm confident a change of leadership and a change of direction are now called for. The company's profits are beyond reproach and our market share is stable. It's time for the powers-that-be at MA to turn their attention to other things. I'm confident I can make the board see the sense in working towards a more equitable arrangement with our suppliers and labour force and to take a more ethical approach to the environment.'

His words did nothing to melt her scepticism. He tried a different tack. 'Why are you so interested in my mother anyway?'

'Because she's a legend. Not just at MA but in the industry. I'm not convinced that anyone can walk in and just overnight change the culture at a company where she's held sway for more than twenty years. You might have the intention of doing exactly that, and I applaud you for it, but I'm less than convinced your board of directors will support you. In fact, I have a feeling they'll shackle you at every turn.'

It wouldn't do to underestimate this woman's perspicacity. Look at what she'd just done. In encouraging him to talk about MA, she'd discovered all of the obstacles in James' path for achieving his vision for the company. She wouldn't sign his contract until she believed he could achieve all that he promised. She might don the 'uniform' of a free-spirited artist, but she had a keen intelligence and he couldn't afford to forget it.

His board *would* shackle his every attempt if he couldn't get them onside, but he had faith in his ability to change their minds. He was far from beaten. 'I think you underestimate how good I am at my job and how persuasive I can be.'

Her eyebrows flew up towards her hairline, and then she swallowed and glanced away.

Christy was going to be key in helping him get his board onside. Her industry contacts and links, her know-how, would help him transform MA, while her status and prestige as one of the brightest new designers on the scene would convince the majority of the board of the efficacy of the new approaches he wanted to implement. Win-win. 'I'm confident I can achieve all that I want to, but I'm not going to pretend it'll be easy.'

'Okay.'

'MA no longer needs to take such an uncompromisingly profit-focused line. Financially the company is doing very well. What's needed now is visionary leadership and I'll do whatever necessary to prove to the sceptics and disbelievers that I can provide that leadership. I'm determined that MA won't be left behind on issues that matter.'

'Good for you.'

She still wasn't convinced, but she'd given him this time in Singapore and he'd find a way to prove to her he could accomplish all he promised. 'Okay, enough about me. Tell me why you started up your own company. Was it something you always wanted to do?'

She picked up her cutlery again. 'Ever since I was a little girl.'

'Why?'

He needed to find out why, and then he needed to find

out why she wanted to sell a company that was on the brink of international success. He needed to find out what she wanted and then he had to give it to her…in exchange for signing his contract.

CHAPTER FIVE

'I'M NOT AVOIDING your question,' Christy said an hour later when they were once again strolling by the waterfront, waiting for the laser show to start. The promenade was lined with people enjoying the warm spring night, the eateries and nightspots teeming, adding colour and merriment.

She felt Jamie glance at her, but she didn't turn to meet his gaze, didn't want him to read her vulnerability because, *of course*, she was avoiding answering his question.

Why had she started her own company?

The simple answer was that she hadn't understood the reality of running a business. She'd been wearing rose-coloured glasses when she'd been dreaming that dream. Back in high school and university the idea had seemed like utter perfection—what could be better than being your own boss, right?

Now that she'd actually had experience at being a small business owner, though, the reality was vastly different. As a small business owner she was responsible for *all* the things. It'd come as a shock to discover she didn't want to be responsible for *all* the things. All she wanted to do was design.

What was more, she sure as heck *didn't* have the business skills to take Beach Monday to the next level.

So hire someone.

She didn't want to hire someone! She wanted…

What? she mocked herself. *A magic solution?* Yeah, like that was going to happen.

So sell the company!

Exactly. She had to sell Beach Monday. But it wasn't as simple as accepting the highest bid. She started to push her hands through her hair, her fingers tangled in the curls, and it took her a moment to untangle them. All the while she was aware of the way Jamie watched her. It made her feel like a worm on the end of a hook.

She couldn't sell without a lot of guarantees—and provisions written into the contract—binding whoever bought her company to the village co-ops she did business with in Ecuador, China and Somalia. The villagers' livelihoods depended on the work her orders generated. She wasn't abandoning them, especially not after taking such pains to initiate and foster those connections in the first place. If she couldn't get a company like MA to honour those commitments then…

She swallowed. Then, she couldn't sell. It was as simple as that. She'd be letting people down and she couldn't bear that thought. She didn't doubt that Jamie meant what he'd said about changing the culture at MA. He'd described the business world as ruthless and cut-throat, but she had a growing suspicion that, while Jamie was wound as tight as a torsion spring, he was also honest.

And he was kind. She was starting to suspect that he wasn't some corporate shark out to take advantage of little fish her. She just wasn't convinced his vision for MA was something he could achieve, despite his best intentions. MA's business model was ingrained into every aspect of the company. Sure, things could change, but not at the click of the fingers—regardless of whose fingers did the clicking.

And she wasn't risking the livelihoods of those who relied on Beach Monday to such a gamble.

'You don't have to answer the question if you don't want to, Christy.' One strong shoulder lifted, sending a ripple of something restless through her. 'It was a personal question—nosy,' he added, giving her an out.

She couldn't drag her gaze from those shoulders. He was wound *really* tight and she wondered what it'd be like to unloose all of that barely contained tension, to spur him to reckless abandon.

Her mouth dried. She'd bet it'd defy anything she'd ever experienced before and—

What are you doing?

She spun away from him, hands gripped together. It took three deep breaths before she could regulate her breathing. Dear God, had he noticed? She had to get a grip. *Quick—think. Say something.*

'Is everything okay?'

She turned back, flashed him a smile. 'Of course.' He'd been asking why she'd wanted to run her own company. *Answer the question.*

She prayed her voice would hold firm and not give her away, because she had no hope of getting her pulse under control. 'My upbringing was about as far from privileged as you can get, Jamie. My father headed for the hills when I wasn't quite five, leaving my mother to provide for us both. Which she did. But with him dodging his child-support payments, and her not really having any proper qualifications, it meant there was never much money coming in. There was enough for essentials but not fancy clothes or beach holidays.' Or art classes.

As if by some prearranged signal, they pulled to a halt.

Leaning on the railing, she stared out at the bay. He leaned on the railing as well, not close enough to touch her, but close enough that she could feel his warmth and inhale the spice of his scent—an exotic blend of sandalwood and amber. It did nothing to slow the racing of her pulse.

'Is that why you created Beach Monday—for all the beach holidays you yearned for as a child?'

His shrewdness took her off guard. She straightened, her stomach fluttering with a thousand nerves. She pressed a hand there, staring at him. This was a man who hadn't paid the slightest heed to the Greek islands when he'd been there or to the beaches on the French Riviera or the Costa del Sol. What on earth could he know about the secret yearnings of her childhood heart and the need to try and right what had felt like an innate wrong in her and her mother's lives?

He straightened too, staring down at her, and his face gentled. 'I think, maybe, that's a yes?'

She had to swallow before she could speak. And then couldn't speak anyway so settled for nodding. The light breeze sent a stray curl fluttering across her face and he reached across to tuck it back behind her ear. A whole different set of butterflies stampeded through her then. Dragging in a breath, she said, 'It's also why I learned to make my own clothes. Hence, discovering I had a knack for design.' She shrugged, feeling suddenly self-conscious. 'It probably sounds dumb to you.'

'It doesn't sound dumb. It sounds like you've been striving for a better life. It's admirable.'

She sent him what she hoped was a wry grin. 'Just call me Cinderella.'

As if in sync they leaned on the railing at the same time again—shoulder to shoulder, fractionally closer than the last time.

Dangerous. The word whispered through her, but she ignored it. They were in a public place. A *very* public place. And this tiny bit of almost touching was companionable, not flirty. Nothing was going to happen.

She pulled her mind back on track before it went off the rails again. 'The thing about not having much money is that you don't have much power either.'

He stilled. 'I never considered it in that light before, but you're right.'

She tried to compartmentalise the distraction of his scent and his heat to a faraway part of her brain. 'I felt that lack of power keenly as a child and I resented it.' She rolled her eyes. 'With the kind of passion only a child can feel. I resented the fact that my mother was always at the mercy of her employers and her roster. She worked in an aged care facility as an enrolled nurse and if she didn't take every extra shift when they asked her to, her hours would be cut to a bare minimum for several weeks afterwards as punishment.'

He swore softly.

'I don't doubt it was a hard world for your mother,' she said, 'but it was a hard one for mine as well.'

'Mine could walk away any time she wanted. Yours couldn't.'

Acid burned her stomach. 'Her lack of options seemed so unfair, but she...'

'She...?'

'She hardly ever complained. And she made things fun. We mightn't have been able to afford fancy holidays, but she'd take me to the beach in summer whenever she could—just for the day. And she made those days feel like holidays.'

'That sounds...' He shifted. 'It sounds really nice.'

'They're among some of the happiest memories I have.'

And she cherished them. 'I used to promise her that when I was queen of the world I'd build her a house on the beach.'

If she accepted MA's offer, she could do exactly that. In fact, she'd have enough money that her mother could retire.

'The two of you are close?'

That made her smile. 'Very.' When she glanced up her smile faltered and she wondered if she'd imagined the wistfulness that flashed through his eyes, but he blinked and the expression returned to one of warm interest and she thought she'd been mistaken.

Or not, she thought a moment later. No matter how hard she tried, she couldn't imagine Denise Cooper-Ford taking Jamie to the beach and building a sandcastle with him or teaching him how to swim. She wouldn't have had the time. She'd have hired staff to do those things. *It doesn't mean they weren't close.*

'I expect she's very proud of you.'

'She's my biggest cheerleader. She's been my biggest supporter all throughout university and then again when I started up Beach Monday. She's so happy that I've been able to follow my dream.'

'I read somewhere you studied part-time.'

Ah, so he'd done his due diligence on her too, huh?

'I worked full-time and studied part-time, which is why I didn't finish my degree until I was twenty-five. I refused to let my mother support me once I'd finished high school. Her emotional support was important, but I figured it was time I became financially independent.'

He straightened. 'You're amazing, you know? You've achieved amazing things. I'm in awe.'

'Nonsense!' She laughed. 'Anyone could've done what I did. And thousands of people do. Every day. It taught me I had the passion to follow through on my dream—and that despite setbacks I can achieve my dreams. It taught me to be focused and determined.'

'And your dream was to create amazing beach umbrellas?'

'Oh, that.' She waved the praise away. 'The umbrellas were an accident. A happy accident, mind. Obviously I wanted to make a living doing something artistic—be some kind of designer—but it wasn't until I took an industrial art class that I found my niche.'

'You've overcome amazing odds. You should be proud of yourself.'

'I am.'

Except she hadn't been entirely honest with her mother. Her stomach screwed up tight. She hadn't confided in her about how much she hated the day-to-day running of Beach Monday.

At first she'd resisted even acknowledging the truth to herself. It'd seemed so fickle of her. She'd worked *so* hard, had put so many hours into Beach Monday's success and to not want to do that any more had seemed the height of folly. She'd tried to learn to love it—to make herself love it.

When she'd no longer been able to lie to herself, she'd had every intention of broaching the subject with her mother. Before she'd been able to do that, though, her mother had fallen ill. Christy had kept putting off telling her, not wanting to worry her. She hadn't wanted her mother misinterpreting this potential change in direction as some kind of panic on Christy's behalf. Her mother's worst fear was that her diagnosis of multiple sclerosis would hold Christy back. As if Christy cared a fig about that even if it should! But it would break her mother's heart if she thought Christy was sacrificing Beach Monday for her.

She pressed her hands together, tapping them lightly against the railing. She had to tell her mother the truth.

She just needed to find the right words first—ones that would allay her mother's fears.

'If you're so close and she's so proud of you, why are you looking as if you're carrying the weight of the world on your shoulders?'

She became aware then that Jamie had angled towards her, still leaning against the railing, but now facing her fully. A frown stretched through his eyes. Oh, those shoulders! And that—

She wrenched her gaze away. 'She's been unwell, and we've both been tiptoeing around, putting on brave faces and not wanting to worry each other.'

He leaned down to look into her face. 'Is she going to be okay?'

He looked so genuinely distressed for her she had to tell herself in the most serious terms possible not to hug him. Instead she nodded. Her mother *was* fine, for the moment at least. 'She's been diagnosed with multiple sclerosis, but her prognosis is good. Except—' she grimaced '—hyper-vigilance is exhausting, and I'm pretty certain she needs just as much a break from it as I do.'

'*That's* why you were so exhausted when you first arrived in Singapore.' He eased back, pursing his lips. 'And something like that is bound to have an effect on your creativity.'

Her shoulders sagged. Her creativity had run screaming for the hills.

'You've been having a tough time of it.'

'No tougher than a lot of other people.'

He ignored that to stare into the middle distance. 'The thought of selling Beach Monday must feel like you're giving up your independence and…your power?'

She shook her head. 'I thought that's how I'd feel, but it's not.'

He raised an eyebrow.

'I don't feel my independence or power is tied to my business. I'm much more than just my business.'

'Of course you are.'

But was he?

The thought came from nowhere.

'I want you to know that if you do sell to me, I'd listen to you. You'd get a say on the direction we should take Beach Monday. Your thoughts would—'

'But not the *final* say.' She wouldn't have any power over the labour force he hired or the suppliers he did business with.

'Your thoughts would matter to me.'

Yeah, maybe, but would they matter to MA's board of directors?

'And obviously in return for that, we'd pay you a generous sum.'

The offer they'd made *was* generous.

He suddenly stiffened and swore. 'What am I doing? I promised myself we wouldn't discuss business tonight. Sorry.' He grimaced. 'It's hard for me to clock off. Work mode is my default setting.'

She planted her hands on her hips and stared at him.

He rolled his shoulders. 'What?'

With a shake of her head, she turned back to the water. The laser light show had just started. With coloured lights dancing on the dark surface of the water it looked like a circus. Ooh…a circus-themed beach umbrella could be a lot of fun. A circus would be good for Jamie. 'I'm thinking you should look a whole lot unhappier about your default setting being work mode.'

She glanced across to find him staring at her. Her gaze lowered to his mouth, and things inside her tightened up.

He had an absolutely perfect mouth—sculpted lips that looked to be the perfect blend of soft and firm.

Dear God. Look away. *Look away!* Evidently it wasn't just her creativity returning, but also her libido. Her lips twisted. How very convenient.

'Was being a big corporate bigwig always your dream?' She needed to stay on task.

When he didn't answer, her stomach took a dive. Did his work define him? Did he feel that his power and sense of self were tied to MA? That'd be an awful way to go through life.

'I can't say I've ever really thought about it,' he finally said. 'It was taken for granted that I'd join the company and eventually become CEO. Molto Arketa is the reason I've lived such a privileged life. I feel…bound to it.'

She noticed his hesitation, but didn't understand it. Any more than she understood his hooded gaze or the way his lips twisted. 'Unlike you, the path was made easy for me.'

'So what, you were lucky. That's not something you need to feel guilty about.'

But she was starting to wonder if that really was the case—was he lucky? What if he was a square peg in a round hole and circumstances had conspired to whittle him into a shape demanded by outside forces? Had he ever had a chance to decide for himself what he wanted to do and what he wanted to be? He'd had all of these expectations placed on his shoulders at such a young age. It didn't seem right somehow. 'If you couldn't be CEO of MA, what would you want to do instead?'

He stared at her as if she'd sprouted another head. 'Why would I want to do anything else? I'm doing precisely what I want to do. Besides, anything else is unthinkable.'

'Why?'

He spread his hands. 'Why would you even ask that

question? I have…so much. And the reason I have so much is because of MA.'

He did. But he didn't seem to be enjoying it.

'I don't know. We just discussed how my sense of self isn't tied to Beach Monday. So I guess I'm wondering if your sense of self is tied to MA.'

He blinked as if the thought had never occurred to him. As if the concept was totally alien. Something inside her started to cry then and she touched his arm. 'Jamie, if MA went under, what would you have in your life?'

He didn't answer.

'I mean, you'd have your mother, of course.'

His bitter laugh had her head rocking back. 'I doubt that very much. Losing MA would kill her.'

The conviction in his voice chilled her. He turned then with icy eyes. 'Surely being committed to MA is a tick in my favour?' He gestured at the bay. 'You're missing the laser show.'

She resisted the urge to shake him. 'I'm not questioning your commitment to MA. Any fool can see how hard you work. I just—'

He raised a supercilious eyebrow. If she'd been its target yesterday it would've shrivelled her to the size of one of the tiny little beads she kept in her workbox, but today she was impervious to it. She'd seen beneath that perfect business exterior and glimpsed the man beneath. He was the kind of man who sent a distressed employee home to recover from a nasty shock. He was a man who'd listened to Christy's practically incoherent ravings yesterday evening and had talked her off a ledge rather than ridicule her or make her feel small. He'd done it all without judgement. This man was innately kind. Couldn't he see he was so much more than his job too?

'You're more than your company, Jamie. I don't care

how big and important MA is. You're a human being who's allowed to have any number of passions and quirks, interests and hobbies outside of your work life. In fact, I think it's a prerequisite.'

'A prerequisite for what?'

'For being a fully rounded human being.' His expression didn't change, her words clearly not striking a chord. She lifted her chin. 'For being a fully rounded and effective leader.'

His eyes narrowed dangerously. 'And how did you reach that conclusion?'

'Because those are the things that make you approachable and will help others relate to you. It creates bonds. And when you make a meaningful bond with another person they'll be happy to follow you wherever you want to take them—they'll take a risk on you.'

He leaned towards her, making her breath catch. 'And where do intelligence and vision and business know-how fit into this utopian hierarchy of yours?'

Utopian? 'They're important too, but you already have those things in spades.'

For a fraction of a second the sudden vulnerability in his gaze made her chest clench, but in the next instant it was gone. 'Look, Christy, I've always subscribed to the belief that one should play to their strengths. I'm not gregarious and bubbly.'

She folded her arms. 'I'm not saying you have to be an extroverted party animal. You just have to like other people. And before you have the chance to misunderstand my words—I already know you like other people.'

'You can't know that.'

'Sure I can. I know because of the way you treated me yesterday. And the way you treated Lien.'

Her mother had instilled in her from an early age to care

about others no matter what. Her mother had been the perfect role model, leading by example, which was why she could now recognise that Jamie did his best to look after others too. But who was looking out for him?

She twisted her hands together. If he wasn't careful, if he didn't ease up and de-stress, he'd be in danger of burning himself out. She didn't want that to happen. She heartily approved of his vision for his company's future. She wanted him at the helm of MA whether she sold Beach Monday to him or not.

She moistened her lips and his gaze lowered to them, his eyes darkening. Need clenched low in her belly, and every nerve in her body fired to life, clamouring for attention and release. They stood toe to toe, mirroring each other's body language, and so close she could feel the barely checked power of his body—it all beat at her in a tempting wave of promise and delight.

She'd thought her attraction was all one-sided, but with a rush of elation realised it wasn't. Jamie found her attractive. He wanted her as much as she wanted him. The knowledge left her breathless. 'You're so much more than the CEO of MA, Jamie. I think you're amazing. I love the plans you have for MA. You should be proud of them and of yourself. But enjoying downtime is important too.'

She touched one finger lightly to his chest, to the spot above his heart, and felt the muscle beneath—hard-packed and solid—and her head spun. 'Don't let anyone steal your tail. Don't let them tell you what you can and can't be. You can be all the things all at once if you want.'

Not breaking eye contact, he slowly shook his head. 'You see things in me that aren't there.'

'I see you through an artist's eye.'

'I think you're seeing what you want to see. You need to be careful I don't take advantage of that.'

His words should've made her cold all over, but they didn't. 'You don't scare me.'

'Maybe I should. I'm not a warm man, Christy. I'm distant and cold—'

'Not warm?' A laugh burbled out of her. 'You're joking, right?'

But the expression in his eyes told her he wasn't. 'You're wrong, Jamie. Very wrong. I don't know who told you that you were cold, but they must've had some agenda of their own.'

'Listen…' She reached up and touched his face, wanting to drive her point home, but the moment she touched him all sentient thought fled. She couldn't remember what she'd been about to say. She swallowed. 'I…'

The light in his eyes flared, and his hands curved around her shoulders. That hot, hungry gaze roved over her face and she was amazed she didn't melt to a puddle at his feet. 'Christy?'

Her name was a groan and a question. She answered it by rising on tiptoe and pressing her lips to his.

She'd been right—his lips were the perfect blend of soft and firm and they turned her world upside down. He kissed her back with a single-minded gentleness that had her melting against him, her hands pressing against the hard planes of his chest, thrilling her palms. He kissed her as if she were made of something fine and fragile—porcelain, crystal, fairy floss—and as if he were determined to take every care and appreciate her fully.

It had her gasping and clinging to him. And then it made her perverse. She wanted to make him greedy and reckless…to lose control. Clenching one hand in the material of his shirt, she anchored herself to him and boldly swept her tongue across the seam of his lips and into his mouth. The hand at her waist gripped her tighter, sending tentacles of pleasure spiralling outwards.

She felt him smile against her lips, and she couldn't help but smile too. And then his hand cupped the back of her head and he kissed her with such merciless thoroughness all she could do was cling to him and kiss him back and pray he'd never stop.

Too soon, though, those lips gentled on hers again as if to quieten the storm they'd created inside her and to bring her back to herself before, finally, breaking contact.

He rested his forehead against hers, as if he needed to catch his breath, before moving away. She focused on unclenching her hands from his shirt.

'You're missing the laser show,' he murmured.

'I don't think I am.'

He smiled, but he moved further away, putting a foot of distance between them, and she glanced up to see consternation in his eyes. A chill speared into her chest.

'I owe you an apology, Christy. That was unprofessional of me. Ours is supposed to be a business relationship, and instead I've taken advantage of—'

'No.' His words froze her to her very marrow. 'Please don't apologise. I'm just as much to blame as you.' More to blame. She'd been the one to initiate that kiss, not him. Dear God. What on earth had she been thinking?

He smiled but it didn't reach his eyes. 'Perhaps blame is too harsh a word.'

She had no intention of getting into bed with the enemy. Not that he was the enemy per se, but talk about conflict of interest! 'Absolutely.' She nodded once, twice…thrice. She couldn't seem to stop. 'It was just one of those things. An impulse of the moment.'

'A lovely moment,' he said, his eyes gentle and his mouth firm.

Gorgeously firm.

Don't think about that. He was trying to tell her that it couldn't happen again. And she agreed with him whole-heartedly.

Christy took another step away, and James scanned her face, something inside him twisting at the stricken expression in her eyes.

Her lips twisted—an attempt at humour. 'But a moment we better not repeat,' she said, not looking at him.

In that moment before they'd kissed, she'd made him forget everything—that he was a Cooper-Ford, all he owed his father and mother, the promises he'd made. He'd simply become a man, nothing more, nothing less. It'd felt liberating. The sense of freedom still clamoured through him demanding more—more freedom, more Christy. He did what he could to leash it.

Christy had made him feel seen—truly seen—and understood. He'd no more been able to stop from kissing her than he'd be able to stop a falling Manhattan skyscraper.

But it *couldn't* happen again.

'I'm not giving my tail away.'

She murmured the words as if to herself, and if he'd been more himself he'd have let it pass, but he was still off-balance from their kiss. 'What does that mean? I didn't understand the reference the first time you made it.'

She shook her head. 'It doesn't matter.'

He bet it did. He bet it mattered a lot. When he didn't say anything, she eventually blew out a little breath. 'Do you know the fairy tale *The Little Mermaid*?'

'The Disney movie?'

'It's a Hans Christian Andersen fairy tale. The little mermaid saves the unconscious prince from drowning when his ship runs aground in a storm. She falls in love with him and asks a powerful witch to give her legs—

there are tests and hardships, in typical fairy-tale fashion, prices to be paid.'

He nodded to tell her he was with her so far.

'The witch tells her that when she has legs, her tail will be gone forever. She'll never be able to return to her own world.'

He found himself fascinated by her story. 'What happened?'

'She chose the legs and went ashore to find her prince, only to discover that he believed another woman had saved his life and that he was marrying her instead. He sends the little mermaid away.'

Jamie's heart stuttered in his chest. 'But where did she go? She couldn't go back home. She—' The full impact of the little mermaid giving away her tail hit him. 'That's an awful story!'

'It's a cautionary tale.' Then she rolled her eyes. 'It's also only one version of the fairy tale. There are others— the most cheerful being she gets the prince, but only for a night, before she has to sacrifice herself. But, in doing so, she wins an eternal soul.'

Acid burned through him. 'You've given away your tail in the past?' The thought of someone taking advantage of her made him want to smash something.

'Not to the same extent as the little mermaid.' She glanced away, her lips pressed together in a tight line. 'When I was at uni I had a boyfriend who stole my artwork and passed it off as his own. He won a university prize, which included a three-month guest residency at a gallery that I'd been hoping to win. Winning that prize was more important to him than I was, apparently. He used me for his own ends, played me for a fool.'

He stared at her, horrified. 'That's… It's appalling.' His

stomach gave a nauseating roll. 'And you think I might be like him? You think I'll steal your work and—'

'No!' She reached out and touched his arm. 'I've absolutely no reason to believe you or MA would ever do anything like that.'

She pulled her hand back, and he didn't know if he was sorry or glad. *Damn it all to hell*, he was getting too involved. He had to pull back. But the thought of taking advantage of her in the way she'd just described sickened him to his marrow.

'Stop looking at me like that, Jamie. This isn't about you. It's about me.'

She looked the teensiest bit cross and for some reason it made him breathe a little easier.

'I came to Singapore to try and clear my head. To work out if I want to sell Beach Monday or not.'

He did his best to channel distance. Remoteness. Coldness.

'Kissing you…'

She gave a shaky laugh and heat exploded through him again.

'Well, let's just say that's muddying my head even further.'

He definitely couldn't kiss her again. She needed some breathing space. It didn't seem too much to ask and—

'Mind you, I think that kiss might be worth a bit of brain fuzziness.'

He choked. *She what?*

She sent him a grin and he couldn't help huffing out a laugh.

'I'm not saying it was wise or that we should ever repeat it,' she said. 'But you're looking far too serious. Come on, let's walk home.'

'Walk?'

She held up her phone. 'Apparently it's only fifteen minutes back to Clarke Quay—and it's beside the river so it should be pretty.'

His heart thudded. Pretty *and* ridiculously romantic. He couldn't recall Singapore being this romantic on his previous visits.

'Thank you for this evening, Jamie—dinner, the view, the light show—it was amazing.'

They turned and made their way in the direction of home, careful not to touch. 'I'm glad you had a nice time.' He had too, he suddenly realised. That might be the oddest thing of all. He'd offered out of duty, but she'd made him forget about duty.

It occurred to him then that too much time spent in Christy's company could be perilous. He was in danger of forgetting his mission.

He made a decision then and there to give Christy the time and space she needed this week, but to absent himself as much as he could. 'You're free to spend the rest of the week however you wish, Christy. There's no need to check in with me. I'm afraid, though, that my schedule won't allow me time off for sightseeing. Focus on recharging your batteries and we'll talk business next week.'

She stared at him. 'Are you sure...?'

He nodded. He was *very* sure.

CHAPTER SIX

JAMES HADN'T MEANT to clap eyes on Christy at all the following day. He'd made his excuses the previous evening with more grace than speed. He'd planned to spend the next few days at the store with Lien. She'd been understandably rocked by the vandalism and he didn't want her working alone. He wanted to introduce her to the security guards he'd hired—one male, one female—and make sure she felt comfortable with them.

He'd wanted away from the disturbing feelings Christy sent erupting through him. Escaping to work, though, hadn't helped him escape those.

When he caught sight of her on the stairs of their apartment building the following afternoon, he should've strode straight across to the elevator and pretended he hadn't seen her. Instead he found himself taking the stairs two at a time to catch up with her. It'd be polite to ask her how her day had been, and if she had everything she needed.

Her tumble of red-gold hair spilled over her shoulder as she peered over the railing to see who followed her. Her face lit up and he had to fight the impulse to take the steps three at a time.

'Hello,' she called out, waiting for him to catch her up and sending him a smile that had his groin tightening.

'Hello, yourself.' He scanned her face and nodded when

she raised questioning eyebrows. 'It's official—Singapore is good for you.'

Her answering smile had his skin pulling tight. Uh, make that tighter. 'I've had such a fun day. Come and see what I bought.'

She flung her door open and he found himself following, intrigued in spite of himself. When what he should be doing was making his excuses and disappearing upstairs. Still, what harm could there be in seeing her purchases and hearing about her day? He was her host, after all.

She dropped her bags to the sofa, upending several of them so that a range of silky bathrobes in a rainbow of bright colour spilled across the upholstery.

'I went to Chinatown. It was so amazing. There's a Buddhist temple that was seriously spectacular.' She pulled her phone out and showed him the photographs. 'And these...' She fingered the material of the robes.

'Are what? Going to make great gifts for your friends back home?' he teased, trying not to imagine her in a vivid yellow one with sprays of blue flowers splashed across it, or the scarlet one bearing spears of fat pink and white orchids.

He swallowed, suddenly parched because he could vividly imagine her in one of those robes, naked beneath. He could imagine untying the sash and letting it fall open to reveal pale flesh, slipping it from her shoulders to drop to the floor and pool at her feet. He'd drop to his knees and bury—

He snapped upright, horrified at how quickly his imagination had taken over. He glanced at her in panic before letting out a slow breath. She hadn't noticed—too intent on her purchases. 'They will make nice gifts, but the colours and the patterns...'

He realised then what had her so absorbed. 'Creative inspiration?'

She nodded.

'Are you ever not creating?' He'd been going to call it work, but it seemed the wrong word to use.

'There are ideas everywhere here. I can't help but feel inspired.' She glanced up, her gaze sharp. 'You've no idea what a gift that is. Thank you.'

She was thanking him? He hadn't done anything!

She pulled out a tiny jade Buddha wrapped in tissue paper. 'The jade at the markets was amazing. Beads and bracelets and pendants.'

He glanced at her purchases. 'You didn't buy any?'

She turned away, but he saw the way she bit her lip. 'I can't spend all of my money on my first shopping trip.'

Her words were light, but he cursed himself all the same. Her world was very different from his and her business had only just started to take off. She wouldn't have too much excess cash and what she did have she wouldn't be able to afford to simply splash around. She'd probably be pouring most of it back into Beach Monday.

'Very true.' He kept his voice light too. 'And if you decide you need jade jewellery, you can simply visit the markets again.'

Her smile was his reward. 'What do you think? Have you ever been there?'

She nodded at his hands, and with a start he realised he still held her phone and was supposed to be looking at her photos of the temple. 'Um…no. But it looks amazing.'

She plucked her phone from his fingers, her eyes narrowing. 'Have you experienced any Singaporean culture at all, Jamie? Or do you fly in, close your deals, and fly straight back out again?'

He loosened his tie. 'I, uh…'

Her hands went to her hips. 'You've not been to the Buddhist temple; you've not been to the Chinatown markets. Have you been on a river cruise or gone to the night zoo, walked through Little India or been inside one of the Hindu temples?'

'I've been for a cruise on the bay.' It'd been with the owner of the centre where the new MA store was located. He'd been too busy negotiating with the other man to spend too much time taking in the scenery, though. 'I've seen the laser shows. I've dined at many of the restaurants at the Marina Bay Sands Hotel, and even swum in their infinity pool. I'm intimately acquainted with the Orchard Road strip.'

Very slowly, she nodded. 'For a moment there I forgot we were from such completely different worlds. You live the high life and I don't.'

A bad taste filled his mouth. The world was inherently unfair and it was only a stroke of luck—an accident of birth—that had made him one of the lucky ones.

She planted her hands on her hips. 'I had a great time last night—it was an amazing experience. But today was every bit as fun.' Golden eyes speared to his, full of challenge. 'Are you up for an adventure?'

He should back off. Instead he found his chin coming up. 'Always.'

'Excellent,' she purred. 'Meet me in the foyer at seven p.m. Dinner's on me tonight.'

Christy glanced around at the crowded food hall and things inside her took flight, just as they had earlier in the day when she'd been walking through Chinatown—taking her time to browse the market stalls and to just…feel free for a few hours from all the worries that had been weighing her down for the last twelve months. Today had been such a delight.

Jamie didn't know what a gift he'd given her. It was why

she'd so foolishly and impulsively invited him to dinner tonight. She'd wanted to give something back.

She shouldn't have done it. They both knew it'd be far wiser to put a little—or a lot—of distance between them until that kiss had become a faint memory. It was why he'd left her to her own devices today rather than accompanying her *to protect his investment*. So why had he accepted the invitation?

Maybe that kiss had already become a faint memory for him? It took all her strength to stop her lip from curling at that thought.

'This place is *hopping*.'

She snapped to at his words. 'It is.' But as her guidebook described it as one of the best food halls in the Arts District that should be no surprise. 'Free table,' she squeaked, pushing him towards a table for two. 'What would you like to eat?'

They'd done two full circuits, just taking in the myriad food options. She'd counted sixteen different vendors in this one hall, all offering a variety of delicious-looking dishes. The vegetables looked fresh and bright, and the scent of cooking spices made her mouth water.

'I don't—' A crafty expression flitted across his face. 'I chose last night, so how about I leave tonight's choice to you.'

It made her laugh. 'Well, I'm going to work on the premise that it's all good.'

'Excellent premise.'

She made for one of the vendors whose display of fresh ingredients appealed to her artist's eye before she could find herself too caught up in Jamie's smile and the blue of his eyes. She chose two traditional specialities, all the while lecturing herself that she was an adult woman and not a giddy adolescent, returning to the table with a laden tray and a renewed sense of resolution.

She set a bowl in front of him—'Apparently we get a free soup with our meals'—before unloading the rest of the dishes from the tray.

He stared at her. She shrugged. 'I don't know, maybe it's a thing. I suggest we just roll with it.'

'Roger.'

'And this is Hainanese Chicken Rice—widely considered Singapore's national dish. And this—' she pointed to the noodle, minced pork and prawn dish '—is Wonton Mee—another local speciality. Oh, and some satay sticks to share because they smelled so good.' And because she didn't know how hungry he was. Last of all she handed him a soda.

He stared at it all, his gaze taking in every detail. 'Which dish do you want?'

'I love the sound of them both. So you can have whichever you want.' She watched his eyes dart from one to the other. 'Or,' she added, 'we can do what my girlfriends and I sometimes do and share.'

'Perfect solution.'

They each pulled the nearest dish in close to sample it, watching each other's expressions. The food was fresh and wholesome and unbelievably cheap. 'OMG,' she muttered. 'This is *really* good.'

He nodded his agreement, reaching for a satay stick. '*Seriously* good.'

When she'd read the words *food hall* in her guidebook it had brought to mind the eating area of her local shopping centre in Australia—a place that served generic fast food. This was fast but there was nothing generic about it.

Jamie gestured at his plate. 'You have to try the Wonton Mee.'

They swapped dishes and ate in silence until Christy couldn't fit another bite in, leaving Jamie to finish off the last of their food 'More?' she asked when he was done.

He shook his head. 'I'm full. I just couldn't bear to waste any of it.' He sat back with a satisfied sigh, glancing around. 'I had no idea this place was almost on our doorstep. It's a gem.'

'I'm guessing it's not the kind of place your colleagues are likely to bring you. They probably think you prefer five-star dining. Oh! Not that five-star dining isn't great—'

'But so is this. It feels *real*. In a way that takeout pizza feels real.'

He liked pizza?

'Thanks for bringing me here, Christy. It's an adventure I'd have not missed for the world.'

The way he looked at her made her toes curl. 'I thought you'd like it.' She fiddled with her shirtsleeves, trying to ignore the temptation curling through her. In this setting, wearing casual clothes and gazing around at everything with a lively interest, he looked disturbingly *real* too, and nothing like the ice prince who'd met her at the airport.

As for their kiss… She'd never experienced anything like it. Not just its intensity and the speed with which she'd been ready to throw all caution to the wind, but its *beauty*. Which was a strange word to use to describe a kiss, but she couldn't think of another that better captured the magic she'd experienced in Jamie's arms.

Except she had to try and put that kiss out of her mind.

With a mental shake, she forced her mind into a different channel. This food-hall experience was such a tiny adventure. Jamie should expand his horizons. 'I think you'd get a kick out of Chinatown too…and the Buddhist temple.'

For a long moment he didn't answer. 'You think I'm nothing more than a spoiled rich kid who doesn't have a clue how to live in the real world without a driver, personal assistant, and his credit card.'

A bitter smile lurked at the corners of his mouth, and she automatically started to shake her head but stopped. What did she really know about him after all?

'Are you?'

'If I said I wasn't, you wouldn't believe me.'

'I suspect you have enough life skills to get by if your credit card happened to be mysteriously cancelled or if your driver and PA were on holiday and out of contact.'

'But?'

She shrugged. *In for a penny...* 'We've already established that your real world is very different from my real world. And that gives the two of us very different perspectives on the lives of the women I've been working with in Africa, China and Central America.'

He leaned towards her, and she had the feeling that his every sense had sharpened. 'And what's your take away from that?'

'That you don't understand the importance to their lives of the work I send their way.'

'Then tell me.'

So she did. She sourced her textiles, beads and other embellishments from village co-ops in Africa, China and Central America, and the trade she sent their way was having a major impact on those communities. In one instance it was helping to improve local infrastructure, like roads and bridges. In one village it meant the younger generation of girls could be sent to school. In yet another, women who had been cast out of their communities due to fistulas—a childbirth injury—were able to get life-changing surgery. These were things that mattered, that made a significant difference to people's lives. It wasn't something she could just walk away from.

When she was done, he dragged a hand down his face. 'You're right. I've no notion of how hard these people's lives are.'

'Neither do I. I've not suffered the kinds of hardships they're facing. And I know it's only a drop in the ocean, but it means a lot to me.'

'I can see that.'

'And whoever I sell Beach Monday to has to promise to maintain those same links, and to continue the education programmes I've helped set in place.'

'That goes without saying.'

Did it? She wasn't so sure. 'What guarantees can you give me that it would continue to be the case? Once Beach Monday is yours, you can do whatever you damn well please.' MA could trade on Beach Monday's good name without lifting a finger to continue her company's good work.

He leaned towards her. 'Christy, it's these very contacts that I want and need. It's why Beach Monday is such an attractive proposition to me. You already have the contacts I want in place. Your stance on ethical issues, the awards you've won, are well known. In buying Beach Monday, Molto Arketa would be tacitly pledging to continue that work.'

'Or, in buying Beach Monday, Molto Arketa could simply be capitalising on Beach Monday's impeccable reputation in an attempt to rehabilitate its own tarnished one. Without any intention of following through on promises made.'

'I could have specific clauses written into the contract legally binding MA to the co-ops.'

Her lips twisted. 'Along with a thousand loopholes for the express purpose of breaking it when things became too hard or not cost-effective enough.'

'I've already told you it's important to me to rebuild MA's reputation. There's no denying that buying Beach Monday would turn public perception around, but it's equally true that I share your vision.'

She folded her arms, resting them on the table. 'What's more important to you, Jamie—rehabilitating MA's reputation or creating a more equitable world?'

'You don't think I can do both?'

And there was her answer. She had the distinct impression that Jamie focused on the wrong things. But she didn't know why. She knew he was kind—she'd had first-hand experience of it. But he was also driven.

Her heart gave a kick and her pulse started to race. What if she could find a way to direct that drive and determination in the service of more altruistic goals?

The idea had her straightening. Well, why not? If she could convince someone like Jamie to support the same causes she did, then the benefit to communities in developing countries would be tremendous. MA's scale was a thousand times greater than hers.

'You know, Jamie, what worries me is that you work too hard and don't take enough notice of the amazing things around you. I don't think you appreciate it the way you ought to.' She leaned towards him. 'Just because you were born to wealth and privilege doesn't mean you're not entitled to a holiday. At the rate you're going, you *will* burn out. When that happens, someone else will be made CEO— one of the old fogeys you're currently fighting, no doubt. I don't want someone like that in charge of Beach Monday.'

Not that it'd be Beach Monday any more. It'd be part of MA.

'Has it occurred to you that you have an over-inflated sense of responsibility to these village co-ops of yours?'

'Not for a moment.'

He nodded as if her words didn't surprise him. 'I don't know how much information you gathered when you did that online search on me and MA, but I'm thinking you wouldn't have had to dig far to discover that my father was…'

A notorious playboy, but she didn't say the words out loud. The man *had* been Jamie's father, and he'd died when Jamie was only twelve—and twelve was an impressionable age. He could've been a playboy *and* a good father. One didn't necessarily cancel the other out.

'He was one of those people who took his good fortune for granted. He went through money like there was no tomorrow and lived like a prince.'

Okay, then. Perhaps *not* such a good father.

'He was selfish and spoiled and lazy…except when it came to pursuing women he wasn't married to.'

Her insides clenched. Denise Cooper-Ford should've kicked his sorry butt to the kerb and divorced him. But she hadn't. Had she loved her husband? Or was it the Cooper-Ford name that she loved?

None of her business.

'When he was dying, he had a change of heart—told me he was sorry he hadn't been a better father, said he wished he'd spent more time with me.'

Her heart burned at the expression in Jamie's eyes. What effect had his parents' tumultuous marriage had on him? He'd been so young. It must've been awful. No amount of wealth could make up for that.

'He made me promise to not make the same mistakes he had.'

She leaned across the table to grip his hand. 'And you haven't—you're neither a spendthrift nor a playboy. But it doesn't mean you're never allowed to let your hair down.'

He squeezed her hand. 'Christy, even as a child I wasn't much of one for letting my hair down.'

'It's never too late to learn.'

She reclaimed her hand. His touch could undo her. And she had no intention of being undone. She'd been proven wrong about men in the past. She was the figurehead of a company that advocated for issues of social justice. She wasn't making a fool of herself over a man again. Not when it had the potential to play out in the rarefied atmosphere of the Cooper-Ford world. She couldn't do anything that would reflect badly on her company.

Jamie's brow pleated, and for a moment she had the oddest sensation that his perfect self had fallen away and what she was looking at now was the real man beneath the façade. And as his eyes met hers, all the noise and bustle of the food hall fell away for a brief moment and nothing existed beyond the two of them. And then one of them blinked—she couldn't have said which—and so did the other, and all the noise and bustle flooded back.

She stared at her hands, motionless in her lap, and wished for another napkin to shred.

'We're taking a table that someone else could use.' He leaned towards her, his eyes intent. 'Would you like to go for a drink?'

She shouldn't. She should make her excuses and go back to the apartment. Alone.

Do you want to say no?

Of course not. It was, therefore, probably imperative that she did.

'I'd like to continue our conversation.'

Conversation?

Oh, yes! They'd been talking about her village co-ops. She'd do everything she could to promote them. 'Please tell me you know some fabulous funky place down on the Quay because I'd kill for a G & T.'

Amusement chased across his face. 'Of course I do.'

Half an hour later they were in an upstairs bar overlooking the river—and the plethora of bright young things thronging the Quay's eateries. It felt like a party. Christy pressed her hands together and stared at it all. 'This is brilliant!'

Noting the serious expression in his eyes, she reined in her enthusiasm for the bar, the Quay, and Singapore itself. 'You said you wanted to continue our conversation. What did you want to ask me?'

'I'm puzzled.' He held his glass of Scotch in his hands. He hadn't yet taken a sip. 'You're proud of everything you've achieved with Beach Monday?'

What a strange question. 'Yes.'

'And you feel strongly about your village co-ops and education programmes and the charities you're involved in?'

'Absolutely.'

That frown deepened. 'Then why do you want to sell? Why hand the reins to someone else? Why give up your control of a company you've built from scratch?'

She stirred her straw through her drink. 'Two reasons. The first is that Beach Monday is on the brink of major international success.'

He nodded his agreement.

'I don't have the business skills to take the company to the next level.'

He leaned back but didn't say anything.

She nodded anyway as if he had. 'I can learn them and I could become good at them.'

'But?'

'But the shocking truth is that I don't want to. I've discovered I've no liking for the business and administration side of things. Which leads me to my second reason. I'm a designer. I want to design.'

His brow cleared. 'And being in charge leaves you no time for that.'

She took a fortifying sip of her G & T. 'It's not only that. Being in charge wrings me dry.' His eyes narrowed and she had no idea if he understood what she meant or not. 'For the last year I've struggled to come up with a single design concept of any worth. Until I arrived here in Singapore, I was starting to worry that my creativity was gone for ever.'

His every muscle stiffened as if in protest. 'But it hasn't. Since you've been here it's been firing on all cylinders.'

'Yes.' She closed her eyes briefly and sent up a prayer of thanks. 'Which proves to me that the business side of things is definitely impacting on my creativity in a detrimental way.'

'It is possible to find a balance, Christy.'

She didn't want to.

'And you've had a lot on your mind as well—your mother's health scare would've had an impact.'

She nodded in acknowledgement. But it didn't change the facts.

'And you could take on a partner—someone to run the business side of things. That would free you up to focus on designing.'

She nodded at that too. It was her Plan B. A plan she had no enthusiasm for.

'But you don't want to.' He finally sipped his Scotch and she did her best not to notice the way his mouth touched the glass. 'You're an all-or-nothing person,' he finally said, setting the glass back down.

She hadn't considered it in those terms before. 'I guess

I am. If I can't sell Beach Monday to a company I trust, however, a partner is the route I'll take.'

Yay. Not.

'But?' Those blue eyes sharpened. 'Why the lamentable lack of enthusiasm? I'd have thought you'd welcome the chance to maintain ties to your company.'

Her chest squeezed tight, making it hard to catch her breath. Beach Monday *was* her baby—the company of her heart. Could she really walk away from it?

She pushed her shoulders back. Of course she could. This was business. 'I have trust issues.' She rolled her eyes in an attempt to make light of her words.

'You think it would be difficult to find a partner you could trust?'

The thought of the entire process—selecting, interviewing, meeting and negotiating—left her exhausted.

'Why do you have trust issues?'

She hesitated, but… It wouldn't hurt to tell him the truth. She couldn't see how he'd be able to use it against her in any way. 'A few months ago I discovered that my office manager, Rosa, was stealing from me.'

His face darkened. 'How?'

'She was in charge of the payroll.'

'And the odd bonus just happened to find its way into her pay packet?'

'On the sixteenth of every month without fail as it turns out. It's the oddest thing, but I really liked her. Who knew thieves could be so personable?'

'Christy, I—'

'What really rubbed salt into the wound, though, was she came highly recommended by a business colleague whom I respected. I've since found out that they'd just wanted to get rid of her from their own organisation.'

He swore, and then leaned across and enfolded the

hands she'd lightly pressed together on the table in front of her between his own. 'I'm sorry that happened to you. It…sucks.'

His descent into childish slang made her smile.

'But, Christy, you learn from experiences like that.'

She pulled away, tugging her hands from his. 'All I've learned is that people can be deceitful and are prepared to take advantage of others to promote their own interests.' Lewis had already taught her that particular lesson, but it hadn't stopped her from making the same mistake again.

She couldn't stop her shoulders from slumping. 'It didn't teach me how to instantly recognise deceit, fraudulence or duplicity. I just now know that it comes all wrapped up in an attractive package deliberately designed to tempt you.'

He blew out a breath. 'And I'm offering you…'

She nodded. 'Exactly.'

'And now you're wondering—'

'If it's too good to be true,' she agreed. 'I'm looking at every possible angle you can screw me over, Jamie.' And she hated herself for it.

'And it looks as if you're enjoying the process about as much as I am.'

His smile was wry and she couldn't help but return it. 'Bingo.'

He stared off into the middle distance. Christy sipped her G & T and then nearly choked when that blue-eyed gaze refocused on her with a new intensity. She set her glass down with a hasty thud. 'What?'

'I'm glad you're so suspicious of me and my motives.'

If she wore glasses, she'd have stared at him over the top of them now. 'Really?' Her voice dripped with disbelief.

'If I can prove to you that I mean exactly what I say, if I can prove that I'm serious about cementing relationships with your suppliers and supporting the programmes you've put into place, then I can also convince my board of the efficacy of my vision. And that will mean I can finally haul MA into the future and secure its place as one of the world's most iconic brands, meaning MA's future success will be guaranteed.'

And yet again she couldn't help noticing that he'd focused on the wrong thing. Was MA's continued success really more important to him than anything else? And more to the point, if that were the case, then...*why*?

Jamie—somehow he was starting to think of himself as Jamie rather than James—knew his proclamation to Christy had been a bold one, but nothing less would win her over.

What was more, he found himself wanting to win her approval, her praise, and her support. When she looked at him he wanted her to feel proud of the association, not wracked with anxiety and riddled with doubts. And he had a dubious suspicion that had nothing to do with business.

He spent the next four days working and trying to keep his mind focused on business, rather than drifting off to the shape of Christy's mouth or the curve of her waist or the way her mane of red curls danced about her face. He continued to gather information about clothing factories in developing countries, and everything he discovered renewed his determination to make grass-root changes at MA. Companies like MA had a responsibility to the rest of the world.

He created a mental checklist of the things he needed to accomplish to win Christy's backing.

He needed to prove to her that he wasn't going to abandon her village co-ops to their fates and replace them with a more efficient labour force.

He had to support the charities and education programmes she headed up. They'd be key in helping him become an industry leader in environmental and social sustainability.

And, finally, he had to somehow prove to her that he was more than the job.

But you're not.

He rolled his shoulders. Garbage. There was more to him than market appraisals and profit projections. Some instinct told him that if he gave his whimsical side a little more freedom, Christy *would* respond to it. He bit back a sigh. Did he even have a whimsical side?

Of course he did. Everyone did. His came to life whenever he so much as glanced at one of her amazing beach umbrellas.

He did his best to try and *loosen up*. In the evenings, he and Christy had fallen into the habit of setting off for some new food hall and sampling whatever new dishes took their fancy. She'd tell him about the exciting things she'd done for the day—she'd visited the Gardens by the Bay and made him want to experience the Supertrees for himself, had spent a magical day at the zoo, and had spent a morning exploring Little India, and an afternoon on a boat cruise.

She'd inspired him so much that during one lunchbreak he'd slipped away from his makeshift office in the apartment to go and check out the Buddhist temple in Chinatown. It had been awe-inspiring, just as she'd said. Walking back home through the crowded streets had made him feel alive, and he'd found himself taking in the shapes and colours all around him. It made him wonder if in Manhattan he always walked with his eyes straight ahead and half closed.

They were sallying forth to sample one of the food halls downtown when Jamie's phone rang. He hesitated, tempted to let it go to voicemail.

'Don't not answer it on my account,' Christy said. 'It could be important.'

He didn't recognise the number. 'Hello?'

'Mr Cooper-Ford, it's Inspector Goh.'

'Hello, Inspector, what can I do for you? Do you have news?' Inspector Goh was in charge of the investigation into the vandalism that had occurred at the MA store.

'I do.'

As he listened to the inspector's report, his gut clenched and his appetite fled. 'I see. Good work. And thank you for letting me know so quickly, I appreciate it. Do you need me to come into the station?'

When the inspector answered in the negative, they rang off.

Christy took one look at his face and led him to a park bench beneath a majestic rain tree with a view of the Victoria Concert Hall. 'The inspector had news?'

He dragged a hand down his face. 'They've made an arrest.'

'So… It wasn't a business rival, a jealous ex, or a disgruntled board member?'

'No.' He had to tell her the truth. There was nothing for it. But he also needed to mitigate the potential damage it could do to their negotiations.

'Was it random after all?'

'I wish it had been, but no.' He turned to face her more fully. 'You'll be aware of the bad press MA received back in February.'

'In relation to the documentary on Bangladeshi clothing factories?' At his nod she continued. 'MA was one of the companies named and shamed for sourcing its labour from factories whose workers—mainly women, I might add—aren't even making a living wage.'

His gut twisted. 'That's the one. And for your information I'm in the process of instituting changes there.'

'Glad to hear it.'

'An activist group has set themselves up in opposition to companies of MA's ilk.'

She nodded. 'Agitating for change.' And then her eyes widened. '*They're* responsible for the vandalism?'

He nodded. Behind the amber of her eyes he watched her mind race and his heart sank.

'This will make the newspapers?'

His lips twisted. 'Undoubtedly.'

While she didn't physically move away, he could feel her emotionally and mentally start to distance herself. 'I don't want my good name or Beach Monday's good name tarnished by yet another MA scandal.'

'I *will* make sure your name is kept out of the papers.'

'How?'

He stilled and then he smiled. 'I'll offer a personal interview.' He'd do whatever necessary to prevent Christy from hightailing it out of Singapore on the next available flight. 'I believe it's time to go public with my plans for MA's future…with my vision for the company.'

Her mouth dropped open. 'Without talking to your board first? They'll have a fit!'

'It's time they had a shake-up.' He was tired of pussyfooting around.

She bit her lip, and then she grinned. 'Okay, I'm so sticking around to see this.'

Some unknown tension inside him dissolved and he found himself grinning back at her. 'Game on.'

CHAPTER SEVEN

THE FOLLOWING EVENING Jamie's gaze remained glued to Christy's face rather than the TV as they watched his televised interview. He wanted to gauge her reaction. If only he could stop focusing on those curls! She had the sweetest ringlet that dangled down the side of her face to brush across her collarbone. He wanted to kiss the spot—

Concentrate!

Mentally he slapped himself. He needed to focus. Not imprint her face on his mind.

He had a feeling it was already imprinted there anyway. He had a feeling he was never going to forget what she looked like in this precise moment. And it was nearly impossible to concentrate with her vanilla-butter-cake scent invading his senses.

When the interview was at an end, she clicked the TV off and tossed the remote onto the coffee table. The movement sent a new wave of vanilla-scented air in his direction. They'd settled on the sofa in her apartment to watch the interview, but he thought now he should've chosen one of the bucket chairs.

'That suit—' he pointed to the now blank screen '—was a damn fine suit.'

'That interview—' she pointed to the TV too '—was a damn fine interview.'

Some of the tension balled inside him started to loosen. As he'd hoped, that interview had helped to mitigate some of her concerns. 'You needn't look so surprised,' he teased. 'I'm good at what I do.'

'You were polished, convincing and *plausible*.'

Her words gave him pause. 'I meant every word.'

She met his gaze. 'I know.'

'None of that was news to you—I'd told you most of it already.'

She moistened her lips. 'But now I believe it with my head too, not just my heart.'

He stared at the shine on her lips, at their plump promise, and need rumbled through his veins.

'But now that you've gone public with your intentions for MA, outlined the direction you want the company to take, you've verbally committed to a course of action, and if you don't follow through there'll be a public outcry.'

He dragged his attention back to what she was saying. 'One that will materially damage MA's bottom line,' he agreed.

'What will your board do?'

'Beside have a thousand fits?'

She grimaced, but a twinkle danced in her eyes. 'You're enjoying this.'

The only answer he gave was a shrug. His board were *not* going to be pleased. They'd rant and rave and try to rattle his cage, but he'd forced their hand. And not before time. He was tired of waiting. MA was profiting at the expense of people who had no power. In all conscience, they could no longer continue the way they were. It was reprehensible.

'My board are going to learn that they have to toe a new party line.'

She nodded, though he sensed her mind racing. But

then her face cleared and she sent him a smile that had his blood heating and his skin going tight. 'You were brilliant.'

The compliment was said with simple sincerity, making his throat thicken. He cleared it. 'Thanks.'

Their gazes caught and held and the room seemed to shrink, and grow warmer. He wanted—

She leapt off the sofa. 'Drink? A soda or an iced water?' she said, her voice too high.

'No, thanks.' He shot to his feet. 'I should be going.'

He hadn't imagined her panic when they'd been in danger of falling into each other's eyes. And he didn't imagine her disappointment at his decision to leave now. He empathised heartily with both.

'You've signed Suki Takaharshi and Danielski?' she said, naming a feted artist and a public relations firm.

She poured herself a glass of iced water and gulped some of it down. He dragged his gaze from the line of her throat. 'I want to sign people who share my vision, whose brand aligns to the one I'm trying to create at MA.'

'Did they know you were going public with this today?'

'I checked with them first—made sure I had their permission.'

'I'm impressed.'

He wanted her to be. 'Thank you for staying and not running back to Australia, Christy, for trusting that I could fix this.'

'You came through when I wasn't sure you could. And you made sure that not so much as a murmur made the headlines about Beach Monday or me. I appreciate that. This entire trip is proving to be a revelation in more ways than one.'

He knew then that he was a step closer to obtaining her signature. It made him want to punch the air in jubilation—

he'd started to earn her trust and respect, had done something to deserve it.

'We should do something to celebrate.' She folded her arms and gave him the once-over. It left him throbbing in places he *really* shouldn't be thinking about. 'I happen to recall you promising me a beach day. I hope you mean to keep your word because that seems a suitable way to mark our ongoing negotiations.'

He recalled that item on his checklist: *Prove to Christy you're more than the job.* 'How does Saturday sound?'

She clapped her hands. 'Perfect.'

The day of their beach trip dawned warm and clear. Of course it did. The apartment complex's concierge had told Jamie it was always summer in Singapore, and he was starting to believe it.

Christy was already waiting for him in the foyer, beach bag over her shoulder, when Jamie arrived. She glanced up, her eyes widening as she surveyed him. She tilted her chin. 'Are you ready to let your hair down for the day, Mr All-Work-and-No-Play?'

'You can call me Mr R & R, because today I'm the King of No-Work-and-All-Play,' he shot back, assuming a swagger. 'I'm going to show you how a beach day should be done.'

She spluttered back a laugh. 'Oh, this should be good.'

Her grin had the blood surging in his veins. Her attention moved to the long thin bag he had slung over his left shoulder and she clapped her hands. 'We're taking a Beach Monday umbrella with us?'

He wanted to high-five someone. 'Of course we are.'

She bounced. 'Which one?'

'Wait and see.'

Her throaty laugh had heat curling around him. He'd

been lecturing himself on the importance of maintaining a fun and frivolous façade for the entire day. So far it hadn't been difficult. It couldn't be this easy, though. He needed to stay on his toes and make sure he could pull this off convincingly.

It wasn't that he wanted to deceive her. He just wanted to prove that…that he could value the same things she valued.

'I take it Robert is on the way.'

'Nope, I'm not a pampered rich kid today. Today I'm just some guy going to the beach with a friend. We're catching the train.'

The train took thirty minutes to reach Sentosa Island. They emerged into the sunlight and were greeted with the sight of Siloso Beach gleaming like a golden promise in front of them. Christy clasped her hands to her chest and stared, her eyes so wide a man could fall into them. 'Oh! It's…*everything*!'

He caught her hand as she made to move down to the sand. 'This is Sentosa's most visited beach, but it's not our destination.'

'Oh, but…' Pausing, she pulled in a breath and nodded. 'Okay.'

'We're heading that way.' He pointed south-east along the boardwalk. 'I know how much you enjoy exploring on foot, but it's warm so if you want to take the bus…'

'Walking will be perfect.'

Her eyes glowed, and his shoulders went back at the realisation he'd put that smile on her face. It felt good, knowing that. *Really* good.

They passed Palawan Beach—the family-friendliest beach on the island—and finally reached Tanjong Beach.

Christy stared around, everything alive in her face. 'It's

gorgeous. What made you settle on this beach rather than one of the others?'

'I'd thought it's the one you'd like best. The guidebook described it as serene and tranquil—well, as tranquil as one can get in Sentosa. There's still plenty of water sports to be had if you're in the mood.' He had the names and number of several operators saved on his phone.

She shook her head, her expression dreamy. 'I just want to swim, lie on the beach, and soak it all up.'

That was exactly what they did. He found a deserted spot at one end of the beach beneath the palm trees and pulled forth the beach umbrella—one from her cocktails and mocktails range. The canopy was a concoction of orange and yellow fizz and bubbles and strategically placed liquorice allsorts while the centre pole was shaped like the stem of a cocktail glass—fun and utterly frivolous. He spread their towels beneath it and then moved back beside her to cast a critical eye over the picture it made.

He couldn't rein in a big stupid grin. 'I can't believe just looking at that thing makes me so happy.'

'It looks perfect here.'

It did. These babies were going to take the world by storm. If she signed with MA he'd make sure of it.

She pulled her sundress over her head and kicked off her sandals. 'Last one in is a...'

Her words stuttered to a halt and he knew it was because he was staring, but he couldn't stop. She wore a crocheted one-piece in a nude colour that almost tricked the eye into thinking she was naked.

'Stop looking at me like that,' she whispered, biting her lip and glancing down at herself. 'It's too much, isn't it? It's the only bathing suit I have and—'

'No! You look great. Really great.'

Her smile when it came was shy. 'Thank you.'

Swallowing, he lectured himself on keeping his hands to himself, before pulling his shirt over his head. Her quick intake of breath as she stared at his naked torso had things inside him heating up. 'We must be crazy,' she whispered as if to herself. He couldn't agree more. They swung away at the same time and started resolutely towards the water in the lagoon.

They swam in the warm tropical water, and lazed on the beach. They devoured the picnic he'd packed. And they touched. Harmless touches. Accidental touches. A touch on an arm to point something out; a sliding of shoulders as they reached for the same bottle of water; fingers brushing against each other's as they passed a towel between them. At one point, Jamie reached out to push a strand of Christy's hair back behind her ear and froze mid-action, but when she smiled at him he completed the move and for a moment everything in the world felt right in a way it had never felt right before.

They sprawled on their towels and talked about everything and anything—their university days, their favourite books and movies; when she found out he jogged in Central Park she made him describe it in detail, and then she told him what she would do on her first day in New York if she ever had a chance to visit. He discovered that she'd worked full-time as a teller in a bank during the eight years she'd spent studying, and that she'd taken on summer jobs as well, waitressing in the evenings or flipping burgers.

He made her tell him what she and her mother had done on their beach days when she'd been growing up. The picture she drew of their relationship had envy twisting in his gut. They might not have had a lot of money, but they'd had a lot of fun…had spent a lot of time together. He wished—

Don't be ridiculous. He'd had an enviable upbringing. It was the height of folly and ingratitude to wish for more.

They read the novels they'd packed. He kept watch when she dozed to make sure she remained covered by the umbrella's shade. With her fair skin she needed to be careful. Staring out at the beach, at white sand and palm trees and an emerald lagoon barely ruffled by a breeze, he let out a long slow breath that had felt caught up beneath his ribs since… He blinked. Since forever.

'What are you thinking about?'

He turned to find those golden eyes of hers watching him, and shrugged. 'I was thinking you were right.'

She nodded with great dignity. 'Yes, I usually am.' And then spoiled the effect by laughing. 'Right about what?'

'I should make time to do more of this.'

She sat up. 'Really?'

It took every ounce of willpower he had not to reach across, curve a hand around the back of her head and drag her lips to his. He forced his gaze away. 'This—' he gestured around '—has been perfect. I can't remember a time I've ever felt this relaxed.' And happy? 'I thought—' He broke off with a grimace.

'What did you think?'

Her voice was soft, and there was no judgment in her eyes. He didn't make a habit of confiding in anyone, but he found himself wanting to confide in her. Some instinct told him she could be trusted with each and every one of his secrets.

She's a business colleague, not a friend.

But she felt like a friend.

'I thought I might find today difficult. I thought it might be hard to relax, to forget about work…to do nothing.'

She nodded as if his words didn't surprise her. 'But you haven't?'

'No.' He frowned. It'd been easy—preposterously easy—not onerous in the slightest.

'And you think that's a bad thing?'

'No.' And maybe that was the most surprising thing of all. 'It feels like it's doing me good.' He mulled that over for a moment. 'Maybe taking a bit of time out isn't as self-indulgent as I thought.'

'Maybe it's necessary.'

He scooped up a handful of sand and watched it trickle through his fingers. 'I'm making changes when I go home.'

Her slow smile filled him with warmth, and something else—optimism. If she moved to New York—if she sold Beach Monday to MA and took up the designer's position he'd offered—they could see a whole lot more of each other. Maybe they could date. He'd never wanted to regularly date a woman before, had actively avoided it, but being with Christy felt like being alive. He didn't want to lose that just yet.

Not that anything could happen until their negotiations here were at an end. It'd be foolish to jeopardise those. Something inside him hardened. And he refused to allow anyone to draw parallels between his behaviour and his father's. He was no womaniser, and he couldn't think of an uglier way to coerce someone into doing business with him than seducing them and playing on their emotions. He'd never do that. Not to anyone, and certainly not to Christy.

'What changes?' she prompted, snapping him back. 'More beach days? Where's your nearest beach?'

'Coney Island, but we have a place in the Hamptons. I could slip away for the odd weekend every now and again.'

'Absolutely! You shouldn't let a place like that go to waste.'

She was right. 'I'm going to try and fit some leisure time into my working week. My job demands a certain amount of flexibility, and long hours, but it doesn't mean

I can't fit in a visit to a gallery or the theatre, or to have a hot dog in Central Park.'

'Sounds perfect.'

He folded his arms and did his best to sound stern. 'You need to fit some of those things into your schedule too, Christy.'

'Well, now… Central Park is a bit more of a hike for me and—'

'You know what I mean. You've spent eight years working and studying without a single holiday. And then you've spent the last two years setting up a brand-new business. It's no wonder your creativity had taken a hiatus.'

'It's hard to find the time and the objectivity when you're in the midst of the chaos, when it feels as if every minute counts or that you should make it count. But a breather really does help.' She chewed her lip, but mischief sparked from her eyes. 'I wonder if I could write off a day at Bondi Beach as a tax expense?'

He laughed, staring up at the perfect blue of the sky. 'It's official, we should make you Supreme Ruler of the World.'

When he glanced back he found her staring at the broad expense of his chest and the hunger that stretched across her face had his hand clenching about his bottle of water. It crackled and she jumped, breaking the moment.

He could recapture the moment. He could lean in close and say something suggestive, staring at her lips with the same hunger she'd just shown. He could ask the question and let her answer it however she wanted—

You're not here to seduce her!

He was here to prove that hitching her wagon to MA's star was the sensible thing to do.

'I think—' She cleared her throat, as if parched. 'I think I need another dip. Coming?'

The water in the lagoon was warm when he needed it to be icy cold, but physical exertion would help. He could swim across from one side of the lagoon to the other—that should help wear him out.

Instead he found himself floating on his back, staring up at the sky and playing Christy's cloud game.

She pointed. 'That one looks like a dolphin.'

He tried to focus. 'That one looks like a plane. A wobbly plane,' he added as the cloud moved and changed.

'That one over there looks like a daffodil.'

They both lowered their arms at the same time and somehow their arms became entwined. He couldn't move away—he wasn't that strong. He wanted to be touching her. Christy slipped her hand inside his. 'Jamie?'

He could barely find his voice. 'Yeah?'

'Thank you for today. It's been a perfect day. One of the best days ever.'

He wished he could give her a hundred such days. He opened his mouth to say as much, and then closed it again. It was the kind of thing a friend would say—a lover—not a business colleague.

'You were going to say something?'

She was attuned to him in the same way he was attuned to her, so it shouldn't surprise him that she'd noticed. 'I was, but I thought better of it.'

'Why?'

If he didn't answer, she wouldn't press him. 'It feels as if I'm walking a fine line between saying something and having it sound like I'm pressuring you to make your business decision in my favour.'

'In MA's favour,' she corrected gently. 'You and MA are not the same entity.'

He was starting to recognise that fact. Not that it changed

anything. He had a responsibility to both MA and his family name.

'If we were just two people enjoying each other's company at the beach, what would you say?' she persisted.

His heart pounded so hard he was amazed a tidal wave didn't form beneath him. 'I wouldn't say, I'd do. I'd kiss you, Christy. Like I've wanted to kiss you ever since I saw you standing in the foyer looking like every dream vision of a beach girl that I've ever had. I'd tell you that not touching you is starting to hurt. But if it's a choice between being near you and not touching or not being near you, I'd choose the former.'

Her grip on his hand tightened until it was a stranglehold. She muttered something incoherent and then she pitched upright. He did too, and they stood in chest-deep water staring at each other and breathing hard. She reached out a hand, planting it on his chest, and the contact had him sucking in a breath. He held himself so taut he almost shook.

Her lips parted, her hunger blatant. She didn't try to hide it. 'Here's what I think. I think that for the rest of today—and tonight—we should pretend that we're just two people enjoying each other's company and nothing more. Everything that happens today has no bearing or impact on our business negotiations next week. Deal?'

Everything inside him clenched up hard. Could they do it? His whole life had been bound up in duty and obligation. Was it wrong of him to want to reach out and take something just for himself? Hunger, need, and desire wrestled inside him with an intensity born of having been kept chained for too long. He'd never wanted anything more in his life than to take Christy home to his apartment and make love with her. Again and again. Until they were exhausted and sated.

To hell with the consequences! 'Today and tomorrow,' he demanded, his voice a harsh rasp. He craved a night with this woman—and another whole day of holiday recklessness before returning to reality. They both deserved it. They'd earned it. And he'd pamper her so lavishly she wouldn't be able to find it in herself to regret it.

Her chest rose and fell. 'Today and tomorrow,' she agreed.

He didn't hesitate then; slipping an arm around her waist, he pulled her flush against him, her softness pressed against his hardness making his head spin.

The hitch of her breath, the way her hands moved across his chest had his libido hitting warp speed. Her lips lifted to greet his, and there was nothing tentative or hesitant in the meeting of their mouths. It flung him out of himself and into a world filled with a million points of light that dazzled and delighted, and pulled him closer and closer to a fire that threatened to consume him.

He lifted his head to drag a breath of air into oxygen-starved lungs. If they weren't careful they'd lose control. And they were in a public place.

Very gently he eased away. Christy splashed water onto her face. 'Wow.' Her voice wobbled. 'Intense much?'

'Off the Richter scale.'

He felt he'd been waiting forever to make love to this woman. Which was crazy when he'd only known her a week. But another few hours of waiting wouldn't hurt. And if they did, it'd be in a good way—the kind of way that had anticipation building between them. Besides, it seemed only fair to give her the chance to change her mind. But whenever their gazes met, he knew she had no intention of changing her mind.

So they horsed around—splashing and dunking each

other—careful to keep their touching light and almost in-nocent, but unable not to touch.

He kept to the plan he'd so carefully worked out the pre-vious day. When the afternoon lengthened, he took her to one of the beach bars for a cocktail and to people watch.

'This is as much of the day as I had planned,' he said. They'd changed out of their wet swimsuits and she wore a pair of cute plaid capris and flip-flops with a big yel-low flower on top that matched the daisies on her sunhat. As cute as it all looked on her, he wanted to tear it off to reveal the naked flesh beneath. And he wanted to touch every inch of that flesh with his hands and his tongue.

He had a feeling she could read that thought in his eyes when she lifted her hair off her nape and fanned her face. 'So you were just going to play it footloose and fancy-free for the rest of the day? How daring of you.'

Her eyes twinkled and her mouth lifted into an irre-pressible smile and he imagined the sounds that would emerge from those tempting lips when he—

'Jamie!'

With a cough, he dragged himself back to the moment. 'Yes. Absolutely. Playing it by ear. If you want to stay and have dinner we can. There's music and dancing a little later too.'

'I'm hungry, Jamie, but not for food. Maybe we could do all of that next Saturday.'

Everything inside him clenched at her unmistakable message. 'The other option then,' he managed to get out, 'is we can leave and head back to the apartment now.'

'Excellent idea.'

Her gaze was fixed on his mouth and he stood before he lost his head and kissed her. The next time he kissed her, he didn't want to stop. Taking her hand, he led her out of the beach bar towards the boardwalk.

They caught the bus to the railway station. It was standing room only on the train, but he didn't mind. Christy stood so close—her back to his front—that whenever the train lurched or jolted her backside would brush against his groin. It gave him an excuse to slip an arm about her waist and hold her there. He relished every moment of the journey.

By the time they reached the foyer of their apartment building, he was on fire. He pushed the button for the lift and then pushed it again and again. As soon as the lift doors closed behind them, he dragged her into his arms and kissed her. The heat they generated was combustible. He burned so badly with his need for her he could barely think straight.

'My floor is closer,' she said, wrapping her arms around his neck and biting gently on his earlobe.

'But the condoms are in my apartment,' he murmured against her lips, smiling at her gasp when he brushed a sly thumb across her left nipple.

The lift door opened and he thanked whatever gods were looking down on them that the corridor was clear. He herded her down the hallway, pressed her back against the door to kiss her thoroughly again—because he couldn't not touch her—while fumbling with his keys.

The door swung open before he managed to get the key in the lock and they'd have both fallen if he hadn't wrapped an arm about Christy's waist and braced his other against the doorjamb. What the hell...?

He glanced up, heat haze shimmering in front of his eyes. When he blinked it away he found his mother's cool eyes travelling over both him and Christy, and the probably faintly ridiculous tableau they presented. And for the moment he hated her for marring a memory he'd always hold dear, for making it seem small and silly.

Carefully, he righted Christy. It was Christy who deserved his care and respect in this scenario, but his mother didn't deserve such bitterness either. 'Christy, I'd like you to meet my mother, Denise Cooper-Ford. Mother, this is Christy Minslow.'

What the hell was his mother doing here? It was an effort to force his lips into the semblance of a smile. 'This is a surprise. I wasn't expecting to see you here.'

'That much is evident, James.'

Jamie's mother didn't sneer, but she didn't smile either. It was all Christy could do to keep her chin from dropping, and to not hide her face in Jamie's shirt. Swallowing, she shook the cool imperious hand that was held out to her and then had to resist the farcical urge to drop a curtsy while she was about it.

Stop being ridiculous! Try and get your brain working again, please, Christy.

It was insanely difficult to think when her body continued to burn from Jamie's touch and his kisses. Denise Cooper-Ford gave off an arctic chill but for a moment not even that could help. But then some of the fog cleared and Christy could finally see the other woman a little more clearly and things inside her clenched.

She wondered if she'd ever met anyone with such perfect posture. This was a woman who could seriously rock a little black suit.

Wow. Just…wow. *This* was the woman who had raised Jamie? She swallowed back the lump that formed in her throat. The woman was so *cold*.

Jamie leaned forward and kissed his mother's cheek. But there was no embrace. She couldn't imagine Denise hugging anyone.

'What are you doing in Singapore, Mother?'

Exactly. Wasn't Denise supposed to be retired?

'The board is organising a coup, James. After your ridiculous interview aired earlier this week, Claude Richardson decided to challenge you for the position of CEO. If you don't do something *immediately*, for the first time in the company's history a Cooper-Ford will not be at the helm of Molto Arketa, and that's not something I'm going to allow to happen.'

CHAPTER EIGHT

'Would that be such a bad thing?' Christy asked, glancing from Denise to Jamie. Their twin expressions of horror had her backtracking swiftly. 'Uh-huh, so that's a yes, then. And, I mean, *obviously* it'd suck if you couldn't make the changes you want to make to the company, Jamie.'

Suck? Had she really just used the word suck in front of Denise Cooper-Ford?

She forged on, hoping to cover her slip. 'We both know they're long overdue, but—'

'It's pushing for these changes that's landed us in this pickle in the first place!' Denise glared at her son. 'How could you have been so reckless, James? I'm beyond furious.'

Christy had to bite back a torrent of indignation on Jamie's behalf. Denise should be…

Darn it, she should be proud of Jamie!

Denise paced, and Christy turned to Jamie. 'All I meant is that you're still the major shareholders, right? You're not going to be thrown out on the street or become destitute or anything like that. And you can keep advocating for the changes you want.'

Something in his eyes lightened and she could've sworn he was about to smile. 'That's very true. And—'

'I refuse to listen to talk like that!' Denise whirled to

face them. 'I will not allow you to walk away without a fight, James. You might've forgotten the promise you made your father, but I haven't.'

Before her eyes, Jamie retreated behind an impenetrable wall, becoming cold and remote. Her heart ached for him.

'Nobody is talking about walking away,' he said.

Denise—*his mother*... She was horrible!

Earlier today Jamie had been enthralled by Christy's childhood stories about growing up with her mother—their days at the beach, their impromptu dance parties, their expeditions into the city to window-shop and then picnic in Hyde Park or the Botanic Gardens. There hadn't been a whole lot of money when she'd been growing up, but there had been a lot of warmth. From what she could see, Jamie had grown up with a lot of wealth and no warmth whatsoever. She wouldn't change places with him for the world. No wonder her simple stories had held him so fascinated.

Her throat ached. She wished she'd told him more stories now—about Christmases and slumber parties and movie nights. She wished she could share every good thing she'd ever experienced with him.

Jamie deserved warmth and love. He deserved to know he was cared for and—

Her heart suddenly stuttered and her mouth dried. Jamie deserved love, sure, but...

She swallowed. She hadn't gone and done the ridiculous, had she? Attraction was one thing, but...love?

Of course not. The idea was crazy.

She swallowed the rock lodged in her throat. 'I guess this means you'll be heading back to New York.' Her heart plummeted at the thought. But *that* didn't mean she was in love with Jamie.

Denise slammed to a halt. 'Absolutely not. We're not returning to New York until we have a game plan.' Cold eyes skewered Christy to the spot. 'And you, my dear, are going to be a part of that plan.'

Ice slid down her spine. *Her?*

Jamie's head jerked up. 'You'll leave Christy and Beach Monday out of this. She won't sell unless I can assure her that MA is serious about implementing more progressive strategies and programmes. What's more, I don't blame her and have no intention of trying to change her mind.'

Wow. All he needed was a white charger.

'Our negotiations will have to be put on hold until we see how all of this plays out.'

The shock on Denise's face had Christy wondering if he'd ever stood up to her so forcefully before.

'What I want to know—' he slammed his hands to his hips '—is what you're doing embroiled in all of this mess anyway. I realise—' his nostrils flared '—that it's probably escaped your notice, but last time I checked you'd retired.'

'James, I—'

'Is one heart attack not enough for you? Are you seriously courting another?'

Christy decided in the interests of tact that now might be a good time to beat a hasty retreat. 'It's obvious the two of you have a lot to discuss. I'll say goodnight. I'll talk to you tomorrow, Jamie.'

With that she turned and fled. She couldn't have fallen in love with Jamie. *She couldn't!*

A text pinged her phone the following morning. Christy pulled it out of her bag with so much haste she nearly dropped it. *Jamie.*

Where are you?

She texted back.

Gardens by the Bay.

Meet me in the grove of Supertrees in fifteen mins?

She sent back a thumbs-up emoji.

When she saw him thirteen minutes later the lines of strain around his mouth and the exhaustion fanning out from his eyes had her wanting to throw her arms around him and hug him.

She didn't. Yesterday she'd been prepared to do so much more than hug him, but in the cool light of dawn—after a mostly sleepless night, and despite the protestations of her heart and the outcry from her body—she knew it would've been a mistake.

Lewis had slept with her, made promises to her, and then shamelessly taken advantage of her before discarding her without a backward glance. Jamie was a hundred times the man Lewis was, and her every instinct proclaimed it. It didn't change the fact it'd be the height of foolishness to allow her own judgement to become coloured by her growing feelings for the man. Jamie and MA weren't one and the same. And while she might view Jamie through rose-coloured glasses, she couldn't afford to do that with MA. If it were just her...

But it wasn't. She had women in remote communities relying on her. The partnerships she'd forged were too important to jeopardise. She would not allow all of her hard work to be destroyed.

She gripped her hands together to stop from reaching for him. 'How are you? I can only imagine the night you've had.'

He waved that away as if it were of no consequence. 'I wanted to make sure you were okay. After yesterday...at the beach. I mean...' He shoved his hands into his pockets. 'If my mother hadn't been at the apartment when we'd got back...'

She nodded. 'We'd have woken up this morning in the same bed,' she agreed. She moistened suddenly dry lips and tried to ignore the clamour of her blood. 'Jamie, I—'

'You're going to say we were saved from making a mistake.'

He glanced away as he said the words and her heart started to race. 'I wish I could make myself *feel* it'd be a mistake.' She sighed, finding a shady spot on the lawn and sitting on the grass. Above them the Supertrees rose up in all of their strange New Age majesty, making her feel disoriented like Alice in Wonderland or as if she were in a science-fiction fairy tale.

After a moment's hesitation, he sat too and she realised he wasn't wearing his suit. She was glad. 'But?' he prompted, forcing her mind back on track.

'I just think our timing is really bad.' She pressed her hands together and then turned to him. 'I like you, Jamie.' It was as much as she was prepared to verbally admit. 'But the business decisions I have to make need to be separate from that.'

'And you don't want to get the two confused—the personal with the professional.'

'And I don't want either of us feeling hurt at whatever decisions we do eventually come to.'

For no reason at all she recalled the speed with which he'd kiboshed his mother's attempts to co-opt Christy to the cause yesterday. Jamie had protected her—championed her. He'd refused to take advantage of her.

'If our negotiations were at an end...' She trailed off with a shrug, feeling heat mount her cheeks.

Finally he shot her a wry smile. 'If I'm not careful I'm

going to be in danger of getting my priorities wrong. I've started hoping you'd sign the contract and take up the offered design position in New York, just so I can see you again—find a way to date you.'

Her heart leapt into her throat. 'Dating the boss?' Her voice came out ridiculously husky.

'Not ideal,' he agreed with a heavy sigh.

And yet she found herself tempted to at least try and make such a situation work, despite the potential perils and pitfalls.

But that would be getting ahead of herself. Which was something she couldn't afford to do. It was time to change the subject. 'Where's your mother?' What strings was Denise pulling this morning?

'I left her at the medical clinic.'

She stiffened. 'Has she—?'

'No.' His lips lifted the tiniest fraction. 'I refused to discuss any matters concerning MA with her until she had a doctor give her a clean bill of health and an assurance that intense business discussions wouldn't harm her health further.'

That made her laugh. 'Good for you.'

'She was forced to step back because of her health and she's had a hard time reconciling herself to that fact. But I'm in charge now.'

And he looked in charge too—confident, assured… powerful.

Hot.

Stop it!

'At least—' he rolled his eyes '—I'm still in charge at the moment.'

She grimaced. 'What's the situation?' She straightened. 'Not that you have to tell me, of course. It's probably confidential—'

'I trust you, Christy. I know you wouldn't betray my confidences. You have integrity, and I admire you for it.'

His praise left her momentarily speechless.

'At the moment it appears the board is split fifty-fifty in favour of me and Claude. The thing is I know the direction in which I'm trying to take the company is the right one. It's the only possible way forward into the future.'

His hands balled to fists and she sympathised with his frustration. His *was* the right way. He had the potential to make a significant impact on the world—one that would have a ripple effect on the rest of the industry. Jamie wanted to bring a social conscience to his company. He shouldn't be hampered in such an endeavour. She wished she could slap some sense into his board of directors. She cleared her throat. Not literally, of course.

'How does your mother think I can help you keep power at MA?'

'Simply that if I sign you, it'll be a feather in my cap—a plus sign on the tally sheet. Everyone knows Beach Monday is on the brink of serious success. Signing your company would be a coup, a triumph. Or as my mother puts it—a genius masterstroke they can't possibly counter.'

'Checkmate,' she murmured to herself.

'No!' His voice was sharp. 'There's absolutely no guarantee that I can win the board's vote of confidence, and I can't pretend there is. If Claude does win the vote then nothing will change—all of my projected sustainability practices and social equity policies will be tossed out like so much garbage. And I won't ask you to sacrifice Beach Monday on anything less than a sure thing.'

The thought of what the likes of this Claude Richardson would do to her village co-ops made her shudder, but…

'But what if I were to sign something agreeing to sell Beach Monday to MA on the proviso that you're the CEO for the next...' she shrugged '...I don't know—five years?'

His jaw slackened. He clenched it again a moment later. 'I can't allow you to do that.'

She raised an eyebrow. 'It's my company. I can do what I like with it.'

'Christy, I—'

'MA's reach is so much bigger than mine could ever be. You have ten times more impact than I could ever hope to have. You can do good things, Jamie. And I have every faith in you that you will.'

'Are you serious?'

Sandalwood and temptation danced around her. She blinked, trying to clear her head. 'I'd want guarantees written into the contract protecting my current suppliers—promises to maintain links with the village co-ops. And I'd want a written guarantee that you'll continue the work of the Beach Monday Foundation.'

He suddenly grinned. 'Considering that as far as I'm concerned they're one of Beach Monday's biggest selling points, then that won't be a problem.'

She found herself suddenly torn between cheering and bursting into tears. Had she really just agreed to sell Beach Monday?

Oh, but think of all the good Jamie could do!

'And I'd have to ask you not to make our deal public until I've had a chance to talk to my mother. I don't want this coming as a bolt from the blue for her. Besides the fact she's been unwell, she's given me so much support through the years and I don't want her to feel left out or not appreciated or to think that I'm treating her differently because she's been ill.'

He placed a hand over his heart. 'You have my word.'

She pulled in a breath and held out her hand. 'Then it sounds like we have a deal.'

Christy took one look at Jamie's face when she opened the door to him the following morning, sensed the fatigue he tried to hide, and wanted to tear Denise to pieces.

She and Jamie had spent the rest of yesterday, after their short interlude in the grove of Supertrees, in his penthouse apartment thrashing out the fine print of their agreement before sending it off to their respective lawyers. Denise had shadowed their every move—questioning, interjecting, arguing and disputing at every opportunity. Until Christy's head had started to throb. The woman had more stamina and persistence than a shark-sized wasp.

Spending yesterday afternoon with her had told Christy all she needed to know about the other woman. Denise was obsessed with MA and it turned her into a relentless bully. Christy, thankfully, had been raised to stand up to bullies, and she refused to bow to the pressure Denise attempted to place on her. But it had been a ridiculously tiring exercise and being in Denise's presence had forced her to call on her every reserve.

And when he was in Denise's presence, Jamie became a different man—cold, analytical, robotic. It was the side of him that made him such an effective businessman, but she hated it. He could be analytical and objective and still maintain his warmth and *humanity*.

But staring at him now, she suspected that cold remoteness was the armour he needed to don when dealing with his mother. He looked *exhausted*. It brought home to her how lucky she'd been in her own mother.

He needed a break—just a few hours would help him unwind and give him a chance to regroup.

'Hey.' She opened the door wider and ushered him in. 'What's up?'

'Nothing. I just wanted to let you know that my lawyer is drawing up the new contract as we speak and will send it off to yours this afternoon.'

'Okay, well, mine has assured me she'll fast-track it as soon as it hits her inbox. If everything is in order, we should be ready to sign it tomorrow.'

She waited for a sense of relief to hit her—relief that she'd finally come to a decision about the future—and kept right on waiting. Maybe that was due to her own exhaustion.

She shrugged off the misgivings that had started to plague her. 'What are your plans for the day?'

'My mother wants to visit the Orchard Road store.'

Poor Lien.

'I was thinking of taking the ferry across to Batam for lunch. Want to join me?'

'Batam? Why?'

'So I can say I've been to Indonesia. It's only an hour's ferry ride.' She sent him a grin. 'And it seemed like a suitably whimsical thing to do. Whimsy is good for creativity.'

He grinned as if her reasoning delighted him, but then it faded. 'My mother expects me to escort her to the store.'

If she thought for one moment that was what he wanted to do… 'Oh, okay.' She turned away with a shrug. 'If that's more important than quietening the sudden attack of nerves of the person you're in negotiations with…'

She could barely keep her face straight as she said the words, and the gleam in Jamie's eye told her he knew it. 'Give me half an hour.'

'You're incorrigible, you know that?' Jamie pulled his hat off his head and raked his fingers through his hair as their gleaming ferry set off for Batam.

She grinned before turning to peer out of the window. Her whole body quivered with interest as she took in the view. They sat opposite one another—'So we can both have window seats,' Christy had said.

The sparkling water and blues skies had a pent-up breath easing out of him. When he was with Christy, he found himself more aware of everything—more in tune with his environment—and in some crazy way it made him feel less solitary.

'After yesterday, I figured we deserved a day off.' She opened her mouth as if to say more, but closed it again.

He had a fairly good idea what she'd wanted to say. 'My mother is intense.'

She glanced back at him. 'Why is she finding it so hard to transition to retirement?'

A weight settled on his shoulders. 'MA was her life.' And it was clear he wasn't living up to expectations. She'd had enough disappointment in her life without him adding to it.

Christy's hair fanned about her face when she shook her head. 'I don't get that. I mean, I love Beach Monday. It's my baby, *I* created it, and a part of me can't believe I've sold it.'

He straightened. Was she regretting their deal?

'But when I think how I'm now free to focus on what I love—I find myself getting excited about the future.'

She didn't look excited. Unease rippled through him. She could've had both. All she'd needed to do was find a business partner. He pushed the unsettling thought aside. She'd considered all her options.

'And there have always been things more important to me than Beach Monday—my mother, my health, my causes. So Denise's attitude is totally foreign to me.'

Balance wasn't something his mother could be accused

of. 'Look, I know my mother is difficult to like. But there are reasons for that. For starters, my father broke her heart.' His hands clenched. 'She loved him, truly loved him. No man has ever come close to touching her heart the way Conrad did. She still misses him. I know she does—every single day—although she never talks about him.'

'Oh, but…' Amber eyes filled with instant sympathy. 'The papers said Conrad kept up his playboy ways after his marriage—that he continued with his drinking and womanising.'

'He did.'

'I thought…' She glanced down at her hands. 'I mean, I figured it was one of those dynastic marriages that was good for business—a mutually beneficial arrangement.'

His stomach churned. 'She married for love. And she thought he'd married her for the same reason. It's not an illusion she held onto for long.' It was why Jamie was *not* letting love into his life. Love ruined lives. He wanted nothing to do with it. He expected to marry—heirs were a duty. Hopefully a joyful one. But his marriage would be based on mutual respect not love. He wasn't raising his children in the same volatile, incendiary environment he'd been raised in. They'd have calm and peace and tranquility.

She pressed a hand to her chest. 'Poor Denise.'

He could barely imagine his mother young and vulnerable now. Her disillusion must've been shattering.

'She never asked for a divorce?'

He was silent for a moment. 'I think she thought—or at least hoped—he'd grow out of his philandering ways. Don't they say love is blind? Maybe she felt trapped. Her parents didn't believe in divorce, so she'd have not had any encouragement from that direction.'

'So she waited and hoped.'

'And threw herself into saving Molto Arketa from ruin, hoping she'd win his approval that way.'

Her hand fluttered about her throat. 'What a horrible situation. For you too.'

He'd been protected by nannies and housekeepers and boarding school, but the sadness in Christy's face made his heart burn. 'Obviously this isn't a story with a happy ending. Her waiting and hoping didn't pay off. When I was twelve, my father and I were in a car accident. He was driving, the car slid on ice and we went down a ravine.'

Her head jerked up. 'I knew he'd died in a car accident, but I didn't know you were there too.'

'My mother managed to keep that out of the papers.' He stared out of the window, but barely noticed the view. 'Somehow I was flung free of the car, but he was trapped and I couldn't get him out. He was bleeding badly from a cut on his thigh. I didn't know how badly at the time. I eventually flagged down a passing motorist but by then it was too late.'

She reached across and slipped her hand into his. 'I'm sorry, Jamie.'

He wanted to reassure her, let her know he was fine, but his ability to smile had fled. He hadn't spoken about this in a long time and remembering had everything inside him clenching up tight. 'He remained conscious right until the end. We talked. He told me he wished he'd lived his life differently. He said…' His heart pounded in his throat. He forced it back down into his chest. 'He said he wished he'd spent more time with me, and had treated my mother with the respect she'd deserved.'

'Oh, Jamie.' Her words were little more than a whisper.

'He made me promise to not make the same mistakes he'd made—to not tarnish MA's reputation like he had, to value and appreciate my good fortune rather than taking it for granted like he'd done. He told me his wild ways hadn't brought him happiness. And he asked me to tell my mother that he was sorry for everything.'

Her grip on his hand tightened.

Despite all of his wealth and privilege, Conrad had never been happy, and that knowledge tormented Jamie. He would never be able to change that fact or make a difference to his father's life. Not now. But he could at least keep the promise he'd made to his dying father and hope it somehow balanced the scales.

'I know it was too little too late, but...' His lips twisted. 'I guess it was better than nothing, right?'

She nodded, but the tears in her eyes had his throat aching. 'I can only imagine how devastated Denise must have been,' she choked out.

The edges of his vision darkened. 'She changed afterwards. Became hard. As if the worst thing that could've happened had happened. Rather than crumble with grief, she threw herself into the business. She took control of the board and steered the company through a seriously difficult time. Under her leadership the company has consistently achieved the highest profit margins in its history.'

Christy released his hand and eased back in her seat. The smile she sent him was warm and full of sympathy, but her eyes remained troubled. 'She found a new purpose.'

'I admire all she's achieved. She had very little support from the board in the early days and has survived three takeover attempts. If she were a man she'd be feted for what she's achieved, but because she's a woman she's called vile names and considered unnatural.'

And now he was letting her down too. MA was the only thing left that mattered to her. He had to find a way to keep control of the company. It'd crush her if he didn't.

And she'd been crushed enough already by Conrad's indifference.

'You're right. It's unfair,' Christy said slowly.

He blinked himself back into the moment. 'But?' he prompted when it became evident she had more on her mind.

She flattened her lips, tracking the progress of a passing speedboat. 'She made a company her life. Companies aren't...' She shook her head, meeting his gaze again. 'I mean, they can't love you back.'

He stared, waiting for more.

'Since Conrad died, it's as if all Denise has let herself care about are profit margins and share prices and sealing deals, rather than flesh and blood people.'

His mother's heart was in deep freeze and he couldn't say he blamed her. 'After seeing what my father put her through, I'm not the least interested in love either.'

She froze at his words, something in her eyes looking suddenly dark and stricken. But then she shook herself and sent him a glassy smile. 'While I'm the opposite and believe people can fall in love and make a lifelong commitment to each other. I'd like to have that. One day.'

Everything inside him tensed. He bit back a curse. He had no right kissing this woman! They wanted different things from life. *Very different.* She was... He swallowed She was *lovely.* Utterly lovely. But he wasn't interested in love or lifelong commitments. Which meant he had no right messing with her life or her heart.

In another couple of days they'd have gone their separate ways. His heart kicked in protest, but he ignored it. The sooner this Singapore interlude was over, the better—for both their peace of minds.

CHAPTER NINE

'YOUR MOTHER IS WRONG.'

Jamie glanced up from his rendang curry—*delicious*—to focus on Christy's face. Always a mistake as he found himself once again getting caught up on the shape of her lips and the arch of her eyebrows.

Half an hour ago they'd explored the magnificent statuary in Batam's awe-inspiring Maha Vihara Duta Maitreya Temple, before retreating to the temple's vegetarian restaurant for much-needed refreshment. Christy had been remarkably quiet as they'd toured the extraordinary complex. Sensing that she was out of sorts, he'd given her space, resisting the urge to engage her in conversation.

His stomach gave a sudden lurch. Was she regretting their deal? Was she having second thoughts?

He set his cutlery down. 'What is it my mother has wrong?' He was careful to keep his voice pleasant, but things inside him clenched. It wasn't fair to say his appetite fled whenever his mother became the topic of conversation, but there was no denying that his enthusiasm for his curry had vanished.

'Yesterday she said that she hadn't forgotten the promise you'd made to your father even if you had.'

Those words had been like a lash of a whip.

'She was implying that if you weren't CEO you'd be

breaking that promise.' Her frown deepened. 'But that's just not true.'

Was she serious? He'd been *given* a business empire. It'd been handed to him on a platter without him having had to do so much as lift a finger. It didn't seem too much in return to tend to it, look after it…protect it. What kind of selfish ingrate would he be to do otherwise?

Her brow pleated. 'You didn't promise your father you'd be CEO. You promised not to make the same mistakes he had, you promised not to drag MA's name through the mud. And you've kept your word.' Her chin was thrust out—testy and belligerent. 'You know what? If she continues to give you grief about your social equity policies you can tell her that what you're doing is keeping your word to your father. Not having a progressive social equity policy *would* blacken MA's image.'

He might not agree with the first part of her statement, but he loved her latter point, and found himself suppressing a grin. Had she spent the last hour and a half in her own head defending him to his mother? It left him absurdly touched. 'Nice point.'

She stared at him for a moment and her face relaxed into a smile. 'Glad we got that sorted.'

He hesitated. She gave so much of herself and it seemed wrong to mislead her in even the smallest way. And despite all of the internal warnings from the cold and sensible self that resided inside him, he wanted her to understand. 'I don't believe my family's expectation that I become CEO of MA is unreasonable.' It was a duty he meant to perform to the very best of his ability. 'It's not a burden.' *Liar.* 'It's a privilege.' *That* at least was true. 'So while it might look like my mother and I are at odds, we're still on the same team. We both want the same things.'

Her smile disappeared and she abruptly turned back to her food.

'You don't agree?'

She merely shrugged. 'I've no right to comment on your relationship with your parents.'

Something in her tone made him frown. 'I'm aware you're not the kind of person who tries to create mischief or cause trouble.' His every instinct told him that. He didn't know why, but he didn't want her guarding her tongue around him. 'Whatever you say, I know it comes from a good place.'

She stiffened. 'Of course I don't want to cause trouble!' Whatever she saw in his face had her hesitating though. Eventually, she pushed her plate away. 'I just think there should be give and take in families. From where I'm sitting it seems to me you're the one who's been doing all the giving, Jamie. I think your parents have been…infuriatingly selfish. I want to shake the both of them. And I don't care what made your mother the way she is—she should be proud of you regardless. What you care about should…' Her hands clenched. 'It should *mean* something to her. She doesn't have to understand it, but she should treat it with respect.'

He blinked. 'I—'

'Have they ever asked you what you want? *No!*' she continued, answering her own question. 'They've laid this path at your feet and demanded you follow it.'

She broke off, breathing heavily. Conflicting emotions pummelled him. He wanted to argue with her, tell her she was wrong. But she wasn't—not completely. His parents hadn't ever asked him what he wanted. But being CEO of one of the world's leading fashion brands—that was an honour. Couldn't she see that?

Was it, though? The thought felt despicably disloyal and reeked of ingratitude.

'Your mother wants to mould you in her own image. But as her choices don't seem to have brought her much happiness, I can't see that they're likely to bring you any either.'

Whoa. 'Now hold on a moment—'

'And *that's* not in the spirit of the promise you made your father.'

He froze.

'He told you the path he chose hadn't made him happy. What if he wasn't warning you against a playboy lifestyle, Jamie? What if he was telling you to be happy?'

His father had regretted taking the MA legacy for granted, and had died before he could rectify his mistake. Jamie wasn't going to let history repeat. Some sense of self-preservation scrambled to the surface then because she was trying to dismantle the very foundations his life stood on. *She* hadn't heard the anguish in his father's voice. *She* hadn't seen the way Jamie's hand-on-heart promise to his father had brought solace to the older man.

'Is all of this senseless supposition because I told you I'm not interested in love? Because, from where I'm sitting, you're drawing an awful lot of conclusions on very little evidence.'

Her eyes flashed. 'You're joking, right? There's ample evidence. What do you have in your life other than MA? Nothing! You're in danger of becoming as obsessed with the company as your mother is. But a company won't keep you warm at night.'

'I didn't say I wasn't interested in romance. And romance *can* keep one warm—very warm—' he kinked a deliberately suggestive eyebrow '—at night.' He wanted to hurt her in the same way her words were hurting him. He loathed himself for the impulse, but couldn't seem to help it.

She waved his words away with a laugh, but the humour didn't reach her eyes. 'Romance is fun but shallow. While love…' Her brows crinkled and her eyes darkened. 'Jamie, love is a normal human emotion."

'I wouldn't describe what happened to my mother as normal.'

She tilted her head to stare directly into his face and then eased back, shaking her head. 'My mother had her heart broken too, but that didn't turn her cold and bitter. Lewis broke my heart and my trust when he stole my artwork, but I've not tarred every man with the same brush. Love is a risk, yes. But it's one worth taking.'

'I'm afraid I don't share your opinion.'

Colour mounted in her cheeks. 'Funny, I never took you for a coward.'

He leaned towards her, deliberately icy and arrogant. 'Is all of this because you had some stupidly romantic hopes about the two of us?'

It he'd been hoping his ugly words would make her backtrack, he'd have been sadly disappointed. She leaned forward too and the scent of vanilla butter cake rose up all around him, leaving him famished. 'We had a tiny romantic interlude, Jamie, nothing more. For a little while I did think it had the potential to develop into something more, something deeper—' she swallowed '—but I was wrong.'

Things inside him started to ache then with a ferocity that made no sense.

'I'm disappointed,' she continued, her amber eyes flashing. 'But I'm not devastated. And certainly not bitter.'

He desperately wanted to rewind this conversation and his own reactions to it.

She glanced at her watch. 'Heavens! Look at the time. If I'm going to the theatre tonight I should catch the next ferry back.' She stood. 'Coming?'

'I'll catch a later one. There's still more to see here.'

With a 'Have fun!' she was gone. And Jamie sat there aching and sore, as if he'd just gone a round in the ring with a heavyweight prize fighter.

After a night spent tossing and turning, Christy rose at daybreak. Unable to face the thought of remaining in the apartment when the walls felt as if they were closing in on her, she tugged on her tennis shoes and headed for a walk by the river. Being near water—rivers, lakes, oceans— usually made her feel better.

But not today, apparently.

She had a feeling nothing could make her feel better. Because yesterday she'd lied when she'd told Jamie she wasn't devastated. Everything inside her felt shattered and broken. Jamie didn't love her—and he never would—and it'd been the height of foolishness for her to have gone and fallen in love with him in the first place.

That forced a laugh from her throat. As if she'd had any say in the matter! She'd no more been able to stop falling in love with him than she could stop the tide from coming in. Her trip to Singapore certainly hadn't gone to plan. One thing was certain, though. Her Singapore idyll was at an end. The minute she signed that damn contract, she was leaving. She'd go home, tell her mother what she'd done, and then she'd lick her wounds in private and make a new plan for the future. If only she could find a single flicker of enthusiasm for the future.

She'd been walking for an hour when her phone pinged. She pulled it out. And then swallowed as she read the message. Her lawyer had just given the go-ahead on the contract.

She stared at the screen and then at the river. She was selling Beach Monday?

Squaring her shoulders, she turned around and retraced

her steps back to the apartment. She'd print off the contract, sign it and then she'd pack and go home.

So soon? It's too soon.

She refused to give into the internal weeping and wailing and gnashing of teeth. A quick and clean break would be for the best.

Forty minutes later, after power-walking back, she strode down the hallway to her apartment only to pull up short when she saw Jamie leaning against the wall beside her door. He straightened when he saw her. 'Hi.'

'Hi.' She kicked herself forward to unlock the door. 'Come in.'

'Your paper came.' He held up a folded newspaper and she gestured for him to put it on the coffee table.

'I, uh...' He shuffled his feet. 'I wanted to apologise for our argument yesterday. I'm sorry I lost my cool.'

Oh, he hadn't lost his cool. He'd channelled icy disdain like a professional. Though she kept that to herself. It was a pity she hadn't been so circumspect yesterday. She'd allowed her concern for him, her horror at the life he was consigning himself to, to override her better judgment. *Fool.*

'It was far from fair. I urged you to share your thoughts and then bit your head off.'

'I should've kept my thoughts to myself. Your relationship with your parents, and how you choose to live your life, is none of my business. I'm sorry. I was out of line.'

'I know it came from a good place, Christy. I know you were motivated by...friendship.'

But they weren't friends, were they? They were business associates. And thinking they could be more was what had led her into this crazy mess. 'Why don't we forget about yesterday—put it behind us?'

He nodded, but his eyes narrowed at whatever he saw

in her face. Before he could challenge her, she held up her phone. 'My lawyer has given our contract the green light.'

He watched in silence as she printed the contract out. 'Are you sure about this? If you need more time to think about it...'

She straightened from where she leaned over the contract, pen poised to sign. 'I'll admit to some nerves and some...' she chewed her lip '...wistfulness, I guess. This is the end of a chapter of my life. I love what I've done with Beach Monday.'

'As you should.'

'But you can take it to a whole other level of success. And MA's sponsorship of my village co-ops and education programmes can do so much good—more than I could ever achieve on my own—so...' She dragged in a breath, her heart beating hard. 'This is the right decision for everyone. You're a man of your word, Jamie, and that means a lot to me.' Despite their differences of opinion on love and happiness, she knew he'd keep the promises he'd made her.

Without another word, she signed the contract, although she couldn't manage a flourish. She held the pen out to him and after the slightest of hesitations he took it and signed as well.

He set the pen back on the table. 'What now?'

She tried to keep her shrug casual. 'Now I go home.'

'I still want to offer you that design position with MA.' He widened his stance. 'We'd be lucky to have you and...'

He trailed off as she shook her head. 'It wouldn't work, Jamie.'

He shifted his weight to the balls of his feet. 'If you're worried about me pestering you or pursuing you—'

'No.' *That* was the problem. The knowledge he wouldn't was a burr in her soul.

As soon as he was back in New York he'd forget she'd ever existed. But if she went to work for MA she'd hear about him, maybe catch a glimpse of him in the distance every now and again. She'd never be able to forget all that he'd come to mean to her. She shook her head again. She wasn't doing that to herself. 'What I need, Jamie, is a fresh start.'

'So—' he shoved his hands in his pockets '—this is goodbye?'

She nodded and held out her hand. 'It's been a pleasure.'

He clasped her hand briefly, his face remote and his eyes cool. 'The pleasure was all mine.'

And then he was gone and Christy was left rubbing her chest where her heart had once been.

Christy couldn't get a flight out until that evening. She had a shower, packed up all her belongings, and had a cup of tea. And still had hours to wait until she needed to be at the airport. Jamie had very kindly organised for Robert to drive her there. Later.

She glanced at her watch. Much later.

Making another tea, she glanced around the room, her gaze falling on the newspaper Jamie had placed on the coffee table earlier. Maybe reading about world affairs would take her mind off her own petty tragedy for a few short hours.

Make up your mind—are the hours short or long?

'Whatever,' she muttered, slamming herself onto the sofa. Whether she considered the hours short or long, after today she'd never see Jamie again. A part of her wanted to be away from here as soon as humanly possible so she could start the grieving and healing process. The sooner she started it, the sooner she'd be over him. Another part of her remained frozen, crippled, unable to move.

No wallowing! She wasn't allowed to wallow until she got home. Pulling the newspaper towards her, she started flipping over the pages and forcing herself to at least read the headlines.

Molto Arketa to ride Beach Monday's sustainability wave!

She'd already flipped to the next page before the words made an impression on her brain. She froze before flipping back. She read the article and her heart started to hammer and her stomach clenched. The article outlined MA's imminent acquisition of Beach Monday and Beach Monday's impressively progressive stance on issues of environmental sustainability, economic efficiency and social equity.

She hadn't had a chance to talk to her mother yet! If her mum caught wind of this before Christy had a chance to contact her, she'd be worried sick. And devastated that Christy hadn't confided in her. She'd be hurt.

Oh, God!

The article went on to say that an internal spokesperson for MA claimed this latest move was a bold statement indicating the company's future direction, praising James Cooper-Ford for his foresight and social conscience, and implying that this move would quell any internal rumblings within the company.

Conscience? Did the man have one? He'd promised her this wouldn't be made public until next week. He'd given his word!

She read a note at the bottom of the article directing the reader to the social pages. Her mouth dried as she turned the pages over, the agitated rustle filling the air, and then froze as she took in a half-page spread romantically linking her with Jamie. There were photos. One was a picture of her and Jamie leaving the MA store on Orchard Road, another in the beachside bar at Sentosa drinking cocktails; and the last—

She covered her face with her hands. The last was of that crazy impulsive kiss they'd shared down by the marina. They looked completely oblivious to the laser light show in the background. Because they had been oblivious! The caption read: Fireworks!

She'd been a fool. A damn fool. Jamie had played her with more finesse than Lewis ever had. And she'd let him! Her stomach pitched and for a moment she thought she might be sick. And then she grabbed the paper and stormed out of her apartment, taking the stairs to the penthouse level two at a time.

Jamie's head came up at the sharp knock on his door.

Adrenaline kicked through him and a wild crazy hope that Christy stood on the other side…that she'd reconsidered his offer about coming on board at MA.

He was on his feet and had the door wrenched open before he was even aware of it.

He'd barely drawn breath when a newspaper was slapped to his chest and Christy advanced—her expression livid and her face thunderous. Her eyes flashed.

Whoa!

'You got what you came for and now all bets are off, is that it? This is the way you work? My God, you had me fooled. You must've laughed your head off when I told you about Lewis stealing my artwork. Did it give you ideas? Did you figure you could go one better?'

He'd seen flashes of temper over the last twelve days, but he'd not seen her lose control completely, and a part of him couldn't help but note how magnificent she looked all fired up.

He pulled his wayward thoughts back. 'Christy, I've no idea what you're talking about.'

With an inarticulate noise of...derision? Frustration? She seized the newspaper from him and spread it out on the dining table.

He took one look at the headline she pointed to and a stone lodged in the pit of his stomach. 'What the hell...?' He seized the paper, his eyes racing over the newsprint. With his heart thumping hard enough to leave bruises, he flicked over to the social pages. He didn't bother reading the article—the pictures told the story. He closed his eyes briefly. 'I knew nothing about this.'

Her snort told him she'd not believe a damn word that came out of his mouth any more, and he couldn't blame her. He'd given her his word, and now—

And now she thought he was like Lewis. She thought he'd used her, betrayed her, and lied to her. She thought he'd sacrificed her and all she believed in—heartlessly and ruthlessly—to achieve his own ends. The realisation left him without breath and he momentarily felt rudderless, as if he'd lost his internal compass. He braced his hands on his knees and tried to get air into his lungs.

'Then who—' her voice was hard '—is MA's *internal spokesperson*?'

He had no idea, but heads were going to roll.

'That would be me,' Denise said, striding into the room. 'So *this* is what all the infernal racket is about?'

He straightened, feeling strangely cold. '*You* did this?' He rubbed numb fingers across his brow. '*That's* why you took the papers into your room this morning?'

She shrugged. 'I knew you'd make a fuss. And I was hoping Ms Minslow would be in the air before she saw the article.'

He unclenched his teeth to say, 'I told you I'd promised

Christy that the news wouldn't go live until next week. *I gave her my word.*'

'But I didn't. This attempted coup needed to be scotched before it could gather any more momentum. I'm sorry if Ms Minslow is displeased, but I took it upon myself to shore up your future.'

He clenched his hands so hard he started to shake. 'This deal with Beach Monday and the internal wrangling of the board have *nothing* to do with you.'

'Stop being ridiculous, James. I'm a major shareholder.'

'But you no longer hold a position within the company.'

'I've given my life to the company!'

'And has it made you happy?'

The words left him on a bellow. His mother paled and he couldn't believe he'd said such a thing to her. But he hadn't been able to shift all that Christy had said yesterday. Her words had been going around and around in his head on an endless loop ever since—piercing his defences and demanding a hearing, an appraisal…and answers. One thing was certain—he did *not* want to become like his mother. *Was* he making a mistake in shutting love so comprehensively out of his life?

He was determined to keep the promise he'd made to his father, but… What exactly had he promised? The question pounded at him.

He ignored his mother and his own internal wrangling to focus on Christy. 'I can't apologise enough. I should've protected you against my mother's insane ambition.'

'Don't you speak about me like that, James!'

He continued to ignore her. 'If there's anything I can do to make it right…?'

She'd lifted her chin, but her bottom lip gave an infinitesimal wobble and regret, guilt and a gut-wrenching pain tore him in two.

'The damage is already done,' she said in a voice he barely recognised.

He'd let her down. She'd not once asked for anything outrageous. She'd done nothing but give, and he felt as if all he'd done was to take and take from her.

For a little while I did think it had the potential to develop into something more, something deeper.

He'd let her down in every conceivable way.

He forced his chin up. At least he could keep the rest of his promises he'd made. 'I swear to you I will abide by our contract. To the letter. I understand you no longer have any faith in my word, but I'm legally bound. You have no need to fear for your village co-ops or education programmes.' He didn't know what else to say to reassure her. 'I will honour all that I agreed to.'

'If you don't, there'll be consequences. I'll be watching. If you contravene the contract you'll be hearing from my lawyers. And I'll go public with my outrage if there's a need to. I can create a media storm.'

He nodded to let her know he understood. He wished she weren't going to be watching from afar, though. He wished—

'Would you like to come on board as a consultant?'

'James, have you taken leave of your senses?'

'No,' Christy said to him, her tone uncompromising.

With what he could only describe as regal grace, she turned to his mother. 'Do you really not care that you just made your son look dishonest and unprincipled in the eyes of a business associate?'

His mother sucked in an outraged breath. 'I made him look strong.'

Christy shook her head. 'You made him look ruthless. It's not the same thing.'

With a shrug of dismissal, she strode across to the door

and he heard her murmur under her breath, 'My mother is ten times the woman you are, Denise.'

All the stories she'd told him about her mother rose up to torment him. 'Your mother—' he swallowed '—if—'

'My mother is none of your concern.'

Her word were an icy lash and it was all he could do not to flinch. 'Christy, if there's anything I can do to make amends…'

She stilled, her hand on the doorknob. 'Anything?'

'Anything.'

She turned and folded her arms. 'Then what I'd like you to do is tear up our contract.'

For one wild moment he considered it. And then all of the responsibility and the duty that had been ingrained in him since birth rose to the fore, making him hesitate. He'd promised his father he'd do everything in his power to look after MA. Before he made a decision as momentous as tearing up their contract, he needed to get it straight in his mind *exactly* what his duty was—to his parents, to MA…and to himself.

Her lips twisted. 'So not quite anything, then. *This* is the world you want to live in?' She gestured around at the penthouse apartment. 'I hope it makes you happy.'

She left and he knew then that this wasn't the world he wanted to live in. The world he wanted to live in had Christy in it.

You didn't promise your father you'd be CEO.

'Where are you going?' Denise demanded as he strode towards his makeshift office.

'To work. While you can pack your things. You're staying at the Marina Bay Sands for the duration of your stay. From there you can't interfere with what doesn't concern you.'

'How dare—?'

'You wanted me ruthless, Mother. This is me being ruthless.' He slammed the door behind him and locked it for good measure.

You didn't promise your father you'd be CEO.

He'd promised to protect MA's reputation. He paced the room. Could he find a way to safeguard that while also following the dictates of his heart?

He pulled to a halt as the vaguest of plans started to form. Was it possible…?

CHAPTER TEN

THE FLIGHT TO Australia took an eternity—as if they were flying through thick treacle or pea soup. Jamie glanced at the flight information on his private television screen to reconfirm that their current ground speed was actually nine hundred kilometres per hour. Admittedly New York to Sydney was a long flight, but this felt as if it were taking weeks instead of hours.

He drummed his fingers against the seat rest. The time gave him too long to brood, too long to second-guess himself...too long to twist his insides into knots. In the last fortnight he'd turned his entire life on its head, with no safety net and absolutely no certainty that he'd achieve his end goal.

He swore and dragged both hands back through his hair. What was he going to do if Christy walked away and told him she never wanted to see him again?

Forcing his head upright before the annoyingly conscientious flight attendant could ask him if he'd like a headache tablet—*again*—he pulled in a deep breath, trying to separate his thoughts and the alternating fears that twisted his gut.

First, and most importantly, the decisions he'd made in the two weeks since leaving Singapore were some of the best and most personally empowering he'd ever made.

Regardless of what happened with Christy, they were still good decisions.

And regardless of what path he chose for himself from this day forward, he'd left MA in good hands. The company had committed to eradicating outdated and exploitative practices. MA would continue to thrive.

And finally, if he didn't attempt to make amends to Christy, if he didn't tell her how he felt, he'd regret it for the rest of his life. He knew that with a certainty that turned his hands to fists. She might refuse his offer. She might walk away from him, but at least he'd know he'd tried. Not that he expected *that* to bring him much comfort, but at least he wouldn't die wondering. He'd know he'd given it his best shot.

One good thing to have come from all of this recent upheaval was his mother had given him her blessing on his current course of action. Even now he couldn't quite believe it. After what he'd done, he'd expected her to shun him for at least a month as punishment or to try and bully him to change his mind—tell him he was making a miserable mistake he'd regret forever, while reminding him of all he owed to her and his father.

She hadn't done any of that. She'd apologised. *Apologised!*

She'd told him that when his father had died she'd felt as if her entire world had collapsed. Her purpose was not only gone, but she'd been forced to face the fact that it had been a sham from the very start. The message he'd implored Jamie to give her when he'd been dying had been an apology, not a declaration of love. He'd never loved her. And he was never going to love her even if he'd survived the accident.

In her grief, and in her horror at the lie she'd told herself for all those years, she'd thrown herself into something she was good at, something that had brought her respect and acclaim—running MA. She'd thought it'd make her feel better about herself. And to a point, it had. But she could see now how closed off she'd become.

She'd told Jamie she didn't want him to lead the same sterile life that she had. She'd told him to follow his heart. She'd told him any price and any risk were worth winning the heart of his fair lady.

He'd never in all of his thirty-four years expected to hear such words on his mother's lips. She'd kissed him then, hugged him awkwardly, and told him brusquely to let her know how he got on and that she was off on an extended holiday tour of Europe to *have some fun.*

He stared out of the window at Sydney Harbour as it came into view—a glorious sight on a late spring morning—and allowed himself a tiny measure of hope. If a miracle such as his mother's turnaround was possible then surely… Surely it wasn't out of the realm of possibility to win Christy's heart.

He didn't expect it to happen overnight—he knew he had a lot to prove to her. And he didn't expect it to be easy. But if she'd give him a chance…

He crossed his fingers as the plane started its descent.

Jamie spent the next two days in conference with his lawyers, going over every aspect of his plan and the new contract he'd had drawn up. He spent every other moment aching to be with Christy, and fighting the urge to throw caution to the wind and just turn up on her doorstep to tell her he loved her.

He'd lost count of the number of times he'd started for the door of his hotel room, only to stop himself. He didn't want to land on her doorstep empty-handed. He wanted to give her something of value.

So, instead, he spent his free hours staring unseeing out of the window at the magnificent view of the harbour and Opera House that was entirely wasted on him, pounding a treadmill in the hotel gym, or taking long solitary walks through Circular Quay, The Rocks and the Botanic Gardens.

From the moment Christy had left Singapore all the colour had bled from his life. In all fairness, prior to Christy he hadn't had a whole lot of colour in it either, but she'd opened his eyes to the vividness and variety that surrounded him. He'd lost that when he'd lost her. When he walked, he did what he could to recapture it, tried to see the world through her eyes, tried to identify the things that would inspire her creativity. It managed to take him out of his own mind for a little while.

Dropping to a park bench in the Botanic Gardens, he stared at the superb view of the Sydney Harbour Bridge, at the way the water glowed orange in the sunset. Barely a breath of breeze ruffled the leaves in the trees above him and the harbour looked momentarily other-worldly. Christy would love this, and he wished so acutely that she were here his hands clenched with the fierce sudden need for her. He'd been an idiot in Singapore. A Grade A idiot. If she rejected him now—

He ran a hand over his face. If she rejected him he'd go home and start over. What he wouldn't do was throw himself heart, body and soul into running MA. What he wouldn't do was go off the rails drinking, partying, and womanising. What he wouldn't do was close himself off from love again.

His phone vibrated. He pulled it out to read an email from his lawyers telling him that everything was in place.

Pulling in a breath, he stood and nodded once. Tomorrow he had a chance to fight for what he wanted. Tomorrow he'd find out for sure if he had the slightest chance of winning Christy's heart.

Christy stared out at the harbour and took three deep breaths in the hope it would fill her with a sense of promise, a sense of enthusiasm. Today could well bring her the new path forward that she'd been searching for. She should be excited.

'Yay.'

But the word fell strangely flat. Nothing could seem to light a fire in the pit of her belly and have her eagerly turning towards the future. Not when she was still so caught up in the past.

It wasn't even three weeks since she'd returned from Singapore. She told herself it was natural to still feel despondent. She missed Jamie as she'd miss the sun or the sky if they were no longer there. As she'd miss the beach!

She shook herself. She was tired, that was all. She wasn't sleeping. And it didn't help that she'd been running herself ragged readying herself for the handover of Beach Monday either.

And that was another thing. Whenever she thought of what she'd done—sold the company she'd started from nothing!—a fresh wave of grief would grip her. Had it been a mistake to sell?

It's too late for regrets now, my girl.

Her lips twisted. What was truly ironic was that her creativity hadn't abandoned her as she'd thought it would in a time of such emotional upheaval. Oh, no. But all of her new ideas—*all of them*—were for beach umbrellas. She couldn't make umbrellas any more—she'd signed a two-year non-compete clause.

So much for a supposedly stellar career in design! It looked as if she was a one-hit wonder and—

Oh, for heaven's sake, stop moping!

She just had to give things a chance to settle down. She'd find her equilibrium again. Squaring her shoulders, she turned towards the office building on Circular Quay— the venue for today's meeting.

Her fingers tightened on the handle of her briefcase. Why hadn't Jamie contacted her, though? She hadn't heard from him. Not even about business. Not once.

She'd gone over and over their conversation on the ferry and during that lunch in Batam, and had berated herself a hundred times. She should've kept her mouth shut and her opinions to herself. But she'd allowed her outrage to get the better of her. She'd been so angry at all that Jamie's parents had put on him, their self-centredness, the silent messages they'd sent him—that he wasn't worth anything beyond his name and what he could achieve with MA. It was such a lie! But one he'd evidently bought into.

To then discover he'd also cut himself off from love… She hadn't been able to bear it.

For him or yourself…?

She had no idea, but what did it matter now? Jamie had all but told her he didn't love her, wasn't interested in letting their relationship deepen into anything more permanent— not that they'd had a relationship per se. A few kisses should never have come to mean so much to her.

If a tiny sliver of hope had stubbornly refused to die after she'd discovered Jamie's attitude towards love, it'd curled up its toes and started pushing up daisies when he'd refused to tear up their contract. That'd informed her with a starkness that could still steal her breath that MA mattered more to him than she ever could or would.

And maybe you need to stop obsessing over this?

Setting her briefcase to her feet, she shook out her hands, reminding herself that today might be the start of a brand-new direction. An anonymous investor had requested a meeting—that had to be a good sign, right?

Seizing her briefcase, she pushed through the door and gave her name at the front desk. A pleasant-faced woman immediately rose from the nearby waiting area. 'Ms Minslow, it's a pleasure to meet you. My name is Carmel. I'm your investor's Australian contact. Please come this way.'

She noted that Carmel didn't mention her employer's name. So far this mystery investor had insisted on liaising through a third-party intermediary. The anonymity puzzled her—unless it was someone big, someone of note, who was slipping into the country under a shroud of secrecy. For a moment her spirits lifted, but it didn't last. The sad truth of the matter was that she'd rather see Jamie.

Maybe that was why she made no push, when Carmel led her back outside, to find out whom she was about to meet. She swallowed, though, when she found herself walking towards the water and a large yacht. 'I hope you don't mind,' the other woman said, 'but my employer thought it'd be more enjoyable to discuss business while cruising the harbour.'

She managed a polite smile. 'Sounds lovely.'

The business advisor she'd hired had assured her this was all normal procedure and that everything was above board. The fact the investor had set up a face-to-face meeting was apparently a very promising sign.

It was time for a new start. It was time to set her face to the future. Squaring her shoulders, she boarded the yacht.

As soon as the crew had cast off—or whatever the term was for setting sail on the harbour—Carmel led her to a large reception room below deck and asked her to wait.

She stood gazing out of a window and tried to appreciate the way the sun sparkled on the water and the way fat
white clouds scudded across a peerless blue sky. But that
sky reminded her of the colour of Jamie's eyes and—

'Ms Minslow.'

She swung around, her breath jamming in her throat.
Jamie!

He stood in front of her in the flesh, living and breathing and larger than life. An ache hollowed out her chest.
It was all she could do not to hurl herself across the room
and into his arms.

Don't make a fool of yourself.

With a superhuman effort she swallowed and managed
a nod. 'Mr Cooper-Ford. This is a surprise.'

Understatement, much?

What was he doing here?

He gestured towards the table. 'Would you like to take
a seat?'

He wore the most beautifully tailored light grey suit that
did incredible things to his eyes. She wore an off-the-rack
navy suit, but the warmth in his eyes told her he saw nothing wrong with it. That warmth had her thighs trembling
and she sat before she could fall. 'So…you're the anonymous investor who contacted my lawyer?' She suddenly
frowned. 'Why the subterfuge?' Her frown deepened. 'And
what kind of investment opportunity do you think the two
of us can engage in?'

She'd ached to see him, but now that he was in front of
her she wanted to scream and berate the fates. What was
the point in seeing him? He would never be hers.

'Ms Minslow, I believe that—*together*—we could
achieve amazing things.'

The unmistakable double meaning in his words made
her swallow. But his continued formality had her grip-

ping her hands together in her lap. His gaze continued to hold hers and she doubted she could look away even if she'd wanted to.

'I'm in Australia for a couple of reasons. One is highly personal.'

Her heart started to pound—hard—and refused to stop.

'And the other is professional. I think it'll be wiser if we dispense with business first.'

Was she the *highly personal* reason he was in Australia? Please, please let her be the highly personal reason.

Business, Christy. Focus on the business.

'Very well,' she agreed, but her voice came out choked and hoarse.

'MA and I have parted ways.'

'What?' She shot to her feet. *'Why?* I—' She slammed herself back into her seat and gulped back a torrent of questions. 'How impertinent of me. I apologise. That is none of my business. But if you and MA have parted company, then…' Her mind raced. 'That means Beach Monday still belongs to me.'

'That's correct.'

The deal hadn't gone through? Beach Monday was still hers?

Yes! She wanted to dance. She was *never* selling her beloved company again.

His eyes twinkled as if he'd read that resolution in her face, and then he sobered. 'You made me realise something while we were in Singapore. You made me realise I'd never considered any other direction for my life than working for MA and eventually becoming CEO there. It made me ask myself that if I were free to choose any other direction, where would I go? Would I want to remain at MA or do something different?'

She could barely take in what he was telling her.

'I asked myself searching questions, like what I'd like to achieve personally; what would I like to be remembered for? All I've ever done is follow the path others have expected of me. My life was one of duty and obligation, but it wasn't one of passion. There was no denying I was good at what I did, but I realised that didn't necessarily equate to happiness.'

'You *don't* want to be CEO of MA?'

One gorgeously broad shoulder lifted. 'It's not a path I'll discount in the future, I'm still a voting member of the board, but while I have the *pedigree*—' his lips twisted on the word '—I don't have the proven reputation on the board to be CEO. Which is why the board didn't have confidence in me. And I find I lack the zeal to prove them wrong.'

Outrage swelled her chest. 'They're just a bunch of old fogeys who can't see beyond their own noses to recognise when they have a person of substance at the helm!' The words were out of her mouth before she was even aware of it. She shifted on her seat at his raised eyebrow. 'I liked the programme of economic sustainability you planned to implement,' she mumbled.

'Which is why I've brought in a replacement who is fifteen years my senior and whose…let's call it *ethical vision*, corresponds with mine. His age and experience have made him acceptable to the board and a five-year tenure has been agreed.'

She stared at him, gobsmacked. 'But why hasn't this made the papers?'

'It goes public the day after tomorrow.'

She slumped back in her seat. Just…wow.

'So now I find myself looking for a project of my own. Because that's what I want to do. I want to strike out on my own. I want to prove that I can be a success without the backing of a company like MA with all of its prestige and infrastructure. I'm looking for a project I can believe in and get behind and help to grow.' He paused, his gaze steady. 'A project like Beach Monday.'

'Beach Monday…? Grow?' she parroted.

'I'd like to be hands-on.'

She tried to ignore the images those words *hands on* evoked in her mind. She moistened suddenly dry lips. 'Does that mean you want to invest in my company?'

'That's exactly what I mean, Ms Minslow.'

She couldn't speak for a moment—couldn't manage a single solitary syllable. But the power of speech hadn't deserted her entirely. 'I don't doubt Beach Monday would benefit from everything you have to offer, Mr Cooper-Ford. What kind of arrangement did you have in mind?' she eventually managed to get out.

'In return for investing this amount of money in your company…'

He wrote an amount down on a piece of paper and pushed it across the table towards her. Her eyebrows shot up towards her hairline. She counted the number of zeroes for a second time. Be cool. *Be cool!*

'Holy crap!' *So not cool.* And she didn't care.

'In return I want a forty-nine per cent stake in Beach Monday. I want to be your business partner.'

'You're serious?'

'Absolutely.'

She glanced at the number in front of her again and frowned. 'This is very generous…too generous.'

'No.' He sounded confident and utterly sure of himself. It was beyond sexy. 'This is business, nothing more, I promise you. I believe in your company and I want to help you take it to the world. Beach Monday is going to be an outrageous success and I want to get in on the ground level. I expect to recoup my money many times over.'

'I'd make you a forty-nine per cent stakeholder for half this sum.'

He tapped the piece of paper. 'While I'd let you wrestle me down to a forty per cent stake for that sum.'

She suddenly wanted to laugh. 'I'm fairly certain this isn't the way we're supposed to do business.'

He held his hand out. 'What do you say? Do we have a deal?'

She found her hand somehow in his. Apparently she hadn't lost the power of movement either, even though she felt as if she had no control of her limbs. 'I'll have my lawyers draw up the papers.'

'Excellent.' He stood. 'It was an absolute pleasure doing business with you, Ms Minslow. I look forward to our partnership.'

'Pleasure's all mine,' she murmured, rising too, her heart careening about inside her chest.

Could they get to the important stuff now—his *highly personal* reason for being in Australia?

'I'll be in touch.' With a nod, he turned and strode away.

Her mouth dropped as she watched him leave. She sat back down with a thump. What did it mean, Jamie showing up like this? Had he and his mother fallen out?

Doh! Well, obviously. Her gut clenched. Had they fallen out because of her? She didn't want that; she'd never wanted that. She knew how important family was to him. She mightn't like Denise, but she hadn't wanted to cause a rift between mother and son. She'd just wanted Jamie to forge his own path.

A rather ugly thought occurred to her. Had he offered to invest in Beach Monday to spite Denise? She dragged both hands back through her hair, only to tangle her fingers in it. With a grimace, she untangled herself.

She wanted Jamie to be here because he'd missed her

and hadn't been able to stop thinking about her. But how ridiculous was that? Because he'd *never* told her he loved her. He'd never even considered it a possibility. So whatever his *highly personal* reason for being here might be, it wasn't to tell her he loved her and wanted to build a future with her.

The day had darkened, though a glance out of the window told her the sun still shone as brightly as ever.

Carmel appeared in the doorway. 'Ms Minslow, a suite has been prepared for your convenience so you can freshen up.'

Really?

'If you'd like to follow me.'

The suite was the height of luxury. And laid out on the bed was the most gorgeous outfit. 'A gift from Mr Cooper-Ford,' Carmel murmured, closing the door softly behind her, leaving Christy alone.

She stared at the outfit. And couldn't stop from reaching out to touch it. For some reason she couldn't fathom, Jamie had bought her a calf-length skirt in a bold print of watermelon slices—the pink of the watermelon contrasting beautifully with the black seeds and the green background. It was fun and whimsical and exactly what she'd have chosen for herself. A simple shell top in a matching pink and green ballet flats completed the outfit.

Christy glanced down at her suit. They'd completed their business. Maybe the change of clothes indicated a move to more *personal* business? Not giving herself a chance to think, she slipped the outfit on and was admiring the effect in the mirror when her phone rang. She pressed it to her ear.

'Christy, it's Jamie.'

His beautiful accent filled her ears and everything inside her tried to take flight. She had to swallow before she could speak. 'Hello, Jamie.' She didn't know what to say. 'It's nice to hear from you.' *Nice?* She mouthed to herself and winced.

'I've wanted to call you for the last nineteen days. I've missed you. More than I realised it was possible to miss anyone.'

His words electrified her. 'Then why haven't you called?'

'Because I've been an idiot.'

She collapsed to the side of the bed.

'Will you have lunch with me in an hour's time?'

'Yes!' She shot to her feet, and then she frowned. 'No.'

'No?' His voice emerged heavy, as if she'd punched the life out of him.

'Jamie, am I your *highly personal* reason for being in Australia?'

'Yes.' He paused and for a moment all she could hear was ragged breathing. 'I've left it too late, haven't I? I've screwed up—'

'No!' With one hand she shoved her suit, tightly rolled up, into her briefcase. 'But if I'm the reason you're here, I don't want to wait an hour to find out why. I want to see you now. Where are you?'

'Up on deck.'

'Don't move,' she ordered, slapping her phone shut and racing out of the door.

She found him at the front of the boat, framed against the Harbour Bridge. He'd swapped his suit for sand-coloured chinos and a turquoise polo shirt. The light breeze ruffled his hair, and he looked like every dream she'd ever had of a handsome prince. She wanted to smile but all her energy was focused on remaining upright.

'Hello again.' A smile hooked up one side of his mouth and she wanted to throw herself at him.

'Hi.' It was nothing more than a breath of air. She didn't know if he'd even heard it.

'Damn it! I had a really cool speech prepared,' he muttered, 'but…' Swooping forward, he cupped her face in his hands, his lips crashing to hers in a fever of need and desire that would have bowled her over if he weren't holding her so securely. Inside her everything tossed and tumbled in a daze of desire and need and a million fizzy bubbles of happiness.

He dragged his mouth from hers and she tried to contain all of those fizzy bubbles. It was just a kiss. It didn't necessarily mean anything. It—

'I've missed you every second for the last nineteen days.'

She blinked.

'Whenever I close my eyes, I see you. When I open them I can still see you…and all I can do is ache for you.'

As he spoke, his brow lowered to hers. She'd entirely lost the ability to speak, to move, to do anything!

'Hell. This wasn't the speech I meant to give. I—'

She grabbed his arm as he straightened. 'But I like this speech. I like it a lot.'

He searched her face and then a grin spread across that beautiful mouth. Taking her hand, he led her beneath the nearby canopy to a sofa, twining his fingers through hers. 'I'm sorry I didn't tear up the contract the minute you asked me to. I…' He shook his head. 'Everything had become jumbled in my mind, and all I could think was I'd be betraying my father. Which I know is nonsense now, by the way. But at the time it felt like a betrayal of everything I'd been given and I couldn't make sense of anything.'

His haggard expression had her hand tightening about his. 'If you had torn it up, I'd fully intended to print another one out and sign it again,' she confessed. 'I just wanted—'

she shrugged '—proof that you cared about something beyond MA.'

'After what I'd allowed my mother to do—making our deal public when I'd given you my word that wouldn't happen—I thought I'd lost every shred of your respect and goodwill.'

'I thought I'd lost yours! I thought I'd alienated you after everything I'd said about your parents. I should've kept my mouth shut.'

'You spoke because you cared. I just didn't want to see what was right under my nose.'

She gripped his hand in both her own. 'Tell me how you managed to extricate yourself from MA. Is your mother still speaking to you?'

She listened as he told her about the decision he'd made to forge a path of his own, and his mother's surprising reaction. She could hardly believe it. 'She gave you her blessing?'

'Fully and without reservation.' He pressed a kiss to her palm. 'You made me see that I have the right to lead my own life. And that in doing so, I won't be breaking my promise to my father.'

It was so much to take in.

'And your mother?' His gaze sharpened. 'I've been in a hundred different kinds of hell thinking we caused problems between the two of you—'

'Well, you can stop thinking it,' she broke in. 'We had a big heart-to-heart when I got home, and I discovered she'd already sensed my lack of enthusiasm for the business side of things. She wasn't as surprised as I thought she'd be at the news.' She shrugged. 'She just wants me to be happy.'

She stared up at him. He hadn't mentioned the L word yet, and she wasn't going to bring it up either. It was enough that he'd told her how he'd missed her. It would do for now.

She hesitated, not wanting to break the idyllic mood but needing to know. 'I have to ask…are you investing in Beach Monday because you feel guilty about all that happened in Singapore?'

'No!' His head rocked back. 'I'm investing in your company for many reasons. Some of them good…and some of them probably not so good,' he added with a grimace.

Tension balled in her stomach. 'Not so good?' she croaked.

'Let me start with the good.' He'd gone a little green, as if he was fighting seasickness, and her stomach churned in sympathy. 'What I need to say first is that I truly believe in Beach Monday. Christy, your designs are amazing. I fell in love with your umbrellas the first time I clapped eyes on them. They made something inside of me want to dance and sing and go on a holiday.'

Her eyes burned.

'I honestly believe that with the business support I can bring to the table, we can launch Beach Monday into the stratosphere. Your design skills and vision partnered with my business know-how and connections…' He spread his hands. 'It's a winning combination. I'm honoured you've agreed to take me on as a partner. And that's the truth. This is a once-in-a-lifetime opportunity, and I mean to make the most of it.'

She nodded impatiently. 'Okay, that all sounds great. Now tell me the not so good reasons.' She needed to know them *now*.

'I dangled this carrot as an excuse to see you.'

'You didn't need an excuse for that.'

'I had nothing else to offer you. I wanted to prove to you that I was a free agent.'

'You didn't have to offer me anything or prove anything to me.'

He met her gaze. 'And I wanted the time and opportunity to win your heart.'

Everything inside her stopped working.

'I'm hoping that working with you will give me a chance to do that.'

She was aware of the breeze blowing a strand of hair across her face, of the water lapping against the sides of the yacht, but she couldn't move a muscle. He wanted…?

'Those are the reasons I made my offer to you, Christy. Guilt had nothing to do with it. I know what I said about not wanting anything to do with love, but I was an idiot. I have a new vision for my future now. And I want that future to be with you.'

All of the things holding her immobile slipped away. 'You…you…' She stood, trembling. He went to stand too, but she pushed him back down and planted herself in his lap. Her heart was too full to speak so she kissed him instead, falling into him with every fibre of her being.

She lifted her head several moments later, breathing hard. 'You don't need the time and opportunity to win my heart, Jamie. It's already yours. It has been ever since you sat in the forest garden with me at the airport and convinced me to stay in Singapore.'

A slow smile transformed his face. 'That's because I was putty in your hands from the moment you saw me at the airport and your face fell when you realised I'd come to meet you. It was humbling, hilarious, and caught me completely off guard.'

'Because *you'd* caught *me* off guard! I wanted to make a good impression.'

'You made an impression, all right.' His eyes danced, but then he grew serious again. 'I know we haven't known each other very long, but I feel as if I've known you forever. Something inside of me recognises something inside of you…and I don't want to live without it again. Christy Minslow, I know it's probably too soon to say this, but I love you.'

The vulnerability that stretched through his eyes caught at her insides. 'Soul mates,' she whispered. 'You're my soul mate.'

'Soul mates.' He nodded. 'I like the sound of that.'

She took his face in her hands and stared deep into his eyes. 'I love you too, Jamie.' She watched his eyes flare with hope and love. 'But I want you to know that you don't need to invest in Beach Monday for me to keep loving you. I—'

He touched his fingers to her lips. 'I know, but I want to. For the business reasons I mentioned. Okay?'

She searched his face and the last prickle of uncertainty melted away and she nodded.

'In a year's time—maybe minus nineteen days—I'm going to ask you to marry me.'

Her breath hitched. 'And after I say yes, can we agree to honeymoon in Singapore?'

He kissed her, his lips curving into a smile against hers. 'Deal.'

'Jamie?'

'Hmm?'

'I really like doing business with you.'

'Ditto.'

And then they didn't speak again for a very long time.

* * * * *

SECRETS OF FOREVER

MARIE FERRARELLA

To
Lucy,
Who knew that 37 pounds
Could tear around the house like that?
We're exhausted, but our hearts
Are smiling!

Thank you, German Shepherd Rescue Society of OC
For bringing Lucy into our lives

Prologue

While Miss Joan's Diner—the only restaurant in the small but thriving town of Forever, Texas—was rarely ever empty, the hours between 11:00 a.m. and 2:00 p.m. were hands down the busiest time of the day. That was usually the time when ranchers and small business owners chose to take a break from their hectic lives and reconnect with friends and neighbors. For the space of an hour or parts thereof, they forgot about deadlines and schedules, or the problems that ranching might generate, and just paused to take a deep breath.

Even so, most of Miss Joan's patrons were usually in a hurry, wanting to eat and go before their self-indulgences created some sort of a problem that left them answerable to either bosses or, on occasion, to themselves.

Miss Joan, owner of the diner for as long as anyone could remember, presided over all this organized chaos with an iron, blue-veined hand, making sure her customers never had anything to complain about, be it the service or the food.

As usual, her full complement of waitresses—four—was on hand during this time frame. While they knew better than to rush her customers, Miss Joan always made sure they kept everything moving right along.

Noticing one of her regulars staring off into space while cradling a cup of coffee in his rough hands, the sharp-tongued woman said, "You want to nurse what's in front of you, Jefferson, go to Murphy's."

Murphy's was the local saloon run by three brothers. When they'd taken over the family establishment after their uncle died, the Murphys had struck a deal with Miss Joan. They'd promised not to serve any food other than pretzels, and Miss Joan had promised not to serve any sort of liquor, not even beer. It was an arrangement that served both establishments well.

Today, for some reason, it seemed as if the diner was even busier than usual.

The noise level was higher. Not to mention the diner seemed hotter than usual. Miss Joan could feel perspiration beading along her brow beneath her ginger-colored hair. She paused just for a second to take in a deep breath.

Something felt off to her and she didn't like it. She just wasn't herself.

The diner owner had just refilled Jerry Walker's coffee cup and turned to replace the coffeepot on the burner when she abruptly froze. Her perspiration intensified. Not only that, but her pulse raced in time with her heart. The latter was suddenly beating so hard, her head felt like it was spinning.

Isolated in her own little world, Miss Joan didn't see one of the waitresses closest to her, Vanessa Aldrich, looking at her, concern etched on her fresh features.

Vanessa had temporarily forgotten about her customer sitting at one of the tables, waiting for his rare steak.

"Miss Joan?" Vanessa whispered. When she received no answer, she repeated the diner owner's name and laid a hand on the older woman's bony shoulder.

Miss Joan all but jumped the way a person did

at the sound of gunfire. "What?" she snapped, doing her best to try to cover up her reaction to what was the most startling moment of physical weakness she had ever experienced.

"Are you all right?" Vanessa asked her.

Miss Joan had prided herself on being equal to and surviving every curve that life had ever thrown at her, including one very big one. Surviving and managing to go on even stronger than before. It was a well-known fact that Miss Joan was the one who provided strength to many people in Forever. She did so while maintaining an air of wry aloofness.

Despite this façade, in times of need or trouble, Miss Joan was always the first person everyone turned to, the first to provide unspoken moral support, not to mention the occasion roof overhead and/or source of much needed employment. It was an open secret that the woman had a heart of gold even though she pretended to remain distant and disinterested even when interacting with her patrons.

The terrifying wave of weakness disappeared as suddenly and mysteriously as it materialized and, within moments, it was as if that debilitating moment had never even happened.

Almost back to her old self, Miss Joan drew

back her thin shoulders and raised her head like a soldier on the verge of battle.

"Of course I'm all right. I'd be even better if my waitresses were moving a little faster instead of stopping to gawk at the woman they work for. Your break time comes *after* the lunch rush, not in the middle of it," she reminded Vanessa as she waved her hand at the man sitting to her right. "Now take Rudy here his steak before it turns cold and Angel has to make him a new one."

"Yes, Miss Joan," Vanessa murmured, hurrying over to her neglected customer's table.

"The girl was just concerned, Miss Joan," Rick Santiago, Forever's sheriff, pointed out to the woman he had known ever since he had been a boy. "There's no need to snap her head off."

Penciled-in deep brown eyebrows drew together over the bridge of Miss Joan's amazingly perfect nose. "There's *always* a need to bite their heads off," she informed the sheriff with no hesitation. "And I'll thank you to let me run the girls in my diner the way I see fit. I don't tell you how to run the town, now do I?"

The sheriff merely smiled because they both knew that was not the case. Miss Joan was the most opinionated person Rick knew. He also owed her a great deal. Everyone in town did. He nodded at his almost empty coffee cup. "How about a refill?"

"As long as you promise to keep your opinion to yourself," Miss Joan said. She positioned her coffeepot over his cup but held off pouring as she waited for Rick's response.

He nodded. "For now," he replied.

Miss Joan sighed. "I suppose that'll have to be good enough. For now," she echoed as she finished refilling his cup.

Rick inclined his head in silent agreement. A draw was the best that anyone could hope for when it came to Miss Joan.

Chapter One

Miss Joan raised her eyes as she straightened the sugar dispenser on the counter.

"If you're expecting me to sprout wings and fly away, you're going to be disappointed, so stop watching me like that," she ordered Cash, her grandson thanks to her finally tying the knot with Harry Taylor some years ago. Making her way over to Forever's other lawyer, one look at Miss Joan's face told everyone within sight of the woman that she looked as if she was loaded for bear. "Don't think I don't know what you're up to," she all but growled, her hazel eyes pinning Cash where he sat on the stool.

"And just what is it that I'm up to, Miss Joan?" the tall, blond-haired young man asked her innocently.

She didn't like playing games. Miss Joan's eyes narrowed like two laser beams as she looked at Cash. This sort of attention made her feel feeble.

"Don't play dumb, Cash. It doesn't suit you. We both know that old man sent you here to watch over me. Well, you're wasting your time, not to mention a perfectly good seat in my diner." Miss Joan nodded at the stool. "A seat a paying customer could put to good use."

"When it starts getting crowded in here, Miss Joan," Cash promised her, "I'll vacate it."

Miss Joan snorted. "Don't you have any wills to write up or update?" she asked, then added, "And I don't mean mine."

Cash laughed. "You're going to live forever, Miss Joan. Grandpa just wants to make sure that you're healthy while you're doing it," he told the town icon with a smile.

Miss Joan cleared away an empty cup left behind by a customer. "Humph. You want to waste your time, you can go right ahead and—"

The lanky woman's words seemed to dribble away as a really sharp, intense pain suddenly stabbed her in her chest, bringing with it a wave of heat accompanied by a weakness she found herself incapable of dealing with.

Miss Joan couldn't seem to catch her breath.

Because she had abruptly stopped talking, Cash glanced up. He immediately saw the change in Miss Joan's face. As usual, he was wearing a suit, but that didn't even begin to stop him. Cash instantly vaulted over the counter to get to her side, managing to acquire a dollop of whipped cream on his trousers as he did so.

He reached the woman just as she looked as if she was going to sink to the floor.

"Miss Joan, what's wrong? Are you having a heart attack?" her grandson asked, putting his arms around the thin, shaken woman as Ruby and Laurel, the two waitresses currently on duty, quickly closed ranks around the diner owner.

Ruby, the older of the two, spoke first. "Get Miss Joan some water," she ordered as she looked at Laurel.

Miss Joan barely heard the young woman, or Cash. They were just noise. Shaken, she was focused on what was happening to her—and frightened. The heated wave had already started to pass and, while not entirely releasing Miss Joan from its death grip, she was doing her best to rally.

Becoming aware of their hands attempting to

hold her steady, she waved away the waitresses as well as her stepgrandson.

"I'm fine," Miss Joan insisted then snapped, "Stop fussing. I'm fine, I tell you." She straightened like a regal queen.

Cash withdrew his hands and released the woman who still appeared to be very fragile to him. He remained close to her.

"No," he told her firmly, "you are *not* fine. In case you missed the message, your body is putting you on notice, Miss Joan, and you're going to listen to that warning, do you understand?"

When he looked as if he was about to take hold of her again, Miss Joan shrugged him off. "What I understand is that Harry raised a grandson who doesn't know how to behave respectfully around his betters," she fired back, deliberately avoiding the word "elders" because she felt it reflected poorly on her.

Cash Taylor was known for his easy-going disposition, but he drew the line when it came to being bullied. "Nonetheless, I want you to go see Dr. Davenport."

Miss Joan was aware that every eye in the diner was on her. She definitely didn't care for this sort of attention.

"*You* go see Dr. Davenport. I don't have the

time," she declared, turning her back on Cash and moving away.

"*Make* the time, Miss Joan," Cash told her in a no-nonsense voice.

Miss Joan slowly turned around and glared at the young man. "If I make the damn appointment, will that get you off my back?" the woman demanded, her tone far from friendly.

Cash's eyes met hers. "Yes," he answered in no uncertain terms.

Frustrated, Miss Joan blew out an impatient breath, a player conceding the game under duress.

"Fine!" she snapped. "I'll make the appointment!"

"That's my girl," Cash said affectionately, planting a kiss on Miss Joan's shallow cheek before she could pull her head away, out of his reach. He knew that Miss Joan wouldn't say that she was making an appointment if she didn't intend to live up to her word. He considered the battle won and went to tell his grandfather.

As good as her word, Miss Joan did, indeed, make the appointment.

The problem was, Cash found out the following week, that Miss Joan hadn't *kept* the appointment. He discovered this when he'd called Forever's lone medical clinic to ask when he could pick Miss Joan up.

The clinic's head nurse, Debi, informed him that Miss Joan had called to cancel the appointment set for later that morning.

Stunned, Cash told the nurse that he was "uncanceling" Miss Joan's appointment and to expect her within the hour. Hanging up, he strode out of his office, disappointed and annoyed.

"You're not really surprised, are you?" Olivia Blayne Santiago, his senior partner, as well as the sheriff's wife, asked when he gave her the update. "Miss Joan never listens to anyone except her own little inner voice."

Cash shook his head. He refused to accept this turn of events. "I just came in to let you know I'll be out of the office for the next hour or so."

Olivia eyed him knowingly from her office chair. "You're going to force Miss Joan to go see Dan, aren't you?"

Cash looked utterly determined. "Even if I have to carry her there myself to do it."

Olivia appeared skeptical. "You might be biting off more than you can chew."

Already on his way out, Cash stopped just short of the doorway. "If anything happens to that woman, I'll have two funerals to arrange, and I'm not up to dealing with that. I'm not ready for that old man to leave me yet," he added bluntly in case there was any question about whom he meant.

Olivia glanced at her calendar. There was nothing pressing on it this morning. "Do you want me to come with you?"

"No, I'll handle it. If any of my clients want to talk to me, ask them to call back this afternoon," he told her. Then he added, "And maybe cross your fingers while you're at it."

Olivia smiled warmly. "Makes holding down the fort a little tricky."

"If anyone can do it, you can," he told the attractive brunette as he left her office.

"Are you taking an early lunch?" Miss Joan asked when Cash entered the diner.

"No," he said, walking up to the counter where she was currently standing, "I'm taking a stubborn grandmother to her appointment at the medical clinic." Cash frowned at the woman. "I'm disappointed in you, Miss Joan. You broke your promise."

Miss Joan raised her chin, a prizefighter spoiling for a fight. "I did not," she informed Cash indignantly. "I promised you I'd *make* an appointment with Davenport and I did. I did *not* promise to keep it," the woman pointed out.

Miss Joan never ceased to amaze him, he thought. The woman could wiggle out of anything.

"The way I see it, you have two choices, Miss Joan. You can either walk out of here with me on your own power, or I can carry you out. Either way, you *are* seeing the doctor."

Miss Joan's eyes darted to her waitresses and then to the sheriff, who had stopped by for a quick cup of coffee before heading out to the Elliot Ranch to handle a local dispute.

"Don't look at me, Miss Joan. I'm on Cash's side," Rick protested.

Miss Joan's face clouded over although, deep down, she hadn't expected the sheriff to answer any other way. "I'm not going to forget this."

"As long as you're around to carry a grudge, that's all right with me," Rick told her. "We're all worried about you," he added.

Word had spread fast about how pale Miss Joan had turned the other day, not once, but twice. No one wanted to witness a repeat performance.

"Listen to me, you two," Miss Joan all but growled. "I am fine." Her tone was crisp, measured. Then she repeated the word—*"Fine"*—with emphasis.

Rick was unmoved and remained seated, nursing his coffee. "We just want to make that official and have the doc tell us so."

"So, which is it, Miss Joan?" Cash asked. "Are you going out on your own two feet, or do I have to carry you?"

Her eyes flashing, Miss Joan muttered a few choice words under her breath as she took off her apron and tossed it on the counter. She knew when she was defeated.

"On my own two feet," she said coldly.

Cash nodded. "Good choice."

Miss Joan gave it one more shot as they walked out of her diner.

"Davenport's a busy man, boy. I don't like taking up his time like this over nothing," she cried.

Cash wasn't buying it. "Attending your funeral will cost him more time," he quipped, escorting the woman to his car.

"Since when did you get so dramatic?" Miss Joan asked.

Closing the passenger door after her, Cash rounded the hood and got in on his side.

"It comes with the territory," he replied. "The sooner we do this," he told her, starting up his car, "the sooner it'll be over."

Miss Joan crossed her arms before her small chest, unwilling to buy into his narrative.

"You don't have to hang around," Miss Joan told her grandson as they walked into the medical clinic. He hadn't left her side since picking her up at the diner.

"I'm afraid we have a slight difference of opinion when it comes to that matter, Miss Joan. You might as well save your breath," he said kindly. "I'm staying."

"This is harassment, you know," she snapped as they entered the semi-crowded clinic. There wasn't a single person there she didn't know, but Miss Joan avoided making any eye contact. She was much too angry to do that.

"No, this is insurance," Cash replied mildly as he nodded at Debi, one of the two nurses sitting behind the reception desk. "I'm ensuring the fact that you're going to be seeing the doctor."

"Dr. Davenport is waiting for you, Miss Joan," Debi said, rising and coming around the desk. "If you'll just follow me."

"Do I have a choice?" Miss Joan asked tersely, glancing over her shoulder at Cash.

"No, ma'am," Debi replied, doing her best not to

smile at the situation. She knew the older woman wouldn't appreciate it. "You do not."

Miss Joan shook her head in disgust. "And to think that I gave this town the best years of my life," she complained, grudgingly walking behind the nurse.

"We'd all like to think that those are still ahead of you, Miss Joan," Debi told her as she led the woman into the rear of the clinic. "You're in exam room one," she said, gesturing toward the room.

It was obvious that Dr. Daniel Davenport was waiting for her, eager to resolve this as quickly as possible. He owed the diner owner a debt because of the way she had treated his wife before they were ever married.

"Hello, Miss Joan," Dan said warmly, taking her hand between both of his. "I promise to make this as painless as possible."

"It's already too late for that," the woman informed him. "Look, I'll save us both some time and trouble. I've had a couple of heart flutters. Nothing serious, but everyone overreacted and made a big deal out of it, including that old man I made the mistake of marrying. Now, I've got a diner to run, so if we're through here—"

Dr. Dan gently took Miss Joan by the arm and led her over to the examination table. "No, Miss

Joan, we are not through here. I need you to sit down on this table and let me examine you."

Annoyed and stymied, Miss Joan exhaled dramatically. "Oh, all right. Just make it quick," she instructed impatiently.

Dan smiled into the older woman's eyes. The lined face of a warrior, he couldn't help thinking. "I'll make it thorough."

Miss Joan scowled, far from happy, but she knew that resistance would only prolong the process, and she wanted to be gone. "Let's get this over with," she ordered.

Helping Miss Joan onto the exam table, Dan flashed a smile at her. "Your wish is my command, Miss Joan."

"Ha! Don't push it, sonny," Miss Joan warned the physician.

It took a lot for Dan not to laugh.

"So, are you satisfied?" Miss Joan asked, buttoning up her blouse. She never took her eyes off Dan. "I assume I can go now, right?"

He made one last notation in the woman's exceptionally thin file. To his recollection, Miss Joan had never been inside his medical center since he had first reopened it.

"No," he answered. "And yes."

Impatience creased Miss Joan's lined forehead. "I'll go with 'yes,'" the woman said, slipping off the edge of the exam table. She turned toward the door.

"I thought you might," he said and then dropped his bomb. "I want you to see a specialist."

Miss Joan raised her eyes accusingly. "I just did," she pointed out. "You."

"No," he contradicted. "I mean a cardiac specialist."

"Forever doesn't have a cardiac specialist," she reminded him tersely.

"No, it doesn't," he agreed, "but—"

"Well, that settles it, doesn't it?" Miss Joan announced. "I can't see one if we don't have one. Now, I've got people waiting for me, so if you don't mind—"

"Oh, but I do mind, Miss Joan," Dan said, catching her gently by the arm and preventing her escape. "You have a big heart, but it's a heart that clearly needs help, and I'm not qualified to do the type of surgery that you need." He watched as shock passed over the older woman's face. "There're some fine cardiac specialists in Austin—"

Miss Joan shook her head, vetoing the idea before it was actually even spoken.

"Unless one of those 'fine' doctors is willing to make a house call to Forever to see me," she informed Dan, "I'm afraid this idea has run its course. So, if you'll just step out of my way, sonny, we can both get on with our lives."

Dan shook his head. "You are definitely one stubborn lady, Miss Joan," he said.

"I never claimed to be anything else, sonny." Her features softened slightly. "Look, I appreciate the corner my grandson and husband just painted you into, but you did your best. You gave me an exam—not that I wanted one—and you gave me your opinion, which I duly noted. Now let me get back to what I do best—"

"Being stubborn?" he asked wryly.

"Being useful," she countered. "Send your bill to Harry," she said, straightening her blouse. "So maybe next time that old man'll think twice before having me practically abducted."

But Dan wasn't ready to give up. He recalled a conversation he'd just had with one of the doctors he had gotten to know well while interning in New York. Back before he had ever come out here and gotten hooked on Forever.

"What if I could get one of those cardiologists to come see you?" Dan asked just as Miss Joan reached for the handle on the exam room door. "If he came here, would you see him then?"

Miss Joan laughed shortly, thinking the chances of that happening were slim to none. Mostly none. She turned around to look at Dan with what passed for her own version of a broad smile on her thin lips.

"Sure, if you can get one to come all the way to our little town to make a 'house call,' then yes, I'll see him—or her. After all, I'm nothing if not reasonable," she told him with a cackle. And then she looked from Dan to Debi, who had remained in the room for the examination. "Now, am I free to leave or do you have an armed guard posted outside this door?" she asked.

"No, no armed guard, Miss Joan. You're free to leave," Dan told her.

Something about the expression on the doctor's face told her this wasn't over yet. But if she pressed the issue and asked, she was fairly certain it would escalate into a bigger discussion, and she had no time for that.

She had people waiting for her at the diner. Probably a lot of people by now.

Chapter Two

Maybe it actually *was* time for a change, Dr. Neil Eastwood thought.

Admittedly, change had been in the back of his mind for a while, ever since his conversation with his old friend, Daniel Davenport. He had felt this restlessness building up inside him for some time but now it seemed to be coming to a head. Neil knew that if he said as much to some of his friends and the colleagues he worked with, they wouldn't hesitate to tell him they thought he was crazy.

Here he was, a skilled cardiac surgeon at the top of his field, associated with the best, most respected hospital in New York City—the city that never slept—and all he could think about was leaving it all behind and starting over somewhere else.

Quite honestly, the feeling had taken root even before he and Judith, his now ex-fiancée, had broken up. But the breakup had definitely escalated this desire for change.

Although she'd adamantly denied it when he'd called her on it, there was no denying the fact that Judith had wanted to orchestrate every minute part of his life. At times, he was still surprised that she hadn't attempted to elbow her way into his actual practice, telling him which patients she thought he should see and which he should turn away.

Judith had made it clear that she'd thought he should only minister to patients who could pay handsomely for his services. Namely *rich* patients. That way, his reputation would continue to grow and he would be able to take on patients who would pay top dollar for his services, no matter what he wound up charging. Judith Monroe had very expensive tastes and although her family certainly had money—old money—she was of the opinion that one could never possibly have *enough* money.

Neil, on the other hand, had not gone into cardiac surgery for the money. Oh, he had to admit that, for a while, it was seductive, almost alluring, to be paid for what he loved doing. But the con-

cept of financial reimbursement had all changed
in one night. He'd been doing back-to-back shifts,
one of which had been whimsically referred to as
the "graveyard," when an ashen-faced father ran
into the ER carrying his five-year-old daughter in
his arms and screaming for help.

As luck would have it, Neil, the only doctor on
duty at the time, turned out to be instrumental in
saving that little girl's life. A little girl who would
have died if not for him. The exhilarating feeling he'd experienced when she'd finally opened
her eyes had been unbelievable. He'd known then
that he wanted to recapture that feeling again and
again.

He'd also known that such exhilaration wouldn't
be possible if he continued to dance attendance
on the rich and famous, monitoring their lab tests
and adjusting their medications just so they could
continue eating and drinking to excess while partying with their friends.

In retrospect, that sort of life, the life that Judith had wanted for him, all felt so meaningless
and utterly empty.

He needed his life to mean something, needed
his existence to make a difference, the way it had
when he'd treated that little girl. He had actually

brought her back from the abyss. By all rights, she had been clinically dead for almost five minutes.

Neil thought of that little girl as his miracle child. When she'd opened her eyes and "come back," somehow, miraculously, there hadn't been any brain damage whatsoever. He had personally tested her for symptoms because he couldn't believe it.

He'd taken that "miracle" as a sign that he needed to shift the path of his life. He needed to dedicate himself to something more worthwhile than what he was doing.

When he'd told Judith about his midnight epiphany and the path he was contemplating taking—operating on patients whether or not they could pay at the time—it had been the beginning of the end for the two of them. Judith had accused him of being crazy, which was immediately followed by a knock-down, drag-out verbal assault where she did the bulk of the railing, not to mention vicious name-calling. She'd called his sanity into serious question, as well.

When that hadn't made him retract his words, she'd played her ace card. She'd threatened to leave because, under no circumstances, could she see herself "shackled to a loser," which she maintained was what he would be if he followed through.

Instead of her rant causing him to "see the light" the way she had expected, Judith's threat had only managed to accomplish his sudden exposure to an invigorating, tremendous sense of relief.

It was as if a huge weight had instantly been lifted off him. No grief, no shock, just a feeling of sweet relief.

He was suddenly free to do whatever he wanted with his life—all he had to do was figure out what that was.

That was when Fate stepped in, Neil thought now, in the form of a phone call.

In his apartment, located a few prestigious blocks from the hospital, he was contemplating his next move, as well as life without Judith, when his cell phone rang. He debated letting it go to voice mail, then changed his mind. He didn't want to put anything off anymore. Whatever was out there, he intended to meet it head-on.

Picking up his cell phone and swiping it open, he announced, "Eastwood."

"Neil?" a deep, familiar voice he couldn't quite place said on the other end of the line.

"Yes, but I'm afraid you've caught me at a disadvantage—"

He was about to ask the caller to identify himself when the person on the other end did just that.

"Neil, it's Dan. Dan Davenport," he added unnecessarily since they had just spoken less than a month ago.

"Oh, wow!" Neil cried. "Funny you should call. I was just thinking about you and the way you had just taken off for that small town to continue your brother's practice. You said it was just until they could find a replacement for him. How long did you wind up staying?" Neil asked, intrigued and amused by the whole thing.

Dan laughed softly. "You know the answer to that, Neil. I'm still there."

"Do you have any regrets?" Neil asked. As he remembered it, Dan was the one who'd had the most detailed plans for his future out of all of the interns. And then his life had taken a sudden, unexpected, detour.

"No, not a single one," Dan answered honestly. "Actually, that's what I'm calling about."

"Not having any regrets?" Neil asked, slightly confused.

"No, about doing the most worthwhile thing with my life that I never initially planned on doing."

Neil experienced an eerie feeling that he was suddenly standing on the edge of the rest of his life.

"Go on," he quietly urged.

"I need your help, Neil," Dan began, warming up to his subject. "There's this venerable old woman in Forever who runs the diner here. It's the only restaurant in town."

As a born-and-bred New Yorker, Neil couldn't envision a place with just one restaurant. "You're kidding," Neil marveled. "Just how small is this place?"

"Small," Dan assured him. "But size doesn't have anything to do with it." He paused for a moment, regrouping. "This would make more sense if you were here, which is what this phone call is actually about. Miss Joan—"

"Miss Joan?" Neil interjected. "Is she a delusional Southern Belle from another century?" he asked, amused.

"Miss Joan is definitely not delusional. It's what everyone around here calls her and it's actually a sign of respect. Anyway," Dan continued, not wanting to keep Neil any longer than he had to, "Miss Joan has developed some cardiac issues. From the exam I gave her, I'd say she probably needs an angioplasty, or possibly a stent put in, or an ablation." Aware that meant burning away some tissues in the heart, Dan conceded, "My experience in these procedures is rather limited and I'd prefer having a specialist look at her to determine the necessary course of action."

So far, this all sounds logical, Neil thought. "So what's the problem?"

Dan gave it to his friend in a nutshell. "We don't have a specialist here in Forever."

"Then have someone in her family—I take it she's not a spring chicken," Neil guessed.

Dan felt it was rather a cold way to assess the woman, but since he was asking for a favor, this was not the time to chastise his friend. "Not really."

"Have someone take her to a specialist," Neil concluded.

"That's the problem," Dan admitted. "Miss Joan claims she's too busy and she won't budge. So I asked her if she'd be willing to see a doctor if the doctor came to see her. I managed to get a grudging 'yes' out of her. Personally," he admitted with a laugh, "I think she doesn't think I'll find anyone."

No mystery there, Neil thought. "I'd say she's right."

Here goes nothing, Dan thought. "I heard via the grapevine when I talked to Wayne Matthews—" a neurologist they both knew "—that you're looking to relocate."

That is only partially true, Neil reasoned. "What I'm looking for is to find a purpose."

Good enough, Dan thought but didn't say. "Well, while you're looking, maybe you could come out here on what I'd consider to be an errand of mercy."

Since Neil wasn't trying to stop him, Dan talked quickly. "Miss Joan is the heartbeat of this town, provided that her heart keeps on beating, of course. If you can come out and give me your professional opinion about her condition, I can personally guarantee that you will have approximately five hundred people eternally in your debt."

"Five hundred people, huh?" Neil repeated, amazed. "Is that how many people there are in your town?" he asked incredulously.

"Yes. Give or take," Dan added.

Neil picked up on the phrase and put his own interpretation on it. "I take it that a lot of people are leaving."

"You'd think," Dan agreed. He'd been guilty of thinking that himself once, but he'd been wrong. "Actually, these days there are more people coming to Forever than leaving. Since I came here eight years ago, more people have moved here than have moved away.

"Anyway…" Dan returned to the reason he had

called his friend. "The problem is, we still don't have a hospital here," he confessed. "So, what do you say? Do you feel like doing a good deed and having everyone in town think of you as a hero?"

Neil laughed. "You know, Dan, I don't remember you as the type to exaggerate. Is that something that comes from living in Texas?"

"No, and I'm not exaggerating. Listen…" he went on, "I'll pay for your ticket and you can stay with Tina and me and the kids when you get here."

Neil read between the lines—or thought he did. "Translation, there's no hotel in town, right?"

"As a matter of fact, there is, and it's a few years old," Dan told him. "I just thought you might like to experience what it's like to *live* in Forever. Hotels are pretty impersonal."

"But you do have one?" Neil questioned, wanting to know just how primitive the town actually was.

"Absolutely," Dan assured his friend.

Neil paused, thinking. "Well, I do have a lot of vacation time stored up." He had been working almost nonstop for a year, taking on extra shifts at the hospital when he wasn't at his practice. "It might do me some good to get away for a while."

"Fantastic! When can you be here?" Dan asked.

Neil looked at the calendar on the wall that dictated his life. There was nothing on it that couldn't be handed over to one of his fellow specialists. "When do you need me?" he asked.

"Yesterday."

Neil didn't detect a smile in his friend's voice. "Is it that serious?"

There was a short pause while Dan was likely thinking of how frail Miss Joan had looked when he'd examined her. More so than usual, though he avoided giving Neil a direct answer to his question. "To be very honest, I'd rather have her examined sooner than later," he told Neil. "Okay, you make the arrangements to fly out, give me the exact details and I'll pay for your car rental when you land."

"Car rental?" Neil questioned.

"I'm afraid so," Dan said. "There's no airport in Forever. You'll be flying into Houston and then driving from there to Forever."

"Uh-huh," Neil replied. "Just one small problem with that plan," he said.

"What?" Dan asked.

"I don't know how to drive," Neil told him.

Dan had difficulty hiding his amazement. "You never learned how to drive?"

"I'm a New Yorker," Neil stressed. Learning to drive had never been a priority to him. "You remember how great the public transportation system is in New York, not to mention we have all those cabdrivers. And now we have all those other independent services practically everywhere you look. The city is crowded with them. There's no need for me to learn how to drive a car."

"I suppose I can see your point," Dan conceded. He had learned to drive because he liked his independence and didn't like waiting for buses and trains, but admittedly that was a personal choice. Dan thought of the patient he had seen just last week for a routine checkup to renew her pilot's license. "I think I might have a solution. Let me make a call," he proposed. "Meanwhile, you do whatever you need to do to get ready to come out here. And, like I said, the sooner, the better."

This was going a little bit too fast, Neil thought. "If I come out, it doesn't mean that I'm staying," he warned, wanting there to be no misunderstandings about the matter.

"Understood. As far as I'm concerned, you're just coming out as a favor to me—and to enjoy a change of scenery," Dan said. "I really appreciate you doing this, Neil."

"Hey, that's why we became doctors, right?" Neil asked. "To make a difference."

That was the way Dan felt now, but it wasn't

what had motivated him to enter medical school to begin with. "Actually, I initially became a doctor because I was hoping to land a position with a prestigious practice and have an excuse to play a lot of golf." Dan chuckled at the man he had once been. "Man, I can't tell you how glad I am that that didn't work out for me. All right, give me a call with all the details when you're ready to come out. I promise it'll definitely be worth your while," Dan concluded.

"Sounds good to me," Neil replied. "I'll talk to you as soon as I get everything in place."

"Count on it," Dan promised.

Neil ended the call, a bemused expression on his face. Funny how things sometimes arranged themselves. Less than a decade ago, he, Dan and Dan's brother had finished up their residencies and were on the brink of launching their medical careers. Of the three of them, only Dan's brother had set his sights on a town in Texas that, from what he had said, was apparently badly in need of a medical professional.

Forever had once had a small medical clinic, but that had closed its doors thirty years prior to their graduation. All set to go there, Dan's brother had agreed to one last night of celebration before leaving for Texas in the morning. Dan had been the one to persuade him to come along and had been driving the car back from the restaurant. Alcohol hadn't even been involved, at least, not where Dan and his brother had been concerned.

The driver that had plowed into them, however, had a blood alcohol content that was over twice the legal limit. He emerged from the accident totally unscathed. Dan sustained several injuries that had landed him in the hospital and his brother had wound up in the morgue. Grief stricken, Dan had decided to take his brother's place in Forever until another doctor could be found to fill the position to be Forever's new medical professional.

Eight years had gone by. Neil assumed that his friend had stopped looking for someone else to take over. He knew that inertia wasn't responsible for Dan still being there. He had to admit that he was more than a little curious as to what had managed to take a man who had clearly had his eyes focused on a lucrative practice to change his mind and allow himself to be won over by a town that contained barely five hundred people.

This was definitely going to be a change, all right, Neil mused. And if nothing else, it would do him some good. This trip would either reinforce this new mindset of his—or it would "bring him to his senses," the way Judith had shouted at him when she'd seen that he was having doubts about the path his life was taking. It had been her attempt to get him back on that path.

Flying down to Forever would allow him to reconnect with a man whom he had once regarded as being one of his best friends.

New York born-and-bred, Neil had never been outside of the state, nor had he ever had any desire to be. This promised to be very interesting.

And, he thought, it would give him the opportunity to make that difference he had been craving to make. That was if he could talk the iconic "Miss" Joan into listening to what he had to say.

If Dan was right, that was definitely going to be a challenge.

Neil smiled to himself as he placed his suitcase on the bed and opened it. He had always liked a challenge.

Chapter Three

Adelyn Montenegro shook her head as she watched her older sister check over her fifteen-year-old Piper Meridian passenger plane. The plane, which Ellie had bought secondhand from Arnie Crawford at a bargain price—and was still paying off—when Arnie decided to retire from his aircraft service, was housed in what had once been a barn. With her grandfather's help, Ellie had converted the barn into an airplane hanger. It seemed to Addie that her sister spent an inordinate amount of time fussing over the old plane.

"I swear, Ellie, you baby that old hunk of tin as if you were involved in a relationship with it."

Addie brushed her straight, midnight-black hair out of her eyes. "Don't you ever get tired of it and just want to go out and have some fun?"

"Leave your sister alone, Addie," Eduardo Montenegro, their grandfather and sole guardian since they were five and seven, chided. Ellie flashed him a grateful look and he smiled at the more industrious of his granddaughters. "I have always taught you girls to follow your dreams and this plane is part of your sister's dream."

"No, Pop," Ellie corrected the gray-haired rancher who, in her opinion, worked far too hard and too long each day, running their horse ranch, "it's just *part* of the beginning of my dream." She stepped back, wiping her hands on the rag she had been using to clean part of the plane's wing, and examining her work. "Someday, I'm going to own a fleet of passenger and cargo planes." She saw her sister roll her eyes at that. "Or at least double what I have now."

Addie sighed. She loved her sister but, in her opinion, there were times when Ellie behaved more like an old woman than someone who was twenty-six years old. "Well, just remember what happened to Amelia Earhart," Addie warned.

"The point is, even *you* know who that is," Ellie said. "And that says a lot."

Addie frowned as she shrugged. "I know who you are, too, but that doesn't do you any good now, does it?" she quipped.

Ellie opened her mouth to send a few choice words in her sister's direction, but Eduardo decided to cut in before this escalated into a real squabble. He loved both his granddaughters, but he had little to no patience for arguments.

"Girls, girls," he said sternly, "if you have all this spare, leftover energy for arguing, maybe you can put it to good use and help me with the horses this morning. They need to be fed, and both Billy and Luke are busy with other chores," he said, referring to two of his ranch hands.

Addie looked crestfallen. She knew there was no arguing with her grandfather when he took that tone. "Yes, Pop."

Ellie, however, couldn't agree to go along with his request. "I'm afraid you're going to have to count me out, Pop," she apologized. "I promised Dr. Dan I'd swing by the medical clinic this morning."

Ever since his son and daughter-in-law had suddenly been taken from him as a result of a car accident, leaving him two little orphaned girls to raise, Eduardo had become keenly in tune to anything that might mean his suffering any further loss.

He looked at Ellie sharply. Was she ill? "What's wrong?"

"There's nothing wrong, Pop," Ellie assured him. "The doc said he just wants to talk to me."

Addie thought it was just her sister looking to wiggle out of chores. "You know," she said to Ellie, "I hear they've got these newfangled things now called 'telly phones,'" she told Ellie. "You pick up a receiver, dial a number and it's like the person's right there in the room with you, talking into your ear. Maybe you could try that," she suggested, catching the tip of her tongue between her teeth.

Ellie gave her sister a dismissive look. There were times when Addie could really get on her nerves. "He said he wanted to talk to me in person. Is that all right with you?"

When Ellie told her that, even Addie looked slightly concerned. "Well, that can't be good," she speculated with a frown. Her eyes swept over her sister. "You feeling okay, El?"

"I'm feeling fine, thank you." She spared both her sister and her grandfather a look. In her grandfather's case, it was to put him at ease. "As a matter of fact, my last check up at the medical clinic had all my tests come back next to perfect."

"You, perfect?" Addie questioned, trying to

cover up the momentary display of concern that had slipped out. "That can't be right."

"Very funny, wise guy," Ellie said. She knew exactly what her sister was trying to do. "Anyway," she said, turning toward her grandfather and doing her best to put his fears to rest, "the doc said he had something to ask me and he wanted to do it in person." She turned to her sister with a big smile. "But Addie here can help you with anything you need. Right, Addie?"

Because their grandfather was still right there, listening to every word that passed between them, Addie couldn't answer Ellie with the retort hovering on her lips, begging for release. So instead she was forced to say, "You can count on me, Pop— even if you can't count on Ellie."

Eduardo's waist had grown slightly wider over the years and his once thick, jet-black hair had grown partially gray at this point. By all accounts, he was still a handsome, virile-looking man more than equal to the task of dealing with his ever-squabbling granddaughters. Each of them in one way or another reminded Eduardo so much of his spirited late son. In a way, it was as if James was still there, he thought, but he couldn't be seen as taking sides in any dispute.

"That's enough, Addie. I know I can count on

both of you, each in your own way. Now, stop wasting time squabbling. Ellie, go see what's so important that Dr. Dan has to see you in person instead of just telling you what he wants over the phone."

"Yes, Pop," Ellie said, hurrying out of the makeshift airplane hanger.

"And, Ellie…" he called after his granddaughter as she left. "If this does turn out to be anything serious, I want you to call me immediately," he told her. "Do I make myself clear, young lady?"

"Yes, sir—and it won't be," Ellie promised just before she picked up speed on her way to the house.

"Didn't you once say that the good die young?" Addie reminded her grandfather. Like Ellie, Addie was protective of the old man, not wanting to cause him any undue concern. However, there were times when she couldn't help herself. "That means that Ellie's gonna live forever, Pop. There's nothing to worry about."

Eduardo sighed and shook his head, his thinning mane of gray hair moving in the autumn breeze as he frowned to himself. On the one hand, dealing with his granddaughters kept him young. On the other, he had to admit that the back-and-forth confrontations were tiring.

I'm too old for this, he thought as he heard Ellie's Jeep engine start up. The constant refereeing was wearing him out.

Ellie, in her Jeep and driving toward town within minutes, had to admit that her curiosity had definitely been piqued. Forever was an exceptionally friendly town where everyone knew everyone else's business. But this was the first time that Forever's doctor, the man officially credited with reopening the town's medical clinic after thirty-some odd years, had ever asked to speak with her in person.

Although she never wanted to cause her grandfather any worries, what she had told him was true. She had just recently had her annual physical for her pilot's license. The results had proclaimed her to be better than all right. She seriously doubted the doctor had made a mistake or overlooked something. He was far too thorough for that sort of thing. Nor would he have knowingly exacerbated her concern that something was indeed wrong by playing any sort of game.

So then, what was this all about? she wondered. No two ways around it, Dr. Dan had definitely aroused her curiosity.

She pressed down harder on the accelerator.

When Ellie walked into the medical clinic, the reception area was crowded as usual. But the moment she crossed the threshold, Debi was instantly on her feet.

"Come on in, Ellie," she said by way of a greeting. "The doctor's been waiting for you. He's with a patient," she told the younger woman. "But he asked that you wait for him."

Ellie glanced at her watch, a graduation gift from her grandfather. Because he was shorthanded, she knew that Eduardo wanted her back as soon as possible, and she had that freight run to make at one. She'd promised to pick up supplies for Jonathan Webber.

This might be cutting it close. "I can come back later if that's convenient—" Ellie began.

Debi was quick to interrupt her. "Dr. Dan really wants to talk to you."

Always accommodating, Ellie nodded. "All right, then I guess I can stay for a few minutes," she conceded. Looking around, she found an empty seat in the waiting area and sat beside Emma Hutchinson, a retired schoolteacher.

"You know," Emma confided to her new seatmate as if they were in the middle of a conversation, "for a sleepy little town, this place has got more commotion going on lately than a bustling metropolis."

Ellie did her best to hide the smile that statement generated. By no stretch of the imagination could Forever, Texas, be described as bustling—at least not in the present century. But Ellie saw no reason to antagonize the grandmother of four by pointing that simple fact out.

Instead she nodded. "I guess it seems that way some days. Especially if you're sitting in the middle of the medical clinic," she added, looking up at Debi. Only halfway into the morning and the head nurse already looked as if she was on the verge of being worn out.

Apparently, Debi had overheard the comment. "You can say that again," she murmured. The sound of an examination room door opening behind her had the nurse looking to her left. "The doctor'll see you now, Ellie." She promptly added, "Exam room three."

Rising, Ellie hurried around the wide reception desk and to the rear of the clinic.

The door to exam room three was standing open and Dan was just coming out to meet her when Ellie reached the hallway.

"Hello, Ellie," Dan greeted the young pilot. "Thanks for coming in so quickly." He stood back so that Ellie could enter. "Why don't you come in and take a seat?" he suggested.

Ellie crossed the threshold, still not sure just

what to think about the unexpected invitation. "Should I be worried?"

The question caught him by surprise. "What? No, why would you ask that?"

Ellie could see no reason why the doctor would ask her to come in—except for one. "Well, I was just here for my annual exam and you gave me a clean bill of health, but maybe there's something that you took a second look at and realized—"

"You're fine," Dan assured her quickly, not wanting her to labor under the wrong impression. "As it turns out," he said, getting right to the point, "I need your help. Specifically, I need to hire you to make a pickup."

The look of relief on her face was instantaneous. She was so busy trying to build up her business and also trying to help her grandfather, she didn't have time to deal with any health issues.

"Supplies or medications?" Ellie asked since the bulk of her flights had to do with transporting freight.

"Neither," Dan told her. "You'll be picking up and flying in a person."

"Oh?"

Rather than satisfy her curiosity, it just managed to raise it. She had never known the doctor—or his wife, for that matter—to have anyone come out for a visit. First time for everything.

Dan could see that Ellie was dying to ask questions. "Let me start at the beginning," he told her. "I'm sure you've heard about Miss Joan and the chest pains she's been having." He knew for a fact that after that first time at the diner, it had become the main topic of conversation whenever the woman was out of earshot. Everyone was concerned.

Never one to take stock of gossip, Ellie was still aware of it. She nodded. "Miss Joan should really listen to you. She's not a kid anymore and she shouldn't just play fast and loose with her health like that."

Dan laughed softly. "The rest of the town agrees with you, but that's not why I'm asking for your help."

Ellie put two and two together. "Let me guess. You want to kidnap Miss Joan and have me fly her to the hospital in Houston so she can be seen by a specialist." She rolled the idea over as she said it and nodded. "I'm your woman."

He laughed out loud at the scenario, although he wasn't surprised that it had crossed the young pilot's mind. "Well, I'm glad you're on board, but, as it turns out, a cardiologist friend of mine agreed to come out here to exam Miss Joan. He's flying in from New York City tomorrow."

Ellie took the information in stride. Now that she thought about it, she was not surprised that the doctor had that kind of pull. "Does Miss Joan know?"

Dan smiled. He was not looking forward to that confrontation, but he was hoping the woman would be reasonable once Neil arrived. "She will."

"So…no," Ellie concluded. This should be good, she thought. "Should I be getting ready to hold Miss Joan down once this doctor walks into her diner?"

"No," Dan laughed. "That's not why I need your services. Like I said, my friend will be flying in to Houston," he told her. "I need you to pick him up at the airport and fly him to Forever."

That sounded simple enough. "I'd be more than happy to," she told him. "But if you don't mind my asking, why isn't your friend renting a car and driving here?" she asked. "That would probably be simpler and that's what most people would do when they make a cross-country trip."

"The problem is Neil doesn't drive," Dan told her.

That really surprised her. Ellie could remember hounding her grandfather to teach her how to drive from the moment she could get behind the steering wheel and reach a gas pedal—with a little help. She had borrowed her late father's boots so that when she stretched, she could press down the pedal. Learning how to drive hadn't been just a rite of passage, it had been a symbol of independence.

"You're kidding," she said. "How has your friend been getting around up until now?"

"He lives in New York. Always has," Dan told her. "The city's blessed with a hell of a lot of public transportation and Neil never found the need or desire to learn how to drive anything except a hard bargain," he quipped. "Anyway, I'm getting sidetracked and I can tell from the sound of her voice that Mrs. Hutchinson is getting anxious," he said, referring to the patient he could hear voicing her impatience in the waiting room. "Can you pick up my friend?" he asked Ellie. "He's arriving at the Houston airport tomorrow. Are you free?"

"For you, Dr. Dan?" Ellie asked with a smile. "Always. I'll need all the particulars—his time of arrival and his flight number. Oh—" she'd thought of something else "—if you have a recent picture of the man, that'll be useful."

Nodding, Dan had already gotten all that. He reached into his lab coat pocket for the information. "He's flying out of JFK tomorrow morning at nine—New York time," he told her, producing the flight number. "And this is fairly recent photo of Neil." Dan held up his cell phone.

Ellie looked at the image on the doctor's phone. That was one good-looking man, she couldn't help thinking.

"Is he bringing his wife?" she asked. Because if he was, that would mean she'd need to prepare two seats on her plane.

Dan thought of the breakup Neil had told him about. "No, Neil's not married."

"Really?" she asked, taking a second look at the picture on the doctor's phone.

He decided to share the information with Ellie. At this point, he didn't think Neil would mind.

"He was engaged for a while, but that seems to be a thing of the past. I'm just lucky he's willing to come out here because Miss Joan really does need to be seen by a specialist. No one seems able to budge her or talk sense into her. Lord knows we've all tried. Harry and his grandson are really worried about her."

Dan shook his head as he approached the exam room door. "She didn't even want to come to see me," he confessed. "Cash threatened to carry her here if she didn't come in on her own power. I'm sure she only agreed to see my friend because Miss

Joan is certain he wouldn't come all this way to make a house call."

"House call?" Ellie repeated, slightly confused by the term.

"That's what they used to call it back in the old days. Before my time," he added in case Ellie was wondering just how old the term was.

She begged to differ with the doctor. "Oh, I don't know about that. When Pop had that appendicitis attack, you came out to see him in the middle of the night."

He remembered. He'd only been in town less than six months. Dan shrugged. "It's a small town. I can't afford to lose any patients."

She wasn't buying the excuse. In her opinion, when they'd made Dr. Dan, they'd broken the mold.

"Well, if you ask me, the town's lucky to have you—and there's no way we're ready to willingly lose Miss Joan." She followed Dan to the door. "I'll be at the Houston airport early," she promised. "And with any luck, I'll give your friend Neil the smoothest ride of his life getting him here." She paused just before leaving. "And if you have any trouble getting Miss Joan in to see your friend," she added, "I'm sure Pop, Addie and I would be more than happy to lend you a hand getting her out of the diner and into the clinic," she told him with a wink.

Dan smiled at the young woman. "I'll keep that in mind," he told her. "Let me know what the charge is."

"Just pay me for the fuel and we'll call it even," she said. "After all, I want to do my part keeping Miss Joan going."

They all did, Dan thought as Ellie left.

"Debi, send in Mrs. Hutchinson. I'm ready for her," he called out just before he went back into the exam room.

Chapter Four

Eduardo made his way to the front door from the rear of the house just as Ellie was about to leave.

"I'm glad that I caught you before you left," he told his granddaughter.

Stopping in her tracks, Ellie curbed the urge to ask her grandfather if whatever this was could wait. She knew that Eduardo wasn't the type to run off at the mouth just to hear himself talk. The man was aware that she was in a hurry to get in the air, so it had to be important.

Biting back her impatience, she turned around to face the distinguished-looking rancher. "Just barely, Pop. What do you need?" she asked, one hand on the doorknob.

"Here, I made this for you," Eduardo told her. He passed Ellie a large placard. Written across it in big, bold, black letters was Dr. Neil Eastwood, the name of the doctor she was to pick up at the Houston air terminal.

Ellie looked at the sign a little uncertainly. "Um, it's very nice, Pop."

Eduardo could tell, by the way his granddaughter thanked him, that she was entirely in the dark about the placard's function. With a laugh, he proceeded to enlighten her.

"This way, if you hold this up in front of the people getting off the New York flight, the doctor who's coming in to see Miss Joan can find you instead of you having to spend a lot of time looking for him." He nodded at the sign. "Something else that used to be done back in the 'old' days," he told her.

"You made this?" Ellie asked, looking the placard over.

"Don't look so surprised. Raising horses and granddaughters isn't the only thing I do," Eduardo told her.

"A man of endless talents," she marveled with a smile. "Thank you, Pop." Ellie brushed a kiss against the man's gaunt cheek. "I appreciate this. It was very thoughtful of you."

The rancher waved away Ellie's words. "I just want you back sooner than later, that's all. Now, take off—literally," he ordered, shooing his grand-daughter on her way. "And don't forget to have a safe flight. Both ways," Eduardo added. Saying that was a superstition of his, and even though he knew wishing her a safe flight didn't guarantee she would have one, he didn't want to take any chances—just in case.

"Always." She smiled at him. "And thanks again for the sign," she said just before she dashed off to her makeshift airplane hanger to get into her aircraft.

The man really did think of everything, Ellie couldn't help thinking as she made her way through the air terminal to where the New York passengers would be disembarking in another few minutes.

The placard she was carrying felt a little cum-bersome, but she didn't want to risk folding it. This way, if it wasn't creased, she felt the sign would be clearly visible when she held it up.

Ignoring the looks several people gave her as she sashayed around, trying to avoid hitting them with the edge of the placard, she found a spot near the front of a group of people. Everyone appeared to be waiting for the disembarking passengers to emerge.

Edging over to the middle, Ellie hoped that the sign would be clearly visible to everyone coming off flight number 324.

The sign was a really good idea, she thought again. She was only five foot four and that didn't always make it easy for her to see people. Ellie picked up the placard and held it above her head. With any luck, the doctor would be one of the first passengers off the plane. If he wasn't, she wasn't all that sure just how long she could hold the sign up before her arms became really tired.

She would have to start working her arms a little more, Ellie thought as an ache began to set in in her forearms. Taking a breath, she braced herself and continued holding the sign up above her head.

Any minute now, she promised herself, doing her best to scan the faces of the passengers emerging out of the passageway.

The flight appeared to be a full one. The disembarking passengers just kept coming, without giving any indication that the flood of people would stop any time soon.

Ellie began to regret not having asked her sister to come with her. Two sets of eyes were better than one and Addie was always looking for ways to get out of working on the ranch. This time it would have been for a good cause, Ellie mused. And more than that, they could have taken turns holding up the sign, which felt as if it was getting very, very heavy.

Several very long minutes later, Ellie began to entertain the idea that maybe this Dr. Eastwood had missed his flight. If he had, that would mean she would have to hang around the Houston airport until later today, or even that she'd possibly have to come back here tomorrow.

Her arms were really aching now. Ellie put down the sign and scanned the handful of passengers still trickling off the New York flight. Just about ready to give up hope, she heard a deep voice from behind her say, "I'm Dr. Neil Eastwood. Are you looking for me?"

Startled and still clutching the sign, although no longer holding it up, Ellie swung around to look at the person who had just spoken to her. She all but smacked the man in the chest with the sign bearing his name.

He stepped back out of the way to avoid the collision just at the last minute, but she still thought that she had hit him.

"Oh, I'm so sorry," Ellie cried, dropping the sign. "Did I hit you?" she asked, embarrassed.

"No, you didn't," Neil assured her. "Would you like to try again?" he deadpanned.

"No. No, of course not," she answered more seriously. "It's just that you startled me," she explained, struggling not to turn red. "I was watching for you, but I guess you must have gotten by me. Good thing Pop made this sign."

Ellie realized that she was babbling, something she had a tendency to do when she was caught at a disadvantage. Now that the doctor had arrived, she folded the placard to make it easier to carry. Tucking it under her arm, she extended her hand to the tall, blond-haired man towering over her.

"I'm sorry for the confusion," she apologized. "I'm Ellie Montenegro. Dr. Davenport sent me to give you a ride to Forever." Somehow, that just didn't sound right to her ear, like something was missing. "That's our town," Ellie tacked on, which still only seemed to make things worse.

The next second, she pressed her lips together. She stopped talking altogether for a moment and took in a deep, cleansing breath.

And then she tried again. "Dr. Dan is going to be very happy to see you. On behalf of Dr. Dan, as well as the rest of our town, I'd like to thank you for doing this—for coming out to Forever to give Miss Joan that much needed heart exam. We would—all of us—" she emphasized, "be very lost without that woman and her glib tongue passing judgment on us."

Amused, Neil inclined his head as if there really was no need to thank him for doing any of this. After all, he was a doctor. This was what he did. Besides, it was fulfilling some inner need of his.

"I'm way overdue for a vacation and I have to admit that Dan made this town sound very interesting." Another word would have been "quirky" but he decided to keep that to himself.

When the woman sent to meet him looked as if she was at a loss for a response, Neil decided that perhaps she needed to be prodded a little. So he did. "Shall we get going?" Neil suggested.

Ellie immediately snapped to attention, embarrassed that she had somehow managed to drop the ball because she was mesmerized by his good looks.

"Yes, of course. I'm sorry, this just threw me off a little. You're actually my first airport pickup," she confessed.

Whenever she flew anyone anywhere, it usually involved dropping them off at a secluded cabin or some other inaccessible place in Texas. She didn't do airport runs. Not until now.

Ellie smiled to herself. Business was expanding.

"Well, then I guess I'm honored," Neil told her. "Speaking of firsts," he said as he started to pick up the carry-on luggage he had temporarily set down, "this is my first 'errand of mercy' flight."

Only half listening, Ellie had put her hand over the suitcase handle, intending to pick it up. When he looked at her in surprise, she told him, "Oh, I can take that for you." She deliberately moved his hands away and caught herself thinking that his hands felt as if they were very large and capable. How was he able to do delicate surgery with those hands? she wondered.

"I can carry my own suitcase," Neil told her, making a move to secure the handle.

But Ellie stubbornly kept her hand where it was, not allowing him take the case from her.

"Dr. Dan said you're a surgeon," she told him. "You don't want to risk hurting your hands."

"It's a suitcase," Neil pointed out. "Not a machete or an anvil. I can certainly carry a suitcase to your car."

"Actually," she corrected him, "We're taking it to my plane."

A plane? That surprised him. Dan had told him

that he was making arrangements to transport him from the airport to Forever. But his friend had said nothing about the arrangements involving a passenger plane. Or, for that matter, a sexy pilot.

"You have a plane?" Neil asked.

Leading the way out of the airport, Ellie happily nodded.

"It's a 2006 single-engine-turbine Piper Meridian." Seeing that meant nothing to him, she quickly added, "It doesn't look like much. But it's very safe."

"A Piper Meridian," Neil repeated. He had never heard of the plane before—at least, he thought she was talking about a plane. Maybe it wasn't safe to make any assumptions. "Is that the name of your airline?"

"No, that's the name of the type of plane I'm flying." Since, in a manner of speaking, he was entrusting her with his life, Ellie felt she owed him a little more of an explanation. "I'm hoping to someday have my own airline. Right now, there's just the one plane."

"Everyone has to start somewhere," he said philosophically. "And this aircraft…it's yours?" he asked, trying to get a handle on the woman he was apparently entrusting with his life.

Her smile was broad as she flashed it at him over her shoulder. "Technically."

That didn't sound all that good. "Technically?" he asked as they went through the airport's electronic doors to the outer area.

"Well, I'm still paying it off," she confided. "I bought the plane from Arnie. He was the one who owned the airline, but he decided to retire early last year. He sold all his planes but the one to another airline. I managed to talk him into selling that one plane to me." She glanced to the doctor. "I guess you probably think that's kind of unusual."

"I've never met anyone with their own aircraft before," he told her, trying to word his response as diplomatically as possible.

Her full lips pulled back into a quick smile. "Well, I've never met a heart surgeon before, so I guess that makes us even," Ellie said.

They crossed to what was a designated airfield reserved for private planes. Ellie gestured over to the side where she had left her aircraft before entering the terminal. The plane looked a little forlorn amid the other handful of planes that had been left there, awaiting their owners.

All the other planes appeared to be a lot newer than hers was. It didn't matter to her. She loved that old aircraft. Ellie waved her passenger over to the Piper Meridian.

"Lucille's right over there," she told him, picking up her pace.

"Lucille?" Neil questioned.

"The plane," Ellie clarified, gestured at the aircraft again.

But Neil was still having trouble assimilating the information. "You named your plane Lucille?" he asked, thinking Dan had obviously failed to mention how unusually colorful these people who lived in Forever were.

"No, I didn't," she told the doctor, which only seemed to further confuse the man. She spoke quickly to rectify that—or to attempt to at any rate. "Arnie was the one who called the aircraft Lucille. I just decided to leave it that way rather than confuse things further by changing her name."

"Afraid you'd confuse the plane if you called it by another name?" Neil asked, doing his best to try to follow the thread of the conversation. She didn't exactly make it easy. Nonetheless, he was amused.

"No, me," she said. When he looked at her curiously, she explained, "I just got used to calling the plane Lucille." They had reached the aircraft and she'd stopped walking.

"Sorry, I didn't mean to make it sound as if I

was making fun of you," he apologized in case that was what she thought he was doing. "Actually, one of the surgeons I work with has a Ferrari he calls 'Big Red.'"

Ellie opened the plane's door and released its stairway. She made no comment about the Ferrari. To her that vehicle was a sinful waste of money, but everyone was entitled to do whatever they wanted with their money—even waste it.

"Go on up," she told the doctor, gesturing toward the opened hatch. Neil looked a little skeptical about the venture. "Lucille doesn't bite," she assured him with a smile.

"I'll hold you to that," he told her before he gamely climbed up the steps that led into the plane. The stairs felt somewhat rickety to him, but he told himself that Dan wouldn't have made these arrangements for him if this method of travel wasn't at least safe.

Dan had sounded rather eager to have him come out to examine this friend of his, so Neil felt it was a pretty safe bet that he wouldn't be risking his life on this venture.

Still, he had to admit that he held his breath with every step he took to reach the inside of the aircraft.

Once he was seated, he heard his "pilot" call up to him, "Don't forget to put your seat belt on."

Taking a breath and thinking he had done smarter things in his life, Neil did as she had instructed. The moment he did, his diminutive pilot, moving agilely, climbed into the plane.

The door slamming shut sounded almost ominous to Neil, like the echo of a death knell. Turning toward Ellie, he asked, "And you *do* know how to fly this thing?"

A whimsical smile played on her lips. "Well, I'd better, don't you think?" she asked him. He looked at her with widened eyes. "I'm just kidding," Ellie assured him with a laugh. "Don't worry, I've logged in a lot of hours flying Lucille. I even have a license and everything," she teased, catching her tongue between her teeth. "And if it makes you feel any better, Dr. Dan cleared me for another year."

"Cleared you?" Neil repeated, obviously confused by the term.

"He said I was fit to fly a plane for another year." Going through her check list mentally, Ellie paused to look at her passenger. "Flying so high above the rest of the world is a wonderful experience, Doctor. There's really nothing that even comes close. You feel like you're one with the universe," she told him.

That revelation didn't exactly fill him with a great deal of confidence. "As long as you *don't* become one with the universe," he told her, thinking that a plane crash could easily accomplish that.

Ellie read between the lines. She needed to make him comfortable about this experience. "Well, I thought you'd want to get to Forever quickly and this is a lot faster than driving," Ellie told the surgeon. "Quite honestly, more people die in car crashes than in plane crashes."

"All it takes is once," he murmured.

"Don't worry," she assured him as the plane revved up. "I'll get you there safe and sound."

But Neil hardly seemed to hear her. At the moment, the surgeon was too busy clutched to his armrests and white-knuckling it.

Chapter Five

If she didn't know any better, Ellie would have said that the muscular, good-looking man in the seat beside her was afraid of flying. In her estimation, he looked almost frozen in place. Maybe he was just uncomfortable. There could be any one of a number of reasons for that. In that case, she decided, it was her job to make him feel more comfortable.

"I take it you don't like to fly very much," Ellie said to him. She raised her voice to be heard above the noise generated within the passenger plane that, unfortunately, was rattling like a blender filled to the brim with cupfuls of loose screws.

It took Neil a second to realize that she was talking to him and then several more to actually make out the words she was saying. He found the noise level in the plane pretty bad.

"Not in a plane that sounds as if it is going to come apart at the seams any second now," he answered. "Are you *sure* this plane is going to make it?" Neil asked, because it certainly didn't sound that way to him.

"Oh, I'm sure," Ellie assured him. "I've flown this little gem when it sounded a lot worse than this," Ellie added.

"Why?" he asked.

For the life of him, he couldn't see taking a chance on flying something that, in his estimation, would have been upgraded in status if it was referred to as a "bucket of bolts."

Ellie shrugged. She assumed that he was asking her why she loved to fly. When it came right down to it, she really couldn't explain why, she just did.

"I guess I just love the freedom of soaring through the sky," she told the doctor. "It's in my blood." Her face brightened as she looked straight ahead through the windshield. "We're almost there," she told Neil, pointing. "If you concentrate really hard, you can almost *see* Forever right there in front of you."

"Forever," Neil murmured, focusing on the word as if it was a prediction. "Yeah, that's what I'm worried about."

"The town," she clarified with a laugh. "Not eternity." He might as well prepare himself, she thought. "Now, I should warn you—"

Neil was instantly on the alert. "Warn me?" he echoed, feeling nerves sprouting in his system. "About what?"

"The weather's a little turbulent right now…" she pointed out, although that was probably unnecessary, given how the surgeon was watching everything intently. "So the landing might be a bit bumpy—"

"But we are going to land, right?" Neil asked, interrupting her.

Ellie spared him a wide grin. "Yes, we are going to land," she assured the doctor, then added, "You might find it reassuring to know that I haven't crashed even once yet."

"All it takes is once," she heard him mutter under his breath.

Her smile grew wider, hoping that would reassure him. To look at the surgeon, Neil Eastwood didn't really appear nervous. But then, looks could easily be deceiving.

"Today is *not* a good day to die," Ellie told him,

putting a spin on an old Native American saying. "So we're just not going to."

He slanted a glance in her direction. It did *not* reflect the soul of confidence.

"You can't guarantee that," Neil pointed out. He grabbed onto the armrests, clutching them even harder as the rickety plane encountered even more turbulence.

Ellie was attempting to compensate for the rough weather, and the winds that had kicked up, by remembering everything she had been taught to keep the aircraft steady.

"Tell you what," she said gamely. "If we crash, I'll return your airfare."

Neil glared in the woman's direction before turning to face front again. He was hardly breathing as he did his best to will the plane to keep aloft.

"I didn't pay any airfare," he reminded her through gritted teeth.

"Well, then I guess I have nothing to worry about," Ellie quipped. "Relax, Dr. Eastwood. I've never lost a passenger yet."

"That doesn't really fill me with that much confidence," he told her. His hands were growing even whiter as he held on to the armrests.

Maybe he should have taken a sedative, she thought. Right now his behavior was making them both tense. And then she breathed a sigh of relief for both of them. The flight was almost over.

"There's Forever," Ellie pointed to the town that lay straight ahead of them. She smiled encouragingly at her passenger, secretly thinking that transporting animals was a great deal easier than bringing in Dr. Dan's friend. "We're coming in for a landing," she announced and then smiled at him. "I can hold your hand if that would make you feel any better."

"You landing this plane in one piece will make me feel a whole lot better," Neil told her, staring at the swiftly approaching ground as they were about to land.

Ellie nodded. "Your wish is my command, Doc."

Mentally, she went through the checklist for a proper, uneventful landing, the way she always did. She did it each and every time she landed even though she knew all the steps by heart.

"Okay, Doc, here we go," Ellie announced, telling him to, "Brace yourself."

"If I were any more braced," Neil answered, "I'd snap in half."

"No, no snapping in half on my watch," Ellie deadpanned. She knew he was kidding. At least, she *hoped* he was. "There's an extra charge for that."

Neil glanced at her. How could the woman make jokes at a time like this? In the few moments that the plane had begun its descent, his stomach had lurched upward and now felt as if it was firmly lodged in his mouth, threatening to gag him.

Neil's entire body was tensed and braced, waiting to feel what promised to be a really jarring impact as the plane prepared to touch down on what looked like the world's shortest runway.

When it finally did land, Neil wasn't sure whether to utter a cry of joy or just shed a few tears of immense gratitude and relief.

The surgeon settled for offering up a few heartfelt, albeit silent, words of thanksgiving. The ordeal was finally over!

With the plane back on Mother Earth, Ellie slowly brought it to a halt then turned off all the plane's switches one by one. When she had flipped the last one, she turned toward her passenger. It was all too obvious that the doctor had definitely *not* enjoyed the ride.

Ellie did her best not to smile. "You can let go of the armrests, Doc. We've landed."

She heard Neil release a shaky breath. Ellie realized that she hadn't heard him breathing during the last part of the landing. Had he really been that afraid?

And then she heard him say, "I guess prayers do get answered," and she had her answer.

"Well, you're proof of that," she responded glibly. Neil looked at her as if he didn't understand, so she did her best to explain. "You're the mountain who came to Mohammed. In this case, Miss Joan was playing the part of Mohammed. Everyone in town knew we didn't have a prayer of getting her to see a doctor anywhere outside of Forever. Just when it all seemed so hopeless, you agreed to fly in and see her."

Neil found he was still trying to release his death grip on the armrests and relax his hands. "I wouldn't have agreed if I had known everything that was involved."

For the moment, Ellie remained sitting in the plane—not because *she* needed to but because she wanted Neil to be able to navigate off the airplane—she didn't want him to suffer the embarrassment of his knees buckling. She'd witnessed it before and she wanted to spare him that.

"Then I guess it's lucky for us you didn't know what was involved—although it wouldn't have been nearly so complicated for you if you had only known how to drive," she diplomatically pointed out.

Neil opened his mouth to argue that point but knew that, in all fairness, he really couldn't. At bottom, he supposed he had to admit that it was his own fault he'd had to face the harrowing flight through the heavens.

"Learning how to drive just went to the top of my to-do list," he assured the pilot.

"I could teach you," Ellie offered cheerfully. "I've been driving ever since I was eleven years old."

Somehow, he didn't doubt it. "Do you drive like you fly?" he asked, even though he wasn't really considering her offer.

Ellie grinned at him. "There's less turbulence on the ground than there is in the air—at least today—so I'd probably have to say 'better.' Think about it."

"Right now," he told her very honestly, "all I want to do is just feel the earth under my feet."

"Hold on," Ellie instructed.

The next thing Neil knew, she had opened the door on her side and, rather than take the stairs, had jumped to the ground as agilely as his Great-Aunt Grace's cat used to when the calico would spring off the kitchen windowsill in the dead of winter.

Craning his neck to catch sight of his pilot as

she disappeared from view, Neil called out to her. "Hello? Ellie?"

Had she suddenly decided to abandon him?

Just as the question flashed through his mind, Neil thought he heard a noise coming from outside the passenger window. Turning his head, he caught a glimpse of jet-black hair flying by. The next thing he knew, the door on his side had opened.

Ellie was on the ground, releasing the door and the steps on that side. She beckoned to him. "C'mon down," she invited.

Neil took a deep breath, focusing on his feet finally being able to touch the ground. Just before he attempted to climb out, he frowned. Why did climbing down look so much more intimidating than climbing up had?

While he supposed that he was as agile as the next person, he really wasn't exactly the last word in gracefulness. He had always been the kind of man who usually looked before he leaped. Right now, looking had a way of interfering with the perfect execution of what he was attempting to do.

Like getting out of a plane without twisting his ankle.

Still, not wanting to fall on his face in front of a ravishing brunette was a definite motivator. Neil braced himself and quickly climbed down, listening to the rickety steps issue their own protest.

And then he was finally on the ground.

No one was more relieved than Ellie was, although she kept that to herself.

"Okay," she said breezily, climbing back up into the plane and retrieving the doctor's suitcase for him. Moving swiftly back out, she put it next to him on the ground. "The rest is easy now."

"Oh?" Neil didn't know whether he should brace himself again or believe her and breathe a sigh of relief.

"Yes. I'm going to drive you into town now to see Dr. Dan."

Ellie led the way over to where she had parked her Jeep this morning. It was still in the field, waiting for her, the way she knew that it would be. She had anticipated having to drive the doctor into town and to the medical clinic once she had flown him in.

Neil examined the vehicle. It was clean, looked as if it had not only some miles on it but some years, as well.

He asked her the same question he had earlier, waiting for an honest answer. "Do you drive as well as you fly?"

Ellie inclined her head. "Almost as well," she answered, tongue in cheek.

"Should I be praying?"

"Only if you want to," Ellie answered glibly. And then she couldn't help herself. She laughed as she threw his suitcase into the back and then climbed in on the driver's side. "I thought all of you New Yorkers were supposed to be fearless."

"We are, but there is a definite difference between fearless and foolhardy. I'm trying to decide which you represent." Neil paused, his eyes washing over her face and accessing what he saw. "I haven't made up my mind yet."

His answer made her grin, not to mention created a tingle that fanned out into every part of her. "I'll take that as a compliment."

"I'm not sure if I meant it that way," he admitted, "but okay. Whatever works for you."

Getting into the Jeep, he buckled up and then looked at his driver. He realized that she was observing him and there was a wide, amused smile on her lips.

"What?" he asked, braced for a flippant answer.

"I think this is going to be a really interesting adventure for you during the next few days," Ellie told him.

His eyes met hers and, for the first time since

it had happened, he was really glad that he and Judith had broken up. "I think it already is," he agreed.

"Glad to hear it," Ellie told him, starting up the Jeep. "Okay, let's go show Dr. Dan that I brought you in safe and sound."

"Well, at least you brought me in," Neil replied, not altogether certain yet about the "safe and sound" part of her statement.

Hearing him, Ellie laughed, and he found himself really liking the sound of her laughter. Unbidden, something warm stirred within him.

Heads turned, the way they always did, when the medical clinic's front door opened. With little to do but read outdated magazines, the patients sitting in the waiting room eagerly looked upon any diversion as a welcome distraction from the tediousness of watching for the minute hand move slowly around the face of the clock.

So whenever anyone new entered into the clinic, all eyes automatically turned toward the newcomer or newcomers.

Ellie Montenegro was a familiar sight in Forever, but the tall blond man walking next to her was definitely not. Several of the female patients in the room sat a little straighter. A few consciously pulled in their stomachs and others just stared unabashedly, memorizing the handsome stranger's every feature—and could, at the very least, recreate his face on paper if anyone were to ask.

Unless Ellie missed her guess, a bevy of questions seemed to be materializing in their heads.

"If you'll just sign in, please," Debi said, addressing the newcomer next to Ellie with a warm, inviting smile.

"Oh, he's not a patient, Debi," Ellie told the nurse before Neil even got the chance. "Dr. Dan is waiting to see him. He's the cardiac specialist the doctor sent me to pick up from the Houston airport."

The moment Ellie told her that, Debi was instantly on her feet.

"Wait right here," Debi told the duo as she quickly went to the back of the clinic.

Dan was in exam room 2 and she knocked on the door twice in quick succession. "Dr. Dan, Ellie is here and she brought that package you've been waiting for."

The door opened almost immediately. "Where is he?" Dan asked, looking over Debi's shoulder as if half expecting his friend to be standing right there. It had been a long time since they had seen one another and, along with wanting Neil to exam Miss Joan, he was also eager to see the man.

"He's in the waiting room right now, along with Ellie," Debi replied.

Dan nodded, pleased that his friend had arrived safely. "Tell him to take a seat and I'll be right out to get him as soon as I finish examining Miss Albright," he told his nurse.

Nodding, Debi promised, "I'll let him know." Making her way back to her desk in the waiting area, she approached the specialist as well as Ellie, who was still waiting there with the doctor. "Dr. Dan said for you to take a seat. He'll be right out to see you as soon as he finishes examining Miss Albright," she told Dr. Dan's friend. "You can sit right over here," she prompted, pointing out two recently vacated seats. "It won't take long. He was just finishing up."

"Thank you," Neil said.

He made his way over to the seats and proceeded to make himself comfortable, trying not to notice that everyone seemed to be staring at him.

At least he was safely on the ground, he thought, trying to take solace in that.

Chapter Six

"Well," Ellie said as she rose even though she had just taken her seat, "I've got to be getting back to the ranch." She was happy to see that Neil's color had completely returned and he no longer appeared to be the worse for his experience.

Neil rose to his feet, as well. "You have a ranch?" he asked. He assumed that her claim to fame was flying freight, and occasionally people, in that little plane of hers—which he had found unusual enough. Apparently, people in Western towns wore a great many hats, Neil thought.

"My grandfather owns the ranch. My sister, Addie, and I live on it and do what we can to help him out," Ellie explained, supplying a thimbleful of background information. She paused, her hand on the doorknob. "If you should need anything else, Doc, Dr. Dan knows where to find me."

"And if he's not available at the time, everyone else in town knows where to find her, too," Eva Whitman volunteered.

Several of the patients in the waiting room nodded their heads, assuring the specialist of that piece of information.

"Good to know," Neil replied cryptically. The cardiac surgeon had to admit that he wasn't exactly accustomed to living in an area where everyone's business was thought of as community property. He politely kept that to himself and nodded his head. Turning to the departing pilot, he said to Ellie, "Thanks again for the ride."

Ellie couldn't help but laugh in response. When the doctor raised a quizzical eyebrow, questioning her reaction, she told him, "You know you don't really mean that, but you're welcome."

He saw dimples in her cheeks and was totally charmed by them, but he had no idea how to respond to her statement—because she was right. The plane ride had come perilously close to making him recycle his last meal, but at the same time, the woman had been under no obligation to make the trip to Houston to pick him up.

Fortunately for him, Neil didn't have to say anything in response because, at that moment, Dan entered the waiting area.

"C'mon in, Neil," he said to his friend.

"Are you expanding your practice again, Dr. Dan?" Silas McCormick asked, raising his voice to be heard above the ongoing din. "It's been a while since you brought in anyone new, like that lady doctor who came here."

Joyce Vance, a widow for the last three years, was quick to attempt to convince the new doctor to put down his roots in Forever. "This is a really great, up-and-coming place to move to," she told Neil. "Am I right?" the woman asked, looking at her closet seatmate as if the answer was a foregone conclusion.

Dan saw the not-so-subtle plea for help written on his friend's face and came to his rescue. "Settle down, folks. Don't scare the man away before he even opens up his suitcase. Dr. Eastwood's only here to examine Miss Joan."

At the mention of Forever's venerable, beloved-if-cranky matriarch, the people in the waiting room became properly respectful.

"About time someone finally gave that woman a

much needed examination. She can't expect to just keep going the way she's been going and pressing her luck." Jonah Timberlane turned toward one of the women in the room. "I was there when she collapsed, you know," he said importantly.

"Almost collapsed," Vic Allen corrected, clearing his throat. "Miss Joan never hit the ground," the retired miner pointed out.

This had all the makings of the breakout of a prolonged argument. "Come into my office," Dan urged his friend, gesturing toward the rear of the clinic. "It's right this way."

"Nice meeting you, Dr. Eastwood," one of the women called out, raising her voice. "Hope you decide to stay here."

Pretending not to hear, Neil didn't answer. But the moment he and Dan left the reception area, he looked at the man ultimately responsible for convincing him to come here for a consultation.

"Are they *always* like that?" he asked Dan a little uneasily.

"No, they're usually a lot more vocal and in-your-business," he told Neil seriously.

Dan managed to keep a straight face for another thirty seconds then laughed. "Welcome to Forever," he told his friend, "where everyone doesn't just know your name, they know absolutely *every-*

thing about you, your family and about your second cousin, twice removed. Why don't you take a seat?" Dan gestured to the chair facing his desk.

Neil sank down onto the chair, shaking his head. "Wow, talk about being nosy."

"These people aren't nosy," Dan told the heart surgeon. "They care. There is a difference."

Neil didn't appear to be all that convinced. "If you say so."

"I do," Dan insisted. He had learned that fact over the years. "That's why they were all so concerned about getting Miss Joan to see a specialist—and why Ellie flew out to fetch you and wouldn't take any money for doing it—outside of being reimbursed for the fuel."

"'Fetch' me?" Neil repeated, marveling at his friend's wording. "Wow, you really *have* changed," he couldn't help observing and then pointing out, "That wouldn't have fit into your vocabulary ten years ago."

"A lot of things aren't what they used to be any more," Dan told the other doctor. "And I have to say that I kind of like the change."

"Seriously?" Neil asked, amazed.

"Seriously," Dan assured him. He didn't want to seem as if he was being Spartan. "Oh, I might occasionally miss having three hundred channels to choose from, but to be very honest, what with my really heavy patient load, my beautiful wife and my very active kids, I don't really even have the time to go flipping through all those channels any more."

"How *is* your wife?" Neil asked.

"Getting more and more beautiful every day," Dan told his friend happily. In his opinion, she had really blossomed in the years they had been together. "You can see for yourself tonight."

"I'm looking forward to it," Neil told him. "And by the way, when do I finally get to meet this Miss Joan of yours?"

"Oh, she's not *my* Miss Joan," Dan assured Neil. "She's everyone's Miss Joan and, at the same time, she's her own person."

Neil laughed softly under his breath. "Sounds like she's quite a character."

Leaning back in his chair, Dan grinned with appreciation. "That's the word to describe her, all right," he agreed. Just then, there was a quick knock on his door. "Come in," he invited.

His other nurse opened the door and partially peered into the office. There was an apologetic look on the young woman's face.

"Dr. Dan, Ms. Whitman is getting a little rambunctious out there."

"Ms. Whitman?" Neil echoed. "Is that the white-haired woman I just met out in your office?"

Dan stood. It was time to get back to his patients. "One and the same," he assured his friend.

"'Rambunctious,' huh?" he repeated, amused. "Now *that* I'd really like to see," Neil admitted. The woman had looked extremely subdued. Apparently, Ms. Whitman was not.

Dan laughed. "Stick around long enough and I can practically guarantee it," he promised his friend as a thought occurred to him and he turned to his nurse. "Trudy, could you call my wife and have her come by so that Neil is able to get settled into the house while he's staying here?"

"Sure thing, Doctor," his nurse replied. "I'll get right on it."

"Dan, I don't need an escort," Neil protested. "Just tell me how to get there and I'll be out of your hair."

But Dan just shook his head. He remembered how disorienting everything out here had been for him at first. "You come from the city where half the streets are sequentially numbered. You don't appreciate that until that's not the case. Trust me, it'll be better if I have someone show you the way."

"Dr. Dan, why don't I ask Ellie to take your friend over to your house?" the nurse suggested.

"Ellie?" Dan questioned. He thought she'd left. "Is she still here?"

"Not 'still,'" the nurse corrected. "She came back, but she just left," Trudy told him. "It seems she forgot to pick up a prescription for her grandfather. I can still catch her for you if you want."

Dan nodded. That seemed to be the best way to proceed. "Please," he urged his nurse. "If you don't mind?"

"That's really not necessary, Dan." Neil was attempting to talk his friend out of doing this.

But Dan was not about to be talked out of it. "Yes," he insisted, "it is." Turning, he looked at his nurse. "Trudy?"

"I'm on it," the woman affirmed, hurrying out the door.

For his part, Neil looked far from happy about this turn of events as he walked out into the reception area.

By the time he had reached it, the woman who had taught him the true concept of "flying by the seat of her pants" had just reentered the clinic. Their eyes met and Ellie grinned at him.

"You know, Doc, we've got to stop meeting like this," she quipped.

"My thoughts exactly," Neil told her without the least bit of a hint of a smile to underscore his words.

"Ellie, Dr. Dan said he hoped you wouldn't mind doing him this one more favor…" Trudy began.

Ellie shook her head. "Not a bit," she assured the nurse.

Neil hated imposing and this felt like a huge imposition. "I thought you said that you had to get back to your grandfather," he reminded Ellie as they walked out the front door.

"Oh, I do," she replied. "But there's no emergency—and Pop will be happy to know that I'm late because of a good cause."

In an odd sort of way, her words rang a familiar bell for Neil. "My father would have never thought that being late for any reason was because of a good cause," Neil told her, thinking back to his childhood. His father had been a parent who had ruled with an iron fist—and refused to put up with anything.

"That's probably because your father didn't grow up in Forever," Ellie told him, leading the way back to her Jeep. "Out here, everyone multitasks."

There seemed to be something wrong with that, Neil couldn't help thinking. "Don't you people wind up burning out early?"

She rolled over his question in her mind. "Another way to look at it is that multitasking invigorates us and helps to inspire us," she told him. She pointed to a far corner of the clinic's parking area. "My Jeep's right there."

"I remember," he told her, his tone slightly dismissive because he couldn't shake the feeling that she was talking down to him.

"I just meant that I hadn't had a chance to move the Jeep yet. I remembered about my grandfather's prescription just when I got to the Jeep and did an about-face to go get it."

Neil realized that the woman was apologizing, when he was the one who owed her an apology.

"Sorry, I didn't mean to snap at you like that," he told her. "I suppose that I'm being a little testy right now."

Ellie didn't want him dwelling on the apology. To her, it was just a waste of energy. "You're entitled," the pilot told him. "This is all kind of new to you."

"It's not *that* new," he insisted. It's not as if he had never apologized for anything before. And then, thinking about his mindset back in New York, he lowered his defenses just a little. "I thought I wanted something new and different, but I'm beginning to realize that I'm not all that crazy about change, after all," he confessed.

Ellie understood perfectly. "Don't feel bad about it. Most people aren't," she told him. "At least, not to begin with. Change means having to give up the familiar, to give up something you're comfortable with. When that happens, there's a part of you that feels as if maybe you're making a mistake—until you find, to your surprise, that you like the change, after all."

That sounded pretty deep, he couldn't help thinking—and totally out of character for this part of the country. "What makes you such an expert on change?" he asked.

"Oh, I'm not," she told him. "I'm just speculating. I like to daydream that I'm going to all these exotic places, but I never have. Maybe that's the real reason why I like flying so much. It gives me the opportunity to pretend I'm going to all these different places but I actually never really have to take off anywhere." She flashed a smile at the doctor as she began to drive over to the Davenport house. "Does that make any sense to you?"

Neil's first reaction was to say "No," but then he gave her words some deeper consideration and wound up surprising himself.

"Oddly enough," he admitted, "it kind of does."

Maybe whatever the pilot had was catching. His brain felt as scrambled as her words had sounded, he couldn't help thinking.

Maybe something else was at fault. "Just how high is the altitude up here?"

She laughed. "Not high enough to play havoc with your brain, Doctor, I promise. You know," she continued, "it's nice that you're open-minded like this."

"Why's that?" he asked, curious to understand what she was going to come up with. He didn't expect actual logic.

"Because it'll help prepare you for dealing with Miss Joan—at least as much as anything could when to comes to the woman."

"You make her sound like some sort of a rare enigma," he said, then realized that he was probably talking over the pilot's head.

It surprised him that he wasn't. "Oh, she's that and much more," Ellie assured him. "A *lot* more."

He thought of all the characters he had encountered during his hospital residency in the ER in New York.

"She can't be that bad," he told Ellie.

"Trust me, she is," she assured him. "Miss Joan is…well… Talk to me *after* you've had a chance to meet her and tell her something that she *doesn't* want to hear."

"That sounds like a challenge," Neil told Ellie.

"Oh, it is," she agreed. "All that and more."

He couldn't really explain it, but for the first time in years, Neil suddenly caught himself looking forward to the encounter.

Chapter Seven

The moment Addie saw Ellie land her plane and then taxi it into the renovated barn, she stopped doing what she was doing. Tossing aside her pitchfork, she ran to the barn so that by the time Ellie got out of her tiny Piper Meridian, Addie was right there inside the makeshift hanger, waiting for her older sister.

"So?" she asked expectantly the second that Ellie emerged.

Ellie dusted herself off. "So?" Ellie echoed quizzically. She had no idea just what her sister was asking her about.

"So what's this new doctor like?" Addie asked

impatiently. "Is he young? Is he cute? Is he easy to talk to? What *did* you two talk about? Do you think he's planning to stay in Forever? Dr. Dan wasn't planning on it when he came, but you know what happened there, so maybe this one—"

Oh, Lord, Ellie thought. Addie had a habit of drowning anyone close by in a sea of words. She held up her hands. "Breathe, Addie. Breathe!" she ordered her sister.

Addie pretended to go through the elaborate motion of drawing in a deep breath and then said, "Okay, so answer this for me—"

Ellie was busy getting her carryall out of the cockpit. Finding it, she slung the strap over her shoulder.

"Yes, he's cute. *Very cute*," she emphasized truthfully. "But I have no idea if he's planning on staying. I don't think he is—"

"But you could be wrong," Addie interjected. It was obvious to Ellie that, sight unseen, Addie had taken an interest in this supposed "new doctor in town" whether he actually was that or not.

"I could *always* be wrong," Ellie allowed.

Addie nodded as she walked out of the hanger with her sister and into the open space. "So what did he talk about?"

Recalling, Ellie smiled to herself. She'd had better conversations with strangers.

"Mainly, he wanted to know when we were going to land and did I think the landing was going to be a safe one," she told her sister. Slipping her hand into her pocket, her fingers brushed against the pills Dr. Dan's nurse had given her.

Pop's prescription, she thought. She wanted to get it to him before she forgot.

Ellie began walking fast toward the house.

Addie was still on the doctor's last conversation with her sister. "What did you do to him?"

"Nothing." Ellie tried not to take offense at Addie's insinuation. "The man obviously isn't used to planes that make loud, rattling noises when they fly," Ellie said with a shrug. "That was probably his first experience with a small passenger plane."

"Poor guy, maybe he needs to be comforted." Addie obviously felt she was just the one for the job. The boys in town who were around her age were all just that—boys. A young, well-to-do doctor was just what she needed to spice up her life. "Where did you say he was staying?" Addie asked, glancing in the direction of town. She gave every impression of being ready to rush right over there.

"What Neil Eastwood needs, Addie," Ellie told her sternly, "is to be left alone. He's going to be dealing with Miss Joan and that's more than enough for anyone to have on their plate at the moment."

But Addie saw it differently and wasn't about to let this opportunity slip through her fingers. "Maybe he needs to have someone offer him a hand when it comes to having to deal with Miss Joan," Addie suggested. "You know, I'm sure he'd be pretty grateful to someone who knew how to deal with Miss Joan—"

Ellie stopped walking and stared at her sister. "And what—that would be you?" she asked, surprised by what her sister was thinking. As far back as Ellie could remember, Addie had been intimidated by the tough-as-nails Miss Joan.

"Sure, why not?" Addie asked, tossing her head and sending her thick, straight black hair flying over her shoulder.

"'Why not?'" Ellie repeated incredulously. It took everything she had not to laugh at the image Addie was attempting to project. "Because the woman would eat you for breakfast and not even notice that she swallowed anything, that's why not."

"Oh, she's not an ogre," Addie insisted, waving her hand at the image Ellie was suggesting.

"No," Ellie agreed, "she's not. But Miss Joan

likes to make people keep their distance—unless she actually *wants* them to get closer."

Addie disregarded the point that Ellie was trying to make. "Maybe Neil would appreciate having a buffer," she said, refusing to give up on creating an "in" for herself with this new doctor.

Addie couldn't really be serious—could she? Ellie wondered. Where was this need to connect with a rich, handsome doctor coming from?

"He's a doctor, Addie," Ellie said, attempting to talk some sense into her sister. "I'm sure he deals with crabby, difficult people all the time. He won't need to have a buffer."

Addie looked at her, pity in her eyes. "Ellie, what happened to your heart?" she asked.

Okay, she'd been patient enough, Ellie thought. Time to stop trying to be diplomatic.

"Nothing happened to it. It's right where it's supposed to be. In my chest. As for you, you're just interested in meeting and cultivating an eligible doctor."

Addie didn't bother denying it. Instead, she raised her chin. "And if I was, what's wrong with that?"

"Nothing," Ellie told her. "If you're attracted to him and not to the *idea* of him. Besides, how do you know he's not married?"

The mere suggestion—something Addie hadn't even thought of—had her looking stricken. "Oh, El, he's not, is he?"

Ellie sighed and rolled her dark blue eyes. "No, Ad, he's not."

"How do you know?" Addie asked suspiciously. "Did he ask you out?" Were they going to be competing against each other? she suddenly wondered.

"No, Addie, he didn't ask me out," she told her sister. "When Dr. Dan made arrangements for me to pick up his friend at the airport, I asked Dr. Dan if his friend would be bringing his wife with him because, in that case, I'd need to clear an extra seat in the plane." She knew Addie would like this. "Dr. Dan said his friend had just recently broken up with his fiancée."

"Nice going," Addie said, impressed by the way Ellie had managed to get the information. She grinned, the dimples in her cheeks springing to life. "He just broke up, eh? The poor man needs comforting."

Ellie rolled her eyes. "Lord, Addie, doesn't your plane ever land?"

Addie stared at her sister. "You're the one with the plane, Ellie."

Ellie shook her head. She was wasting her time.

"Never mind. I've got to give Pop his pills," she said, holding up the medication.

Both sisters had always agreed that their grandfather's health was always their first priority.

"Okay, but don't forget that after that, you promised to help me pitch fresh hay in the stalls," Addie reminded her.

But Ellie had to bow out. "Sorry, Ad. I can't. I've got a couple of errands to run and then I have to get ready."

Perfectly arched dark eyebrows drew together as Addie gave her sister another questioning look. "Ready for what?"

"Dinner," Ellie replied innocently. "I've been invited out for dinner," she said, knowing that it wasn't going to die there.

"With who?"

"With 'whom,'" Ellie corrected.

"A grammar lesson?" Addie asked. "You're giving me a grammar lesson? Now? Seriously?"

"Seems appropriate," Ellie told her sister.

Addie's patience was swiftly evaporating. "An *answer* would be appropriate, El."

"I guess we'll just agree to disagree on that point, little sister," Ellie said cheerfully. "Now, if there's nothing else, let me go and give this to Pop so I can get on with my errands."

Addie made a sharp, guttural noise under her breath. Was Ellie attracted to the visiting surgeon or not? "Damn it, Ellie, you can be so very infuriating at times!"

Ellie flashed Addie a complacent smile as she passed by her sister. "Then I guess my work here is done," she said, her eyes sparkling with humor.

"C'mon, Ellie, who are you having dinner with?" Addie called after her, but Ellie managed to put a lot of distance between them very quickly as she headed toward the ranch house.

Walking in, Ellie found her grandfather in the kitchen, sitting at the table and nursing a cup of coffee that was swiftly disappearing.

Not his first, or his second, of the day, Ellie was willing to bet.

The man looked up when he heard his granddaughter enter.

"Did you find your doctor?" Eduardo asked.

"Not 'my doctor,' Pop," she corrected, thinking of Addie and how much her sister would have liked to have fielded that question. "But yes, thanks to that sign you made for me, I did. And here—" she dug into her front pocket and took out the prescription she had picked up for him "—I also got these for you." She handed the packet to her grandfather.

He frowned at the offering and didn't attempt to

take it from her. "I told Dr. Dan that I didn't have the money for that right now, Ellie."

He could be so stubborn, she thought. "You didn't pay for that, Pop."

"I'm not having you pay for it, either, Ellie," Eduardo insisted. How would it look to the men if he had her paying for things? Or to Ellie, for that matter?

"I'm not," Ellie assured her grandfather.

"Oh, so then you stole it," Eduardo said loftily.

She knew that the thought of accepting charity rankled her grandfather. He thought nothing of doling it out, but the man balked when it came down to accepting it.

"No. Dr. Dan said to think of it as a way of thanking me for going out of my way and bringing his friend to Forever to examine Miss Joan." She paused, looking at her grandfather. "Pop, you are the dearest person in the world to me—and to Addie," she added seriously. "And neither one of us is about to have your pride be responsible for putting your life in any sort of danger." She couldn't read her grandfather's expression. "And if that's being disrespectful, then I'm sorry, but there you have it. So please take your medication and stop giving me a hard time about it. I've got more than I can handle with Addie driving me crazy all the time," she told her grandfather. "Now, is there anything else?"

"No, not at the moment," Eduardo answered, the corners of his mouth curving affectionately. "You're a good girl, Ellie."

Ellie grinned at him. "You're just finding that out now, Pop?" she asked, pretending to ask the question seriously.

The gray-haired gentleman waved her off. "Go, do whatever it is you have to do. I'll have a couple of the boys pick up your slack. Oh, one last thing…" he said as another question occurred to him.

Ellie paused, waiting. "Go ahead."

"This specialist that Dr. Dan managed to get to come out," he began.

"What about him?" she asked, doubting her grandfather's questions were on the same level that Addie's had been. He, undoubtedly, had legitimate questions.

"Do you think he'll be able to get Miss Joan to listen to him, provided that what he has to tell her isn't something she would actually *want* to hear?" he asked, curious.

Eduardo wasn't saying anything that Ellie hadn't already wondered herself. Miss Joan wasn't exactly the easiest person to handle.

"Well, if he doesn't turn out to be forceful

enough to get her to agree to getting treatment—and I think that there's probably a good chance that he will have to—there's all the rest of us around to gang up on the woman and *make* her listen to reason." She paused then said, "At bottom, Miss Joan is a reasonable person," Ellie insisted.

Eduardo smiled, nodding. "While that is true," her grandfather agreed, "there's something that you have to understand."

Ellie wondered if this was something her grandfather was relating to himself and that she wasn't going to want to hear.

"What?" she asked cautiously.

"As a person begins to grow older, fear has a way of interfering with common sense. Maybe Miss Joan is afraid to let those scary thoughts in because, if she does, then they might just stand a better chance of coming true." He looked at her, trying to gauge her reaction to what he'd just said. "Does that make any sense to you?"

"Too much, actually," Ellie admitted.

He smiled at his older granddaughter. "What that means is that we're all going to have to be there for her, like you said. Just the way that you were for me." His eyes narrowed. "Don't think I've forgotten what a bully you can be when you want to be."

She put on an innocent expression. "I don't know what you're talking about," she told her grandfather with a laugh. And then she brushed a kiss on his cheek. "I'll see you later on tonight, Pop. And do me a favor, tell Addie that I'll make it up to her."

"Make what up to her?" Eduardo asked, curious what she was talking about.

She merely smiled at the man. Ellie didn't want to get into it because she was fairly sure that her sister wouldn't want their grandfather teasing her about the possible infatuation Addie might be harboring, sight unseen, for Dr. Dan's friend.

"She'll know," Ellie told her grandfather. "Now I'd better go before I wind up being late to the Davenport house for dinner."

Eduardo smiled to himself, pleased that his older granddaughter was actually taking a little time out for herself to socialize instead of just working around the clock. Heaven knew that Ellie deserved a little "me" time. She certainly was more than entitled to it, Eduardo thought.

Ellie had barely had enough time to take care of the handful of chores she had promised herself to do before she left the ranch house.

Avoiding Addie had been trickier, but somehow, Ellie'd managed to accomplish that, as well.

At the last minute, before she headed toward the Davenport house in town, Ellie swung by the Murphy brothers' saloon. She wanted to pick up a bottle of Pinot Grigio. Personally, Ellie didn't care for the taste of wine, but she knew that other people did. Even if the bottle wasn't opened at the table today, she was fairly confident that it would be put to good use somewhere down the line. She didn't feel right about showing up for dinner empty-handed.

Standing at the doctor's front door, she rang the doorbell. Several seconds went by and Ellie began to wonder if she had misunderstood the doctor's invitation and it had been for a different day. But then the door began to open.

She'd expected to see Dan or his wife on the other side of the entrance. Or, just possibly Dan's stepson, the little boy who had initially been the reason Dan's wife, Tina, had gone through Forever and why her older sister, the sheriff's wife, had come out here looking for Tina in the first place.

It occurred to Ellie that it had been a while since she had seen any of those people. She really needed to find a little time to catch up, Ellie thought. Addie was right, she was much too busy working at one thing or another to stop and enjoy the company of old friends. That needed to stop, Elli silently lectured herself as the front door finally opened.

It wasn't any member of the Davenport family who'd come to the door. Instead, the person she was looking at across the threshold was Neil.

Chapter Eight

It took Neil a second to process the fact that the woman who had flown him from the Houston airport—and was responsible for an unsettling amount of turmoil in the pit of his stomach, thanks to that flight—was standing right in front of him.

"Did we make arrangements to have me fly back to Houston?" he asked Ellie. "Because if we did, then it was premature. I haven't had a chance to meet and examine Miss Joan yet."

"Well, I can't say that I'm really surprised," Ellie told the specialist. "Miss Joan can play really hard to get when she wants to."

"What are you doing, standing outside, Ellie?"

Tina Davenport asked, coming to the door and standing beside her husband's guest. "Come in, come in," she invited, pushing the front door further open for Ellie and gesturing for her to come in.

"Dan said he'd be here shortly. He's running late. Big surprise there, right?" Tina asked with an infectious laugh. She had been a doctor's wife now long enough to take it all in stride without blinking an eye. Tina glanced at her watch. "He did say that if he's not here within fifteen minutes, we should go ahead and start dinner without him."

That didn't seem quite right to Neil. The whole idea of his coming out was to visit with Dan, as well as to help him out with his contrary patient. "Oh no, I can wait," Neil assured his hostess.

"So can I," Ellie said, adding her voice to the doctor's.

"Well, you two might be able to wait," Tina told her dinner guests, "but if I don't feed them," she nodded toward the children who seemed to have just appeared in the room. I could be accused of trying to starve my children."

Tina ruffled her oldest son's hair. The boy wrinkled his nose and, in typical teen fashion, pulled his head back.

"They look pretty healthy and well-fed to me," Neil said, winking at Tina's daughter.

"That's because they can periodically consume their weight in food like hungry little shrews," Tina told her guest. "Good thing they run around as much as they do and wind up burning it off."

Suddenly, her five-year-old perked up, cocking her head to one side and listening. And then she grinned from ear to ear. "Daddy!" the little girl happily cried as she ran from the living room all the way to the front door.

"Jeannie, you know what Daddy and I said about you running to the front door!" Tina warned as she quickly went after her daughter.

"You said *don't*!" Jeannie answered her mother dutifully.

"Sit, I'll go get her," Neil volunteered, on his feet and pursuing his friend's youngest before she could make it to the door.

Because his legs were so long, he was able to catch up to the little girl quickly.

Tina's eyes met Ellie's as she smiled. "I like him," she confided, lowering her voice so that it wouldn't carry any further than just between the two of them.

Ellie tactfully made no comment. She merely smiled in response.

The next moment, there was no need for a reply. Dan's big, booming voice was heard greeting each of his three children. He walked into the living room carrying his youngest in his arms while his middle son had his arms wrapped around his father's leg, apparently hitching a short ride back into the living room.

"And there's my lovely, long-suffering wife," Dan said, setting his daughter down. His son uncurled his body from around his leg while Neil stood back and observed it all. He envied his friend.

"Hi, honey," Dan said, pausing to brush a quick, affectionate kiss on Tina's cheek. "Sorry I'm late," he apologized. His glance swept over his friend, and his guest, as well, the apology meant for all of them. "It just couldn't—"

"—be helped," Tina concluded with a patient, weary smile. "Yes, dear, I know." She glanced toward Neil and Ellie. "That's what he says almost every night," she told them as she walked out of the room. "Dinner will be on the table in five minutes."

"Maybe I should go help her," Ellie said to Dan as she started to follow Tina into the kitchen.

"Don't you dare," Tina called out. "From what

I hear, you work hard enough. Consider this your break."

Dan smiled, his eyes meeting Ellie's. "I'd listen to her if I were you. Tina's one tough little cookie when she wants to be. She likes doing things her way." He chuckled. "I think that comes from having spent some time under Miss Joan's wing when she first came here and settled in Forever," Dan confided to Neil.

Neil shook his head. "This Miss Joan must really be something else," he commented. "I'm really looking forward to finally meeting her."

Hearing him, Ellie laughed in response.

"What's so funny?"

"Nothing," she answered. "Just be careful what you wish for," Ellie told him. She saw Neil's brow rise in a silent question. "Don't get me wrong. Miss Joan is a generous soul, but getting her to see reason can prove to be a very frustrating thing. 'Obedience' isn't a word that's part of her vocabulary—at least not when it's applied to herself," she told Dr. Dan's friend.

Neil looked at Dan for verification. "She's not wrong, you know," Dan assured him.

"Come, sit," Tina urged. "Before everything gets all cold."

Neil followed Tina into the dining room. The

others came behind him. "But she did say that she was willing to see me, right?" he asked Dan.

"What she said," Dan told his friend honestly, having his youngest in tow as he went into the dining room, "was that she 'might' be willing to see a specialist if he came to Forever to see her."

"What is that supposed to mean?" Neil asked. "Is she going to have to be hog-tied before I can conduct any tests on the woman?"

"So you *have* met Miss Joan," Ellie pretended to conclude.

The expression on Neil's face was a cross between confusion and concern. "Are you serious?"

"Ellie is just trying to lighten the moment," Tina explained, giving the pilot a warning look. "Miss Joan isn't that bad. I think her problem is that she just doesn't want to be thought of as being mortal—like the rest of us."

"Personally," Dan interjected, "I think Miss Joan is just afraid that something *might* be wrong and if she submits to these tests, then that fear might be confirmed. If she avoids having the tests, then her fear won't be confirmed."

"But that doesn't change anything," Neil said. "She's just avoiding finding out the truth."

"Treating the woman is going to require patience and understanding—in other words, your lightest touch." Dan nodded. "All right, enough shoptalk," he told the others, rising at the table. He wanted to be in a better position to cut the roast Tina had prepared. "Here, let me cut a piece for you. You'll find that Tina makes a really mean roast and you're going to need some decent red meat to help you face up to dealing with Miss Joan."

"Okay, now you're just exaggerating," Neil said, waving away Dan's prediction. "But I do have a huge weakness for roast beef. It has to be my favorite meal."

"I know," Tina told her guest. She glanced toward her husband. "Dan told me. That's why I made a roast—to celebrate your first visit to Forever."

Neil inclined his head. "I do appreciate that. And the fact that you made mashed potatoes and gravy, as well," he noted, looking at what Tina had set out on the table.

There were a number of bowls, all containing different vegetables that, by the looks of them, had been freshly picked from Tina's garden. In his estimation, Dan was truly a lucky man. His ex-fiancée had never once even attempted to cook for him. The closest Judith had ever come was to order takeout. At the time, he had thought nothing of it, but now he felt that home cooking was a way of displaying affection.

"Tina, everything looks delicious," Neil told his hostess.

"Wait until you taste it," Dan said with pride.

"I can't wait," Neil replied.

"Thank you. I had help." Tina smiled at their guest.

"And by help, she means the kids," Dan told Neil. "I'm afraid that by the time my day is over, all I have the energy for is walking in the door and taking off my shoes." He grinned, adding, "Sometimes not even taking off my shoes."

Neil helped himself to some of the baby carrots, green beans and mashed potatoes. "Remember when you had plans to open a practice on Park Avenue?" Neil reminded his friend.

A faraway smile curved Dan's lips as he nodded at something that sounded like it came from a hundred years ago, or at least another lifetime. "I do."

"Ever wish you had followed through on that?" Neil asked, curious.

To Neil's surprise, Dan never hesitated. He just shook his head. "No. Treating people's imaginary illnesses wouldn't have been nearly as satisfying as the kind of medicine I'm practicing these days.

Granted, a lot less hectic. But it definitely wouldn't have been as satisfying," Dan confided.

"You're serious?" Neil looked directly at Dan. "No regrets?" he asked, studying his friend more closely. "None whatsoever?"

"No," Dan said. "None. My only regret is that there aren't somehow more hours in the day."

"Well, you could achieve that, in a way, by having another doctor working with you at the clinic. I mean, besides Dr. Alisha," Ellie specified, referring to the ob-gyn who had begun working there a few years ago.

Dan chuckled. "I can just see how that ad would read. 'Want to work long hours for very little monetary pay? Compensation would be made in the form of an incredible feeling of well-being and a sense of contribution.'" His eyes met Neil's. "I really don't think that would entice too many people to relocate to Forever." Dan laughed to himself as he thought of his recent communication with Neil. "The only reason I got you to agree to come out here to see Miss Joan was that you felt you needed a change. Now that you're here, you're probably rethinking your decision on the matter."

Neil lifted a shoulder in an evasive half shrug. "Well, we'll see how this all works out," Neil said without committing himself to the situation one way or another. Feeling that the conversation needed a change of pace, he turned his attention to Dan's wife. "The roast beef is really excellent."

"Thank you," Tina replied. "I actually learned how to cook while working at Miss Joan's Diner."

"You worked at Miss Joan's Diner?" Neil asked, surprised.

"I think, at one point or another, most of the young women in town had some sort of a job working at her diner," Tina told him.

Neil looked at Ellie. "But you didn't, right?"

"Actually, I did work there a couple of summers when I was a sophomore and a junior in high school. Pop thought it would be good for me to earn some extra money doing something outside of the family ranch."

Neil rolled the information over in his head. "Your father sounds like a pretty understanding man."

"'Pop' is my grandfather, not my father," Ellie corrected. "But you were right about the other part. He's very understanding."

"Maybe he can talk to this Miss Joan and get her to go along with having those tests done," Neil suggested. And as he said that, another thought occurred to him. "What if it turns out that Miss

Joan is going to need surgery? Even a simple procedure," he pointed out. "What then?"

Dan didn't want to worry about that yet, although he was fairly certain that was going to wind up being the case. "We'll cross that bridge when we come to it," he told his friend.

Neil looked at Dan. "Are you sure we'll be able to?"

"Am I sure?" Dan repeated. "No. Hopeful, yes. You know, I've found that a lot of things that have transpired here in Forever depended entirely on faith. Worrying about how things might turn out too soon never does anyone any good—least of all, me. I've found that I'm at my best when I'm in a positive frame of mind."

Personally, Neil thought, he couldn't operate that way. Obviously, Dan not only operated that way, he seemed to thrive on it. He definitely seemed to be happy about the way his life was going. A great deal happier than Neil was. In a way, he envied Dan.

Tina and Dan made a point to urge Ellie to take Neil outside while they cleared away the dishes and washed them. When Ellie protested that she wanted to help and that it should be Dan who went outside with Neil, the doctor countered her objection.

"This is only a two-person job," Dan said. "Four people will only manage to get in each other's way. Take him outside," Dan instructed Ellie then turned toward Neil. "Go outside and see what it feels like to breathe in some totally decent night air. Ellie, I'm handing him over to you."

Ellie inclined her head and promised agreeably, "I'll try not to lose him. C'mon, this way," she urged the cardiologist.

It took only a few seconds outside of Dan and Tina's house for it to hit Neil. "Wow, it's incredibly dark out here at night."

"I guess this is a far cry from 'the city that never sleeps' for you, right?" Ellie speculated. "There really aren't any lights out here. Once the sun goes down, that's it."

"I never really thought about that," he admitted.

"You have to be really careful out here," she warned him. "One misstep and you can wind up twisting your ankle."

"Maybe I should have brought a flashlight with me—if I had thought to pack a flashlight," he added. When he had agreed to the visit, he hadn't really thought about what he might be getting himself into.

"That's all right, don't worry about it," Ellie assured him. "I've gotten pretty good about being able to see in the dark."

"You're a bat?" Neil asked, amused.

She took his question in stride. "You learn how to compensate. And you also learn how to take very small, measured steps," she added with a grin that Neil was able to hear in her voice rather than actually be able to see.

The next thing Neil knew, she was reaching for his hand. It was a pleasant surprise; one that actually caught him off guard.

She seemed to sense his surprise because she told him, "I'm not getting fresh, Doc. I just don't want to be the one responsible for getting Dr. Dan's friend hurt," she explained good-naturedly.

The simple act of holding her hand like this created a pleasant, warm sensation within Neil that had him totally flummoxed. Slightly embarrassed, he thought he needed to offer some sort of protest. "I'm not that much of a klutz."

Neil had no sooner said the words than Ellie felt a tug on her hand as he came close to tripping over the root of a tree. He would have fallen if she hadn't gripped his hand really hard to keep him upright and on his feet instead of letting him land spread eagle on the ground.

To keep him upright, Ellie instinctively yanked

him toward her. Unprepared, Neil found himself falling into her, their bodies colliding against one another and fitting surprisingly well.

It was hard to say who was the more surprised by what had happened, and which of them ultimately wound up enjoying it more.

Or what happened next.

Chapter Nine

One moment, Neil was vainly trying not to embarrass himself by tripping in front of the sexy pilot. The next moment, before he actually realized what was happening, he and said sexy pilot were sharing a kiss. "Sharing it" because it was hard to say who kissed whom first—or if there was an instigator responsible for initiating the first move or if this explosive kiss just happened by spontaneous combustion.

However it came to pass, both participants silently agreed that it was more than just an unexpected, exceedingly pleasant surprise.

It was something akin to the first discovery of fire.

At least, Neil felt that way.

When their lips parted and Neil drew his head back, he wasn't even aware that he was grinning from ear to ear—but he was.

"Well, that was certainly unexpected," he murmured when he was finally able to form words.

Ellie's heart was hammering so hard, its beat was practically the only thing she was aware of for several moments. "You'll find that most things that happen in Forever generally are," she told him.

They hadn't even known each other for the span of a day. This wasn't his usually mode of operation and he hardly recognized himself.

"Was I taking advantage of the situation?" he asked Ellie uncertainly.

"Only if you pretended to trip," Ellie told him with a smile.

"No. I hate to admit it, but I really did trip," he admitted, glancing up at the sky. No one ever enjoyed being thought of as a klutz.

"Then, no, you weren't taking advantage of the situation," she said. It surprised her—and also touched her—that he would even think of apologizing.

The sky above was studded with an amazing patchwork of stars. It seemed like the perfect night for two people to get to know one another better, he couldn't help thinking as he looked back at Ellie. "What if I kissed you again?"

"*That* might be viewed as taking advantage of the situation," she told him.

"Then you think that I should trip again first?" Neil asked innocently.

"I think we should be getting back to the house before Dr. Dan and Tina come looking for us and find us sharing more than just an innocent evening stroll." She had no sooner said that than Ellie thought she heard the front door open and Tina calling out to them.

"Ellie, Neil, did you two get lost out here?" Tina asked.

Ellie exchanged looks with Neil. "Speak of the devil," she said to her companion in a low voice, amusement evident in her tone.

Neil raised his voice to answer Tina. "No, we're out here. I'm just noticing how dark everything gets once the sun goes down."

"Quite a culture shock after the bright lights of Broadway," Dan admitted, coming out to join his wife. He slipped his arms affectionately around her waist and pulled her to him.

The next moment, Jeannie burst from the house to join her parents. "Are we playing a game out here?" she asked, eyes wide and hopeful. She was quickly followed by her older brothers. Both seemed just a little more subdued in their comments as they joined the adults.

"Yes, honey," Dan said, putting his hand on his daughter's shoulder to guide her back into the house. "We're playing a game. It's called 'herding your dinner guests back into the house.'" Every word was wrapped in affection.

"All right, you two," Tina announced into the darkness. "Everybody back into the house. My dessert has jelled and is ready to be consumed."

Being young enough to still display enthusiasm over the simpler things in life, Jeannie cheered and clapped her hands together in anticipation. Her older brothers, however, refrained from showing that sort of reaction, although, Neil noted, their pace did pick up a little.

Tina, without a doubt, everyone agreed, made the world's most heavenly desserts.

When dinner and dessert were finally over and it was time for Ellie to leave, Neil insisted on walking her to her vehicle. That freed Dan and Tina to tackle the simpler things in life that they looked forward to: tucking their children into bed and, in Jeannie's case, reading to her until she dropped off to sleep.

The two boys insisted that they were much too old for such "baby things," although they asked to have their door left open so that they could overhear Dan reading to their sister. As far as Dan was concerned, this was what everything else was all about. It was one of his favorite parts of the day.

"I appreciate you being chivalrous," Ellie told Neil as he walked her the short distance from the Davenport house to her Jeep, "But you really don't have to do this. This isn't the kind of neighborhood you're used to," she pointed out, thinking of what she'd heard went on in some New York neighborhoods. "I'm perfectly safe out here walking to my car."

Maybe he was being overly cautious, Neil thought, but that didn't change anything for him.

"Humor me," he told her. "Old habits die hard—and if you're afraid I'm going to use this as an excuse to kiss you again, you don't have to worry," he assured her with a mile. "You're safe."

Ellie cocked her head and peered up into his face. "Are you saying that you don't want to kiss me again?" she deadpanned.

"No, what I'm saying is that…" Neil's voice trailed off as he realized he had managed to paint himself into a corner. "There's no graceful way out of this sentence, is there?"

Ellie grinned at him. "No, not really." Her eyes twinkled in amusement. "Don't worry, Doc. I'm just having a little bit of fun at your expense." And then she grew serious. "So, when are you going to be seeing Miss Joan? Do you have a time yet? Maybe I can sell tickets," she teased.

He looked at her in disbelief, not entirely sure that she *wasn't* serious. "Are you people that hard up for entertainment?"

"Don't sell entertainment short," she quipped, attempting to keep a straight face. And then she told him honestly, "I'm just curious as to who's going to come out the winner here. For Miss Joan's sake, I hope it's you. I wasn't at the diner when Miss Joan nearly passed out," she confided, "but I know some people who were. The upshot of it was that Miss Joan looked frightened. That is not a usual occurrence and *none* of us wants to see her like that again. The woman is the town's rock.

"So," she continued, "if you need a little moral support in bearding the lioness in her den, all you have to do is just say the word and I'm there for you. So are a lot of other people."

Neil thought of the conversation he'd had with Dan when he'd agreed to come to Forever in the first place. "Well, from what I gather, Dan intends for the two of us to go to the diner tomorrow to try to sweet-talk this woman into coming back to the clinic."

Sweet-talking Miss Joan into anything she wasn't entirely sold on doing might prove to be very difficult, Ellie thought.

"She's light enough to be carried if necessary," Ellie pointed out.

Neil laughed at the picture that created. "I think there are laws against forcibly taking a patient in to be examined."

She rolled that over in her mind. "True, but around here, the sheriff enforces the law and Sheriff Rick wants to keep Miss Joan healthy and around just as much as the rest of us do."

Neil nodded. "Maybe she'll surprise us and listen to reason," he speculated.

"Maybe," Ellie agreed. After all, miracles did happen, she added silently as she put her hand on the handle of the Jeep's driver's-side door. "Well, I'd better get going before Pop starts to think I lost my way getting home." She paused for a moment. "If I didn't say it before, Doc, welcome to Forever."

For some reason, Neil couldn't shake the feeling that the words almost sounded like a foreshadowing.

He was letting his imagination run away with him, he thought. The next moment, Neil flashed her a smile. "Thank you."

Opening the driver's-side door, Ellie paused for just a second before getting in. With a quick movement, she brushed a quick kiss against Neil's cheek and then got in behind the steering wheel.

In the blink of an eye, she started up her Jeep and, before he could even process what had just happened, she was gone.

Neil stood there watching her taillights become smaller and smaller until they disappeared completely. He could still feel the warm imprint of her lips on his cheek. Had she kissed him to let him know that she hadn't minded his kissing her earlier? Or because she'd absolved him of that and wanted him to know that they were now even?

Neil lightly glided his fingertips along his cheek as if to press the sensation she'd created there into his skin.

His mouth curved in a slightly bewildered smile.

He was glad that he had come here. He had begun to feel lost and alone after his breakup even though he had been the one to instigate it. He was now beginning to think it was the best thing that had ever happened to him.

The following day, though no one had said a word to Miss Joan about her pending interaction with the cardiologist, somehow she knew.

The moment Dan Davenport and another tall, good-looking man walked through the door into the sacred territory known as Miss Joan's Diner—followed by a few other patrons of the establishment, including Ellie Montenegro—her rail-thin body went on the alert.

Miss Joan raised her hazel eyes up from what she was doing at the counter to hone in on the stranger entering her arena.

She then looked at Dan and nodded, saying, "Hi."

The rest of the diner went deadly silently.

"What can I do for you and your friend, Doc?" she asked in a voice that said she already knew what was coming but wanted to hear them say it.

"You could come back with us to the medical clinic," Dan told her politely.

She looked at him sharply, warily. "And why would I want to do that?"

Dan patiently reminded her of the conversation they'd had the other week. "Because you said you would submit to an examination and tests if I got a cardiologist to come out here to see you."

The expression on Miss Joan's face told Dan she didn't see things that way. "No, I said I'd see him. And, as far as I can tell, that's exactly what

I'm doing right now. I'm *seeing* him," she pointed out, her voice tight.

This is just wordplay, Neil thought, and they were wasting time, something he had always felt was a precious commodity.

"Miss Joan—" Neil began patiently.

She turned her eyes on him sharply. "Don't you 'Miss Joan' me, sonny. We haven't even met yet."

Neil suppressed a sigh. "Fair enough," he said, extending his hand to introduce himself. "I'm Dr. Neil Eastwood," he told her.

Miss Joan's eyes narrowed. "Look, Handsome, just because you've got those dimples in your cheeks when you smile doesn't mean that I'm about to peacefully trot off to the medical clinic and let you play doctor with me," she informed him, a warning note in her voice.

"There won't be any 'playing' involved, Miss Joan," Neil respectfully intoned.

With one hand fisted at her hip, Miss Joan gave the man a steely look meant to put him in his place. "Damn straight there isn't going to be any 'playing.' I'm too for you, kid. And too much woman, to boot," she added with a nod of her head. "Now, I've got a diner full of hungry people to feed," she informed him. "So if you don't mind—"

"Oh, but I do mind," Neil said, cutting her short.

"From everything that Dan told me, you are at risk of having a cardiac episode that isn't slanted to have a happy ending if left unattended."

Miss Joan raised her chin defiantly. "Don't you have enough of your own patients to take care of without coming out here, trolling for more?" she asked.

"Yes, I have a lot of patients," Neil agreed. "But, in all honesty, I've never had one the whole town seems to be so worried about."

Miss Joan looked around the diner, glaring at the patrons as if to silently tell them to butt out. "And you still don't. Now, order something or leave," she told him sternly, "because you're taking up space and it's approaching my busiest time of day."

Ellie stepped forward. "What are you afraid of, Miss Joan?"

"I'm not afraid of anything," she snapped a little too sharply.

"All right, then fine…" Ellie said, approaching the counter and Miss Joan. "If you're not afraid, have the Doc run some tests. If he doesn't find anything, everyone's happy and he'll go away." She paused, exchanging looks with Dan. "And if he does find something, he would have caught it early and whatever's wrong can be fixed. Again, everyone's happy."

"I'm not happy," Miss Joan growled.

"You'd rather be sick?" Ellie questioned the older woman.

"I'd rather be left alone," Miss Joan all but barked.

"And you will be, darlin'," Harry, Miss Joan's husband said, adding his voice to the others as he walked into the diner. His eyes never left his wife's face. "Just as soon as you have the tests done."

Miss Joan's angry gaze swept over all the people within the diner. Like a creature backed into a corner, she lashed out.

"Is this the thanks I get after all these years of serving you people, of listening to you whine and complain and giving you a shoulder to lean on? Having you all suddenly decide to gang up on me like this and kicking me when I'm down?" she demanded.

Rather than waste his breath by arguing with the woman, the sheriff, who was also there, told Miss Joan, "Yup," as he came forward. "Now, the sooner you stop being so stubborn, Miss Joan, the sooner you can have these tests done and the sooner you can get back to work," he concluded.

Miss Joan uttered a guttural sound steeped

in frustration. She looked stymied and far from happy at the turn of events. She was usually accustomed to bullying her way out of things as a last resort, but it just wasn't happening this time.

"And my agreeing to this blackmail is the only way I can make you people stop harassing me?" she asked.

"The only way," the sheriff assured her.

"Because we're not going to back off until you submit," Dan told her in no uncertain terms.

Miss Joan thought of something. "You don't have the kind of equipment you need to run these tests," she pointed out. "And I am *not* about to take off to go to some big-city hospital because some cute, big-city doctor thinks he can get me to—"

Neil cut her short before she got too wound up. "I can have whatever's necessary for the tests brought out here," he told her.

Confounded and exasperated, Miss Joan raised her chin defiantly, a fighter looking for a fight. She didn't believe him.

"How?" she challenged.

"I have connections," Neil assured her. "If need be, the necessary equipment for the tests can be flown out here," he told her. "Now, will you say yes?"

"You're not going to stop flapping those gums of yours until I do, is that it?" Miss Joan asked.

Neil held his ground. "That's about it."

Ellie found herself very impressed. She wouldn't have thought the surgeon would stand up to the iron-willed Miss Joan. She'd thought he would back off at the last moment.

"Tell me, when did talking a patient to death become a required course for a medical degree?" Miss Joan asked.

"Since they made you, Miss Joan—and broke the mold," Neil answered. And then he smiled at the crusty woman. "We wouldn't want to risk losing a one of a kind," he told her.

Miss Joan sighed. "I'd better say yes before I wind up in a diabetic coma with all this sweet talk and sugarcoating going on," the woman declared, waving her hand at Neil and, in essence, surrendering. Ever practical, she demanded, "How long are these tests going to take?"

"It'll take up to a day once the necessary equipment comes in," Neil told her.

Rather than say anything to Neil, Miss Joan turned her head toward the kitchen. "All right, I know you heard every word, Angel," she called out to the young woman who did all the cooking. "When these witch doctors are ready to run these voodoo tests of theirs, I'm putting you in charge of my diner."

"Yes, Miss Joan," Angel Rodriguez complacently called back from the kitchen.

"Okay, boys, the ball's in your court," Miss Joan announced to Dan and Neil. "Now, until you get everything here so you can take those damn tests, let me get back to doing my job," she ordered. So saying, she turned her back on the doctors and did just that.

Chapter Ten

Since she had only come to lend her support and not to actually get anything to eat or drink at the diner, Ellie left.

But she didn't go very far. She hung around because she wanted to tell Neil how impressed she was with the way he had handled Miss Joan. She had seen a lot of people shot down by the dictatorial diner owner.

"Masterfully done," she told the two doctors as they walked out of the diner and down the front steps. "You two handled Miss Joan like pros. Kindly, but firmly," she added with approval.

"Your input helped," Dan told her, grateful she

had thought to show up and add her voice to all the others.

"Yeah, well, we're not exactly home free yet," Neil pointed out.

Ellie put her own interpretation to his words. "You don't think you'll be able to secure the necessary equipment to conduct the tests that you'll need to evaluate her condition?" Ellie asked.

Neil looked at her. Her question had caught him off guard since that wasn't his point.

"Oh, I'm fairly sure I can get what I need. It might take a little doing, but it can be managed," he said, thinking of his network of fellow surgeons.

Confusion creased her forehead. "Then what?" she asked.

Neil voiced his concern to both Dan as well as to Ellie. "I'm thinking beyond that. What if Miss Joan doesn't like the results the tests yield? What if the tests point to her having to have a procedure done, like an angioplasty or an ablation, or something more serious?"

"Like a bypass?" Dan asked.

Neil nodded. "Like that. Then what?"

There was no sense in worrying about what hadn't come to pass yet. "One step at a time," Dan told him. "First, let's get those tests done. Contact those people you know and see what it takes to get everything set up," he advised his friend.

What Neil needed, Ellie thought, was something to divert him. "And after you make those calls and while you're waiting for the equipment to arrive, why don't we see about getting you those driving lessons we talked about?" Ellie suggested.

Well, he hadn't seen that coming, Neil thought. "As I recall, you were the one who did the talking. I just listened."

"But you didn't say no. C'mon, learning how to drive is all part of asserting your independence, Doc," Ellie coaxed. She glanced at Dan for his backing as she continued talking. "Don't you want to come and go as you please?"

The eager pilot was forgetting one crucial point, Neil thought. "To do that, I'd have to have a car," he pointed out.

When he saw the smile that slipped over her lips, he knew that this wasn't going to be his way out of the lessons. "The town mechanic runs a garage," Ellie told him. "I'm sure that he'll be more than happy to set you up with a loaner—provided you know how to drive."

Neil looked toward Dan for help, but his friend was already on his way back to the medical clinic. "You're on your own here, Neil."

Neil sighed. "Are all the women in this town so pushy?" he asked Dan.

Dan laughed. "I'm afraid so, buddy. It's all part of being strong and independent."

"You should have warned me," Neil called after him.

His friend merely smiled at the protest. "Then you wouldn't have come."

"You're right," Neil agreed, raising his voice so that it would carry. "I wouldn't have."

Ellie took hold of his arm, directing Neil toward the clinic. "But you're here now and you might as well make the most of it," she told him. "C'mon, I'll come with you to the clinic and wait while you make those calls to secure the equipment you'll need so you can conduct those tests. And then," she concluded happily, "I'll give you your first lesson."

Neil looked at her skeptically. "I don't know about this…"

"I do," she countered firmly. "And if you're worried about anything happening, Dr. Dan'll treat you at the clinic," Ellie told him. "No waiting," she teased to cinch the argument.

"No waiting," Neil murmured under his breath as if he didn't view that to be a selling feature. Resigned, he decided to go along with this for the time being, but he was far from thrilled. "You know," he told her as they went to the medical clinic, "I've been skydiving a few times."

That surprised her. "Oh?"

"Yes," Neil acknowledged. "And somehow that seemed a lot safer to me than what you're proposing."

"Don't worry," she assured Neil as they approached the clinic directly behind Dan, "I'm not going to have you going any faster in my car than you're totally comfortable with."

Neil gave her an extremely dubious look. "I sincerely doubt that."

To Neil's surprise, after he placed his phone calls to make arrangements for the loan of the medical equipment, the driving lesson went surprisingly well. Contrary to what he had expected, Ellie turned out to be a very patient, very thorough, teacher. She didn't point to any of his shortcomings and set a pace for him that he found exceedingly comfortable. She only went on to the next new point after he had mastered the last one. And although he felt himself having a little difficulty with a couple of the executions, she never once made him feel as if he was failing in the endeavor.

"Okay," Ellie announced as Neil made his way

back to the spot where they had first begun the driving lesson.

"Okay?" he questioned, confused by what she was telling him. For his money, he just felt as if he was getting started.

"Yes. I think you've done enough for one day," Ellie said. In no way was she being judgmental. On the contrary, she sounded as if she was congratulating him.

He looked at her in surprise. "You're kidding," he protested.

Ellie grinned. Things had gone better than she'd hoped and she really felt good about this—as she hoped that he did.

"Doc, you've been driving for almost two hours. You don't want to overdo it." She could see he was about to protest that he wanted to continue. While that made her feel very good about the whole endeavor, she really did need to stop the lesson now. "Besides," she told him, "I have a delivery to make in half an hour and I've got to get ready to leave."

"Are you driving somewhere?" Neil asked. It was hard to miss the hopeful note in his voice. "Because if you are, maybe I can—"

"I'm flying," she told him, cutting Neil's offer short.

"Oh." He looked disappointed, even though he

attempted to cover his reaction. "Well then, I guess I can't come with you."

She surprised him by saying, "Sure you can." She knew he hadn't wanted to hear that, but she teased him by continuing. "There's no passenger on this flight, so you're more than welcome to come along."

"Let me rephrase that," Neil said. "I'd *better* not come. I survived one flight, I don't want to push my luck," he emphasized.

She could only interpret that one way. "You really think I'm going to crash?"

His answer surprised her. "No, I really think I'll embarrass myself and throw up. I narrowly avoided it the last time."

Ellie laughed. Apparently, they had crossed a new threshold when it came to honesty. "I don't think you're giving yourself enough credit, Doc. Besides, how will you ever earn your 'sea legs' if you don't keep challenging yourself?" she asked.

"Hey, dealing with Miss Joan was challenge enough," he told her. That was definitely enough challenge for anyone. "And I did let you take me out for a driving lesson."

Ellie inclined her head, giving him the point. Neil was right. "Sorry, I tend to get greedy when things are going so well," she apologized. "All right, Doc, where do you want me to drop you off before I go pick up the freight for my run?"

That was easy enough to answer. "The medical clinic will be fine—but if you're pressed for time, I can walk there."

She pretended to take offense. "Are you trying to tell me that you don't want my company?"

He stared at her. Where had she gotten that idea? "No, I'm trying to be thoughtful."

And then Ellie smiled at him and he realized that she was pulling his leg. He also realized that he was really getting to like that smile.

"So am I," Ellie said. "Sit tight, Doc. I promise to get you there with no bumps, no bruises, and totally in one piece."

And then she winked.

It was the wink that did it. It alerted Neil that any way he looked at it, this woman was going to be quite a handful. She represented the unexpected and, after being micromanaged to the nth degree by his ex, he had to admit that this was really a pleasant change. A *very* pleasant change. And he welcomed it.

"If you're interested, I'm available for another lesson tomorrow, same time, same place," Ellie told him as she let him out at the medical clinic. "Unless one of your doctor friends come through with that mobile treadmill and that EEG machine by tomorrow."

"I think at the very least it's going to take another day or so," he told her. Then added with a smile, "So, if you're up for a lesson, so am I."

Ellie nodded. "Okay, I'll be here." She beamed at him as he closed the passenger door and turned toward his destination. "You did well today, Doc. Really well."

One compliment deserved another, he thought. And, in his opinion, she had made something he had put off indefinitely seem very easy. "I had a good teacher."

Ellie smiled as she nodded. "Maybe next time, you'll let me teach you how to fly."

"Let's just put a pin in that for a while," Neil told her. There was such a thing as getting too ahead of himself, he thought. Flying a plane had never been on his list of things to do. Ever.

"Oh, but you don't know what you're missing," she told him.

"Yeah, well let's just keep it that way for a while," he told her. Mentally, he added, *For a long while.*

Ellie made no comment. She merely smiled and, he had to admit, though no words were exchanged, her smile did unnerve him.

He honestly didn't know if that was a good thing or not.

* * *

Ellie went ahead and made her run, picking up some much needed supplies from a store located more than seventy-five miles away. The supplies were for Ramona Santiago Lone Wolf, the town's vet.

Driving her ancient station wagon, Mona met Ellie in the open field located just behind her vet facility.

"I appreciate you getting these to me so quickly, Ellie," Mona told her as she got out of her vehicle. "There are times when I really miss Doc Elliott," she said, referring to the old town vet. "I never used to feel that I was operating without a net when he was around. He always seemed to know what to do, what to say. And I could lean on the man," she said wistfully.

Ellie was unloading her plane, piling the supplies on top of one another. She knew exactly how Mona felt. She had the exact same feelings when it came to her grandfather.

"I guess that happens to everyone eventually. It's the way of the world." She smiled at the pretty veterinarian. "Old Doc Elliott must have been an endless source of information for you."

"Oh, for everyone," Mona agreed. "There wasn't anything he didn't know about animals.

Not to mention that the man was also like the town historian. Do you know that he was the only one in Forever who could remember when Miss Joan first came to live here?"

Now that she thought of it, she had heard something to that effect. The woman was so much of a fixture in Forever, it seemed as if she had always lived there.

Ellie paused, trying to remember details.

"Wasn't she married back then?" Ellie asked. "Something about a husband and a baby boy who both died in some sort of a natural disaster, or something like that? A flash flood, I think, was the way the story went." As she talked, bits and pieces of details came back to her. "That's why she was so closed off for so long and why it took Harry more than thirty years to convince her to marry him.

"That would almost be romantic if it wasn't so sad," Ellie commented. With a mighty effort, she deposited the last of the supplies from her plane onto the ground.

"If I remember it correctly, it wasn't a flash flood, it was a car accident," Mona told her. "Miss Joan's husband was pretty much of a scoundrel and he ran off with Miss Joan's sister. Zelda or Zoë or something like that," she said, totally surprising

Ellie. "Doc Elliott said that her husband took the baby because he was trying to get back at Miss Joan for giving him such a hard time. As if anyone would applaud a womanizer," the woman said in disgust.

"And they were killed in a car accident?" Ellie asked, still attempting to absorb the information. In all the years she had lived in Forever, she had never heard this story. She was still a little doubtful about how true it was. Not that she didn't believe Mona, but it just seemed so unusual that there was never any mention of it. "Are you sure about this?" she pressed.

Mona nodded as her voice took on a somber tone. "The baby died instantly. Miss Joan's husband lingered for a few days before succumbing to his injuries."

"And the sister?" Ellie asked, stunned by this revelation.

"Not a scratch," Mona declared. "She was the one who was driving."

Ellie felt almost numb. She tried to reconcile the information with the woman she had known all her life. "How awful." She couldn't help ask, "How come I've never heard any of this before?"

"Out of respect for Miss Joan," Mona told her, "Doc Elliott didn't want the story getting around."

Okay, she could understand that. But something else was bothering her. "So then why did he tell you?" she asked. It didn't seem to make any sense.

"He told me because he thought it might help me out. I was going through a tough time. I won't go into any of the details," Mona told Ellie, "but suffice it to say that it did help. And, out of respect for Doc Elliott, I never told anyone."

"Until now?" Ellie questioned. Again her curiosity was raised. "Why say anything now?"

That was simple enough to explain. "Because sometimes secrets can eat up our insides. I think that maybe it would do Miss Joan some good to own up to this. Maybe she can even finally call a truce with her sister."

"A truce?" Ellie questioned. This seemed to be getting more and more involved.

"Yes, according to what Doc Elliott told me. When her sister came to see Miss Joan to try to tell her how very sorry she was for everything that had happened... How she would give anything if none of it had ever happened..." Mona then repeated in an aside, "Like I said, Miss Joan's husband was a scoundrel and he turned her sister's head and talked her into running off with him." Then concluded, "Miss Joan told her to get out. That she never wanted to see her again."

"And did she?" Ellie asked. She couldn't imagine never speaking to her own sister, no matter what Addie might be guilty of doing.

"Nope," Mona answered. "Not that anyone ever knew about any of this. I mean, nobody but me even knew she had a sister, and that was just because of what Doc Eliott told me. The woman left town a long time ago. From what Doc Elliott told me, the story died down, time passed and Miss Joan just became the Miss Joan we know today."

"How do you know this even happened?" Ellie questioned.

"Because Doc Elliott wasn't the type to make things up, even for a good cause, like to help me deal with things." Mona took in a breath. She had spent enough time in the past. "All right, let's get this all back to my clinic and I'll settle up with you there. I've got horses to treat if I don't want this thing to spread and we wind up with a full-fledged epidemic on our hands."

Ellie nodded but, unlike the sheriff's sister, her mind wasn't on sick horses. She was still focused on what Mona had told her.

"You want me to keep this between us, Mona?" she asked the vet.

Mona thought the matter over for a moment.

"Actually, you do what you think is best. Maybe

it's about time someone go looking for Miss Joan's sister and, if she'd still alive, bring her back here so that fences can be mended. I'd say that thirty or more years is definitely enough time to have passed." She looked at Ellie. "Don't you think?"

"Oh, more than enough time," Ellie agreed, nodding her head.

She couldn't wait to get home to tell Pop about this new-old development.

Chapter Eleven

Ellie went over what she wanted to say to her grandfather a number of times in her head as she drove back to the ranch. But when she finally arrived and found him in the tack room, she could only blurt out, "Pop, how long have you lived in Forever?"

Eduardo was focused on repairing an old, beloved saddle whose leather had become extremely worn in places. Ellie had offered to buy him a new one, but he had turned her down. Not because he hadn't wanted her to spend the money but because the saddle had a great many memories associated with it. Too many to mention, or recreate, he'd mused.

Surprised by the question, Eduardo looked up.

"You know the answer to that as well as I do, Ellie. I came here when you were six and Addie was four. Your father and mother had just gotten into that terrible car accident." He set down his tools and gave his granddaughter his full attention. "Being notified about that accident had to be the very worst day of my life. But that day became the best day of my life because that was the day I became the guardian of two precious little girls."

The events were foggy and jumbled in her head, but Ellie could still remember some things. "I remember that Miss Joan came and got us in the middle of the night. She took Addie and me to her place, right?"

"Right." Eduardo studied his granddaughter, wondering why she was asking after all this time had passed. "Where is this going, Ellie?"

She wanted to get a few things straight first before she went on to tell Pop what she had found out. "There wasn't anyone else living with her at the time, was there?" She didn't remember that there was, but she could have been mistaken.

"No, there wasn't." Eduardo rose from the seat

where he was sitting and faced his granddaughter. "Again, where is this going?"

Rather than beat around the bush, Ellie decided to dive into the subject headfirst. "Did you know that Miss Joan has a sister?"

Eduardo frowned slightly, the lines in his forehead deepening. "No, you're mistaken. I heard that she had a son, a toddler actually, and a husband. They both died in some sort of flash flood many years ago, but as far as I know, no one has ever asked her about it and she never volunteered any information. I certainly never heard about a sister. Why?" He cocked his head, looking at his granddaughter intently. "What did you hear and who did you hear it from?" he asked. He knew that gossip was alive and well in Forever, as well as thriving here some of the time.

Ellie didn't want to name names yet. "I got it from a very reliable source who heard it from someone she trusted—"

"Ah, third-hand information." Eduardo nodded knowingly. His eyes narrowed slightly. "You know what I think of that sort of thing, Ellie."

"Yes, I know, but there has to be some way that we can check this out, some sort of records that can be accessed to see if this information can be verified," she insisted. "It *might* be true," she stressed, more than willing to give the possibility of Miss Joan having a sister the benefit of the doubt.

Eduardo gave his granddaughter's question some thought. "Well, you could try asking the sheriff's wife, Olivia, to look into the matter. She's a family lawyer and, if anyone would know how to access this kind of information, she would. But this seems very important to you—why now?"

"Pop, Miss Joan might be facing a medical crisis…and you know her. If it comes to that, if she needs an operation and has to go to a hospital to get it, she's not going to want to hear about it. If she has family somewhere, like a sister, and we could find that person, maybe she could talk Miss Joan into having the procedure done," Ellie argued.

"Ellie, you are presupposing that she is going to need surgery and that she is going to refuse to have it done," Eduardo said. "Miss Joan is not a stupid woman," he reminded his granddaughter. "Why don't we just wait and see what those tests tell the doctor?"

That was simple enough to answer. "Because I don't like waiting to the last minute. I believe in being prepared. I always have."

Eduardo shook his head and laughed softly under his breath. "Lord, but you are your father's daughter," he said fondly. "He was always obsessing over things like that when he was your age, too."

Ellie liked hearing that she had something in common with her father. For the most part, both of her parents were mere shadows in her memory. And that only made her that much more committed to following through on this new mission she had set up for herself.

Miss Joan had been there for her and for her sister, even though Addie had no memory of the time. As for her, Ellie could actually remember Miss Joan coming into her home and telling her and her sister that they were going to be staying with her for a while. When she had asked why, Miss Joan had gathered the two of them onto her lap, held them close for a moment and said that they were going to be with her until their grandfather came for them. She was the one who'd broken the news to them that her parents had "gone to heaven."

Ellie vividly remembered the scent of cinnamon when Miss Joan had given them the news and she remembered seeing tears in the woman's eyes as she'd spoken.

Beyond that, there were only disjointed bits and pieces floating through her mind. But Ellie knew she owed the older woman a great deal.

Looking back now, knowing what she had just

learned, Ellie realized that Miss Joan had been re-living her own tragedy because of what had happened to her and Addie.

If there was even the tiniest possibility that any of old Doc Elliott story was true, Ellie owed it to Miss Joan to track down what had happened to the mystery sister. She couldn't shake the feeling that this might actually help things in the long run—as long as that sister were still alive.

"Thanks, Pop," she said. "I'm going to go see if I can catch Olivia in her office." With that, she walked out of the tack room.

Eduardo nodded. "Let me know if there's anything I can do," he called after her.

"I will," she promised. *Provided there is anything to be done*, she added silently.

Ellie rehearsed what she was going to say to Olivia at least three times before she got to the woman's law office in the middle of Forever. As it turned out, when Ellie told the woman about her discovery, Olivia was surprised, to say the least.

After listening to Ellie repeat the whole story, the family lawyer was silent for several seconds then said, "Well, I can definitely look into this for you. I have a few ideas where I could try to find out if there's any truth at all to the information.

Do you want me to let Cash in on this?" she asked since Cash Taylor was not only her law partner, he was also Miss Joan's husband's grandson. Olivia assumed, because Cash hadn't said anything to her, that he was in the dark about this, as was his grandfather.

"Well, if this does turn out to be true," Ellie said, knowing that Olivia was a little skeptical, though for her, the feelings that it was true were growing stronger and stronger, "then he and Harry are going to need to be filled in eventually."

"You know how private Miss Joan is," Olivia pointed out. "She might not like anyone knowing. If this does turn out to be true, there's a reason no one's ever heard about it."

"I know. But I'm willing to bet that nobody in town likes the idea of living in a world without Miss Joan if we can possibly help it. And something tells me that we might need a lot of ammunition on our side to convince that woman to agree to have the surgery—if that does turn out to be the case," Ellie amended.

Olivia nodded. "You have a point. I'll get on this right away," she promised. "But if I hit a wall, then I'm going to ask Cash for help," she warned.

Ellie nodded. "Sounds fair." And then she got down to practical matters. "Look, I can't pay you up front, Olivia, but maybe we can come up with some sort of a weekly arrangement so that—"

Olivia looked at Ellie, a somber expression on her face. "Are you trying to insult me?"

Ellie stared at her. "No, of course not. Why would you even ask something like that?"

Olivia drew herself up in her chair, her posture military-rigid. "Because you're making it sound as if you have a monopoly when it comes to caring about Miss Joan—and you don't," the woman informed her. "Miss Joan, whether she likes it or not, is community property. *All* of us owe her something. *All* of us care about the woman because, for one reason or another, at one time or another, Miss Joan was there for each and every one of us when we needed her most."

Ellie smiled at the lawyer who had hit the matter right on the head. "I didn't intend any disrespect, Olivia."

Olivia nodded her head. "I know that, but sometimes things need repeating." She looked down at the notes she had made to herself while Ellie had told her what she knew. "I'll let you know as soon as I find something—and, Ellie," she called after the pilot who was already at the door, ready to leave.

Ellie turned around, waiting.

"Good call," Olivia told her. "I've got a feeling we're going to need everything we can gather together in our arsenal to get that sharp-tongued, stubborn old woman to listen to reason."

Ellie smiled at Olivia and nodded. "I know."

Ellie wanted to tell Neil about this latest potential development with his patient, but she was forced to wait until the following day when they were to meet for the doctor's next driving lesson.

She swung by the Davenport house that following morning to pick him up. Ellie fully intended to tell him about Miss Joan's possible mystery sister the moment she saw him. But Neil looked so anxious to get behind the wheel for another driving lesson that she decided to put her news on hold. It could keep until another couple of hours had passed.

"You know, I am really surprised that you never decided to do this on your own," she told Neil after he very neatly parked her Jeep in the spot she had pointed out. The man, she thought, was a natural. "You're really good at it."

He almost beamed in response to her compliment. "Thanks. But I honestly never wanted to before." He tried to make her see it from his point of view. "Between taxis, buses and trains, there was never any need for me to learn. You teaching me has put a whole different spin on things," he confided. "For one thing, you make it look like fun."

They were parked over to the side of a road and there was no one else around. Alone like this with her had Neil feeling all sorts of romantic inclinations again. "You make a lot of things look like fun," he confessed.

Despite the fact that the Jeep was opened up, Ellie suddenly felt a lot warmer.

She was allowing herself to be distracted, she upbraided herself, and right now, as drawn to Neil as she felt, she couldn't afford that to happen. "I have some news about Miss Joan for you."

She caught him off guard, but he had his own news and he had a feeling that his was better. "So do I, actually. One of the people I went to medical school with went into the same branch of medicine I did and, after he graduated, he relocated not too far from this section of Texas.

"I kind of got him through medical school," he added, "and he feels he owes me, which in this case is a good thing. When I contacted him, he agreed to let me borrow the equipment I need to conduct Miss Joan's tests and assess the results. Everything I need will be here by tomorrow. I'll have to work fast because the loan is only for the day—but that should give me more than enough time to ascertain if Miss Joan has some sort of coronary issue going on or not."

Finished with what he had to tell Ellie and happy things were going so well, Neil asked, "All right, what's your news?"

"I found out that Miss Joan might have a sister," Ellie said.

He wasn't sure why that would be viewed as good news one way or another.

"Well," he allowed slowly, "I suppose that's good news in case Miss Joan winds up needing a kidney, but otherwise—"

Ellie realized that he didn't see the possible problem this sort of news could very well avert. She filled him in.

"This might be the person we need to help tip the scales in case you do need to operate on Miss Joan. The woman can be exceptionally stubborn and maybe the promise of being reunited with an estranged relative might be what we need to get her to agree to having the surgery."

"You really believe that?" he questioned. "That turning up with this so-called 'mystery' person will make her listen to reason?"

"I *have* to believe that," Ellie told the surgeon. "Sometimes faith is all we have to get us through things. I believed that Dr. Dan would find a way to get a cardiologist to come take a look at Miss Joan and here you are," she grandly announced.

Neil laughed, shaking his head. "I don't know how to argue with that."

"Then don't," she told him. "There's no point in arguing, anyway."

"Say, would you like to come with me to the diner so we can tell Miss Joan the news?" he asked, feeling that if Ellie was so involved in this, she should be there for the highlights.

She wasn't sure what he was referring to. "About finding out that she has a sister, or about the necessary lab equipment coming tomorrow morning?"

"Why don't we tell her about the latter and hold off telling her the other news until this 'sister' is actually located and on her way here?" Neil suggested. "Think of it as our possible ace in the hole."

She thought of that as an unusual way for him to phrase it. "You play poker, Doc?"

Amused, Neil smiled at her. "On occasion."

"I would have thought that someone like you would prefer playing a more cerebral game, such as bridge or chess."

He didn't want Ellie harboring a stuffy image of him. "Actually, I find poker to be more down-to-earth and exciting," he told her. "Maybe while I'm here, after everything is over with, you and I can play a hand or two."

Ellie smiled at the thought. "Maybe," she agreed. "But right now, I think you should tell Miss Joan to get ready for those tests tomorrow. By the way, did I hear you right? Did you say something about your friend shipping out a portable treadmill machine?"

He nodded. "You heard right," Neil told her.

That was both good and bad. Good, because it was obviously necessary and bad because… "She's not going to be thrilled about that."

"I don't need her to be thrilled," Neil said. "I just need her to agree to do it."

"Isn't that test for younger people?" Ellie questioned, anticipating Miss Joan's reaction.

"It's for anyone with a heart who is able to walk," Neil told her. "And from what I've observed, Miss Joan can not only walk, she can get around rather fast for a woman her age."

Ellie raised her hand to stop him. "Word of advice."

Curious because he hadn't said anything that unusual, he said, "Go ahead."

She couldn't keep the grin off her lips. "If you want to stay alive, I'd stay away from using terms like 'a woman your age' when talking to Miss Joan unless you want to observe being vivisected up close and personal by a layperson."

Neil laughed, waving his hand at her advice. "I'm sure that Miss Joan's bark is worse than her bite."

"I wouldn't put even money on that if I were you," Ellie told him.

Neil read between the lines. "She means a lot to you, doesn't she?"

Ellie saw no reason to deny it. "Miss Joan is the closest thing that Addie and I have to a mother. You'll find that a lot of people in this town feel that way."

Neil nodded. That was becoming very clear to him. "Then I'll be sure that all the tests are performed carefully and correctly," he promised. "Now, let's go and beard the lioness in her den."

"You drive," Ellie told him, remaining seated where she was.

Her suggestion pleased him. He felt like a student who had just graduated after taking an accelerated program. "All right," he said, restarting the engine, "I will."

Chapter Twelve

Ellie was thoroughly convinced that Miss Joan had some sort of special radar that managed to alert her to things, even though it didn't seem really possible.

Despite the fact that the diner was relatively full and she wasn't even remotely looking in their direction, somehow the woman just seemed to know the moment they walked in.

Setting down a pair of menus in front of two of her patrons seated at the counter, Miss Joan didn't even look Ellie and Neil's way when she asked, "You two here to eat, or did you come for the sole purpose of bending my ear?"

To his credit, Neil recovered from the unexpected confrontation first. "A little of both," he answered truthfully.

Miss Joan moved over to the couple. "Well, if you're here to eat, you're more than welcome to sit down because, after all, that's the business I'm in. But if you're here to use that as an excuse just to bend my ear and try to talk me into something, you know where the door's located," she told them. "And just in case you forgot—" Miss Joan gestured toward the door "—there it is."

Neil looked at Ellie. "You in the mood for steak?" he asked. Then, before she had a chance to answer, Neil made the decision for them; he needed leverage to use with Miss Joan. If they were eating her food, then she had to be more receptive to what he was saying. "We'll take two of your finest steaks."

Miss Joan gave him a withering look, as if he should know better. "There is no 'finest.' All the steaks here are good, sonny."

Neil never missed a beat. "Then it shouldn't be any trouble picking out two of them for us," Neil told her. "I like mine rare. How about you, Ellie? How do you like your steak?"

"Tasting like a chicken," she answered.

Neil looked at her, confused. "What?"

Rather than explain it to him, she looked at Miss Joan. "You have any of that fried chicken you had on the menu the other day?"

"We might," Miss Joan answered evasively. Then, because it was Ellie, she warmed up a little. "I'll have Angel check. If she doesn't have any, she can whip up a batch. That okay with you?" Miss Joan asked.

That would definitely give Neil more time to talk to the woman, Ellie thought as she slanted a glance at Neil. "That'll be perfect," she told the woman.

"What do you want to go with that?" Miss Joan asked the duo, pretending that she believed they were there for lunch.

"Whatever you pick will be fine," Ellie said, determined to be easy.

Neil nodded in agreement. "What she said."

Miss Joan planted herself directly in front of them, one fisted hand on her waist. "Okay, now you two are just trying to butter me up. Just what are you really after?" she asked.

"A really good meal," Ellie returned guilelessly. "Doc here thinks that New York diners have cornered the market when it comes to serving really great, inexpensive meals, and we know better than

that, don't we, Miss Joan?" she asked in a con-
spiratorial voice.

Miss Joan's frown went clear down to the bone.
"You must think I was born yesterday," she accused.

"No, we don't," Ellie protested, deliberately assuming a wide-eyed expression.

"But you do look young enough to pass for
that," Neil said innocently, tongue in cheek.

Miss Joan's eyes narrowed as she gave him a
piercing look. "Don't try to flirt with me, sonny,"
she warned the cardiologist.

"I wouldn't dream of it," Neil told her. And then
his voice turned more serious. "But I am going to
tell you that my friend came through."

"Good for you," Miss Joan responded cryptically. "Your orders will be up very soon," she told
them as she began to walk away.

Neil rose a little in his seat as he called after
her. "What time will be good for you?"

Turning, Miss Joan studied him for a long moment then said, "That all depends. Good for what?"

Okay, this had gone on too long, Ellie thought.
The doctor's patience could only be pushed so far
before he lost it. She answered for him. "To do the
tests he came out here to do, Miss Joan."

Miss Joan raised her chin a little. "What if I say 'never'?"

Ellie looked at the woman in surprise. This was something new. "Miss Joan, you can't go back on your word."

"Sure I can," she contradicted. Asserting herself, Miss Joan said, "I can do anything I damn well please. I haven't had another one of those fluttery incidents since the baby doctor here arrived in town."

"Doesn't mean it's not going to happen again," Neil pointed out. "And having the proper equipment shipped out here like this is the most convenient I can make it for you."

"That's not true," Miss Joan replied, her eyes meeting his. "It would be more convenient for you to forget about this whole thing altogether. So how about it?"

Ellie answered for him, feeling that since she'd known Miss Joan a lot longer, she was in a better position to become tough with the older woman. "I can get Harry and Cash to strong-arm you," Ellie told the woman.

Hazel eyes held Ellie prisoner.

"You can get them to *try*," the older woman informed her haughtily.

Ellie's voice softened as she tried another approach. "Miss Joan, you mean a great deal to all of us. Please, please just agree to go along with having these tests done," she pleaded. "Who knows, maybe you will be in the clear once they're done and then everyone can drop this whole subject."

The expression on Miss Joan's face was dubious, but she threw up her hands in exasperation. "All right, all right! I'll have the damn tests done—and *then* we *will* drop the whole subject," she declared.

Maybe, Neil added silently. "All right, how does tomorrow morning at 9:00 a.m. sound?" He reasoned that everything would have arrived and been set up in Dan's office by then.

"Lousy," Miss Joan answered honestly.

Neil glossed right over that. "If we get started by nine, we should be finished before your noon rush hour starts," he proposed.

Unwilling to commit, Miss Joan just shrugged. "We'll see."

Neil frowned. "Miss Joan—" he said, a warning note in his voice.

She blew out an exasperated breath. "All right, all right! If it gets you people off my back, I'll be there tomorrow at nine."

"Why don't I come by the diner and pick you up?" the doctor proposed.

Miss Joan pretended to take offense at the suggestion. "You don't trust me?"

Neil smiled at her. "No further than I can throw you," he answered good-naturedly.

Miss Joan actually chuckled under her breath at that. "You're smarter than you look, sonny. I'll go see how Angela is doing with your order," she announced, slipping into the small kitchen.

As she walked away, Neil caught a glimpse of Ellie beaming at him. "What?"

"Nicely played, Doc," she said. "I think Miss Joan actually respects you."

"I think that just might be Miss Joan's way of accepting the inevitable," Neil pointed out. "She's an intelligent woman. I think she knows that she can only put this off for so long."

Ellie laughed at his naïveté, which she found adorable. "Miss Joan knows no such thing. You have no idea how far that woman can push her unique brand of stubbornness. At bottom, the only thing I can hope for is that, worse comes to worst, everyone will gang up on her and force that woman to agree." She wasn't even thinking as far as having an actual procedure performed. "Well, at least she's agreed to submit to the tests."

Neil eyed her knowingly. He knew that they were both thinking the same thing. "Unless she changes her mind by tomorrow," he sighed, shaking his head. Why had he even gotten himself into this? Since he had, he was now committed. "We're just going to have to make sure she doesn't."

"Do you need a hand getting everything set up at the clinic?" Ellie asked, more than ready and eager to help out in any way possible.

"As it turns out, I've got a lot of volunteers," Neil told her. That, in turn, had surprised him. He wasn't accustomed to such a communal effort. "You're right. Everyone really cares about Miss Joan." He paused, reflecting for just a second. "This is a really nice place."

And then, just like that, he changed his focus, moving on to something more personal. "You know, I could use some company tonight," he told her, taking her up on her offer to help out.

She thought she heard something in his voice, something he wasn't aware of. "Are you nervous?"

He backed off a little. "No." Then he told her, "But I still wouldn't mind some company. If you're not doing anything," he qualified.

Ellie was about to answer him, but the sheriff chose that moment to come up behind them. He placed a friendly hand on Neil's shoulder, isolating Neil's attention and turning it toward him.

"I'm afraid we've got other plans for you,

Doc," Rick told him, surprising both Neil and Ellie, as well.

Neil turned on his stool and gave the sheriff a curious look. "What kind of plans?"

It had taken some preparation and coordination, but Rick made it sound as if it had all been spontaneous and spur of the moment.

"Well, the Murphy brothers are throwing a little party in your honor at Murphy's tonight," he said as if he and Dan hadn't been the ones to get the ball rolling. "And it won't be much of a party if you don't attend."

"A party?" Neil echoed, surprised at the whole idea. Had he missed something? "Nobody said anything about a party."

"That's because this was all just one of those last-minute deals, just like these tests for Miss Joan," the sheriff explained. And then Rick smiled. "It's our way of saying thanks for coming out all this way to see the cantankerous woman and going through all this extra trouble to make sure that she's going to be around for a long while.

"Yes, Miss Joan," Rick said as Miss Joan came out of the kitchen and gave him what passed for a dark look, "we are talking about you."

"Well, stop it. Unless you don't want to keep on

eating here," she warned. "And since this the only place in town where you can get a decent meal—"

"—at least one you have to pay for," Ellie said, adding her two cents and earning a dour look from the woman.

Rick knew that Miss Joan had overheard everything—he firmly believed the woman had ears like a bat—so he didn't bother repeating himself or attempting any sort of a further explanation.

"You're welcome to come, too, you know. As long as you promise to leave that viper tongue of yours home, Miss Joan."

"Meaning you want me to keep quiet? Humph. What fun would that be?" she challenged.

Laughing under his breath, the sheriff looked at Neil. "I sure don't envy you, Doc. You're going to have your work cut out for you tomorrow with this one," Rick predicted. "That's part of the reason the Murphys thought you might appreciate attending a party tonight." It was also, he added silently, the main criteria behind having it now rather than later. "Six o'clock work for you?"

He'd had a totally different, more intimate sort of evening in mind, but this could work, too, Neil thought. He was rather flattered by the gesture, actually. However, he didn't want to presume too much.

"You really don't have to do all this, you know," he told the sheriff.

"Sure we do," Rick said. "Tell him, Ellie." The sheriff turning to her for backup.

"What he's trying to tell you…" she explained, wondering why the sheriff would think it would sound any better coming from her, "is that what we lack in volume, we more than make up for in enthusiasm." She took a quick breath. "Like I said, everyone cares about everyone else if you're part of Forever." She thought for a moment then decided that maybe this would bring it home for Neil. "It took Dr. Dan a while to get used to that idea. But once he did—" she smiled "—there was literally no going back for him. And thank goodness, because we needed him as much as he needed us. Still," she allowed, "Forever isn't for everyone." She didn't want him to think she was attempting to railroad him into something. "There have been people born here who couldn't *wait* until they were old enough to get away. Some of them, though," she had to add honestly, "eventually did come back."

"Well, right now I'm just going to go to the party and enjoy myself—within reason," Neil qualified. When she looked at him quizzically, he explained. "Something tells me I'm going to need all my wits about me for tomorrow when I'm conducting those tests on Miss Joan."

Ellie nodded her head in agreement. "You really are a quick study."

After the impromptu early lunch, they both went their separate ways: Neil to consult with Dan and Ellie to the ranch to tell her grandfather and sister about the party that was being thrown at Murphy's.

It had been a while since her grandfather had socialized with his neighbors and she knew he could use the diversion. As for her sister, she knew that Addie was always up for a party. If she found out that Ellie hadn't told her about it, she would have been one very unhappy sister and an unhappy Addie was not something that any of them could easily put up with.

Besides, she knew that Addie wanted to meet this new doctor and, even though she found herself getting more and more attracted to him, far more than she thought she would be, Ellie definitely didn't want Addie thinking she was attempting to hide the man from her.

"A party?" Pop questioned when she told him. "For this doctor friend of Dr. Dan?"

Ellie nodded. "It's to say thanks. I think it was the sheriff's idea. Rick's and the Murphy brothers," she added, spreading the credit around. "I think they're hoping that if they do everything they can to make it hospitable for the Doc, he'll keep that in mind when he's dealing with Miss Joan." She smiled at her grandfather, her voice filled with affection. "We all know she can be pretty rough on a person if they're not used to her ways," Ellie said.

"Well, I don't care what the reason is, I'm always up for a party," Addie said, listening.

"And here I thought you wouldn't want to go," Ellie deadpanned.

Addie looked at her sister as if she had grown another head and then waved a dismissive hand. "Very funny, El. Ha, ha." She then turned to her grandfather. "So, do we all go together, or should I drive in separately?" she asked, a hopeful note in her voice.

"Why don't we all go together?" Pop suggested. "Like a family."

"Works for me," Ellie agreed.

"Yeah, me, too," Addie said with a sigh that belied the truth behind her words.

Chapter Thirteen

In the end, Ellie did wind up taking her own vehicle to the party at Murphy's. She had forgotten all about an errand she'd needed to run and hadn't wanted to make Pop and Addie arrive at Murphy's late just because she would be.

By the time she arrived at the family type saloon, the parking had quickly filled with vehicles and the air resounded with the music that Liam, the professional musician in the Murphy family, was performing with his band.

Ellie could feel the music before she even got out of her Jeep.

Entering the packed establishment, she quickly

scanned the immediate area to see if Neil had arrived yet. He had, as had Miss Joan, who was there with her husband, Harry. Besides Harry, there were several other people milling around the diner owner.

Ellie realized from the evident body language that this was a party with a duel purpose. It was to say "thank you" to the cardiologist going way out of his way to ensure Miss Joan's health and it was for Miss Joan, as well, to show the woman how loved she was by everyone and how much she meant to the people of Forever.

If it turned out that Olivia wasn't able to locate Miss Joan's mystery sister, Ellie hoped this would be enough to cement the argument that Miss Joan couldn't just blatantly ignore the test results if they wound up pointing to her needing surgery. Her life wasn't her own to do with whatever she chose to do with it. Like it or not, her life belonged to all of them.

Spotting her family, Ellie waved at Pop. When he saw her, Eduardo immediately waved back. He was busy talking to Julia Anderson, recently widowed in the last year. Addie, as usual, was in the center of a group of young men. The girl was a regular walking–guy magnet. Ellie would have been worried about her sister if it wasn't for the fact that Pop kept such a sharp eye on her.

Too sharp in Addie's opinion, Ellie mused, but any young man who was worth her attention would easily endure Pop's scrutiny. It was a small price to pay to have a vivacious young woman in their life.

"I see you finally made it."

Ellie nearly jumped when she heard the deep voice behind her.

Between the loud, throbbing, pulsating music and her own thoughts, Ellie hadn't heard anything, least of all Neil coming up behind her until he was right there, less than an inch away.

Startled, she had to catch her breath as she swung around to face him. "You know, if you ever get tired of being a surgeon and decide to take up a second career, you might give cat burglary a try. You've got sneaking up on people down pat."

He laughed. "How long have you been this jumpy?"

"How long have you been in town?" she countered archly.

A deep smile curved his lips. "Should I be flattered?"

The noise level had increased again, drowning out his words. Ellie was forced to point to her ear and shake her head to let him know she hadn't heard what he'd just said.

Leaning in, Neil tried again, this time whispering the words directly into her ear. "Should I be flattered?" he repeated.

The warmth of his breath curled along her neck and cheek, and Ellie had to struggle not to shiver in response. It was even more of a struggle to attempt to keep her wits about her and not go with the gut reaction that made her want to kiss him.

From out of the blue, a sadness took hold of her. They were just getting to know one another, with the promise of so much more, but he would be leaving soon. And then what?

She had no answer.

"You can be anything you want to be," Ellie finally responded. Desperate to change the subject, she looked around the crowded saloon again, hoping to have something present itself.

"What are you looking for?" he asked. Again, he was forced to bring his mouth close to her ear so that she would hear what he was asking her.

Ellie raised her voice as she answered him. "I know that the Murphys and Miss Joan have an agreement about who serves what at their separate establishments, but I thought that since she was attending this party here, she might have brought some food with her."

Rather than say anything, Neil took her arm and directed her attention to a table set up in one of the far corners. It was loaded with all sorts of quick snacks. There were platters of tiny quesadillas, enchiladas and small, edible flour "baskets" filled with salads comprised of three kinds of peppers, tomatoes and shredded Romaine lettuce. There was also a mouthwatering selection of three kinds of meat.

"For snacking," he explained. "If the Murphys and Miss Joan ever decide to join forces and form one large establishment, nobody is ever going to get any work done again," Neil predicted.

She laughed. "You're probably right."

Rather than head over to the table, Ellie turned on her heel and went in the complete opposite direction.

"I thought you said you were hungry," Neil said. "Why aren't you getting something to eat?"

"No, I asked if Miss Joan had brought any food. I was just curious. I can eat later," she assured Neil. "Right now, they're playing one of my favorite songs," she told him, cocking her head to listen as she allowed the beat to get into her hips and direct them. "Do you dance?"

"Not well enough to put me on Broadway," he answered. "But yes," Neil acknowledged, "I do."

That was when she presented herself to him by putting out her hands in a silent invitation to dance. "I happen to know there are no talent agents here tonight, scouting Murphy's, so you're in the clear. You don't have anything to be embarrassed about."

Neil grinned warmly at her, his eyes sparkling. "Well then, I guess I have no excuses left."

And with that, he slipped one arm around Ellie's waist, took hold of her hand with his other hand, and proceeded to dance with her to the heart-racing tempo.

When the number ended—and Ellie felt as if she had just covered the entire floor three times over—the band struck up another song, the beat even more compellingly arousing.

Neil cocked his head, his eyes silently asking her if she wanted to continue dancing. When Ellie smiled her response, her eyes crinkling, it was all that he needed. The next number started and he didn't even bother asking her. They just continued dancing.

But after the third dance ended, Ellie held up her hand and cried, "Uncle!" as she struggled to catch her breath.

Neil pretended to take her literally. He scanned the immediate area as he asked, "Where?"

Ellie didn't answer that. Instead, she just told him, in small gasps, "I think I need some air."

Neil dropped the pretense. He nodded and, taking her hand in his, led Ellie outside as if he were the town native and she the visitor.

"Fortunately," he responded, "fresh air is something that Forever seems to have in absolute abundant supply." He pushed open the door and the difference was immediately evident.

The rush of cool air felt wonderful against Ellie's flushed skin. For a moment, she allowed it to work its magic. She couldn't trust herself to carry on a conversation that didn't sound as if she was being pursued by stampeding horses and gasping for air.

"Where did you learn how to dance like that?" she finally managed to ask him.

Neil debated giving her a flippant, witty, noncommittal answer. But Ellie didn't strike him as the kind of woman he could just lie to or make up something for, just for the sake of sounding clever. That had never been his thing anyway.

So he told her the truth, even though it painted him in less than a flattering light.

"There was this girl in high school I was trying to impress. Rhonda. She took my breath away every time I looked at her. Someone told me that she liked to dance, so I got my mother to get me lessons."

Instantly, Neil became more human to her. Ellie could even see him in her mind's eye, pining after an unattainable girl. "And did you impress this girl?"

"No. She never even looked my way. When I asked her to go to the dance, she looked at me as if I was crazy. That's when I found out she was going with the captain of the football team. The guy had shoulders out to here," he told Ellie, holding his hands as far apart as they would go to show her just how wide those shoulders were. "I swear," he said with a laugh, "you could use those suckers as a diving board."

"Well," Ellie declared with a shrug, "her loss. A heart surgeon and a fabulous dancer. If you ask me, that's a killer combination," she told him.

"And soon to be a fantastic driver," he added. "Don't forget that," Neil reminded her, amusement curving his mouth again.

Ellie felt as if his smile had nestled directly into her chest, all but weaving its magic all through her system.

"Well, let's hold off on the 'fantastic driver'

part," Ellie advised, pointing out, "You haven't quite gotten there yet."

"But I will," he said confidently. "All I need are a couple more lessons from this fabulous, sexy teacher I have—" he looked at her and the way that the moonlight danced along her skin "—and I'll be ready for the Indy 500."

They were standing some distance away from the entrance. Out here, their main source of light came from the full moon. The semidarkness only added to the vulnerability she was experiencing.

Ellie was treading on very dangerous ground right now. If she had a brain in her head, she would get herself back inside the saloon and seek the company of others.

But she didn't.

Not just yet.

Instead, her eyes met his. "'Fabulous, sexy teacher,' huh?" she repeated.

"That's right," he confirmed.

"Are you taking lessons from someone else besides me?" she asked innocently, amusement shining in her eyes.

"No," Neil answered, turning his face toward hers as he lowered his voice to just slightly louder than a whisper. "Just you."

"Then maybe you should have your eyes

checked before you start giving Miss Joan those tests tomorrow. That is, if you want to actually be able to see the results."

"There's nothing wrong with my eyes," he assured her quietly. "I see everything just fine."

His gaze slid slowly over her face, appreciatively taking in every supple inch of her body. Making each of them warm in their own way.

"Just fine," Neil repeated as if reciting the two words like a prayer.

His eyes never left her face.

Ellie could feel her heart pounding in her throat now, threatening to take away her very last fragment of air.

"Maybe this party the sheriff threw for you is a good thing," she told him breathlessly. "You obviously don't get out very much."

But Neil had a very different opinion on the matter.

"You don't have to sample every single cookie in the box to know if the one you have is extremely sweet and the best tasting one you've ever had," he told her, his voice so low that part of her thought she was imagining the words rather than actually hearing them.

If her heart began pounding any harder, it was going to create a hole in her chest and just fall out, she thought. Even in the darkness, she knew it was only a matter of seconds before he became aware of what it was doing, how hard it was beating.

And why.

She needed to save herself before it was too late.

"Maybe we should go in," she told him.

"Maybe we should," Neil agreed.

Instead of doing that, Neil slid his fingers along her cheek, tilting her head ever so slightly. And then he slowly inclined his head and his lips met hers.

Just like that, time stood still as the kiss between them blossomed and grew until it couldn't be measured in any breadth and scope.

Ellie's mind stop protesting; stopped attempting to put the brakes on. Instead she allowed herself to be wildly, breathlessly, swept away down an uncharted river she had never even imagined in her wildest dreams existed.

Rising up on her toes, she slid her arms around his neck, felt herself eagerly responding to the heat of his body. Not just responding, but finding herself wanting more.

Eagerly.

Where had this come from? And why, in heaven's name, now?

And why with a man who couldn't possibly

want to stay in this small town once his job was done—which would be very, very soon?

It just didn't make sense, Ellie silently argued. She had always been so sensible, so practical, far more levelheaded than her years. Her behavior now was totally against type.

And yet, she realized, it didn't have to make sense. Not really. It just had to *be*.

This had to be.

Oh, Lord, Ellie thought, she was losing her mind. All that time she had spent up in the air was unraveling her.

The worst part was, she didn't care. She wanted to grab whatever happiness she could for however long she could.

Neil had come here looking to help, to make his life mean something. Maybe he was even looking for answers… But he hadn't come looking for this, certainly not this. And he knew that he hadn't come to Forever with any plans for remaining in this tiny dot of a town outside the length of time it took to get that old woman back on her feet and in her customary fighting form. Finding love— certainly not a soulmate—or even finding "like" had never entered into the picture.

So what was he doing out here in the shadows,

with his lips pressed against hers and his pulse all but going into orbit?

This was insane. This was ridiculous.

This was—

Heaven.

Nothing but sheer, unadulterated heaven in its purest form. And he could see why someone could become addicted to it, give up everything as long as it could be assured that, in the end, *this* would be waiting for him.

He kissed Ellie harder.

For the first time in his life, he could understand the term "head over heels."

But understanding and allowing were two different things and he had to remember that he had responsibilities and obligations. And those came first, before his own indulgences, he silently insisted.

Even so, all he wanted was to get one more minute with her. Just one more…

Chapter Fourteen

"Hey, Neil, you out here?" Dan called out. He had stepped outside of the saloon and was standing in front of the entrance, squinting into the darkness and trying to make out a lone, tall figure that might, in all likelihood, be his friend.

Hearing Dan, Ellie drew back, creating a small space between herself and Neil. "I think you're being paged," she told him.

Neil sighed. It was just as well, he thought. Right now, Ellie was far too tempting and part of him was worried that if he didn't rein himself in, he could easily get carried away. There was just something about this adventurous pilot that he found exceedingly attractive.

He sighed and drew back. "So it would seem," he agreed. Raising his hand, he called out to Dan. "Over here."

Dan immediately started walking toward the sound of Neil's voice. He only stopped short when he realized that Neil wasn't alone.

Well, this is interesting, Dan thought. "Oh, I'm sorry. Did I interrupt anything?"

Ellie thought fast and came up with a cover story that she felt saved all three of them from any embarrassment.

"Your friend wore me out with all his fancy dancing, so I came out here to catch my breath. New York training had the Doc feeling I shouldn't be out here alone, so he volunteered to come with me." And then Ellie deftly changed the subject. "Is everything okay?" she asked. Her mind immediately went to why Neil was in Forever in the first place. "It's not Miss Joan, is it?"

Dan laughed. "Only if you're referring to her being in rarer, sharper-tongued form than usual. No," he continued, glancing at his friend, "I came out here to find Neil because it was nearly time for me to give the toast."

"The toast?" Neil repeated suspiciously. In his

opinion, enough attention had been sent his way. This had to be about his patient, or at least he hoped so. "You're talking about the one for Miss Joan, right?"

"No, I was referring to the one that is intended to include both of you. Actually," Dan confessed, "I can't take credit for this. The toast is more Rick's idea than mine. And he's the one who's going to be giving it," he explained.

Neil was already shaking his head. "I think, if it's all the same to you, I'll pass."

"Funny, those are more or less the same words that Miss Joan used a few minutes ago," Dan told him. "If you ask me, you two are a match made in heaven. You think alike."

"Nobody's asking," Neil commented pointedly, frowning at the idea of being the focus of a toast.

That was the point when Ellie decided she needed to step in. "C'mon, Doc," she urged, slipping her arm through his and tugging him toward Murphy's. "You can't insult everyone by not going in and listening to them tell you how grateful they are that you came. That's what this whole thing is about, you know."

"Sure I can," Neil countered.

Her eyes met his with a silent challenge. "Then how do you expect Miss Joan to go along with everything if you, the reasonable, big-city surgeon, doesn't?"

Dan laughed, tickled by the way Ellie had managed to turn the situation around. "She's got you there, Neil," he told his stubborn friend.

Neil sighed, mentally surrendering. He found Dan's choice of words rather appropriate as he left the shadows and began to walk toward the saloon. "Yes," he agreed with a sigh that seemed to come from the very depths of his soul as he glanced in Ellie's direction, "she does."

Ellie was positive that she was reading far too much into his words than he'd ever intended, but she still couldn't shake the feeling that there was more to them than was implied strictly on the surface.

The moment the door to the saloon was opened, everyone inside turned to the three people who were entering.

Applause and cheers greeted Neil and he found himself being separated from Ellie and Dan and tugged toward the center of Murphy's. All those bodies in one place made the atmosphere feel a great deal warmer than he had anticipated.

He had been brought in and placed right next to Miss Joan.

Her hazel eyes went over him slowly, pinning him in place.

"I see they got you, too, sonny," Miss Joan said. "I would have thought someone as clever as you would have been able to make good his escape," she commented. "Maybe you're not as clever as I gave you credit for."

Miss Joan's husband sidled up to Neil. "Don't let her get to you," Harry whispered to him. "She just doesn't know how to deal with all this attention being showered on her." He smiled fondly at his wife. "You'd think she would have gotten used to it by now."

"Sure I know how to deal with it," Miss Joan contradicted. "I just walk out on it." But when she moved to do so, she found herself surrounded by well-wishers who blocked her path. Miss Joan pursed her lips in a disapproving frown. "You'd think that grown people would have better things to do with their time than drink and give aimless speeches."

"Right now," the sheriff said, coming up between the two guests of honor, "I can't think of a single one. Everybody—" Rick raised his voice to address the room "—lift your glasses high and give your heartfelt thanks to Dr. Neil Eastwood," He turned toward Neil. "Dr. Neil left his cushy Sixth

Avenue life to come out here and make sure that Miss Joan continues giving us her sharp-tongued commentary on everything we're doing wrong." He raised his glass a little higher as he declared, "We don't know what we'd do without you and we hope it's another fifty years before we have to start worrying about finding that out."

And then he positioned himself between the two and looked out into the crowd. "To Dr. Neil and Miss Joan!" the sheriff declared.

Anything else he might have said was drowned out as a resounding chant of "To Dr. Neil and Miss Joan!" was loudly declared at just the right intervals to sound like an uncoordinated cacophony of high and low voices, some melodious, some shrilled, none of them blending harmoniously.

The only thing they all had in common was the love that was woven through them.

The party went on for more than another two hours. The time was filled with good conversation, good food and just enough drink to make it all go down easily.

The sheriff, who had helmed the entire event from start to finish, was there to help when it came time to close the party down, as well. Rick was there predominantly because he didn't want to take

any chances that either party would be too inebri-
ated to oversee the various tests scheduled for the
next morning or too unable to take said tests in the
first place. What he was looking to prevent was a
problem with the readings.

Rick was afraid that if Miss Joan became in-
toxicated, the true readings that would be necessary to make an accurate determination wouldn't
be able to be taken.

"Well, I guess I should thank you for this," Miss
Joan muttered. Her eyes swept over the sheriff as
well as two of the three Murphy brothers, Matt and
Liam, as she and her husband had begun to make
their way slowly over to the door.

Rick waved away her thanks. "There's no need,"
he told her.

Miss Joan eyed him with an annoyed air. "Well,
you boys might have been raised in a barn, but me,
I was raised with old-fashioned manners. You always say 'thank you' to the person who went out
of their way for you—even if you didn't want them
to in the first place," the woman added pointedly.

Rick smiled. "And we call *that* a backhanded
compliment," he commented to his sister, Ramona.

"You're free to call it anything you want," Miss
Joan informed him.

Placing his still powerful hands on Miss Joan's

shoulders, Harry tactfully ushered her toward the door. "I'd better get her home before she stops being so humble and nice."

"Watch your step, Old Man, or you're sleeping out in the henhouse tonight," Miss Joan warned. "With the chickens."

Unfazed, Harry merely laughed. He'd heard it all before. "That's the price I pay for wanting fresh eggs in the morning," he told Neil with a wink as he and Miss Joan left the premises.

Ellie couldn't help the grin that came to her lips. "I'll bet you don't have anything like that back where you are."

"No, we do not," Neil agreed. He'd had a really good time tonight. Far better than he would have ever expected. "I'd better call it a night myself," he told Ellie, although it was obvious to anyone paying attention that the surgeon was really reluctant to go.

"We should be going, too," Dan agreed. He had one arm around Tina as he gently ushered his wife and children before him in the general direction of the entrance. "Big day tomorrow." Slanting a glance at Neil, he added with a kindly grin, "No pressure intended."

"Right," Neil laughed. Like that changed anything. "None felt."

"So, is the appointment for the tests still set for tomorrow at 9:00 a.m.?" Ellie asked, looking from Neil to Dan.

"We figured that would be a good time so that Miss Joan doesn't decide to get a head start flying the coop," Dan told Ellie. Neil nodded his agreement.

Ellie quickly reviewed her schedule in her head. She didn't have anything for the morning and, even if she had, she knew it would be a simple enough matter to reroute a pickup flight to a later time.

She smiled to herself. That was what made currently being the only air service in town, however small it was, such a good thing.

"Need a cheering section?" she asked, looking from one doctor to the other.

It appeared that Ellie and Neil had taken to one another and Dan, for one, was quite happy about the idea.

"Sure," Dan said, answering for his friend, and then specifying, "A quiet cheering section."

"Never intended anything else," Ellie assured Dan. She turned toward Neil, not wanting to horn in unless he gave his permission, as well. "How about you?"

"How about me what?" he asked, thinking he might have lost the thread of the conversation.

"Do you have any objections to my hanging around the medical clinic tomorrow while you run your tests on Miss Joan?"

"Objections?" Neil echoed with a dry laugh. "Hell, no. We might even need you to hold her down," he said. "There's a likely possibility that Miss Joan might change her mind about being so 'agreeable' by morning when the chips are finally down."

Dan's wife, Tina, had a different take on the situation. She had known Miss Joan longer than Dan had. "I think that if Miss Joan was going to disagree about anything," she said, speaking up, "it'll be about having a procedure done at all if those tests actually point to her needing surgery."

Dan nodded. "Right, as usual, my love," he said. But rehashing all this now was moot. They needed to wait until tomorrow, "Okay, let's get these sleepyheads into bed," he said to Tina.

With that, he bent down and picked up Jeannie. The little girl looked more than happy to rest her head on her father's shoulder. She was asleep before he even managed to take two steps.

"I can remember doing that with your sister," Eduardo whispered to Ellie as he and Addie walked by, on their way out. After meeting Neil,

Addie had decided the doctor was more suited to her sister than to her and had quietly stepped back.

"Not with her?" Neil asked, looking at Ellie.

"Ellie?" Eduardo repeated incredulously as he laughed at the suggestion. "You are kidding, of course, yes? This one," he told the cardiologist, nodding at his older granddaughter, "was much too independent to ever let on that she was too tired to walk. She would have continued walking home until she fell on her knees in an exhausted heap."

"Your memory is going, Pop," Ellie told him, trying to look stern, but the affectionate laugh gave her away.

Not playing along, Eduardo shook his head. "My memory is as sharp and clear as it was on the day you came into my life."

Neil would have enjoyed staying around these people and listening to their stories until well into dawn, but he needed a clear head for the morning and that required sleep. It wasn't just that the woman he would be working on was so important—as far as he was concerned, every patient he dealt with was equally important… It was just that so many eyes would be trained on him, figuratively rather than literally, and he didn't want to even remotely run the risk of something, however minor or unintended, going wrong.

As he had already told himself, every patient was important, but Miss Joan was especially important, which was why he had to be at his best. Neil couldn't afford to just phone this in—not that he ever would—but this time he had to be even more vigilant than usual.

Belatedly, he focused on the present and announced, "I'll walk you all to your car." His words were intended not just for Ellie but for her family, as well.

Ellie answered first. "You don't have to," she told him. "I know where my Jeep is and so does Pop—and Addie," she added belatedly when her sister gave her an annoyed look at the accidental exclusion.

"Old habits die hard, remember?" Neil asked her, reminding her of what he'd said when she had pointed this out the other day.

"Let him do what he feels is right, Ellie," Eduardo gently prodded. "Nothing wrong with good manners."

"I wasn't inferring that there was, Pop," she told her grandfather, further pointing out, "Just that he needs his rest, so he is free to skip this part of his ritual."

"Now who's acting like an overprotective

mother hen?" Addie asked her sister with a knowing smirk.

Pop came close to telling Addie, "Leave your sister alone," but he managed to bite it back at the last minute, aware that neither granddaughter would appreciate the comment for different reasons.

So instead, he paused to shake Neil's hand. "Good luck tomorrow and remember Miss Joan's bark is worse than her bite."

Neil laughed. "Can I quote you on that?"

"Don't you dare," Eduardo told him with a wide, good-natured smile.

Neil merely nodded. "I didn't think so."

Miss Joan was clearly an enigma and he really wasn't a hundred percent sure just how to read her, so he decided that it was better to err on the side of caution than to just forge right in and lose the battle altogether.

Chapter Fifteen

In hindsight, Neil would think later that day, it hadn't gone well.

He supposed that what had caused him to let his guard down in the first place was that getting Miss Joan to initially cooperate and submit to having the battery of tests had gone better than he had expected.

Once the morning arrived, however, and despite the last-minute decision to switch the venue from the clinic to Dan's cabin where he and Tina occasionally retreated when they wanted peace and quite, Miss Joan had showed up on time, accompanied by her husband, Harry. And, with an amazing minimum of grumbling, the woman had agreed to carry on with the planned testing.

The tests included an EKG, a treadmill test and, finally, an EEG—performed when Neil was dissatisfied with the results obtained from Miss Joan's treadmill test.

"Don't know why you need to make a woman my age gasp for breath because you want to have her running on a piece of moving machinery, something I'm never going to need to do in my life," Miss Joan said tersely. "But, hey, if it makes you happy, I'm willing to do it." She frowned, looking down at all the wires that Debi had attached strategically to her chest and arms for an accurate reading. "But having all these funny little electrical round things attached to places that should remain private except between a husband and his wife, creating zigzag patterns on a ticker tape while you force me to walk, just seems like a big fat waste of time," she complained.

"And as for this last one," she declared when Neil performed the EEG. "That fancy camera work to see if my heart's beating? Well..." she snorted. "You don't want to *know* my opinion of this one."

Neil merely offered her what passed for a smile as he reread the all the test readouts. He had hoped against hope that he was wrong, but it certainly didn't look that way.

This isn't good, he thought, raising his eyes to look at his patient.

Finished, Miss Joan had had gotten up off the gurney brought in for expressly this purpose and was buttoning up her blouse, glad to be putting it all behind her.

"But at least everyone and his brother," she was saying, "is going to stop pestering me to have these damn things done." Dressed and ready to leave, she looked at Neil. "We done here?" she asked him, fully expecting a positive response.

Neil didn't answer at first. He had seen an anomaly on the treadmill readout, one he had been afraid he would see. At the very least, it indicated that Miss Joan had a blockage and needed to have an angioplasty done. In addition, because of the arterial fibrillation, an ablation, where some of the heart tissue would have to be cut away, might also be called for.

"No, Miss Joan," he finally said, not relishing what he needed to tell her, "I'm afraid that we are *not* done here."

She watched him for a moment. Something that Ellie could have sworn that looked like fear flashed through her eyes before a somber expression set in.

"Maybe you don't understand," Miss Joan stated firmly. "We're done here." With that, the woman headed for makeshift testing room's door. "You had your fun, you played doctor," she told him crisply. "Now I've got to get back to my life."

Neil raised his voice, thinking that would stop her in her tracks. "Miss Joan, you have a blockage, not to mention a serious case of A-fib taking a toll on your heart. You need to have an angioplasty performed and probably an ablation, as well."

Miss Joan's expression was dark as she turned to look at Neil. "You are trying my patience, sonny. Can those things you just came up with, those fancy words, can they be done right here in Forever?"

"No, I'm afraid not," he told her. "Forever's clinic doesn't have the facility to perform those procedures," he said as kindly as he could. He wasn't used to having to justify his recommendations, or to having to baby his patients. "You'll need to go to a fully equipped hospital for that."

She raised her chin defiantly. "Well, I guess that answers that, doesn't it?" Miss Joan paused to give him a look that her husband had once said could have stopped a charging rhino dead in its tracks. "In case I haven't made myself clear," she informed him, "it's not happening." And with that she swept out of the room that contained all the equipment and into the outer one where her husband and Ellie were waiting. Ellie had wound up keeping the man company because he had struck her as being uncharacteristically nervous.

"Miss Joan!" Neil called after her.

The woman just continued walking. "Go tend to people who want to be fussed over. That's not me! We're done here," Miss Joan announced in no uncertain terms.

She whizzed by Harry and Ellie without a single glance in their direction.

Harry jumped to his feet, incredibly spry for a man his age. "Miss Joan?" he called after his wife.

Miss Joan just kept walking. "I'm finished playing games," she merely told her husband as she made her way out of the cabin, slamming the door in her wake.

Bewildered, not to mention worried and more than a little frightened for his wife, Harry looked at Neil for an explanation as to Miss Joan's behavior. "What you just found, is it bad, Doctor?"

It wasn't Neil's habit to disclose a diagnosis to anyone beyond the patient involved. But this was a case he had gone into knowing that he would undoubtedly need help managing the patient and, in doing so, rules he always adhered to would be bent and even broken. In view of that, he felt he had the right to disclose at least this much to Miss Joan's husband. A lot of people cared about this sharp-tongued woman.

"It's what we thought," he said, referring to what he had previously shared with Harry. "Your wife needs to have surgeries."

Harry took a deep breath, trying his best to brace himself. "More than one?"

Neil nodded. "I'm afraid so."

"And if Miss Joan refuses to have these surgeries performed?" Ellie asked, feeling that Harry needed to be prepared for the worst case scenario.

"She'd be literally rolling the dice as to how long she can keep going without suffering some sort of dire consequences," Neil answered, hoping that would give the man the ammunition he needed to make his wife realize she was being recklessly foolish.

Harry sighed haplessly. "I'll work on her," he told the doctor. "But you have to understand that she is one stubborn old woman. I know from experience that nobody is going to make Miss Joan do anything she doesn't want to do."

His shoulders slumped in what amounted to a parenthesis; he looked like a man who felt he was facing a losing battle.

"Thanks for everything, Dr. Eastwood. You did your best," he told Neil as he left the cabin to try to catch up to his wife.

Neil shook his head, totally mystified. He didn't like things that didn't make any sense. "It's not as if we don't have the technology to help her," he said to Ellie, clearly frustrated. "We do. We can."

"We'll work on her," Ellie told him, moved by how deeply affected he seemed by Miss Joan's behavior. "And by 'we,' I mean everyone in town. We'll get Miss Joan to come around."

He eyed her skeptically. After the performance he had just witnessed, he doubted it could be done. "You actually believe that?"

"We have to," she told him simply. And then Ellie glanced at her watch. Talk about bad timing. "I've got a delivery to make."

"Go," Neil told her, waving her on her way.

But Ellie noticed that the surgeon was making no effort to leave with her. She couldn't very well tell him to leave the cabin, but she didn't like the idea of his hanging back.

"You'll be all right?" she asked, concerned.

"Always have been," he replied in a distant voice.

With that, Neil turned his attention to the equipment brought into the cabin. He needed to get it ready for transport when the van's driver arrived. The guy had to take it back to the physician who had temporarily loaned the equipment to him.

Ellie hesitated. He couldn't do all this alone, she thought. "Look, I can stay awhile and help you. I'll just make a call and postpone the delivery run—"

"No," Neil said, stopping her before she could continue. "You take care of your business. I'd rather be alone right now, anyway," Neil told her.

Ellie was surprised at the extent that his words stung, but she did understand how he felt. Given his position and the breadth of his knowledge, she was sure that Neil was accustomed to having people obey his recommendations without question. He was not accustomed to being ignored like this.

This was a whole new world for him, she thought as she quietly left him to pack everything up and, more importantly, to sort out his feelings about what had just taken place.

The delivery run took her longer than Ellie had anticipated. After she was back, there were chores at the ranch she needed to catch up on. She knew that her grandfather wouldn't say anything, but she felt guilty about not doing her share.

It was after seven before she had time to turn her attention back to Neil. She hoped he had come to terms with today's events and had had found a way to deal with them. This wasn't over by a long shot, even though it might have felt that way to him.

Ellie stopped by the medical clinic, thinking she would find him there with Dan even though it was technically about to close down for the night.

She was disappointed.

"Haven't seen him in the last couple of hours," Dan told her as he saw his last patient of the day to the door. "After Neil packed up all the equipment he'd borrowed to do Miss Joan's tests and it was picked up, he said he had somewhere to be. He told me that he'd be by my place later on tonight, possibly a lot later." Dan looked at Ellie with compassion. "I think this thing with Miss Joan hit him kind of hard. He's not used to having his advice ignored," he sighed, empathizing with his friend. "He's frustrated that she won't listen to reason."

Ellie nodded. "It's a large club."

"I know, right? But Neil's a grown man and he'll work this out for himself," he assured Ellie and then confessed, "I just hate having put him in this position. I really thought she might listen to reason once she agreed to being examined." Dan began closing up, thinking this was early for him.

"I'll let Neil know you were looking for him once he turns up," he promised.

Ellie nodded as she left the clinic. But she wasn't patient enough just to sit around, waiting for Neil just to turn up. He'd looked really upset and she wanted to comfort him.

The man had to be somewhere, she reasoned.

Ellie swung by Murphy's, thinking he might want to get an anonymous drink to kill some time.

But he wasn't there.

She took a quick look into the diner, thinking that maybe he had decided to give talking Miss Joan into having the surgeries one more try.

But he wasn't at the diner, either.

She left before Miss Joan saw her, not ready to confront the woman just yet.

Okay, so where was he?

Ellie doubted that he would go wandering around the countryside, not without having a destination in mind. As far as she knew, there was only one place left to try before she gave up her search.

Operating on instinct, Ellie swung by the ranch house to pick up a few things from the refrigerator and the pantry, and to pack them into an old basket that she and her sister used to use for picnics. Mentally crossing her fingers, Ellie drove back to Dan's cabin. It was the only place she could think of where Neil might feel comfortable enough to just hang around while he tried to figure out what to do about Miss Joan.

Approaching, Ellie saw one lone light in the window and knew she had guessed right.

Parking her Jeep, she took the picnic basket with her and presented herself at the front door. She knocked. There was no response, so she knocked again. And then a third time.

"I'm not going to go away, Doc," she announced, about to knock for a fourth time.

That was when the door finally opened. Neil stood in the doorway, his body prohibiting entrance. Looking at her, he shook his head. "You people are a really persistent bunch, aren't you?"

"You're just picking up on that?" she asked with a grin. Raising the basket she was holding to get his attention, she said, "I figured you hadn't eaten anything yet and Dr. Dan wouldn't want you starving while you were his guest, so I brought food."

Neil eyed the basket, making no effort to take it. "Is that from Miss Joan's Diner?"

"No," she told him. "It's from my kitchen. I figured you wouldn't eat anything that came from her diner right now and the bottom line here is that I really want you to eat."

Neil frowned and then stepped back, allowing

her to enter. He shut the door behind her. "Why would that matter to you?"

"Ouch," she cried, dramatically placing her hand over her heart. "That's kind of cold," Ellie told him. "You really have to ask?"

Neil sighed. He wasn't behaving like himself, he silently admonished. "Sorry. This thing with Miss Joan has really set me off."

"The way she's behaving is nothing personal against you," Ellie insisted.

Coming into the outer room, she set her basket down and proceeded to take out what she'd packed, which included some pieces of fried chicken, side dishes of potato salad and carrots, as well as something to drink, plates, utensils, napkins and two glasses. She set them all on a makeshift table. "Like most of us, Miss Joan doesn't like facing her own mortality. Her thinking is if she doesn't admit there's something wrong, then whatever is wrong can't kill her."

"Except that it can," he said. "Miss Joan is too smart a woman not to know that," he insisted.

"She does know that," Ellie assured him. "But give her time. She needs to work this through at her own pace," she told Neil. "Meanwhile, everyone is working on her to make her realize that having this operation is the lesser of two evils—

the bigger evil in this case being dying," she concluded flatly.

"Now, you do your part and eat, Doc, or when we finally *do* get through to that stubborn woman, you might not be up to doing what actually needs to be done," she told him.

He looked at the food she had put on the table. "I'm not hungry."

She wasn't buying it. "The hell you're not. By my calculation, you haven't eaten since early this morning. By now, you should be ready to chew on cardboard. Sit," she ordered, pointing to one of the chairs at the table. "Eat."

He looked at her as if he couldn't believe what he was hearing. "I—"

"Don't talk," Ellie cut in. "Eat. Now," she told him.

Because the whole scenario struck him as almost ludicrous, Neil found himself grinning at Ellie in response.

"Yes, ma'am."

Ellie nodded, pleased. "Better. Just so you know, you can't be engaging in a battle of wills with Miss Joan. Trust me, you'll be a casualty in that war. The woman has had years of practice at it and she'll win, hands down."

He saw no point in arguing with that. She was

probably right. "I can't believe how someone who knows that there are all these people around who care about her the way they do can willfully disregard her health like this."

Ellie waved her hand at his statement. "Oh, believe it," she told him. "We all told you how stubborn that woman can be," she reminded him.

"I know, but…" he sighed.

Without thinking, he picked up a piece of fried chicken and took a bite of it. The moment he started chewing, he looked up at Ellie, traces of surprise on his face.

"Hey, this is good," he told her. "You made this?"

"Yes. You sound surprised," she observed.

"It's just that…well, you've got all these other things that you're good at, like flying a plane. I didn't think you'd be good at doing domestic things, too," he confessed.

"You mean like cooking," she guessed with a smile. "Or, by 'domestic things,' are you referring to making beds and doing laundry?"

He knew when he'd made a mistake. "I'm tripping over my own tongue."

"That's okay," Ellie said. She thought of when Neil had kissed her and felt a warm shiver undulate down her spine. "It's rather a nice tongue, so you're forgiven."

He laughed. "You have a way with words," he told her. "I guess there's nothing you can't do when you set your mind to it."

Ellie cocked her head, looking at him, bemused. "Is that a challenge?"

"I don't know," Neil replied honestly. "It might be." His eyes met hers. "Do you want it to be?"

She could feel her heart actually skip a beat as her skin heated so quickly it took her very breath away. She was acutely aware of the fact that the ball had just been lobed into her court and it was up to her to either let it fall at her feet or to return it.

Ellie more than happily returned the serve.

Chapter Sixteen

Getting up from her seat, Ellie came around to Neil's side of the table.

She wove her arms around his neck and said, "Yes," in a low, breathy whisper just before she brought her mouth down to his and kissed him.

By turns surprised and then exceedingly pleased, Neil pushed his chair away from the table and pulled Ellie onto his lap. He managed all this while never removing his lips from hers.

The kiss deepened.

It continued to grow in intensity, making Ellie's head spin so much, she felt as if she had lost her bearings, not to mention any grip on reality.

For a second, she couldn't even remember where she was.

All she was aware of was Neil, who was setting her whole body on fire.

Neil kissed her over and over again, making the entire world fade away until it was nothing more than a pinprick in the scope of the universe.

Yes, he had kissed her before and it had been a really, really wonderful experience. But this was on an entirely different level.

This was something spectacular and oh, so hot. Her pulse was beating so hard, the rhythm reverberated throughout.

Though her breath was growing shorter and shorter, Ellie didn't want to break away and come up for air. She definitely didn't want what she was experiencing to stop.

She closed her arms around Neil's neck, huddling her body closer to his, glorying in the warmth transferring from his body to hers.

Neil was aware that he was pressing his advantage and a sense of propriety was telling him that he really should be putting the brakes on before this went too far—if it hadn't already.

Maybe it was his state of mind, but he just couldn't help himself, couldn't keep from absorbing and glorying in everything that this woman had to offer.

Her sweetness. Her sustenance. The delicious ripeness of her mouth pressed against his.

Oh, Lord, her wonderful mouth.

He couldn't get enough of her, feasting on everything Ellie had to offer and craving more.

Even so, Neil forced himself to pull back. As wonderful as this was—and this *was* wonderful— he felt he wasn't allowing her to think, much less to say no if she was so inclined. Neil didn't want to overwhelm her, he wanted her to want him of her own free volition.

Drawing his head back, he asked her, "Do you want me to stop?"

Ellie stared at him, bewildered. She couldn't understand why Neil would ask her that. "Why? Did I do something wrong?"

"You?" he questioned, stunned. The woman had to be the closest thing to perfect he had ever encountered. "Lord, no. I just didn't want to railroad you into doing something you might not want to do."

She didn't think she could be so touched while lost in the wild throes of overwhelming desire, but she was. He was being gallant. More than that, he was actually willing to step away if she didn't want this to happen—which just made her want it all the more.

Ellie could feel herself growing very, very warm as passion swept through her.

She framed his face with her hands, already making love with him in her mind, and warned, "You just try to stop now and see what happens."

Neil grinned then, his heart swelling. The emptiness he had been harboring began to evaporate. This was, he couldn't help thinking, exactly what he needed both to help him cope with the events that had transpired this morning as well as to finally come to terms with what had gone down between him and Judith. He had been right to end his soul-draining engagement and now he could see why. Because it left him open to the promise that Ellie bore within her.

She was his destiny even though he hadn't seen it at the time. It was both unnerving and exhilarating.

"You're a scary lady, Ellie Montenegro," Neil told her.

Her eyes were filled with laughter as she replied, "You have no idea, Dr. Eastwood."

"Okay," he declared. "Enough of this chitchat. More kissing."

And with that, Neil kissed her again, harder and

with even more enthusiasm than he had displayed the last time.

Her head began spinning again. All the available oxygen was being sucked out, leaving her caught up in a world filled with only him. A sensation she desperately wanted to continue.

By degrees, Ellie became aware that he was picking her up, aware that he was carrying her to the other room while her mouth remained sealed to his, affording her the very sustenance she needed to thrive.

When Neil finally drew his lips away from hers, she almost felt bereft. But then that feeling faded as he began to trace his lips along her neck, her throat, the planes of her face. Anointing all of her and making her desperately eager for more.

Ellie gave back as good as she got. For every place along her body that Neil kissed, she returned the favor. She was almost desperate to devour him with her eager mouth, wanting to do to him what he was so clearly doing to her.

She was acutely aware of the fact that when it came right down to it, she hardly knew Neil, but that didn't really matter. Her *soul* knew him, *had* known him, she felt.

It made no sense in reality—wouldn't have made any sense to her had someone said this to her only a short while ago. And yet, in her heart, she knew that what she felt was true.

And if what was happening between them never went anywhere beyond tonight, she would deal with that later. Right now, the only thing that mattered was this moment, this man. This wondrous feeling that was exploding within her and creating incredible rainbows in her soul.

Ellie gloried in his artful hands, which touched her everywhere, caressing her, possessing her, making her feel incredibly beautiful, cherished and wanted.

Her heart pounding, she was only vaguely aware of unbuttoning Neil's shirt, pushing it away from his wide shoulders and down his arms. She was eager to feel his naked body beneath the material. Eager to touch and caress. And possess him.

She could feel him doing the very same thing to her as she undid his trousers, tugging them away from his torso.

Ellie could hardly recognized herself.

She had never behaved this way before. But then, she had never *felt* this way before. It was as if some sort of wild animal within her had been set free, given the go-ahead to behave in a manner that was completely foreign to her.

Ellie didn't even want to think what had to be

going through Neil's mind about her right at this moment. About what he thought about her wanton behavior. All that was secondary to this moment, this sensation, this man who had lit her fire and managed to set her off this way—making her sizzle.

She wanted more. More of this fantastic sensation. More of *him*.

Neil couldn't even begin to describe what he was feeling right now. This woman with the adorable face was behaving in ways he wouldn't have ever even begun to imagine.

She took his very breath away. It was like handling liquid fire, trying desperately to contain it without getting burned, and yet being utterly fascinated by it.

Neil was creating havoc within her as he was covering her eager, throbbing body with a network of hot, openmouthed kisses. With each one, though it didn't seem possible, he only managed to fuel his desire to higher and higher levels.

He was making her crazy, Ellie thought. He was blotting out her very thoughts with what he was doing, leaving her to be a throbbing mass of pulsating, yearning desire.

Working his magic, he had managed, by using

his clever mouth, to bring her up to one climax and then quickly to another.

It was all she could do to keep from screaming out loud.

Ellie bit down on her lip, holding in her exploding joy as it seized her—but it wasn't easy.

After each episode, she fell back on the gurney, exhausted beyond her wildest imagination as well as incredibly sated.

The second time it occurred, she didn't think she would be able to even move, but at the same time, she felt guilty that she had received all the pleasure and he hadn't.

When she realized that Neil was beginning to undertake the same path again, Ellie put her hands against his shoulders and stopped him. And then, before he could say a word, she drew him up to her level.

"Together," she breathed. Her meaning was as clear as she was able to make it, given the fact that she was having trouble dragging in air.

"Whatever you want," Neil told her. There was a gleam in his eyes as he slowly dragged his body up along hers, arousing both of them as he did so.

Neil was more than ready for her, but even so, he wove a wreath of kisses all along Ellie's face and neck one more time before he finally united them and entered her.

And then he began to move. At first slowly, then faster and faster, until they found themselves racing, breathlessly, to the final pinnacle, the final all-engulfing explosion. When it came, wrapping itself around both of them, the impact was so surprisingly powerful it all but disoriented them.

They clung to one another, holding on tightly and relishing every single nuance about the moment.

Ellie felt like there were stars exploding in her head, dancing through her very system. Everything else she had ever felt before paled in comparison. She held on to him, clinging to Neil and to the moment, wishing with all her heart that it would never end.

But she knew it had to. And when it did, the sadness that drenched her was all but overwhelming.

Ellie hung on until she managed to surface from the sadness, her breathing coming in short spurts until she finally managed to steady her pulse, getting it down to a normal rate.

Neil's arm tightened around her, holding her close to him. The feel of his heart beating against hers was incredibly comforting, more than she had ever thought possible.

Ellie sealed the moment to her, preserving it so that she could remember this in the times when Neil would no longer be there with her.

"Well, I have to admit that I never saw the day ending like this," Neil said, lightly kissing the top of her head.

"Is that a good thing or a bad thing?" Ellie asked him.

"It's an unusual thing," he answered because although, quite honestly, he had wanted to make love to Ellie practically from the first moment he had first laid eyes on her, he hadn't really thought he would wind up doing it. He had felt that Ellie seemed to be out of his reach.

"Oh," she replied, thinking that perhaps he was already putting distance between them.

He thought he could detect a note of disappointment in her voice and he certainly hadn't intended to offend her in any way.

"But it's definitely a good thing," he told her with a broad smile. "A very good thing," he stressed. "In fact, it's so good that I'm thinking of getting my strength up for seconds," he teased.

"You need to get your strength up?" she asked.

He struck her as being such a hearty, robust speci-
men of virile manhood.

"Hey, don't kid yourself, fly-girl," he told her
with a straight face. "You took a hell of a lot out
of me just now."

She was trying to follow him. If he was drained,
why did he want to go another round? "But you
want to go again?"

"Oh, I definitely want to go again," Neil said
with enthusiasm.

"Mmm," she murmured, turning her nude body
into his. "So just how long do you think you'll need
to get your strength back up?"

He pretend to think. "Hard to say," he answered,
his voice trailing off.

Ellie began to kiss him, at first with small, but-
terfly kisses then she progressed to longer, deeper
ones that crisscrossed his face and torso, anointing every part of him.

"Is it getting any easier to say?" she asked Neil
as she went on kissing him.

"Not yet," he answered, his voice catching.
Then he changed that answer to, "Well, maybe just
a little easier." And then that changed to, "I think
it might be soon. Very, very soon," he amended,
as she continued kissing his face and throat, then

worked her way—slowly—down along his chest, moving ever lower.

Ellie could feel his heart pounding beneath her parted lips.

"In my humble opinion," she told Neil, "I think you're going to be ready for round two…oh, just about any minute now."

As she said it, she feathered her fingers along his nether regions, mischief in her eyes as she grinned wickedly. She could feel his response to her growing as she stroked.

He caught her hand before she could continue. Ellie was really making him crazy, he thought, wanting her more with every passing second.

"You keep doing that, Ellie, and I'm not going to be responsible for whatever consequences are going arise," he told her.

She pretended to think it over and her wicked smile grew wider. "I think I'll take my chances," she told him with a laugh.

Catching her up in his arms, Neil rolled over onto her.

"Round two," he announced, his eyes shining as he went on to make love to her.

Ellie didn't waste her time with a verbal response. In her opinion, actions spoke louder.

Much louder, and their time together was growing shorter and shorter.

She fought off and blocked the pang that threatened to seize her.

Everything had grown so complicated but she couldn't think of that now.

She just wanted to make love with Neil now. She would think about all the rest later.

Much later.

Chapter Seventeen

"You're getting in kind of late, aren't you?" Eduardo commented when Ellie drove up to the ranch house in her Jeep and got out.

Her grandfather was sitting on the front porch in the weathered rocking chair that he had once carved for his daughter-in-law when she was first pregnant with Ellie. It was close to midnight and she had thought that Pop would have been in bed by now.

"I was getting a little concerned," he went on to tell her.

She came up the porch steps and stopped at his chair. "Pop, I'm a big girl now," she reminded him affectionately. "You don't have to worry about me."

"Doesn't matter how 'big' you are or how old you are," he told her matter-of-factly. "I'm always going to worry about you and your sister. It's what family does," he said simply. "So, is everything all right?" Eduardo asked.

He wasn't the type to pry. Ellie was right, she was past the age where he felt he needed to be overly protective of her and keep track of what she did. But at the same time, he was determined to always be there for his granddaughters should they ever feel that they needed him.

She decided that since he had waited up, he deserved to hear part of the story. "Dr. Eastwood finally got to run those tests on Miss Joan."

Eduardo nodded. He'd hoped that Miss Joan would live up to her word. "So how did that go?"

Ellie sighed. "Not well," she confessed. "The test results showed that she needs to have surgery and she didn't want to hear about it. Dr. Eastwood isn't used to being disregarded and I think her reaction really bothered him. I tried to make him feel better about the situation by telling him that it wasn't him, it was just Miss Joan being Miss Joan," she told her grandfather.

If he suspected that anything else happened beyond that, she knew he wasn't going to push the matter. It was an unspoken agreement between them.

"Well," Eduardo said thoughtfully, "he knew that going in."

"Yes," she agreed, "but knowing something and being confronted with it are two very different things. It hit him hard. He felt he should have been able to convince her to have the procedure."

"So, were you able to make the good doctor come around and feel better?" Eduardo asked.

It was hard to keep the smile from her face, but she didn't want to have to explain about that, too, so all she said was, "I think so."

Eduardo's eyes met hers. She could see that she hadn't completely convinced him, but he wasn't about to push the matter.

"Good," he pronounced. "Get some sleep, Ellie. Maybe things will look better by tomorrow."

That had always been her grandfather's guiding mantra, she thought. "Maybe," she echoed. "G'night, Pop."

He rose slowly from the rocking chair, his limbs not as cooperative as they used to be.

"Hold on, I'm going to call it a night, too," he said, walking into the house with her.

Ellie's cell phone rang early the next morning. She was groping around for the device she'd left on her nightstand before she was fully awake.

Finding it, she held it up to her ear. "Hello?" she mumbled thickly.

"I found her!"

The woman's excited voice echoed in Ellie's head before she could make any sense of the declaration or discern who the caller was.

"Found who?" she asked, sitting up as she dragged one hand through her hair, desperately trying to bring consciousness to her brain along with it.

"Zelda. I found Zelda," the woman on the other end cried. And then, in case Ellie was still only half-awake, she added, "Miss Joan's sister. She's alive!"

Ellie blinked as she realized who was calling her—and why. "Olivia?"

"Of course it's me. Who did you think it was?" The lawyer didn't wait for an answer as she continued with her effusive narrative. "I located Miss Joan's sister," she repeated. "I had a long talk with her, told her what was going on with Miss Joan, and she's more than willing to come out and talk to her sister. She is concerned, though, that Miss Joan might not want to talk to her."

The full import of what Olivia was telling her was taking root.

"Don't worry about that part. I'll take care of

it," Ellie told the lawyer. "You did the hard part. You found her," Ellie declared. "How *did* you manage to find her?"

"Networking," Olivia answered glibly. "By the way, I heard about Miss Joan's reaction to the test results yesterday."

Ellie suspected that by now probably half the town, if not more, had heard about Miss Joan's stubborn refusal to have anything done to alleviate her condition. But now that Olivia had been able to actually find the woman's sister, this gave them a measure of hope that they would be able to get Miss Joan to come around and change her mind.

She was aware that this was a long shot, but at least now there was one.

"I'm sending Cash out to bring her back to Forever," Olivia was saying. "Any way you look at it, this is going to prove to be very interesting," the sheriff's wife told Ellie.

Ellie couldn't help but laugh. "You do have a way of understating things, Olivia. Well, I'd better get up and get dressed. Eastwood is going to want to be there for this auspicious reunion. And who knows, maybe this really will get Miss Joan to finally come around."

"One can only hope," Olivia replied wistfully.

* * *

Ellie never dawdled in the morning, not even when she was a little girl getting ready for school. She had always been too conscientious. However, this had to be the fastest that she had ever gotten ready in her life. Less than ten minutes after she had received the phone call from Olivia, she was up, dressed and out the door with a piece of toast in her hand.

Eduardo had just come down the stairs when Ellie hurried past him to get out the front door.

"Hey, where's the fire?" he asked.

She didn't want to stop, but she did. She wasn't in the habit of ignoring her grandfather.

"Olivia found Miss Joan's sister. Cash is being sent out to bring her into town and I just wanted to tell Neil the good news that all isn't lost."

"Oh, so it's Neil now, is it?" Eduardo murmured to himself with a knowing smile. "Interesting," he commented, nodding his head as he went into the kitchen. "Very interesting."

Ellie lost no time driving to the Davenport residence in town. She knew for a fact that Dan was always up early because he needed to get to the medical clinic and open it for business. It had been that way ever since he had first arrived in Forever and reopened the clinic. Ellie also knew that with three children, Tina was perforce an early riser, as well.

She had no idea what Neil was accustomed to doing, but she knew he'd welcome this news and would want to hear it as soon as possible.

Ellie only needed to ring the doorbell once and the door flew open.

Tina's youngest was standing in the doorway. The moment Jeannie saw who it was, an amazingly sympathetic look came over her small face as she asked, "Are you sick, Ellie? Do you need to come in and see my dad?" The girl obviously associated anyone who came to their house with being a potential patient of her father.

"No, honey. I'm just here to give your dad and his houseguest, Dr. Eastwood, some really good news," Ellie told the little girl.

"What news is that?" Neil asked, coming into the living room and joining Jeannie and Ellie.

He smiled broadly at Ellie. The events of yesterday evening were still very much on his mind and he found himself reliving them over and over again—and wanting to generate even more memories.

Assuming that Ellie might be there for that very same reason, Neil started to tell her, "You know,

I don't have anything really planned for today, so if you're interested—"

But he wasn't able to get any further than that because Ellie blurted out, "Olivia's located Miss Joan's sister. Cash is on his way now to pick her up and bring her back here."

It suddenly occurred to Ellie that she didn't even know where the woman lived or how long it was going to take Cash to get her and bring her back to Forever.

"You really do keep managing to surprise me," Neil told her with a shake of his head. He was aware of why they had been looking for the other woman and he honestly hadn't held out much hope for success, but then, he had been wrong before. "You think this long-lost sister that's been turned up can talk some sense into Miss Joan's head?"

"To be honest, I have no idea," Ellie admitted as Jeannie stood in the room, taking everything in, happy to be there with the adults. "But it's worth a try. I think finding Zelda—"

"Hold it. Her name is Zelda?" Neil questioned incredulously. "You mean like in that game?"

Ellie was aware of the fact that the name was not exactly a common one anymore and that the mention of it tended to bring up images of a video game, but that couldn't be helped.

"Everyone's got to be called something," she told him with a shrug. "The important thing is that she's on her way here and she might be able to get Miss Joan to listen to reason."

Neil had his doubts. "What makes you think Miss Joan will listen to her any more than she'd listen to anyone else?" he asked.

"Hope," Ellie answered simply.

He hadn't been here all that long and already he'd known that was going to be her response. "Ah, that old chestnut," he said, nodding. He wasn't trying to belittle her belief, he just didn't put as much stock in hope as Ellie did.

Ellie shrugged, dismissing his attitude. "Better than nothing."

"That's true," he said. "Okay, let's hope that your old-fashioned theories bear fruit because, frankly, the longer Miss Joan waits to have this done, the more of a risk she's running of having a fatal heart attack or something along those lines."

He wasn't saying anything that Ellie, as well as the others involved in Miss Joan's world, didn't already know.

Olivia decided that it was for the best if Dan and Neil met Zelda first before they descended on Miss Joan with her in tow.

Zelda turned out to live in a small suburb outside of Dallas. She was a tall, thin woman with a gaunt face, salt-and-pepper hair and dark eyes that looked as if they could bore right into a person's soul. There was an overwhelming sadness about her.

"Look," Zelda told the two doctors, "I appreciate what you people are trying to do, but I seriously doubt that I can talk Joan into anything. We haven't spoken to one another in over thirty years, not since—" She stopped for a moment then changed direction. "Well, not for over thirty years," Zelda repeated. She became even more solemn. "Her last words to me were 'I never want to see you again. Ever!' That's not exactly somebody who would be willingly convinced by anything I had to say."

"A lot of time has passed," Ellie reminded Miss Joan's sister. "Maybe Miss Joan is ready to forgive and forget, she just doesn't know how to go about it. Did she even know how to contact you?"

Zelda shook her head. "No, but I doubt she even tried." She was long past tears, but the solemnity she bore went deep. "I can't even blame her. What I did was pretty unforgivable."

Neil paused, scrutinizing her. He had seen that look before, on the faces of people resigned to living a life in perpetual hell for something they felt they had done, something they were guilty of.

"Let me ask you something," Neil said.

Zelda raised her chin, bracing herself. "Go ahead."

"Have you forgiven yourself?" he asked.

Zelda squared her shoulders, looking like a woman who was about to become extremely defensive. But then it was as if the air had just been let out of her. "No, I haven't."

"Don't you think it's about time that you did?" he asked. "Because, if you can't forgive yourself, then how is Miss Joan supposed to forgive you?"

Zelda shrugged, a hopeless expression on her face. "I guess that, deep down, she's not," she answered.

"That's not going to help her any," Neil told the estranged sister. "And, deep down, under all this, Miss Joan needs help. I think the fact that she does might be scaring her most of all."

Zelda sighed, mentally taking a step back. "Well, if you really believe that I can actually help, then count me in. I want to be able to help Joan in any way that I can because I can never make up for what happened."

"You need to put that behind you," Ellie told the woman. "What counts now is the present and, after that, the future. Everyone in this town cares about your sister. In her own unique, inimitable way, she has made a big difference in a lot of people's lives. They don't want anything to happen to her if it can, in any way, be prevented."

Zelda nodded. "Understood. I'm willing to do anything I can," she repeated.

Neil nodded. "All right then, let's do this," he told Zelda and the others.

The noonday rush had just concluded and activity at the diner was settling down when Ellie and Neil walked in.

Miss Joan looked up, her expression impossible to read. "I thought there was a disturbance in the atmosphere."

She still didn't look entirely friendly, as if she was holding herself in check. "If you two are hungry, take a seat. But I'm telling you that if you're here to try to talk me into letting you operate on me or alter me in any way, you're just wasting your time and your breath. I don't want to be cut open, and if that means that my time is limited, well so be it. I've made my peace with that and you should, too. Now—" she looked from one to the other "—what can I get you?"

"A better attitude," Ellie told her.

"Sorry, fresh out of that. And my attitude is my own business, missy," she informed Ellie.

"That would be fine if there's nothing to be done for you, Miss Joan, but there is and it's not even anything major," Neil insisted.

"That's a matter of opinion, sonny." She gestured toward herself. "These are all original factory parts and they're staying that way."

"I see nothing's changed. You always were as stubborn as a mule," Zelda said as she entered from the side and walked up to the counter. The woman had managed to slip in unnoticed because Miss Joan had been so focused on the two people talking to her.

Miss Joan paled the moment she heard her sister's voice. And then her eyes narrowed into small slits. "What the hell are you doing here?"

"Trying to talk some sense into you," the other woman answered. "You have people here who care about you, who are used to putting up with your abuse just because they're worried about you and want you to be well. Don't you realize how important that is? How precious? How can you even *think* about throwing all that away because you're too afraid to listen to reason and have some simple procedure done?" Zelda asked.

As the others looked on, they saw Miss Joan's face grow red as fury set in.

"Get out of here!" Miss Joan shouted at her sister, pointing to the door. "Get out of here this minute!" And when no one made a move, she all but growled, "I mean *now*!"

Chapter Eighteen

Rather than leave, Neil took a step forward. He didn't handle this sort of stubbornness well and he was on the verge of having it out with Miss Joan. And at this point, he had nothing to lose.

Sensing what was about to happen, Ellie put her hand on his forearm, silently stopping him. When he looked at her, she slowly moved her head from side to side. This wasn't the time or the place for this sort of confrontation. Too many people were in the diner and she knew that Miss Joan wouldn't appreciate this kind of public display. They could try talking to her later, when she was relatively alone. That was their only hope of getting through to the woman.

For a couple of moments, Neil appeared to struggle with indecision but then he finally relented. He blew out a breath and, in an effort to hold on to his temper, he turned toward the door.

"Let's go," was all he trusted himself to say at the moment.

Meanwhile, Ellie hooked her arm through Zelda's and turned Miss Joan's sister around toward the door, as well. She urged the woman to leave with them.

"You know this just isn't right," Neil said heatedly as they walked out of the diner. "I never met anyone so damn bullheaded, so incredibly perverse—"

"I know," Ellie agreed. "But we can't kidnap Miss Joan and force her to have the surgery," she pointed out. She shrugged as she went down the front steps. "Who knows, maybe if we leave her alone, she'll come around on her own."

"And maybe pigs'll start flying," Neil retorted, still angry.

"Well, if I were you, I wouldn't hold my breath in either case," Zelda advised, a really sad expression on her face.

All three reached the bottom of the steps, and were about to head into the parking lot, when the diner door slammed against the opposite wall behind them.

They all turned in unison when they heard Laurel, one of the younger waitresses, plaintively cry, "Wait!" as she came running down the steps, trying to catch them before they left.

Ellie barely got the words "Why, what happened now?" out when Laurel came running up to them, looking terrified.

"It's Miss Joan!"

Neil took the steps two at a time, reaching the diner door in the blink of an eye.

"What happened?" he asked, repeating Ellie's question as he, Ellie and Zelda poured back into the diner.

Laurel was right behind them. "Miss Joan just grabbed her chest and keeled over. She didn't even say a word, she just went down," she cried breathlessly. Grabbing Neil's arm, she was in a state of panic as she looked at him with wide, frightened eyes. "She's not—not—not—"

The young woman couldn't bring herself to even frame the question.

The other waitress on duty, Vanessa, was kneeling on the floor beside Miss Joan's still body, holding her hand and desperately trying to bring the older woman around.

"I think I found a pulse," Vanessa told Neil as he knelt next to her.

Relieved to have the doctor back, the young woman scrambled to her feet to give him room.

The diner owner was on the floor, looking so incredibly pale, she had everyone thinking the worst had transpired.

All eyes were on Neil. No one spoke, no one even dared breathe, as he quickly examined Miss Joan, taking in her vital signs and trying to assess her condition.

Unable to keep silent any longer, Zelda finally demanded, "How is she?"

The expression on Neil's face was grim as he looked at Miss Joan's sister and then at Ellie. "It's not good," he answered. "I need to get her to a hospital as fast as possible."

"The closest hospital to Forever is over fifty miles away," Angel told him. Like everyone else at the diner, Miss Joan's cook had ventured out from where she was working and gathered around the fallen woman.

"You go fast, the ride there will kill her," Ed Hale, one of the many regulars at the diner, predicted.

"Yeah, but if he drives slow, she might die on the way," Allison Farrow argued.

"I can fly her there," Ellie told Neil. Her mind racing, she made a mental note of everything that needed to be done. "Someone get Harry," she ordered as she headed for the door. "He needs to know about this. Angel, you call Cash," she told the woman. "Tell him what happened." The last person she looked at was Neil. "I'll be right back," she promised. And then she raised her voice. "I need everyone to clear their cars out the parking lot. I'm going to have to land my plane there," she told the people in the diner just before she raced out of the front door.

Zelda suddenly came to life. The diner's patrons were all looking at one another, their concern all but paralyzing them. No one was making a move to get to their vehicles.

"You heard her," Zelda said in a voice that could have easily been mistaken for Miss Joan's. "Get those cars out of the way right now! She's gonna need to land her plane." Turning to Neil, Miss Joan's sister asked, "What can I do?"

Neil was working over Miss Joan, trying to make sure that her heart was not going to stop again. He didn't want to press his luck.

He barely glanced at Zelda, afraid to look away from the pale woman on the floor.

"I think you already did it," he told the woman.

Zelda knelt beside her sister and took hold of her hand, squeezing it as tightly as she dared. Her eyes began to fill.

"Damn you, old woman. You can't die before you forgive me, you hear me? Don't you dare die on me!" she ordered, tears sliding down her thin cheeks.

One of the diner's patrons had gone to the medical clinic to get Dan. The latter all but burst in through the door.

"What happened?" he cried as he knelt on the floor beside Neil in front of Miss Joan.

"She had another attack," Neil said, summing it up simply. "This one was a lot stronger than the last one. There's no way to avoid it, she's going to need an operation," he told Dan. "Ellie went to get her plane. In all likelihood, we're fighting against the clock. We're going to have to fly Miss Joan to the hospital."

And then, since he was relatively unfamiliar with the hospitals around that region, Neil asked, "What's the name of the best hospital in close proximity?"

Dan didn't even have to think. "That would be Lincoln Memorial. They've got a great cardiology department. I know one of the doctors there," Dan added.

"I think you'd better call them," Neil told him, never taking his eyes off Miss Joan. The woman was barely holding on. "Tell them we're bringing them a cardiac patient and we're going to need to use one of their operating rooms stat."

Harry came in at that moment. He was clearly terrified when he saw his wife on the floor of the diner.

"Can you save her?" he asked Neil, his voice trembling as he bravely fought not to break down. He knew he needed to remain stoic for Miss Joan's sake.

"I damn well am going to try," Neil answered, momentarily looking up and exchanging glances with Dan. "I'm going to need you to come with me," he told Dan. He felt that if they were both there, accompanying the woman to the hospital, Miss Joan had more of a fighting chance to survive than if only he was with her on the flight, even though it was going to be a short one and he was bringing an oxygen tank and a defibrillator with him.

Dan offered the other doctor an encouraging smile. "That goes without saying, Neil."

"I have to come, too," Harry told them, speaking up. "I'm her next of kin." The phrase all but stuck in his throat and he nearly broke down as he'd said it, but he managed to push on. "I have to be there to give my permission so you can do whatever you have to do to save this cantankerous woman who is the love of my life. It took me years to convince her to marry me. I can't lose her now." Unable to hold it together any longer, Harry quietly began to sob as he struggled to get himself back under control.

"I'm coming, too," Zelda declared as she came back into the diner and picked up the thread of the conversation. "No way she's going anywhere without me," she informed the doctors. "By the way, the parking lot's clear."

Hearing Zelda's statement about coming with them, Neil looked as if he had his doubts. "How many people can Ellie's plane hold?"

"Six," Ellie answered as she quickly crossed the diner floor back to Neil and Dan. "It can hold six." She immediately looked at Miss Joan. She had never seen the woman look so ashen. "How is she doing?" she whispered, as if afraid that anything louder might affect Miss Joan in an adverse way.

"Better once we get her to the hospital," Neil answered. "You know how to get to Lincoln Memorial?" he asked, not wanting to take anything for granted at this point.

"I know how to get to anywhere in this state,"

Ellie assured him. Ready to go, she looked around. "Do you have something you can use as a gurney for her?"

Neil shook his head. "We don't have time to look for anything." He made a judgment call. "I'm going to carry her. She doesn't weigh that much."

But Dan moved in. "It's better if I take her feet and you take the upper torso. Once we have her off the ground, *then* you can carry her," he told his friend, adding, "No offense, but we don't want to risk the chance of dropping her."

Neil opened his mouth to argue that, if anything, the woman was a lightweight, but he knew that Dan was right. He didn't want to take any chances.

Meanwhile, as the two physicians sorted out just how to carry Miss Joan to the plane, Ellie dashed out of the diner and hurried back to her plane. Opening the doors, she waited as Neil brought Miss Joan down the diner stairs and to the plane. Dan had quickly gotten into the plane so that he could help with the transfer.

Harry hung back, not wanting to be in the way. But he stayed close enough to what was going on to be there for the woman he loved.

"Miss Joan would have a fit if she saw this plane in her parking lot," he commented to Ellie, struggling again not to let his emotions get the better of him. But it wasn't easy.

"She can take my head off once she gets well again," she told Harry with a smile. Then she gripped his hand, squeezing it. "And she *is* going to get well, Harry."

Harry nodded numbly. "I know she is," he answered even though they all knew there were no guarantees to be had.

On her way to board the plane, Zelda paused only once, eyeing the small passenger plane skeptically.

"Is this thing safe?" she asked uncertainly, the question intended for no one in particular.

"It's safer than walking there," Neil told Miss Joan's sister.

Hearing him, Ellie smiled at Neil. Given his reaction when she had flown him here from the Houston airport, he had undergone quite an about-face in attitude.

Neil and Dan were both now on the plane. Zelda had followed, reluctantly clambering on. She had taken a seat and then strapped herself in as if she expected to accidentally fall out of the plane in mid-flight if she wasn't secured.

Ellie turned her attention to Harry, silently offering to help him board the plane. But he shook his head, turning down her offer.

"I can manage," he told her. "You just concentrate on getting us there. Please."

"Consider it done," Ellie told him. Saying that, she circumvented the perimeter of the plane, making sure she had shut and secured all the doors. Satisfied, she finally got onboard herself.

"Okay, people, we're about to take off," she told her passengers. And then she looked over her shoulder at the one passenger on board who counted right now. "How's she doing?" she asked Neil, nodding toward Miss Joan.

"She'll be doing a lot better once we get her to Lincoln Memorial," Neil answered. "Did you already call it in, or whatever it is you have to do?" It occurred to him that he had no idea what the proper protocol was for bringing in a plane—or even if there was one when it came to landing it near a hospital. Some had helicopter pads on their roofs.

"I've already alerted the hospital that we're bringing in a critically ill patient and that we're flying her there on a plane, not a helicopter. They gave me instructions where to land. There'll be an ambulance meeting us there."

"An ambulance?" Zelda cried, frowning. "I

thought the whole idea was not to have to waste time driving my sister there."

"It is, but there's no place to land the plane," Ellie explained as she swiftly went over her checklist in her head one last time. "Don't worry, the landing field is half a mile from the hospital," she told Zelda then promised, "They'll have Miss Joan there in no time."

"Hope you know what you're talking about," Zelda commented, grabbing her armrests as the plane taxied the short distance and then took off.

Neil focused on his patient and not the dip in his stomach just then.

"Don't worry, Zelda. She always knows what she's talking about," he assured the woman. For just a split second, he spared Ellie a quick glance and an even quicker smile.

She didn't know what had made her do it, but she had turned around just then and caught the look that Neil gave her. There were no words to describe how that made her feel or how empowered.

She realized just how much Neil had come to mean to her in an incredibly short amount of time. She would have one hell of a time trying to come to terms with life once he went back to New York.

Now wasn't the time, she told herself.

"It's going to be all right," she promised Harry

and Miss Joan's sister, who had grown eerily quiet. "We're almost there already."

"Yeah, well, I'm not going to be happy until this flying matchbox lands in one piece," Zelda commented.

"Amen to that," Ellie thought she heard Neil murmur under his breath.

She had no idea why, but both comments made her want to laugh—but she didn't.

"Hang on, everyone. Just a few more minutes," she promised. "I can see the airfield up ahead."

"Make sure you land in it," Zelda told her sharply.

No doubt about it, Ellie thought, this woman was definitely Miss Joan's sister. She wouldn't have thought that the world had room for two Miss Joans, but obviously she had thought wrong.

Chapter Nineteen

As she sat there in the Lincoln Memorial OR waiting room, Ellie concluded that waiting was very possibly the hardest thing in the world to do. She felt as if she had been sitting in that room an inordinate amount of time, waiting for the surgery to be over and for Miss Joan to be wheeled into Recovery.

Until that came to pass, she wouldn't be able to breathe easily.

For the most part, she and Dan had spent the time since Miss Joan had been wheeled into the OR attempting to comfort Harry and Zelda, assuring Miss Joan's husband and her sister that everything would be all right. Though he tried it hide it, Harry looked as if he was really frightened about the outcome while Zelda just appeared to be in varying states of anger.

Ellie had a feeling that if the tables had been turned, Miss Joan would have handled the situation pretty much the same way.

Ellie was also very glad that Dan had elected to remain at the hospital with everyone once Miss Joan had been taken into surgery. He was able to bring the voice of reason and common sense to the scene, helping Miss Joan's relatives cope.

Because of his familiarity with Miss Joan's condition, not to mention his rather high standing in the cardiac surgeons' community, Neil was allowed to be part of Miss Joan's surgical team. The last she had seen of him, Neil had disappeared behind the operating room doors to scrub up.

By her watch, that had been over five hours ago.

During that time, Zelda had come close to wearing a path in the tiled floor with her endless restless pacing. For the umpteenth time, the woman looked toward the doors that led into the operating room.

"Something's gone wrong and they don't want to come out to tell us," Miss Joan's sister accused nervously.

Ellie glanced at Harry, wanting to shield the man at all costs.

"Don't go there," she told Zelda, her voice sounding a great deal stricter than it normally did. "Not until we know that for a fact—and we *don't*."

Zelda opened her mouth, looking at Ellie in surprise. But then she closed it again, backing off. However she continued to look disgruntled.

"Nicely done," Dan whispered to Ellie, who was sitting next to him. "I didn't know you had it in you."

Ellie's mouth curved slightly. "Neither did I," she admitted. And then she quickly jumped to her feet when she saw the OR doors opening. Neil came into the room.

The heart surgeon was instantly surrounded by the five people in the waiting room.

"How is she?" Harry asked, clearly afraid of the answer but even more afraid of continuing to be in limbo.

Neil did his best to summarize what had gone on in layman's terms. "Miss Joan's had an angioplasty and I also performed a partial ablation. That should take care of her blockage as well as get her atrial fibrillation under control," he told Harry and Cash, who had driven to the hospital to be there for his grandfather. Neil forced a smile to his lips.

"With any luck, she should be up and about, chewing everyone out in next to no time."

Cash breathed a heavy sigh of relief.

"Heaven help me, I can't wait," Harry said. And then he surprised Neil by throwing his arms around the surgeon and hugging him with all his might. "Thank you," he cried, his voice all but breaking. "Thank you!"

Zelda nodded, although she remained where she was and didn't attempt to hug Neil. "What he said," was all the woman added.

Neil nodded, beginning to understand the way the woman operated. "Miss Joan's in Recovery now, but you can all go see her once she's out."

Suddenly feeling wiped out, Neil sank onto the closest chair. A lot of time had gone by. Beyond the hospital windows, dawn was beginning to slowly give light to the world.

Ellie changed seats, taking one next to Neil. Dan, she noticed, tactfully let them have their space, choosing to remain with Harry, Cash and Zelda.

"Can I get you anything?" she asked Neil. "Coffee? Tea? Something to eat from the vending machine—although I have to warn you, the selection is rather limited."

Neil shook his head, turning her down. "Just sit here with me and let me savor the moment."

Her mouth quirked into a quick smile. "That, I can do," Ellie responded. "I've always had a weakness for heroes."

Neil shook his head, rejecting the label. "Just doing my job."

"And being a hero," she insisted, pointing out, "It's not everyone who can ride to the rescue."

Neil was too tired at the moment to argue.

Less than ten minutes later, Cash's wife, Ramona, finally arrived. The vet had driven in following an emergency surgery of her own.

After anxiously asking about her husband's stepgrandmother, and finding out that Miss Joan had responded well to the surgeries, she hugged Cash and looked extremely relieved.

Turning to Ellie, Cash told her that he could take Harry and Zelda back with them when they were ready to leave, freeing Ellie up to leave now.

"I know that Dr. Dan probably wants to get back to the clinic and you probably need to get back, as well," he said to Neil.

"As long as you give us a ride to my plane, I can take it from there," Ellie told Cash.

Ramona glanced at her husband, noticing that some of the color was returning to Harry's face. "Is Miss Joan conscious yet?"

Zelda spoke up before Harry or Cash could. "She's still in Recovery."

Ramona nodded. "Then we have some time," she said. Cash looked at Ellie and the two physicians. "Ready whenever you are," he offered.

All three were on their feet immediately.

"Are you sure you're up to flying?" Neil asked Ellie once they had arrived at the airfield and Cash and Ramona were on their way back to the hospital.

"Don't worry," she assured him. "I can do this with my eyes closed."

"If it's all the same with you, I'd really rather you did it with your eyes open," Neil told her.

Ellie laughed. "I can do that, too," she responded with a grin. "Besides, I'm not the one who was on my feet for over five hours in the operating room, saving a life."

"Like I said, just doing my job," he told her. "Now, I know of two pretty tired men who would really be grateful if you went ahead with yours and got us back to Forever," he said, glancing at Dan. The latter merely nodded his agreement.

"Gentlemen, your chariot awaits," she told her passengers whimsically, gesturing toward the front of her plane.

* * *

Compared to their flight to the hospital, the return flight seemed completely uneventful and over before it had gotten underway. Suppressing a smile, Ellie noticed that Neil hadn't turned pale even once during the trip. By the time the man was ready to go back home, he would be an old hand at this. She had no idea why that made her feel so incredibly sad, but it did.

Neil, Dan and Ellie were unprepared for the fanfare that greeted them when they finally returned to Forever. It seemed as if half the town converged around them, seemingly popping out of nowhere.

They were immediately beset with questions about Miss Joan and it felt as if everyone wanted to buy each of them celebratory drinks at Murphy's. Most of the offers were politely declined after the first one or two had been placed in front of them.

Nothing dampened the celebration, though. Everyone, it turned out, had been extremely worried that Miss Joan wouldn't make it.

The questions and impromptu celebrating didn't die down until way into the evening.

Dan never managed to get back to his clinic. To compensate, most of his patients demurred, saying that whatever had brought them to the clinic could definitely keep for at least another day if not two. The patients unable to wait were seen by Dan's associate, Dr. Cordell.

When the celebrating finally wound down and everyone began returning to their homes, Ellie turned to Neil. "I can drive you over to Dan's house," she offered. Dan and his wife had already left, but Neil had been prevailed upon to hang back awhile longer.

Instead of saying yes, Neil laced his fingers through Ellie's and suggested, "Why don't you drive us over to Dan's cabin instead? I think I've gotten my second wind."

It wasn't hard to read between the lines. Ellie smiled at him. "Oh, so I take it you still feel like celebrating?"

"You could say that, yes," Neil answered, a sexy, incredibly mischievous smile curving his mouth.

"Works for me," she told him. Walking to her vehicle, they got in and Ellie started up her Jeep. "I've always wanted to know what it felt like to be kissed by a hero."

"Oh, I intend to do a lot more than that," he told her. "And I'm not a hero," he said again. "Just a guy who was lucky enough to be in the right place at the right time."

"I don't think Miss Joan will see it that way," Ellie told him as she pulled up in front of the cabin. "Trust me, as long as you're in Forever, you're going to be on the receiving end of a whole lot of free meals at the diner."

"Then I'd better look into having some of my pants let out," he said as he unlocked the cabin door and led the way inside.

For just a moment, Ellie could feel her heart leap. But the next moment she warned herself not to read too much into Neil's words. All the surgeon was saying was that he would be here for a little bit, nothing more. He definitely didn't mean what she wished with all her heart that he meant.

Just for now, though, she decided to pretend that he did. After all, she had nothing to lose.

Neil closed the door behind him, flipping the lock and hearing it click into place.

"It occurred to me that if Miss Joan hadn't been as hearty as she was—and if you weren't there to fly all of us to the hospital, she could have easily died."

"But she was, and I was, so she didn't," Ellie said, catching her breath as Neil started undressing her.

She would really miss this when he left—

Ellie immediately upbraided herself for focusing

on negative thoughts. She needed to focus only on the good parts, she silently insisted. There would be time enough to focus on negative thoughts later.

"But what about the next time?" Neil asked.

Her pulse launched into double-time.

"Dan and Alisha will deal with that when it comes up." This wasn't where her head was at right now, she thought, responding to Neil. She started to remove his clothing. "Stop talking."

His grin was positively wicked. "All right."

For a while, he did stop talking, losing himself instead in her and glorying in the way she made him feel—as if he was ten feet tall and totally invincible.

When it was over and, shrouded in the misty afterglow of lovemaking, lying together on the gurney that they had turned into a makeshift bed, Neil returned to the subject that had been at the back of his mind for most of the day.

"Forever needs a hospital."

The statement, coming out of the blue the way it did, caught Ellie completely off guard. It took her a moment to be able to respond.

"No argument," she agreed. "Do you have a solution?" She was kidding.

But he wasn't.

"I have a trust fund," he told her.

"Sure you do," she said, nibbling on his shoulder affectionately.

She was distracting him and he wanted to get this out before he got really carried away again.

"No. I do," he told her. "I really do." What she was doing was making his eyes roll back in his head, and he needed to tell her this part so she would understand.

"I'm an only child. My parents were very well off, and add to that my mother's great-aunt—Aunt Grace—who never had any kids. She was always too busy making her money work for her and, apparently, it worked very, very hard. When she died, she left all her money to me."

Ellie pulled herself up on her elbow and looked at him, an eerie feeling that she was on the cusp of something really big emerging, though she was afraid of getting carried away. "What is it that you're saying?" she asked in a small voice.

"I'm saying that I have enough for some serious seed money to put into starting a hospital here in Forever," Neil told her. "And I honestly think I know enough people to contact who will put up the rest of it."

"You're talking about getting money together to build a hospital. Here. In Forever." Ellie didn't know if she was asking, or reiterating, as she stared at him. Being nude under the sheet didn't exactly help her thinking process, either.

"You're a little late to the party," Neil told her with a smile, "but yes, that is exactly what I'm talking about."

Ellie realized that she wasn't absorbing this. "But why?"

"Because it really hit me today that the next time someone needs an emergency operation, there might not be enough time for you to fly them to Lincoln Memorial or some other hospital. They could die because there isn't a hospital here."

"That's all well and good, but this is all going to take time," she pointed out. "Lots of time."

"I am aware of that. I was kind of good in math that way. Not brilliant," he allowed, "but good enough."

Ellie put her fingers on his lips to still them. Hope began to rise within her. "You'll have to be here at least part of the time to oversee this project, won't you?"

"Nothing gets by you, does it?" He laughed. "I will," he answered. "Probably all the time I'm not here, I'll be out there, hitting up friends for donations," Neil told her.

"Wait. Wait!" she cried, trying to get this all

straight in her head and at the same time to not get too excited because it really *couldn't* be what she thought it was—could it? She drew her courage together and forced herself to ask, "So you're staying in Forever?" Even as she asked, she braced herself for a negative answer.

"Uh-huh."

Her eyes widened. "Really?" she cried, her heart beating hard.

"Really," he echoed.

She threw her arms around his neck, kissing him soundly. She was prepared to continue and make love with him all over again, but he surprised her by catching hold of her arms and pulling them away from him.

"There's one more thing," he told her.

Ellie felt a knot suddenly materialize in the pit of her stomach, pulling tightly and somehow managing to steal all the air from her lungs. She tried to brace herself for what she felt was coming, but she knew she really couldn't.

"What?" she asked in a shaky whisper.

Holding her hand and still very naked, he slipped out of bed and down to one knee, and said, "Elliana Montenegro, will you do me the supreme honor of becoming my wife?"

She didn't know whether to laugh or cry—or get her hearing checked.

"What?" she asked, stunned.

"You don't have to change your name if you don't want to. Because yours sounds so lyrical, I understand you wanting to keep it, but I'd really be very happy if you said yes—"

"Yes!" she cried, hardly believing her ears. The man she had found herself falling in love with was actually asking her to marry him. How wonderful was that? "Yes, I'll marry you."

"Really?" he cried, surprised. "Because I thought I'd have to do a lot more convincing, or that you'd tell me you had to think about it or—"

"Please stop talking!" Ellie pleaded. "I want to start practicing for the honeymoon and I can't if you're talking."

He grinned at her, loving her so much that it actually physically hurt. "Yes, ma'am."

Neil noted, with pleasure, that her smile went all the way up into her eyes. Capturing his heart, it took him prisoner.

As did Ellie when he started kissing her again.

Epilogue

Years later, whenever she talked about it, Miss Joan told people that she'd nearly had to die to bring Ellie and Neil together—but it had been worth it. The woman thought nothing of taking full credit for the young couple getting married because, in her mind, she really was the one person responsible for the two of them meeting in the first place.

When Neil and Ellie went back to Lincoln Memorial to see how the woman was doing after her surgery, even in her weakened state, the sharp-tongued diner owner only needed to take one look at the duo to discern that there was something different going on between them.

"So, what's going on, you two?" she asked in a raspy voice.

Neil took the question at face value, but Ellie wasn't so sure. This was Miss Joan asking and the woman had an eerie way of knowing things before they were ever made public.

"We're just happy that you've pulled through and are going to be all right," Ellie said, hoping that would satisfy Miss Joan's question.

She and Neil had decided to get married as soon as they found the time, but for now, they were both agreed that they wanted to hang on to this special secret just a little while longer.

"Is that your story, too, sonny?" Miss Joan asked, turning her eyes on Neil.

"Yes," he answered, doing his best to sound as innocent as possible.

Miss Joan frowned. "Look, I didn't escape the Grim Reaper's clutches just to have you two blow smoke up my butt."

Exhaling a very short breath, the woman looked at her husband, who was also in the room and hadn't left her side since she'd been brought in. "How about you, Harry? You know anything?" But even as she asked the question, Miss Joan answered for him. "No. Of course you don't. That's okay. I didn't marry you for your ability to see through people's fabrications. I married you for your sweet innocence and kind heart."

She paused to clear her throat and then continued as if nothing had happened. "You're not leaving here, you know—neither one of you—until you've come clean."

Ellie knew the woman meant it. Rather than engage in a battle of wills, she told Miss Joan, "Neil asked me to marry him."

"Yes. And?" Miss Joan asked, waiting for Ellie to get to the point.

Ellie's smile was brilliant as she answered, "And I said yes."

Miss Joan huffed. "Well, it's about damn time," she said as if the union Ellie had just told her about had been a forgone conclusion to her. "And just to prove that there are no hard feelings about you dragging Zelda back into my life, I'll be the one throwing the wedding for you two."

Because the first part of her statement was even more mind-boggling than the second part, Neil had to ask, "Wait, does that mean that you and your sister have patched things up?" Because if they had, he felt as if this was a really big deal, given

the anger he had seen on Miss Joan's face the day
Zelda had walked into the diner with them.

"Well, right now there's just Scotch tape, not
duct tape, holding everything together, but I guess
you could say that," Miss Joan allowed magnani-
mously. She pulled her blanket up closer around
her. "I'm letting her work at the diner for now.
She's on probation," she added. "We'll see how
it goes."

Ellie smiled. She had a good feeling about this, she
thought, exchanging glances with Neil and Harry.

"But enough about that," Miss Joan said
abruptly. "I need to start making plans for your
wedding. The end of the month should work…"
she decided, then continued talking.

Yes, Ellie thought as the man who could create
upheavals throughout her body with his mere touch
reached for her hand, lacing his fingers through
hers, the end of the month would definitely work
for her.

* * * * *

MILLS & BOON

Coming next month

THEIR ROYAL BABY GIFT
Kandy Shepherd

The woman's wet dress clung to her body making no secret of her curves. She was a scandal in the making.

He grabbed a striped towel from a stack on a nearby lounger and threw it around her shoulders, another one around himself. "Keep your head down and walk as quickly as you can," he said.

She attempted a faster pace but stumbled and he had to put his arm around her to keep her upright. He scarcely broke his stride to pick up the phone she'd dropped when she'd fallen.

"Are you hurt?"

"Only…only my pride."

"Are you staying at this hotel?"

She shook her head and wet strands flew around her face, sending droplets of water on him. "I…I only came here for lunch. My hotel is in the older part of town."

"I'm in the penthouse here. There's a private elevator down to my suite. I'll take you there."

"Please." She was still shivering, and her eyes didn't look quite focused.

He had to get her—and himself—out of here. Edward kept his arm around Ms Mermaid as he ushered her to the discreet private elevator. If people didn't recognise him, a scandal could be averted.

Within minutes they were in the expansive suite where he was living while his Singapore house was being gutted and refurbished. He slammed the door behind them and slumped in relief. No one with a camera could follow him here. He turned back into the room. Then realised he had swapped one problem for another. Standing opposite him, dripping water on the marble floor of his hotel suite was a beautiful stranger—and her presence here could so easily be misconstrued.

"Thank you," she said. "I could have drowned." Her eyes were huge, her lush mouth trembled. Hair wet and dripping, makeup smudged around her eyes she was breathtakingly lovely. A red-blooded male, no matter how chivalrous, could not fail to feel a stirring of attraction. "I…I can't swim, not enough to save myself. But you…you saved me.".

Continue reading
THEIR ROYAL BABY GIFT
Kandy Shepherd

Available next month
www.millsandboon.co.uk

COMING SOON!

We really hope you enjoyed reading this book.
If you're looking for more romance, be sure to
head to the shops when new books are
available on

Thursday 29th
October

To see which titles are coming soon, please visit
millsandboon.co.uk/nextmonth

LET'S TALK
Romance

For exclusive extracts, competitions
and special offers, find us online:

f facebook.com/millsandboon

y @MillsandBoon

◉ @MillsandBoonUK

Get in touch on 01413 063232

For all the latest titles coming soon, visit
millsandboon.co.uk/nextmonth

MILLS & BOON

THE HEART OF ROMANCE

A ROMANCE FOR EVERY KIND OF READER

MODERN

Prepare to be swept off your feet by sophisticated, sexy and seductive heroes, in some of the world's most glamourous and romantic locations, where power and passion collide.
8 stories per month.

HISTORICAL

Escape with historical heroes from time gone by. Whether your passion is for wicked Regency Rakes, muscled Vikings or rugged Highlanders, awaken the romance of the past.
6 stories per month.

MEDICAL

Set your pulse racing with dedicated, delectable doctors in the high-pressure world of medicine, where emotions run high and passion, comfort and love are the best medicine.
6 stories per month.

True Love

Celebrate true love with tender stories of heartfelt romance, from the rush of falling in love to the joy a new baby can bring, and a focus on the emotional heart of a relationship.
8 stories per month.

Desire

Indulge in secrets and scandal, intense drama and plenty of sizzling hot action with powerful and passionate heroes who have it all: wealth, status, good looks…everything but the right woman.
6 stories per month.

HEROES

Experience all the excitement of a gripping thriller, with an intense romance at its heart. Resourceful, true-to-life women and strong, fearless men face danger and desire - a killer combination!
8 stories per month.

DARE

Sensual love stories featuring smart, sassy heroines you'd want as a best friend, and compelling intense heroes who are worthy of them.
4 stories per month.

To see which titles are coming soon, please visit

millsandboon.co.uk/nextmonth

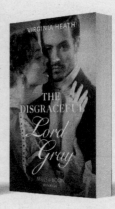

MILLS & BOON

HEROES

At Your Service

Experience all the excitement of a
gripping thriller, with an intense romance
at its heart. Resourceful, true-to-life
women and strong, fearless men face
danger and desire - a killer combination!

MILLS & BOON
MEDICAL
Pulse-Racing Passion

Set your pulse racing with dedicated, delectable doctors in the high-pressure world of medicine, where emotions run high and passion, comfort and love are the best medicine.